FORSAKEN OUTPOST

KEN LOZITO

ACOUSTICAL BOOKS LLC

Published by Acoustical Books, LLC

KenLozito.com

IF YOU WOULD LIKE TO BE NOTIFIED WHEN MY NEXT BOOK IS RELEASED VISIT

WWW.KENLOZITO.COM

Paperback ISBN: 978-1-945223-81-5

CHAPTER 1

As the *Pathfinder's* systems continued their slow collapse, Connor Gates wondered which would run out first: the ship's power or his crew's hope.

In his many years of military service, Connor had learned that time could escape him. It didn't matter whether there was a lot going on or very little. Time had a way of passing at an alarming rate, no matter how well prepared he was. He stood on the *Pathfinder's* bridge, a large amber holoscreen hovering before him. Various sub-windows had populated, showing data feeds that told him the status of the wayward ship, and almost all the data pointed to the fact that their time surviving on this ship was running out.

Connor averaged about five hours of sleep a night, but in the days following their escape from the Aczar world, Ichlos, it had been less. It wasn't just him but the entire rag-tag "crew," although he hesitated to use that word. The *Pathfinder* had no crew, just a group of people who'd happened to be on the ship when a major breakthrough in their hyperspace technology came to fruition—one that might've had a little help from a frustratingly mysterious alien race they referred to as the Phantoms. The Phantoms existed outside of normal space—n-space but had the capability to function within n-space whenever they wanted. Despite all of Connor's security precautions to hide the research that was being done with the Infinity Drive, the Phantoms had figured out what they were doing and intervened. Noah thought the Phantoms were trying to help them, that as desperate as things were on this ship many thousands of light-years from home, things could've been much worse. Connor could see Noah's point, but he still reserved judgement where the Phantoms were concerned. Noah was among the best people he'd ever known, though his good nature sometimes blinded him to certain truths. Noah wasn't naïve, but in Connor's experience, powerful, intelligent, alien species had their own motivations for the actions they took, and that didn't always coincide with the betterment of everyone involved.

The door to the bridge opened and Louis Maclean (Mac) walked in. Mac's right hand started to rise but then stopped.

"Good morning, General Gates," Mac said as he walked over.

Connor didn't have access to military records, but he knew a veteran of the Colonial Defense Force (CDF) when he saw one.

"Good morning, Mac."

Mac was a cook and commanded the kitchen. He looked around the bridge with a bit of uncertainty.

Connor waved him over. "I'm almost positive nothing else is going to break if you walk past a few workstations."

Mac chuckled and rubbed his bald head. His thick gray eyebrows knitted together in amusement. "Sorry, General." He shook his head. "Once in the CDF, always in the CDF."

Connor smiled and tipped his head to the side. Then he switched off the holoscreen. "What's dragged you out of the kitchen at this hour?"

"It's our guests, sir. You asked me to set aside some of our supplies so they could convert it to make food for themselves," Mac said.

Connor nodded. "Is there a problem?"

Mac shrugged. "Maybe. I'm not sure. We gathered plants and other things from their planet because it was compatible with our own processors." He paused for a second with a thoughtful frown. "I don't know anything about Aczar physiology, but the amount of supplies I set aside for them, they've hardly used."

"Are you saying they're starving?"

Mac lifted his palms. "I don't know. They're not complaining. If anything, they seem content, but I'm not sure about that. Their expressions are hard to understand. It's just strange. Most things that talk and move that fast have high metabolisms, but not the Aczars. When I asked Phendran about it, I got the impression he was amused by my question. But he assured me that this situation was going to be short term, and they could endure it."

Connor nodded slowly, finally understanding what Mac was implying. "I see."

"I just figured that with everything they've done to help us escape, they deserved better than to simply 'endure' being our guests. I'm just not sure how to convey that to them. I'm not an ambassador."

"Neither am I."

Mac stared at him for a second, one eyebrow arched. He looked unconvinced.

"Alright, I'll talk to Phendran about it. Maybe something is getting lost in translation. They might be concerned about *us*. Our provisions aren't what I would call extensive."

Mac sobered. "No, not by a long shot. At least I don't need to worry about feeding the prisoner."

Connor had the impression there was more that Mac wasn't saying. Their prisoner, Salpheth, was trapped in an energy sphere in the secondary power-core. Salpheth was a Phantom, some kind of ascended being, but he'd been left behind by his own race. The Aczars had imprisoned him for hundreds of years. They'd kept him alive, and Salpheth had manipulated their species into a dogmatic condition that prevented the development of technology to explore the galaxy. The Aczars and Salpheth had been in a stalemate for a long time. Connor learned that Salpheth had escaped his prison a few times, and it had caused a significant upheaval in Aczar society. Salpheth, who many revered as a deity of some kind, a holder of higher knowledge, had tried to steal the *Pathfinder* to escape the Aczars. But there were some Aczar who'd been brave enough to question Salpheth's motivations.

Connor was still trying to understand his new alien friends. They'd helped Connor and the others escape just as a civil war had begun on the Aczar homeworld.

Connor and Mac left the bridge.

"Is there anything else, Mac?" Connor asked.

Mac was a man of many skills and had a keen sense of putting things in order. Connor appreciated his unique perspective, even here, out in the middle of nowhere.

"No, that should do for now. If there's anything I can do to help, you just say the word."

"I'll do that."

"I'll leave you to it, sir," Mac said and quickened his pace.

Connor went into the conference room near the bridge. The metallic band on his left wrist warmed for a moment, and Connor glanced at it. During their escape from the planet, Phendran had given Connor a piece of his Saruvian Robotic Assistant (SRA) so he could interface with Aczar technology. Things had happened so quickly that Connor hadn't had the chance to return it. When it was discovered that Phendran and some of the other Aczars who'd helped them escape were stranded in space near the ship, Connor had them brought aboard. He'd wanted to give the SRA fragment back to him at that point, but Phendran refused. The SRA had changed and requested to stay with Connor. He could've refused, but the SRA was an interesting piece of alien technology. He supposed it was a form of artificial intelligence, but the Aczar viewed their SRAs as a partnership, treating them as equals.

Aczars used their SRAs as both a tool and a weapon, and Connor suspected there were other functionalities that he hadn't had the chance to explore. Connor's SRA was still in a learning mode and had limited communication with him. Phendran assured him that this was to be expected. Aczars bonded with their SRAs almost from birth. It was used in their education and defense. The SRAs were high powered and could change forms through the re-alignment of their matrix. It was made from some kind of metallic alloy but was also a machine.

Connor's SRA was learning about him, but it also showed him things, as well, and helped bridge the communication gap between Humans and Aczars.

Phendran sat in the chair and his feet didn't reach the ground. Aczars were short—just under five and a half feet tall—thin, with furry brown hair. They had large, tan-colored ears that extended from their heads and ended in triangular points. They also had hooked snouts, and their mouths moved rapidly as they spoke. Their movements were fast and energetic.

Phendran wore a uniform with metallic accents and sleeves of bright chrome. His SRA was part of the clothing he wore. Three other Aczar sat nearby.

Phendran looked at Connor and spoke. "I detect a power spike in your SRA."

The Aczar had stopped speaking before the translator finished.

"It became warm for a second and I wasn't sure why," Connor replied.

"Your SRA was acknowledging our presence," Phendran said, and his head tilted slightly. "And it has a general approval of some-thing that has transpired."

Connor frowned. "It didn't tell you what?"

"It's no long part of my SRA."

Connor wondered how his SRA would react if it *didn't* approve of something he did? Would it try to stop him? Would it interfere? He was cognizant of the security risks, but given the current situation, he'd take all the help he could get.

Noah looked away from the holoscreen he'd been staring at and gave Connor an appraising look. "You just make friends wherever you happen to be."

Connor chuckled as he sat next to him. "It beats the alternative, although the jury is still out on some of the recent developments."

Noah glanced at Phendran for a second, then looked at Connor. "You don't think they'd pin that one on us, do you?"

"Our going there was a catalyst. No matter how you look at it, our presence was a factor. And if they ever learn that Salpheth is our prisoner, they'll demand his immediate return."

Noah pushed his fingers through his hair for a second and shook his head. "It'll be nice to have those kinds of problems."

Phendran peered at them, and some of the other Aczars spoke quietly to each other.

"This recent exchange is a bit confusing for us," Phendran said.

"He means that if...*when* we have those kinds of problems, it'll mean we've overcome the problems we're facing today," Connor replied.

Phendran considered this for a half-second and then glanced at his companions. "We now understand."

One of the Aczars sat with his arms crossed. He seemed to regard his surroundings with some disdain.

Connor looked at him. "Noxrey, you look like you have something to contribute."

The Aczar just looked back at Connor. "I have no comments to share."

Not all the Aczars were happy to be there. The very foundation of their society forbid space travel. Phendran was a Loremaster and had extensive knowledge about his species' history. Connor found that Phendran made him more open-minded about things, particularly where Salpheth's manipulation of his entire species was concerned.

The other two Aczars, Kholva and Vorix, were students of Phendran's, whereas Noxrey was more of an engineer. They'd all helped Connor and the others escape, but their ship had been caught within range of the Infinity Drive and had traveled with the *Pathfinder* thousands of light-years away.

Glenn Rhodes, a director of the Colonial Requisitions Department, also at the table was. He'd been part of the team, inspecting Connor and Noah's R&D project for the Infinity Drive. Rhodes had been difficult to deal with in the beginning but had been of more help as he accepted that the events that led them there hadn't been because of any negligence on their part.

Captain Tyler Kincaid sat to Connor's left. He'd been assigned to Connor's protective detail, responsible for security matters.

"We should get started, General," Kincaid said.

"Alright," Connor said and looked at Noah.

His friend's expression became sober. "Lots of updates, and none of it is any good. Our nav systems still can't pinpoint our location."

"It's been over two days. No indication at all?" Rhodes asked.

Noah leaned forward, raising his hands. "For all intents and purposes, our nav system is designed for a much smaller region of space because of what our current capabilities have been. Obviously, things have changed, and the shortcomings of our nav system will need to be addressed."

Connor regarded his friend for a moment. "What kind of issue is this? An issue with resources like available cycles from the computer core?"

"I wish it were that simple. Look, Salpheth fed some kind of coordinates into the nav system. I have no way to recall them, so unless you ask him, we might never figure it out."

Trusting their prisoner to disclose that information wasn't Connor's first choice.

"I cannot recommend that course of action. Salpheth cannot be trusted," Phendran said.

"It might be our only option," Rhodes replied.

"I might be able to provide an alternative," Phendran said.

Connor raised his eyebrows. "Okay, what do you mean?"

"I have access to data of the surrounding star systems around Ichlos."

Noah's eyes widened for a second. "So do we. In fact, we tracked the stars upon arriving at your planet."

"I understand that, but the data I have is from our entire time on Ichlos," Phendran said.

"Really? That's amazing. Why didn't you tell me before?" Noah asked.

Phendran was quiet for a moment and looked as if he wasn't sure how to respond.

"Where is the data?" Connor asked.

A flicker of understanding registered on Phendran's face. "It's in my brain."

Rhodes blinked and looked at Connor for a second. "In your brain?"

Phendran nodded. "Yes, as Loremaster, we practice special memory techniques to function as a living archive."

Rhodes's mouth hung open, and he leaned back in his chair.

"A living archive? Are you saying you carry the entirety of Aczars' knowledge inside your..." Connor said and lightly tapped the side of his head.

"Yes, only certain Aczar are able to do this," Phendran replied.

Connor wasn't sure if the translator was working. All their own considerable knowledge could never be held by anyone. This was why they had specialists, and even then, they were experts in very specific areas. Only by working together could people expand on the knowledge they'd gained.

"I see this is a cause for hesitation," Phendran said.

Connor glanced at the others for a second. "I've seen your technology. It's very impressive. I'm at a loss as to how you could store all that information in one person's mind."

"But it's not just one person's mind. It's shared, and my SRA helps bridge the gaps. The knowledge I have isn't always readily available. I must focus on retrieval, and this can take some time."

"But don't you use…" Connor began to say but then stopped. "We use machines to hold our data. It frees up our minds for other things. Don't you use machines for data storage?"

"Ah, I see the disconnect," Phendran said. "We do use machines as well, but they are jointly controlled by Loremasters and our Council. As I've said before, I have data from our observations of the great expanse."

"Are you able to share it?" Noah asked.

"I've been working on doing that with my SRA. The problem is making the data available in a way that your nav system is capable of processing," Phendran replied.

Noxrey stared at Phendran. "The archives are only for the Aczar."

Connor frowned for a second. "I don't understand."

Phendran regarded his companion. They could communicate with each other through their SRAs, and he wondered what they were saying.

Noah looked at Connor. "What's going on?"

"They're discussing the matter among themselves," Connor replied.

He waited a minute and then gestured toward Noxrey. "I get the sense that you don't want to be here."

Noxrey blinked and stared at Connor. "It is forbidden for us to traverse among the stars."

"And yet, here we are," Connor replied. "You want to go home. That can only happen if we work together."

"General Gates," Phendran said, "there are restrictions on Loremasters sharing our knowledge."

"What kind of restrictions?"

"The kind that results in severe consequences. However, if I comply with those restrictions, the result could also be construed as severe."

Connor nodded once. "We have a saying: Damned if you do and damned if you don't."

"Our language accounts for similar sentiments," Phendran said.

"There are more than just the limitations of our nav system," Noah said.

Connor looked at him and nodded for him to continue.

"Our power core is degrading fast."

"Faster than before?" Connor asked.

Noah nodded. "Yes. Essentially, we're trying to do more with less. The result is that core degradation increases. We need to find a way to refuel it."

"Is that even possible?" Rhodes asked. "I didn't think the ship was ready for that."

"It's not," Connor said.

"Not traditionally. Those refinement systems had been taken out of the ship and…well you know the rest," Noah said.

Rhodes nodded. "It was being scheduled. So, how do you propose to refuel the power core?"

"In emergency situations, it is possible to use our current power core as a means to refine other fuel sources. Doing that results in a lot of waste, but it'll help in the short term," Noah said.

Connor stared at him and heaved a sigh. "Doing that requires the secondary power core as a backup."

The secondary power core was currently home to their prisoner.

"Right, and we can't risk it because of Salpheth. So, I'm proposing we don't use it."

Connor blinked. What Noah was proposing was extremely risky. It could leave them stranded if things went wrong.

"I know what you're going to say," Noah said. "If I could come up with a better option, I would have. In fact, this might be our only option."

Connor considered for a few moments and then looked at Phendran. "Is this something you could help us with?"

"I'm afraid we have no knowledge of spaceships," Phendran said.

"Yes, but you do know about generating power. A lot of power in a compact form."

Phendran considered this and then looked at Noxrey. "You might be able to help them."

Noxrey looked at them.

"I could go over how our power core works. Maybe it'll spark a thought about it," Noah said.

Silence.

"It'll help you get home," Connor said.

Noxrey looked at Connor and then at Noah. "Very well. I will try to assist."

Noah stood. "We should go there now."

Noxrey hopped off the chair and followed him out of the conference room.

"General Gates," Phendran said, "I wish you would reconsider your position on allowing us to join you during your interactions with Salpheth."

"It's not that I doubt you. You're free to observe us through our monitoring systems. However, I don't want Salpheth to know that there are any Aczars here on the ship."

"I don't understand why you delay."

"Because right now, Salpheth believes he only has us to deal with. Once he learns about you, he'll change how he approaches us. I want to get a baseline to compare when we *do* reveal that you're here."

Phendran slowly nodded. "Very well. Remember, you cannot trust anything he says."

Connor would never forget it. Salpheth was the most dangerous thing on the ship.

CHAPTER 2

MAJOR ETHAN GATES stood before a large wallscreen. His ready room aboard the *Ascendant* had space enough for a desk and a lounge area for small meetings. There was only so long he could endure sitting at a desk and found that he preferred standing for more than half his work sessions—a trait he'd gotten from his father, General Connor Gates.

He stared at the status window of the teams deployed well into the Oort Cloud of a distant M-class star. The star system's barren worlds held no interest for him. The stellar probe's analysis had confirmed what the onboard scanners detected. The star system's farthest regions, barely under the influence of the star, were home to densely packed rock and ice. Not an ideal place to investigate the Vemus, but this was where the analysis of certain anomalies had led them. The teams he'd deployed reported in as they made their way through the area to investigate several large masses that might contain remnants of Vemus exoskeletal material.

Ethan glanced at the report he'd been working on. He needed to send the update to COMCENT for their exploration task force, which would then be relayed home. They were more than eighty light-years from New Earth; the nearest subspace relay station was over twenty light-years from their current location. More stations were coming online as they explored deep space.

He brought up the ship's status in a sub-window. The *Ascendant* was part of a new class of exploration cruiser that was built on the foundations of the CDF's Valkyrie class heavy cruiser. His trained eye sought out the hallmarks of the warship's foundational design that had been used for his ship. The *Ascendant's* shape was that of a long, flattened tube, with more observation areas than any warship would ever have, but his ship still had teeth. Their armament was in specialized attack drones, HADES VI missiles with fusion warheads, mid-range rail guns, and other shortened-range energy weapons. They didn't have enough firepower to fight a war, but there was enough to hit an attacking force so they could make a strategic withdrawal from the situation. The *Ascendant's* strength was in its drive-core, which increased their operational space significantly over earlier exploration efforts. His command was tailored toward deep-space exploration, but it still functioned as part of a task force of ships that was spread over a vast region of space.

A chime came from the door to his ready room.

"Come in," Ethan said.

"Good afternoon, sir," Major Will Qualmann said as he stepped into the room.

His executive officer (XO) was a few inches taller than Ethan. He was lean, dark-skinned, and had a resonant voice.

Qualmann glanced at the wallscreen for a moment, and his hawk-shaped nose crinkled as he smiled a little.

"I know," Ethan said. "I'm still going."

Ethan had scheduled time for a climbing session in the fitness center. He'd had to cancel his last three sessions, which became a problem because of the limited slots per day. Ethan hated missing appointments, but he found that priorities tended to shift when one was in command of a ship.

"You might notice that there's a betting pool giving the winners three-to-one odds on whether you'll show up this time," Qualmann said.

Ethan chuckled. "Maybe I should hold off for better odds, then clean up."

Qualmann arched an eyebrow. "And take advantage of your crew?"

Ethan shrugged. "*I* didn't tell them to start the betting pool."

"Indeed," Qualmann replied.

Ethan regarded his XO for a second, eyebrows knitted suspiciously. "You've got credits riding on this."

Qualmann's expression was carved in stone. "I cannot endorse wagering on whether the commanding officer of the *Ascendant* is going to renege on his time slot."

Ethan pursed his lips a little. "We could make this interesting."

Qualmann's eyebrows rose.

"A race."

Qualmann grinned. "Sure. I'd like to see how the new Mark VII MPS suits stack against your hybrid capabilities."

Ethan's Vemus hybrid capabilities enabled him to augment his body, making it stronger, enabling him to hold his breath for very long periods of time, and he'd been using it as part of his hyper-focused work sessions. It hadn't enhanced his intelligence at all, but he got more done.

"I didn't think Dr. Lorenco was performing the upgrades to the neural implants that could leverage the Mark VII's capabilities."

"She's finished reviewing the research and cleared the protocols for anyone who has the current implants."

Ethan had seen a video of the Mark VII MPS suit operating autonomously, and it was impressive.

"Could be interesting," Ethan said.

"That it could, but alas, I have the afternoon watch, so your humbling will have to wait."

Ethan snorted. "Still hate that I won the last time?"

"I viewed it as a learning experience, an opportunity for improvement."

"That's not what you said before. You said I cheated."

Qualmann sighed. "Yes, but your response made me reconsider."

Ethan frowned as he tried to remember what he'd said. "Oh, you mean my saying that if you're not using every advantage within the rule of engagement, you're asking to lose?"

Qualmann tapped the side of his head. "That's the one." He glanced at the wallscreen for a second, his expression becoming serious.

"None of the teams are overdue," Ethan said.

"It's a mess."

"High risk, high reward."

"Mention the possibility of a remnant of the Vemus out there and the hybrids insist on being part of the away teams."

"They're the most experienced in dealing with the Vemus if we cross paths with them," Ethan said.

Qualmann considered that for a few seconds. "It's almost as if they don't know who they are without searching for the Vemus. It's the cornerstone of their existence."

"For some, it is," Ethan replied. "Others view it as their duty to protect others from the threat of the Vemus."

"Yes, it's similar to why people join the CDF. However, the expectation is that hybrids will move away from these traditions that drive them, allowing them to grow beyond what happened to them on Earth."

"That's just it. Being a hybrid is something they must live with, whereas everyone else can forget it."

Qualmann stared at him for a moment. "And you?"

"I'm something in between. I didn't grow up in the same kind of world that Cyn did. I was turned into a hybrid to save my life, so my perception is different from theirs."

"That's gotta be challenging. Your wife is out there while you're here," he said, gesturing toward the wall screen.

"I've been out there. So have you. No need to be on every away mission," Ethan said and scratched his chin. "But, yeah. Our line of work is dangerous."

"Don't worry, sir. I've got your back."

A comlink chimed from the bridge as a sub-window came to prominence on the wallscreen.

"Major Gates," Captain Seana Brett said, "we've detected an anomaly through our comms array. The signal is weak, but repeating, and is believed to be of alien origin."

"How far away is it coming from?"

"Seven light-years. The detection was pieced together from the outer bands of our subspace frequency. I think it could be a distress beacon of some kind," Captain Brett said.

"On my way," Ethan replied.

He and Qualmann left his ready room and entered the bridge.

Captain Brett gestured toward the main holoscreen. "I've updated the tactical plot with the alien signal detection, sir."

Ethan looked at the main holoscreen. The signal's source was the ship's computer's best guess as to the origin of the signal.

"Can we send a general acknowledgment reply along the same subspace frequency?" Ethan replied.

"I can try, sir. It's an alien signal, so we don't know the language. I can take what we've received so far and repeat it back to them. Perhaps we'll get a different reply from them as some kind of confirmation," Captain Brett replied.

"Do it," Ethan said.

Qualmann looked at him. "Premature to send the First Contact package."

Ethan nodded. "Let's see if we get a response first."

He watched Captain Brett. She had short blonde hair and pale skin.

She looked at him. "Package ready, Major."

"Send," Ethan said.

"Message sent," she replied.

Ethan looked at Lieutenant Anson Gooding. "Ops, request a status update from the away teams. Advise them…" he paused for a second. "Find out if they've detected any Vemus activity."

"Understood, Major. Sending status update request to all away teams," Lieutenant Gooding replied.

Ethan glanced at Captain Brett, and she shook her head.

"If we get a reply, that'll be another species you'll be credited with as being part of their First Contact," Qualmann said.

Ethan shook his head. "I don't have any credit for encountering a new species. And I doubt Vemus remnants really count."

"Yes, they do. They're of alien origin. Just because there was no meaningful communication resulting from that contact doesn't mean it doesn't count."

Ethan's eyebrows flicked up once. "We were fighting for our lives."

"I've read the reports."

"Yeah, well, let's hope this isn't like that."

"Major Gates," Captain Brett said, "there was a pause in communication, which I presume means that it received our signal, but nothing else has changed. It could be an automated signal."

Qualmann nodded. "A ship's distress beacon would last longer than the survivors, unless they had some kind of stasis technology. This is worth checking into."

"Agreed," Ethan said and asked Lieutenant Gooding for an update.

"Away teams report no Vemus contact. No confirmation of exoskeletal material found, sir."

"Understood. Recall all away teams. We're cutting the mission short," Ethan said.

"Yes, Major. Relaying updated orders to the away teams," Lieutenant Gooding replied.

The decision to end the mission early wouldn't be well received by the hybrids. Qualmann was right that they could be overzealous in their pursuit of the Vemus and would insist on performing a thorough check of this region of space before they'd admit that the anomaly detected hadn't panned out the way they'd all hoped.

"Major," Lieutenant Gooding said, "Comms request from away team Charlie."

Qualmann let out a quiet chuckle.

"Unless they have actual evidence of Vemus activity, they're to return to the ship. Advise them to log all areas of interests that have not been investigated and we'll make the case to return here at a later date," Ethan replied.

"Yes, Major," Gooding replied.

Qualmann eyed Ethan for a moment. "You already have us going to investigate this alien signal?"

"Not yet, but it's highly likely," Ethan replied and looked at Captain Brett. "Do a thorough analysis on the signal. I want to propose a mission to investigate it to Colonel Phillips."

"Yes, Major," Captain Brett replied.

Ethan looked at his XO. "We're out here to chase something bright and shiny."

"You should use that exact phrase in your mission request to Colonel Phillips."

"It does add a bit a flare to it."

Qualmann chuckled.

A message appeared on his wrist computer and Ethan read it, his expression sobering.

"What is it, sir?" Qualmann asked.

Ethan quickly reread the messages. "It's from COMCENT and my mother. My father is missing."

Qualmann frowned. "Missing? I thought he was on New Earth."

The message had come through COMCENT, indicating his father's disappearance was officially recognized by the colonial military.

"Something happened at an R&D facility, and a ship to be used with an experimental Infinity Drive is missing."

"Someone stole it?"

Ethan scanned the message and shook his head. "The message doesn't say."

"That could mean they didn't detect anything," Qualmann said.

"It's not just my father but a group of other people as well. They have no idea what happened to them. They detected no ships were detected in the vicinity."

"When did this happen?"

"Over six weeks ago," Ethan replied. "Captain Brett, you have the conn. Let me know when all the away teams are back aboard the ship."

"Yes, Major, I have the conn," Captain Brett said, and moved to the command station.

Ethan returned to his ready room and brought up the message from COMCENT.

"I can leave you alone if you need," Qualmann said.

Ethan shook his head. "No, come in."

"You'd think that if someone like your father was missing you'd have heard about it before now."

Ethan thought for a few moments. "Not necessarily. The investigation is ongoing." He continued reading the message and sighed. "Noah Barker is among those who are missing, along with protective details assigned."

Qualmann peered at the message, "Only a fraction of the crew was aboard the ship? Says it was during a retrofit of a retired Falcon class CDF frigate."

"My father is involved in a lot of things. If they were experimenting with the Infinity Drive…" Ethan said and paused for a moment. He walked to his desk and pulled out a bottle of bourbon, pouring two cups and handing one to Qualmann. "The alien Vemus wasn't the only species we encountered on the planet in that report you referenced earlier. My father encountered a species we call Phantoms. They've taken an interest in…well, us. People I mean. They were responsible for our interstellar probes making it to Earth about sixty years before they were supposed to arrive."

Qualmann sipped his bourbon. "Do you think they're involved in your father's disappearance?"

"Possibly. I don't know. There's no proof of it… just a missing ship, which could mean that there was some kind of breakthrough or malfunction with the Infinity Drive."

Qualmann frowned. "While in dry dock at a research facility on New Earth? That kind of work would've stuck security measures in place." He sighed. "I doubt it's a malfunction."

Ethan frowned. "Why?"

He shrugged. "Malfunctions are more destructive."

"Because there was no explosion means it wasn't a malfunction?"

"Yes, actually. That's exactly what I mean. What kind of research were they doing?"

"I don't know the specifics, just that they were exploring theories on how to make the Infinity Drive better. The message references something the Phantoms said to my father."

"What did they say?"

"They were perplexed as to how our FTL technology worked."

"I remember learning about those space probes. Our FTL technology is great. Look how far we've come."

"They implied that it was limited, so my father began a project to revisit the development of the Infinity Drive."

"How'd he go about doing that?"

"By recruiting the man who invented the technology. He's also a close family friend, and he's also missing. Their disappearance has gotten the attention of a lot of important people."

Qualmann exhaled through his nostrils. "I bet, but he's still missing."

Ethan bobbed his head once.

"So, what are you going to do?" Qualmann asked.

"What do you mean?"

"Are they recalling you?"

Ethan shook his head. "No, I've been informed. When they learn more, they'll let me know."

Qualmann blinked. "Don't you want to return home and search for him?"

"Abandon my command?"

"Yeah, but this is your father."

Ethan thought about that for a minute. There were more qualified people searching for his father already working on this. By the time he returned to New Earth, what would've changed? He still had the message from his mother, which would probably include everything the official notification lacked. If she wanted him to return home for some reason, how could he deny that kind of request? But he doubted she'd make it.

"It would take us a month just to get home. I'm not going to abandon my command, but that doesn't mean I'm not worried about my father. Don't misunderstand me. I want to find him."

Qualmann looked unconvinced.

"Look, this isn't the first time my father has disappeared, as in some alien race has taken a particular interest in him. Wherever he is right now, he's doing everything he can to come back home. He'll find a way. It just might take him a little while. Somehow, he'll either return or send a message."

"I wish I had that kind of faith," Qualmann said, then shook his head. "I guess it makes sense. After all, we're talking about the Great Connor Gates, father of the Colonial Defense Force, and one of the men personally responsible for humanity's survival."

Ethan had accepted long ago that his father cast a very large shadow, and he doubted he'd ever exceed it. His father had told him it was because of the circumstances he'd found himself in. Ethan was determined to make something of his life. For him, that meant exploring the mysteries of the galaxy, but he'd be lying to himself if he said he wasn't worried about his father. His father had saved his life, but the fact was that the galaxy was huge. He had no idea where to begin a search, and he knew better than to make snap judgements about how best to help find him, but that didn't make wanting to do something about it any easier.

"I can take the next watch if you need some time with this," Qualmann offered.

"Negative. I'll be fine, but thanks for the offer."

CHAPTER 3

Connor supposed he was getting used to the nearly empty ship. The quiet corridors and empty lounges reminded him of the days when they'd first started constructing their own ships in the CDF. The designs of these ships brought in more material comforts than were thinkable during the humble beginnings of the CDF fleet.

He snorted. The "fleet" they'd had during their first war with the Vemus was hardly more than a battle group with a few dozen actual ships and a much smaller core group of warships.

The *Pathfinder* was an older ship and had been in service for over twenty years. He knew the history of the ship. It had been among task forces that scouted enemy star systems in alternate universes during the Krake Wars. Sometimes, as he walked through the quiet corridors, he tried to imagine the people who'd served on this ship, and he couldn't. He had no idea who they'd been. If they'd been back home, he could've brought up the records that showed the commanding offers and crew rosters. He didn't know every member of the CDF, but there had been a time long ago when he *had* known them all. He'd recruited them, drawing upon the colony's finest to forge them into the fighting force they'd so desperately needed.

It was the soldiers from those early days whose voices he sometimes heard during the quiet moments. It was difficult to remember all their faces, but for some reason their voices stayed with him, though they didn't haunt him as they once had. He was at peace with his past. Now, all he wanted to do was return home. Sometimes, he heard a certain comforting voice that encouraged him. It was quiet and soothing. When he woke during those brief moments when sleep hadn't completely given way to wakefulness, he heard his wife—a faint echo of her laugh coming from another room in their home on New Earth. This made him miss Lenora all the more. He knew she'd be worried about him, but he also knew she had absolute faith that he'd do everything in his power to come back home. He tried to imagine his homecoming, seeing Lenora again and telling her what had happened. He could guess her reaction, but he wanted to see it for himself. He wanted to hold her in his arms. He wanted to share their morning coffee before they left for their respective jobs. And most of all, he wanted to be off this ship.

He was careful to keep these thoughts to himself. The others looked to him as a source of stability and stalwart determination that would get them through this. But no matter how busy they were with trying to keep the ship operational, the stress still gnawed away at them all. After escaping the Aczar homeworld, that stress had increased significantly.

He walked to the workshop near the robotics maintenance area and found Rabsaris Husker hunched over a workbench. Next to him was Sergeant Brent Seger.

Rabsaris had his hands inside a repair drone almost to his elbows, looking over at a small holoscreen that showed the inside of the drone. He finished what he was doing and stepped back from the bench.

"That ought to do it. Go ahead and initiate the startup routine," Rabsaris said.

Seger closed the panel and started the repair drone, which went through a quick self-diagnostic. It was in the shape of a large spider, with four legs and two arms. The bronze-colored body was about two meters in diameter.

The repair drone stepped off the large workbench and walked past Connor.

Rabsaris raised his chin toward Connor. "That's Naya's repair drone for main engineering. One of the actuators for two of its legs was sticking. It was becoming more of a hindrance than a use."

"Oh, I know she'll appreciate that," Connor replied.

Seger grinned. "Only if it does the job. I'm going to go help her out, unless there's something else you need from me, General?"

"No, go. I know Naya's working on the power relays," Connor said.

Sergeant Seger left and Rabsaris looked at Connor.

"I think Naya is trying to recruit him."

Connor grinned a little. Seger was dark skinned, about average height, and muscular. "He's got a talent for it."

Rabsaris nodded. "That and a keen propensity for weapons systems. A good man to have watching your back."

"That's why he has his current job."

"I'm glad you came by. I was just on my way to the power core," Rabsaris said.

They left the workshop and walked down the corridor.

"I wanted to check with you to get a feel for where we're at with repairs." Connor said.

Rabsaris was quiet for a few moments. "We're doing what we can. I suggest we close off portions of the ship that we don't need to use."

"Reduce our footprint?"

Rabsaris nodded. "Anywhere we can conserve power will only help us. This ship was supposed to have a crew of a hundred and fifty. There are only eighteen of us. Some areas we can seal off and others can be available as needed. Any idea how much longer we'll be out here?"

"We need to figure out our location relative to New Earth."

Rabsaris frowned. "Won't you return Phendran and the others to their world?"

"Eventually. The best thing we can do for them is to return home, evaluate everything we've learned, and outfit another ship to make the journey that would bring them back home. It won't be a quick thing, either. We're flying blind out here."

"Blind and losing power. You know, there are emergency protocols for restricting people to certain locations. If it comes to it, we could survive here using only ten percent of the ship. Cut power to everything else. That might make a difference."

Connor nodded. "It might come to that, but I don't think we're there yet."

"Understood, sir. Let me know if you want me to pursue it. And as far as repairs go," Rabsaris said with a shrug, "we're using band aids on systems that need to be replaced. They'll keep working, but eventually there won't be much we can do with them."

Connor looked away for a second, thinking about his son. "You should've seen what the hybrids did to extend the life of their ships. They made scavenging for resources their highest priority because their lives were on the line. I keep thinking about what some of them would suggest in this kind of situation. We take so much for granted sometimes."

"I'd heard about that."

They'd made their way to the power core where Noah, Phendran, and some of the others were working. Connor checked the security feed for the secondary power core and saw Jorath standing guard at the corridor leading to it. He had his workstation open. If their prisoner attempted to escape, they'd initiate a purge of the power core that would send Salpheth into space.

"There is no reason it shouldn't work," Phendran said.

Noah nodded. "You're right. It was something I was working with."

Connor joined them, and Noah smiled. "You're going to love this. We," he said, gesturing toward Phendran, "have figured out a way to extend subspace communications."

"How far?"

"Have you heard the expression 10x?"

Connor's eyes widened. "Ten times? You've increased the range of subspace comms by a factor of ten?"

Noah nodded. "Yes. We won't be able to contact home or anywhere near it, but it does open some possibilities." He opened a comlink to the bridge. "Captain Kincaid, initiate a broadcast. The new protocols are ready."

"Wait one second," Connor said. "Just to confirm, you've managed to increase the range of subspace communications, but does it require more power?"

"That's the beauty of it. It doesn't. Phendran helped with that."

Phendran looked up at Connor. "Once I saw how the system worked, I was able to identify ways to increase efficiency of the power consumption. You were well on your way to making these improvements on your own. I just gave a nudge in the right direction."

"I appreciate that," Connor replied. "Alright, go ahead."

"Yes, General," Kincaid said, his voice coming over comms. A few moments later. "Hmm. Uh, General, I think you're going to want to come to the bridge. We're receiving some kind of auto-mated response. More than one of them. They keep coming in."

"On our way," Connor replied.

They left the power core and headed for the bridge. Rabsaris went to main engineering to help Naya with maintenance.

Connor glanced at Noah, who had a holoscreen open over his wrist computer. He peered at it for a few moments and then closed it.

"He wasn't kidding. The new subspace protocols are definitely getting a response."

"The question is: who is responding?" Connor said.

They entered the bridge. Kincaid and Cassidy Rhodes were sitting at a pair of workstations. A star chart of the surrounding area was showing on the main holoscreen.

"General," Kincaid said, "the small data points represent the automated response to our broadcast."

Connor studied the main holoscreen for a few seconds and then looked at Noah. "What does that remind you of?"

Noah's eyebrows knitted together. "Communication relays or buoys. They function as repeater signals that extend the range of communications."

Connor nodded. "And they're subspace capable."

Cassidy cleared her throat. "Does that mean the signal will keep getting repeated until it reaches a station or something?"

Connor leaned toward the main holoscreen. "Sometimes. That's assuming there are no breaks in the chain or some kind of security protocols get activated. Some of the data points just stop. The range is pretty significant, too."

Noah looked at Kincaid. "Have you received any other kind of response?"

"Negative. Just the acknowledgment and the confirmation that our broadcast was relayed farther down the chain."

Connor was quiet for a few moments, thinking. Then he looked at Phendran. "Were you able to figure out a way to share the data you have with our navigation system?"

"It's ongoing. We've been focusing our attention on extending the life of your power core," Phendran replied.

Noah came to stand next to Connor. "What are you thinking?"

"We need to figure out where we are, but I also don't think that is a mere coincidence," Connor said, gesturing toward the main holoscreen.

"You think Salpheth was heading somewhere specific?"

Connor nodded once. "That's exactly what I was thinking. He just needed this ship to take him somewhere he could secure a better alternative. Given his history, I think it's a safe bet that he's patient and methodical."

"So, what are you going to do?"

Connor glanced at the others for a moment. "I'm going to have to talk to Salpheth."

"General Gates, I must caution you," Phendran said. "Even when Salpheth is sharing the truth, it will contain the stain of deception. He will only do things that increase his own gains."

"I appreciate the warning, but I've dealt with people like that before."

"Will you allow me to accompany you to your confrontation with Salpheth?"

Phendran's choice of words was always purposeful and incredibly accurate.

"No, but I want you to observe it from here. Noah will make sure you can hear everything Salpheth says. You'll be able to communicate with me should the need arise," Connor said.

"I understand, General Gates," Phendran said.

"Captain Kincaid, you're with me," Connor said.

Kincaid stood and followed Connor out of the bridge.

CHAPTER 4

CONNOR AND KINCAID made their way to the secondary power core.

Jorath looked over at them in surprise. He was an Ovarrow, a species native to New Earth. His brown skin was almost pebbled, like that of a reptile, with pointy protrusions that stemmed from his shoulders and elbows. Jorath had long arms, and his large hands ended in stubby black claws. A brow line extended to both sides of his head, and a wide mouth held frown lines that went toward his powerful neck. He worked for Glenn Rhodes and was assigned to his security detail. Anytime high-ranking officials visited remote areas, a member of their staff had weapons training and general security practices so they could function as escorts. Jorath was a former member of the Mekaal, or Ovarrow military, that had been absorbed into the Colonial Defense Force.

Connor had interacted with quite a few Ovarrow over the years. Many of them were highly disciplined and adhered to a strict compliance policy, and he knew Jorath would follow the instructions of his mandate almost to the letter. While Connor could appreciate that kind of discipline, it also became a hindrance when dealing with more complex issues that required out-of-the-box thinking.

"General Gates, I'm not due to be relieved for three more hours," Jorath said.

"I've come to speak to Salpheth."

Jorath glanced at Kincaid. "I understand. Will Captain Kincaid be joining you?"

"No, actually, he'll be joining you here while I go on inside," Connor said.

"Very well," Jorath replied. His gaze went to Connor's middle.

He was looking to see if Connor carried a sidearm. It didn't matter to the Ovarrow that a sidearm would be mostly useless against Salpheth.

"What is the status of the prisoner?" Connor asked.

"The containment field is active, and Salpheth mainly stays right in the middle. He rarely moves, and sometimes I think he only does it when he thinks I'm watching him," Jorath said.

Connor frowned. "He can't see you out here."

"I know that, but it still happens."

"I think he's just trying to manipulate you into thinking that. Salpheth can't see outside of the room the containment field is in, not to mention the door in between. Don't give the enemy capabilities that haven't been already proven."

"Understood, General Gates," Jorath said.

Connor looked at Kincaid. "Initiate security protocols. If anything goes wrong, I want the entire system purged."

"Yes, General," Kincaid said.

Connor trusted Kincaid to get the job done. He wouldn't hesitate. None of them could afford to allow Salpheth to escape.

Connor walked down the long corridor and opened the door to the secondary power core. The door slid to the side, and a bright amber glow filled the space. He stepped inside the room, and the door shut behind him. A red warning light flashed near the ceiling, indicating a system purge was imminent.

A grayish humanoid figure floated inside the sphere. The figure lifted its head, aware of Connor's presence. Even within the energy field, Salpheth's body glistened with a white light. His torso was bare, and he had wide, large, teardrop-dark eyes that regarded Connor intently. The edges of his thick lips turned up. Salpheth lifted his elongated head, which shifted the pale flaps of skin that ran down his back, disappearing from view.

"Have you come here to beg for mercy?" Salpheth asked.

Connor grinned. "That's funny because I was coming here to offer you the same chance."

Salpheth didn't reply, so Connor continued. "You see, I'm starting to think you're more trouble than you're worth. I'm going to offer you a chance to convince me otherwise."

Silence continued to mushroom between them in a pregnant pause, which Connor had no trouble stretching out as long as possible. They both knew that Connor had the upper hand, even if it ensured neither would survive. Connor could give the order and purge the power core, sending Salpheth into space. Then, they could take their chances on finding a way home, so that tilted the odds a little in Connor's favor over Salpheth's. However, Salpheth either knew where they were or had a better idea than anyone else on the ship, including Phendran.

"What is it you want from me?" Salpheth asked.

Connor stepped closer to the energy field. "I bet you've had to ask that a lot over the years while the Aczar held you prisoner."

"They are irrelevant."

"You mean, *now* they are irrelevant because you're stuck here with us?"

"The Aczar are a very astute race. I enjoyed the challenge they presented."

Connor bit his lower lip for a second. "If you want, I could send you back to them."

Salpheth regarded him for a long moment. Somehow, he could make his body become completely still, almost like a statue, and Connor wondered what he was doing when that happened. The Phantoms had left Salpheth behind, and Connor didn't know why. He doubted Salpheth would give him an honest answer if he asked.

"I don't think so," Salpheth said.

"Why not? I bet they'd be overjoyed to have you back with them. After all, you're their 'Great Mentor.'" He inhaled a deep breath and sighed. "That is, until some of them began to rebel."

"Maybe that was by my design."

Connor simply stared at him, waiting.

"These comments don't serve any purpose except to stretch my patience."

Connor shrugged. "Maybe that's all I want from you."

"Doubtful."

"It almost worked, you know. You almost got away with it. You hid yourself on our ship, waiting until we finally escaped. Then, you could take our ship and go wherever you wanted to go. I'm glad your plan failed, but it does create an issue that must be dealt with."

Salpheth moved toward Connor, coming right to the edge of the energy field. He was humanoid but on a much larger scale. He stared down at Connor for a few seconds and somehow adjusted his size to become equal with Connor. He probably sensed that Connor wouldn't be intimidated by a little thing like size. Sometimes he was brave, and other times the enormity of the standoff pressed on him long after it was over.

"Finally, you've come to your senses. Now are you ready to negotiate?"

Connor tilted his head to the side a little. "So, you're willing to negotiate?"

"Of course. Neither of us gets what we want if things stay as they are," Salpheth said.

Connor thought that Phendran would have a few things to say about that.

"I can see that you don't believe me."

"I don't believe you," Connor confirmed.

"If your ship fails, I'd be just as stuck as you are but for much longer. My guess is that you're in a location far between stars and your options are limited."

He chuckled. "That's as general a statement as anyone could make. This ship is in deep space, so of course we're at a place 'between stars.' You're going to have to do better than that."

Salpheth regarded him for a moment. "All you have to do is tell me what you need."

"Or you could just volunteer something you already know I need."

A deep laugh bubbled out of Salpheth. "Very well, General Gates. I propose an alliance." He paused for a second, staring at Connor. "A temporary one. Together we can overcome the challenges we face."

"What kind of challenges do you think we face?"

"This ship is in disrepair, and your power core is degrading quickly. At its peak it would've met your needs, but now, not so much. It's going to make you desperate." He arched an eyebrow. "Maybe even desperate enough to come speak to me. From what I've seen of your ship, it's in need of repair. Also, based on the limitation of your current navigation system, I'd say that you have absolutely no idea where you are. Therefore, it becomes impossible for you to return to your home. Have I missed anything important?"

Connor smiled wolfishly. "As a matter of fact, you did. I could jettison you from this ship anytime I want. How long would you survive in space all by yourself? I doubt that this would appeal to you, so maybe I wouldn't be so smug about the current state of this ship. Right now, I'm trying to decide whether you're worth keeping around, and you're not really giving me much of a reason." Connor stepped back and turned toward the door.

"Wait," Salpheth said. "My offer of an alliance is sincere. If you gave me access to your nav system, I could help you pinpoint your location."

Connor shook his head. "Do I look foolish enough to do that? Seriously, I'd rather take my chances than allow you to have access to any system on this ship."

"Then what do you propose?"

"Tell me where you were going. You entered coordinates into our nav system that were erased after the Infinity Drive came online."

Salpheth's gaze narrowed. "I need time to consider your request."

"You have ten seconds."

Salpheth stared at him.

Connor opened his comlink. "Captain Kincaid, stand by to purge the secondary power core."

"Yes, General. Ready when you give the order, sir."

Connor raised his eyebrows and waited for Salpheth to respond. Salpheth might believe he was bluffing, but he wasn't. Sometimes, dealing with the enemy wasn't worth the risk. Getting rid of Salpheth would alleviate some of the tension on the ship, including himself.

Connor stared at him and opened his mouth to give the order.

"I think it's time for us to make our positions known," Salpheth said.

"No, I want those coordinates or I'm going to kick you off my ship."

Salpheth glared at Connor with soulless, dark eyes. "I needed your ship to take me to a place where I could secure better accommodations. I want to be free of you, just as much as you want to be free of me."

"I could've guessed that. You haven't told me anything I didn't already know. What did you intend to do after you got where you were going?"

Salpheth regarded him thoughtfully for a few moments. "I'm surprised you haven't guessed."

Connor speared a look at him. "Captain Kincaid—"

"I intend to find those responsible for leaving me behind. I believe your species is familiar with the concept of retribution."

Connor frowned. "You want revenge."

Salpheth leaned toward him, his face coming dangerously close to the energy field containing him. His features darkened and his expression became menacing with the promise of severe violence. "You have no idea how much I've considered it. You could say it sustained me during my time with the Aczar," he said in an almost detached sort of way. Then he leaned back and his expression became more passive. "Now, I've laid out my intentions for you to judge."

Connor was quiet for a few moments while he considered it. The comlink with Kincaid remained active, and he knew the CDF captain was waiting for Connor to give the order. Salpheth saw them as a means to an end, but if they became an obstacle to overcome, things would get worse. The trouble was that he wasn't sure what would come of it. If he purged the power core, leaving Salpheth in space, and the Phantom somehow survived, he could include all of humanity in his promise of vengeance.

There was so much that Connor didn't know. Perhaps the ship's point defense systems were enough to destroy the Phantom—but what if they couldn't? The Phantoms were a species he didn't understand. Salpheth had a physical form, but he could also exist in different forms. The other Phantoms Connor had encountered resided outside of n-space. They'd used a machine, some kind of construct, to interact with him. And what if the only way for them to get home was to work with Salpheth?

"Stand down, Captain," Connor said.

"Understood, General," Kincaid replied.

Connor looked at Salpheth. "I'll consider your offer."

Salpheth floated toward the center of the containment field. "I look forward to our next exchange, General Gates." Salpheth closed his eyes, and his body became completely still.

Connor left the secondary power core. He stood outside as the door closed, pausing to get his bearings, then walked down the corridor to the others.

Kincaid gave him a once-over. "Remind me never to play poker against you, sir."

"Did you accomplish your objective, General Gates?" Jorath asked.

Connor exhaled through his nose. "I know more than I did before going in there. So, yeah. Now we need to decide the next steps."

Jorath regarded him for a long moment. "The Krake used to manipulate us. Make promises. Pit various factions of my species against one another. It was madness. Those were dark times for us. My impression of Salpheth is that he operates in a similar manner. His stated goals are simple, yet his motivations and true objectives are more complex."

"Would you trust him?"

Jorath shook his head. "Never, and he doesn't expect you to. I don't know what the most prudent course of action would be."

Connor chuckled a little. "Me either. Thanks for your input."

Jorath nodded. "I will stay here for the remainder of my watch."

Connor and Kincaid left him and went to the conference room near the bridge.

CHAPTER 5

"General," Kincaid said, gesturing toward the Mess Hall, "we all need to consume our designated rations to maintain peak performance."

Connor looked at him for a second. "Did you just quote actual regulation to me?"

He smiled. "Close enough, sir. The meeting can wait a few minutes," Kincaid said, and then pursed his lips. "We could just have it here. We're not the only ones who probably need to eat."

Connor sighed, knowing Kincaid was right. "Go ahead and let the others know."

Kincaid sent a message and then joined Connor.

Mac had prepared some kind of protein-rich pasta with an imitation cream sauce that reminded Connor of Alfredo, but not quite. Mac had converted the supplies they'd gathered from the Aczar homeworld into something they could consume. They could survive on it, and Connor had eaten worse meals while on deployment.

They sat and quickly consumed their portions while the others joined them. Phendran and the other Aczar didn't eat. They didn't have to, having already met their nutrition requirements for the day. They waited patiently for the others to finish their meal, and even though the Aczar didn't consume much food, they had a healthy respect for coming together during a meal. It was a tradition their two species shared.

Connor frowned in thought, and Noah arched an eyebrow at him.

Connor shrugged his shoulder. "I was just thinking about how other intelligent species we've encountered have similar practices to what we do. You know, coming together to share a meal."

Noah nodded. "Makes me wonder about the Phantoms. Does Salpheth need food? How does he sustain himself?"

Phendran looked at him. "He consumes energy."

"Is he feeding off the containment field?" Noah asked.

Phendran nodded. "Yes, but the amounts are quite small."

Connor frowned. "Does he ever increase his consumption rate?"

Several of the others watched with eyebrows raised in concern.

"Do not be worried that he will devour the energy field. He can't do that. It has to do with the way he absorbs the energy. The left-over particles are reabsorbed into the field, so there isn't any degradation."

"That's impressive," Noah said. "I was worried there for a moment."

Seated at the other table were Glenn Rhodes and his daughter, Cassidy. Naya and Seger joined them, along with Rabsaris.

"It's just going to be us," Connor said.

"I'll give the others a status update after this," Noah said.

Connor nodded. "Thanks. Well, you all observed my meeting with Salpheth. I'd like to hear your thoughts on what he said."

Rhodes cleared his throat and shook his head. "How can we trust anything he says?"

The question was echoed by some of the others, and Connor waited, knowing the value in letting the others express themselves.

Noah raised one of his palms into the air. "We're never going to have a sure thing here."

Connor nodded. "No, we're not."

"I can't see allowing Salpheth access to the nav system," Rhodes said.

"Agreed," Connor said and looked at the others. "It's important to remember our goals. We want to get home safe." He looked at Phendran and the other Aczar. "Return you to your planet."

Phendran nodded. "Your assistance is very much appreciated in that matter."

Rhodes gave Connor a considering look. "If you could have anything at all to help you make this decision, what would it be?" he asked, and he tilted his head to the side. "Outside of finding our own way home. I think we could all agree on that."

A few chuckles came from the others, and Connor considered the question for a moment.

"I wish we knew a way to contact the Phantoms. Outside of finding our own way home, that's something I think would be of benefit to us."

Noah heaved a sigh and nodded. "They followed you the last time. There is no evidence that they were able to follow us this time, though."

"Yeah, I think they would've contacted us if they could." Connor sighed. "And I think they'd know how best to deal with Salpheth."

"I wouldn't be so sure about that," Noah said. Connor arched an eyebrow. Noah shrugged. "They were the ones who left him behind. Or at least someone did. They just cast him out. They might not know any better than we do."

"So, he was exiled or something. We've done the same thing to our criminals," Connor replied.

"Yes, we've exiled extreme criminals, but we also supplied them," Noah said. "And we create a way for them to return to our society. We make allowances for repentance after they've faced the consequences of their actions. We haven't left one of our own on a world surrounded by an alien species who then kept them prisoner."

Phendran and the other Aczar looked at Noah in surprise and a little alarm.

"I'm not judging what your ancestors did. I'm merely stating the facts as I know them. Am I wrong?" Noah asked.

Phendran shook his head. "You are not incorrect."

"We need to be careful not to oversimplify historical events," Connor warned.

Noah nodded. "I understand that. Salpheth can assert whatever he wants, but he's also a product of what his life has been. I think it's important to remember that when we interact with him."

"Be that as it may," Rhodes said, "if we cooperate with Salpheth, we're putting our lives in the hands of something we can neither control nor completely understand. How can that end well?"

Noah was about to speak but stopped.

Connor gave him a companionable nod. His own thoughts had taken him to the very same sentiment. "It's complicated, isn't it?"

"Not the way I see it," Rhodes said. "We'll never be able to trust him. Therefore, we shouldn't put him in a position where he can be a threat."

"So, you would just eliminate him? Dump him out in space and move on?" Noah asked.

Rhodes frowned. "It's what General Gates was going to do."

Noah shook his head. "No. He would do that to protect the rest of us, and so would I. Has anyone considered that maybe we should try to understand Salpheth before we decide what his fate should be?"

Connor knew his friend. Noah wouldn't give up on anyone if there was a chance they could be redeemed. It was something

Connor admired about him, but in this he couldn't agree. "I'm not sure we can understand Salpheth to that extent. He doesn't have the same moral foundation we do. His actions and the things he says prove that."

Noah looked away for a few moments, thinking. "Let's flip this around. No, bear with me for a moment," he said as some of the others started to groan.

"Go on, Noah," Connor said.

"Salpheth needs a ship. He's already admitted it. Wherever he was going would've had to give him what he needed. So, wherever he was going has some kind of ship or other method of transportation."

Rhodes considered it for a moment and frowned. "He's been imprisoned for how long?"

Connor looked at Phendran.

"Over fifty generations have passed. About one thousand years," Phendran said.

Rhodes's eyes widened and he looked at Connor. "Is the translation accurate?"

"I'm willing to take it on faith. Regardless, math unit conversion aside, it's been a long time," Connor said. He looked at Noah and gestured for him to continue.

"That's exactly my point," Noah said. "Salpheth doesn't trust anyone. He's been abandoned or exiled. Amounts to the same thing. We would call it abandonment issues. Maybe we could get him to trust us."

Connor gave him a pointed look. "I'm not going to let him out of the containment field. That's a leap of faith I won't take."

"No, of course not. Neither would I. He's offered to work with us, so let's work with him. Give him the opportunity to prove who he is," Noah said.

Phendran's large ears fluttered irritably. "This course of action is unwise. General Gates, you should rid yourself of Salpheth as quickly as possible. With the advancements in your subspace communications, you have options for figuring out where Salpheth was going."

Noxrey growled a chittered response to Phendran, and the translator only was able to interpret the end. "You go too far!"

"Things will never be as they once were on Ichlos, Noxrey. Even if Salpheth were to return, the evidence of his manipulation of our species is overwhelming. It's time for us to be rid of his influence and make our own future," Phendran said.

Noxrey glared at him for a few seconds, then said. "We should discuss this elsewhere."

"Very well," Phendran replied.

The other Aczar stood and left the Mess Hall.

Phendran stopped at the entry and looked at Connor. "General Gates, we need to confer among ourselves. I don't envy the decision you must make. If you were to give me and mine a vote, it would be for you to return us to our planet."

"I intend to do that, no matter what happens now," Connor said.

"I leave you to it," Phendran replied and left.

Rhodes looked at Connor. "Shouldn't they have an escort?"

Connor smiled. "They do. Sergeant Seger slipped out after Noxrey left. He'll keep an eye on them."

Rhodes looked over to where Seger had been, then shook his head. "I completely missed it."

An uneasy silence settled on them, and that was what Connor wanted. This was a very difficult decision he had to make, and now the rest of them understood it better than they had before.

"Okay, I need some time to think about all the things that were brought up here. All of you made good points, some I'd already thought of and other things I hadn't considered. In the meantime, I'll be on the bridge. If anyone comes up with another solution, that's where you'll find me."

Connor stood.

Noah looked up at him. "Connor, I'm not suggesting that we forget about how dangerous Salpheth is. What I *am* suggesting is that if we treat him with a little humanity, maybe it would be reciprocated in kind."

Connor smiled. "I know, Noah. You're my moral compass."

Noah shook his head and grinned.

Connor didn't. "I'm not kidding."

Noah's eyebrows raised in surprise, and Connor left the Mess Hall.

Kincaid followed him out. "I get the sense you'd like some time alone, General. I'll wait outside the bridge."

"Negative, Captain. You'll be my sounding board," Connor replied.

CHAPTER 6

ETHAN REVIEWED the protocols for contact with a previously unknown alien species. The introduction to the sections for First Contact gave a brief history of how these protocols had come to be. However, since it was the colonists who had been the first to establish contact with multiple alien species, those experiences dictated practical changes to protect the people involved. They hadn't encountered an intelligent species that was completely peaceful, and Ethan had no illusions that whoever was at the other end of that distress beacon might be dangerous. But whoever they were, they needed help.

By the end of his watch, the away teams had returned to the ship. He scheduled a meeting with his senior staff and went to his office near the bridge. Colonel Phillips had already given preliminary approval of the mission, and Ethan needed to send the specifics of their plan up the chain for official approval to be logged.

He ate dinner alone at his desk. Cynergy had only just returned to the ship and needed to get cleaned up. Spending more than a day deployed on a shuttle with minimal creature comforts tended to make one ripe by the end.

He considered playing the message from his mother again but decided not to. It answered some of the questions he had as to what was being done in the search for his father. There really wasn't anything he could do, but he felt a pang of guilt at not being there for his mother and sister. They weren't alone, but he wanted to be there for them.

Ethan closed the holoscreen over his desk and stood. The muscles of his shoulders were a little stiff from his workout earlier. He'd managed to get some downtime. Actually, he'd taken the time to blow off some steam, and the results were a more focused mind.

He left his office and went to a nearby conference room. Will Qualmann was sitting at the dark table with Captain Seana Brett and Captain Tom Washburn.

The edges of Ethan's lips lifted at Qualmann's arched eyebrow. Qualmann had lost the bet, and they both knew it.

Seana noticed the exchange and frowned. "Did something happen?"

Ethan sat in one of the burgundy chairs and smiled. "Some of us are learning the price of betting against their commanding officer."

Washburn looked at Qualmann and laughed. "You got caught up in that?"

Qualmann tipped his head to the side. "I had three-to-one odds. I thought it was worth it."

Washburn shook his head. "I thought you knew him better than that by now," he said, gesturing toward Ethan. "He gets cranky when he hasn't exercised."

Seana sighed, looking amused, and Ethan gave her a wink.

The door opened, and other attendees arrived. Cynergy came over and sat next to him, squeezing his shoulder a little as she sat down.

Wade Walsh strode in, grinning. "Thank you, Major Gates," he said and threw a prideful look at Qualmann.

"You win some; you lose some," Qualmann replied.

Cynergy frowned and looked at Ethan.

"I'll tell you later," Ethan said, and turned to address the others. "I'll keep this as brief as possible, but we've got a new mission. Lieutenant Brett, please begin."

For the next ten minutes, Lieutenant Brett went over the data she'd collected and analyzed about the alien distress signal.

"Just to clarify," Cynergy said, "we're assuming this is a distress call."

"There is a high probability that the signal *is* a distress call. I'd hesitate to refer to it as a mere assumption," Lieutenant Brett replied.

Cynergy nodded. "I understand that, Lieutenant. I'm not implying that this discovery is less than what it is. However, we have no idea how long the signal has been active. What we know is that it repeats." She looked at Ethan. "Have you considered that this is some kind of lure for an ambush?"

Cynergy and other hybrids were not part of the colonial military, but they had decades of experience in a long war of survival with the Vemus.

"We don't know for sure. We won't know until we get there and assess the situation," Ethan replied.

"I'm glad to hear that," Cynergy said and looked at the others. "Our experience with the Vemus is that while they are most often a hive-intelligence, they're also not beyond setting traps. They've used distress beacons to lure us to an area, only to attack."

Benjamin Horak, the lead science officer, raised his hand to speak. "We don't know whether this alien signal has anything to do with the Vemus."

Cynergy glanced at Lieutenant Brett for a second and shook her head.

"What brought us here was the detection of Vemus exoskeletal material," Cynergy said.

"Which has not been confirmed, and there is a significant likelihood of this detection being a false positive," Ethan said.

Cynergy's gaze narrowed. "We didn't get a chance to finish our assessment."

"Understood," Ethan said and looked at the others. "The alien signal has the higher priority."

Wade cleared his throat. "Do you think we'll be able to return here to complete the investigation?"

"We'll mark the location and upload your current findings to COMCENT," Qualmann said. "As for whether it will be us who return here, it's too soon to tell."

Wade looked at Ethan. "Is this true? That we might not return here?"

Ethan considered it for a moment. "Yes. There are other leads for us to follow."

"But this is related to the Vemus," Cynergy said.

"Tracking the Vemus is still a priority, but think this through. Best case scenario we find some small remnant, and the data gleaned from it doesn't lead us to any further conclusions. If there were actual ships trapped in that mess, we would've detected them." Ethan paused for a second and looked at the others. Some were in agreement while others looked frustrated. "The simple fact of the matter is that we can't be everywhere at once. Our interstellar probes are constantly on the move, sending us new data."

"And," Qualmann said, "it's going to take us about a week to reach the source of the distress beacon."

Vemus infestations eventually led to the creation of an alpha, who would then organize the resources and technology on a planet to build a fleet. That's what they'd discovered on other worlds that suffered from an infestation. Earth's experience with the Vemus was different in that scientists were able to change them to pursue humans across the stars to the colony. It's not clear what the Vemus would've done had they succeeded in taking over New Earth. Would they have reverted to some kind of latent protocol that compelled them to travel to the source of all Vemus?

"This is for the away team that just returned," Ethan said. "Use the computing core to conduct your own analysis of the data you've collected. Build a case for returning here, and I promise that it will be considered. I can't commit anything else at this time."

Cynergy looked away from him, and Benjamin Horak cleared his throat.

"Tracking Vemus alphas has proven to be much more difficult than many people thought it would be."

"Okay, I'll bite," Ethan said. "Tell us something we don't know."

Several chuckles sounded around the conference table.

Horak bobbed his head once. "It's interesting. They limit themselves to the technology available. It could be that there are many alphas out there traveling slower than the speed of light. That would make any journey take thousands of years to complete, if not longer. It's just not an efficient system."

"Unless there is hierarchy," Cynergy replied.

"I'm aware of the hierarchy theory, where Vemus alphas are not traveling to the source of all Vemus but to a presumed super-Alpha responsible for a particular region. Once absorbed into the hive or a collective, they go on up the chain until they reach the ultimate source of the Vemus," Horak said.

"It's a good theory, but it has to be proven," Ethan said.

"Which is why we ought to pursue every lead that involves the Vemus. The future of the Confederation depends on it," Cynergy replied.

"We're actually quite lucky," Horak said, and the others stared at him. "If this Vemus hierarchy does prove to be accurate, I'm actually encouraged by the fact that we haven't found any alphas near Old Earth or New Earth. This discussion would be different if that were the case."

"Going back to a slow method of travel," Ethan said. "That supports that the Vemus are operating under their own time…" he paused for a second. "I hesitate to say 'constraints' because I don't think that's appropriate. I think the Vemus just do things like a biological machine that doesn't know any better."

Qualmann cleared his throat. "Sir, we're getting off topic."

Ethan nodded. "Right, thanks for that. Travel time to the source of the signal will be five days. Then, we'll do another assessment of the region before committing to any kind of close contact."

They went through a few more line items, and Ethan noticed that the hybrids at the meeting had settled into a disappointed silence. He'd spent a lot of time among hybrids and was one of them, but sometimes he felt as if he were on the outside. It had been years since he'd been turned into a hybrid, and in many ways, he was still an outsider. Many of the hybrids who joined the Confederation exploration initiative were determined to assist in hunting the Vemus. Their expectations were that the Vemus should've been found in other star systems near Old Earth, but that hadn't happened. Instead of being relieved at learning this, their frustration had increased. As a group, the hybrids on the ship had become more serious. They'd changed in the time the CDF had liberated Earth from the Vemus, and sometimes Ethan wasn't sure that the changes in the hybrids had been for the better. He agreed that the Vemus were a threat and that they shouldn't ignore them, but that didn't mean they should blindly pursue the Vemus to the exclusion of all else.

CHAPTER 7

THE MEETING ENDED, and while Ethan walked with his wife through the ship's corridors, an uneasy silence settled between them.

They reached their quarters and Cynergy looked up at him. "Ethan, I need to clear my head."

"I could go with you."

She shook her head. "No, that's fine. You've had a long day, too. I just want to be alone for a bit."

She stepped in for a quick hug and then he watched her leave.

Ethan entered their quarters, and the ceiling's ambient lighting brightened. The glossy, pale walls reflected the light, giving their quarters a warm, welcoming feel. It was essentially an apartment. Spacious living quarters had been provided for all on the ship. This was deemed essential for long-term exploration initiatives and was a necessity he appreciated.

He walked into the living room and sat down. The smart cushion realigned to support him, and Ethan glanced at the holoscreen on the wall. It showed a large panorama of the ship's external video feed, which displayed a breathtaking expanse of stars. He sat there for a few minutes, allowing his thoughts to come and go. He dozed for a bit and then looked at the time. An hour had passed and Cynergy still hadn't come back. He'd never get to sleep without them talking.

He stood and left their quarters. It was past twenty-two hundred hours, and the lighting in the corridors was dimmer than normal for the late evening hour. He walked the corridors of the ship, making his way to the maintenance workshop near the primary hangar bay. He found Cynergy working at one of the benches.

She sensed his approach and turned toward him.

"I had to clear my own head," Ethan said.

He closed the distance between them and wrapped his arm over her shoulders. She leaned into him, and for a moment there was peace between them.

"I missed you," he said.

"I missed you, too."

He dragged over a stool and sat. "Why do I feel like you're avoiding me?"

"I'm not avoiding you," she said a little too quickly and looked away. "It's my turn to perform maintenance checks on our equipment."

Ethan arched an eyebrow, staring at her.

She sighed. "I just wanted some alone time."

"You know, it's not the end of the world that we didn't find the Vemus here."

"We'll never really know, will we?"

"I know you like to be thorough."

"So do you, Ethan. It's why I'm surprised by this."

He regarded her for a moment. Her long, dark-blonde hair was tied back into a loose ponytail. She stared at him, her honey-brown eyes a mix of warmth and frustration.

"Cyn, the detection criteria for exoskeletal material are prone to false positives. It's not the fault of the probe's evaluation parameters; it's because the exoskeletal material is like camouflage. It resembles naturally occurring structures in space. It could be any chunk of rock or ice that's large enough to be a ship. The data from the scans didn't indicate a hidden power signature of any kind."

Her lips compressed for a moment. "That's true. We should cut short any search effort where immediate gratification doesn't occur."

"You're being unreasonable."

She lifted her chin with a sneer, but then it fizzled out. She reached out to take hold of his hands. "Ethan, I'm sorry. I don't mean to be so hard on you. I know you're in command of the ship and there are protocols you need to follow. But I'm worried that cutting this effort short will lead to other things being cut short. Before we all know it, no one is searching for the Vemus."

"It wouldn't be such a bad thing," Ethan said, and her hands stiffened in his. "Hear me out. I'm not suggesting giving up on the Vemus. Believe me, I'm not. But it shouldn't be the cornerstone of all our exploration efforts."

"How long will it be before the Confederation changes its priorities? Soon, no missions will be authorized for exploration until we've spread out enough to make it worthwhile."

"Don't you think you're being a little too cynical about this? No one is proposing that."

She looked away from him for a moment. "I just don't want us to be blindsided again. Humanity was blindsided, and it nearly wiped us out the first time. It was something we all had to live with —until you guys came back. We have different perspectives on this. I hope the Confederation doesn't lose sight of that."

Ethan gently rubbed the top of her hand. It was cool to the touch. She seemed to be cold a lot lately.

"What if the Phantoms are right about us not being able to handle the Vemus? They suggested that we build ourselves up before pursuing them."

She inhaled. "And in the meantime, the Vemus are allowed to conquer an untold number of worlds? Is that fair?"

"I think you're oversimplifying the matter."

"Or maybe you're not thinking it through."

"I *have* thought about this, just as much as you have. It's not fair that other worlds will become victim to the Vemus, but is it our responsibility to ensure that everything that happens in the galaxy is fair? Kinda a tall order, since we haven't seen hardly any part of it. Plus, our population is extremely small."

"So, you're saying we should stop?"

"No, that's not it. Slow down maybe," Ethan said and paused for a moment. "Why does it have to be one or the other? Why shouldn't we take a measured approach?"

"Because that's how things usually are. We either search for the Vemus to better understand them so we can protect our future, or we don't. How else are we supposed to look at it?"

"What if we don't find them?" he asked. She considered it for a few moments, but didn't reply. "We stay out here for years, decades even, and we never find so much as a hint of them around. Would you be satisfied, then?"

"I don't think it will be that long."

"The other concern that comes up in us searching for the Vemus is leading them back home. Sometimes, when you kick the proverbial hornet's nest you not only get stung, but you bring down the entire nest down on yourself."

"I understand."

"Are you sure?" he countered. She frowned for a moment. "Me and every other CO with a ship has standing orders to prevent the Vemus from taking captives at all costs. This includes eliminating the prisoners."

"I knew they were discussing that, but I didn't know they'd moved forward with it."

"It's not just a failsafe measure. It's meant to make us cautious about the risks we choose to take. If you were captured, I'd be put in an impossible position."

The edges of her lips lifted a little. "Well then, I better make sure I never get captured."

"This is more serious than you realize. My superior officers aren't messing around with this. There's a cost to what we're doing, and sometimes I'm not sure it's worth it."

"It *is* worth it. Protecting future generations is worth it."

"Yeah, I just don't like it. I never thought I'd say this, but sometimes I hope we never encounter the Vemus again—not a remnant, an active infestation, or something we haven't even considered yet." He sighed.

"I understand, Ethan. Sometimes I hope the same thing."

His eyebrows raised. "Really?"

She nodded. "Of course, I do. So do the others."

"I'm surprised to hear you say that."

"Well, it's true, but I don't think it'll be that long before we find them again. I know the odds are against it, but I just believe it."

"Is that why it's so frustrating when you don't find them? There is a danger in believing that the enemy lurks around every corner. We need to balance our approach to this."

"I know, and you're right. We can be intense when it comes to the Vemus." She eyed him for a moment.

"That's funny because I thought I was speaking with my wife and not the others."

"Well, I'm aware of how some of the others regard the hybrids."

Ethan leaned in a little and stared at her. "I'm still just speaking with my wife, and the other hybrids will have to find a way to cope on their own."

Cynergy smiled and kissed him. He held her for a few moments, and the tension drained out of them.

He released her, and she regarded him for a second.

"You sound a lot like your father sometimes."

"That's good."

She smiled. "I meant it as a compliment. It just takes me by surprise sometimes."

Ethan looked away for a second, and Cyn frowned. "What's wrong?"

He exhaled softly. "He's missing. My father is missing and they're unable to locate him." He proceeded to tell her about the report he'd received.

"The whole ship is missing?"

He nodded. "Parts of the docking clamps and partial sections of the facility where the ship was being retrofitted. One of the prevalent theories is that somehow the I-Drive was engaged."

"On the planet? I didn't think that would work on a ship that size."

"Ordinarily not. The power core is too small, but the ship was in the middle of a major upgrade and was attached to the facility's main power core."

Cynergy's eyes widened.

Ethan was aware of certain weapons development theories that proposed the use of the I-Drive as a weapon. Instead of propelling a ship through space, it could use gravitational forces to destroy a target. In theory, with enough power it could have destroyed a planet.

"The facility didn't have enough power to destroy the planet. It could've wreaked havoc on the region, but that's why the facility was thousands of kilometers away from any inhabited city."

She shook her head. "That's one way to think about it. What if the nav system had the ship going along the planet? It could destabilize the planet's crust."

"Yeah, or the nav system could've taken them through the planet. They're not sure of the destructive power, but it would've meant that anyone on the ship would've been killed instantly."

"Oh, Ethan," she said. "But that didn't happen, which means something else did."

"Yeah. The CDF deployed scout ships that have been searching for them but haven't found anything."

"Maybe it's something they haven't considered yet."

Ethan frowned, shoulders slumping a little. "Like what?"

She shrugged. "I don't know. When nothing makes sense, it's time to consider other options."

"I've been trying to do that, and I keep coming up short."

Cynergy stood and pulled him to his feet. "Maybe you just need to sleep on it. Come on, let's go back to our quarters."

CHAPTER 8

CONNOR SPENT most of the day on the bridge. Kincaid joined him for a couple of hours, and then Connor sent him away. Throughout the day, various people stopped in to offer a few ideas about what they could do but didn't offer anything he hadn't already considered.

Glen Rhodes and his daughter, Cassidy, were on the bridge with Connor. Cassidy was quiet as her father had settled into a frustrated silence.

"I don't think there is a single right answer," Connor said. "I'm considering the least bad option we have. No matter how you slice it, we're on a lifeboat out in the middle of nowhere."

Rhodes gave him an appraising look. "Have you sailed before?"

Connor chuckled and shook his head. "No. Been on a few research submarines once."

Rhodes raised his eyebrows. "Really? When?"

"On New Earth. Went through the first Arch Gateway discovered at the bottom of a lake."

Cassidy frowned and glanced at her father.

Rhodes blew out a breath. "I remember when that happened.

You've been part of most of the pivotal moments in our colony's history."

"Just lucky I guess."

Cassidy stared at him. "Have you ever written any of it down?"

"A journal?" Connor asked. She nodded, and he shook his head. "Not much. Some video logs and such. Haven't looked at any of those things in a long time. I've been busy."

"Have you considered adding them to the Colonial Archive?" she asked.

"Cass," Rhodes said.

She frowned. "What?"

"It might be a sensitive subject."

She blinked and looked at Connor. "Oh, I'm sorry. I didn't even think about that."

Connor waved away the comment and looked at Rhodes. "I appreciate that, but she's right. It might be time to review some of those things and decide what's worth preserving."

She smiled. "For what it's worth, I think all of it would be a very good thing to preserve."

She reminded Connor a little bit of his own daughter. "Are you thinking of changing careers?" he asked. "Switch to archivist for a while?"

Cassidy grinned and looked at her father for a second. "I don't know. I never thought about it." Her expression sobered. "There's a lot I haven't thought about."

"We'll be fine," Rhodes said, and she looked at him. "I believe it. You should, too."

"I do," she replied. "It's just that sometimes…" she shrugged a little.

"Me, too," Connor said. The others looked at him. "I'm just as human as the next guy. Anyone who says they never experience doubt is either lying or selling something."

They were quiet for a few seconds.

"I do think Noah has a good idea about how we should interact with Salpheth," Cassidy said. She looked at her father. "I know you don't agree."

Rhodes sighed. "Noah is a brilliant man. A bit of an idealist but not without a healthy dose of realism. Would you agree with that?" he asked, looking at Connor.

"He'll never give up on you, even if you cross the line. I've seen him overcome so many things. People who…" Connor shook his head. "Doesn't matter. Noah will always seek to find a solution that preserves the integrity and soul of everyone around him. It's a very good thing, but sometimes it becomes an impossible task."

"You'd know a thing or two about that," Rhodes replied.

"And everyone will have their own interpretation of whether you made the right call. It's just the way it is."

Rhodes stood. "We'll leave you to it. Unless you'd like us to stay?"

Connor shook his head. "I'll be fine."

Rhodes regarded him for a long moment. "Before all this happened," he said, gesturing in the air, "I didn't completely appreciate your position—how difficult it is to take the lead, even when others think they could do a better job. For what it's worth. I'm glad you're here, General Gates. I'll support whatever decision you make."

Rhodes extended his hand toward Connor, and he shook it.

After Rhodes and Cassidy left the bridge, Connor thought about how all their interactions had changed. They'd gone from a group of strangers tossed into an almost impossible situation, not trusting anyone, to a more seasoned respect for each other. Connor wasn't immune to snap judgements or even a few unhealthy biases, but he tried to limit them where he could.

Phendran and Noah entered the bridge.

"Still here, I see," Noah said.

"How else were you going to find me?"

Noah snorted. "Phendran wanted to speak with you."

Phendran studied Connor for a moment.

Connor glanced at Noah. "The comms buoy network we detected hasn't changed. No more came online, and there has been no response to our communication attempts."

Noah nodded. "It could be automated like ours are."

"Could be a remnant of what was once available. The only way to know for sure is if we go to the nearest one and check it out."

Noah slowly bobbed his head. "And it could be taking us even farther away from home."

Connor looked at Phendran. "I know you want to return home. How are the others doing?"

"They're worried. Noxrey in particular, but Kholva and Vorix show signs of increasing apprehension because of our current predicament," Phendran replied.

Connor regarded the Aczar for a long moment. "And you?"

Phendran sighed. "I share their concerns. Like you and the others, we're worried we will never return home. Even if we were to make it to your home world, can you guarantee that your government will behave any differently than we did when you visited Ichlos?"

"We would. Phendran, we have experience working with alien species. If you help us return to New Earth, we will take you back to Ichlos."

"Yes, but how long will that take?" Phendran asked.

"That I don't know," Connor replied.

Phendran looked at Noah. "Do you know?"

He shook his head. "This is experimental technology. We'll need to perform analysis and testing to ensure that it works as we expect it to. Then, we'll need to outfit a ship for the journey."

Connor nodded. "It's going to take some time. I'm not sure how long, but it won't be years."

Phendran considered this for a few moments. "Considering

how our Ruling Council was going to treat you, I'd say that is more than fair."

The Aczar government was going to take the *Pathfinder* away and dismantle it. They told them that they would be able to live out the remainder of their lives on Ichlos, but Connor knew better. Ichlos's atmosphere was toxic to both Humans and Ovarrow, so they'd never be able to survive. The only reason Phendran and the others were able to survive on the *Pathfinder* was because their SRAs helped them adapt to the artificial atmosphere on the ship. The method was complex, and it stretched the capabilities of the SRA by increasing the synergistic relationship between the artificial intelligence and the Aczar host.

"Phendran, I give you my word that you will not be stranded on New Earth," Connor said.

Phendran looked confused. "The translation is puzzling me."

"I promise that I will personally see to it that you and the others go home in the event that the leadership on my home world begin to delay their efforts to do the same. Within reason. Can you accept that?"

Phendran was quiet.

"You should believe him," Noah said. "Connor is known to always keep his promises."

Phendran looked up at Connor. "Very well. I accept your promise."

Connor was glad Phendran had been reassured by what they'd already agreed upon. It would be better for everyone if they all worked together.

He looked at the main holoscreen, which showed where the comms buoys had been detected. They stretched out for hundreds of light-years.

"Picking one of these at random doesn't seem like a good idea. The ship is barely holding together as it is," Connor said.

"The hull will hold together. It's the critical systems I'm worried about," Noah replied.

Connor turned toward him. "Even if we're able to refuel our power core somehow, how many times do you think we'd be able to use the I-Drive? The drive core is an issue as well, and we can't maintain it because…"

There was no reason for him to say more. Noah knew as well as he did that they didn't have the means to perform any kind of maintenance tasks required for optimal functionality from the I-Drive. That was when failures occurred. Even now, they were taking a significant risk when using it.

Noah shrugged. "Two more times, then we'd have to reassess."

Connor looked at Phendran. "Do your archives have any information on the kinds of ships the Phantoms used?"

"No, there is no information like that."

Noah frowned. "But your ancestors traveled to Ichlos. Wasn't that knowledge preserved?"

"Yes, but the details were removed. It was decided that we would abandon any and all developments of technology that would temp our species to leave our planet."

Connor sighed. "We're going to have to deal with Salpheth. He has the knowledge we need. And we have the transportation he requires."

"He did offer to help," Noah said. "I know we can't trust him, but it's not like he wants to die out here any more than we do."

"And he'll say anything he has to in order to get out of his cage," Connor said.

Noah's gaze sank a little. "Yeah," he replied. "So, how are you going to do this?"

"I think he'll know if I lie to him, so I was thinking of just being completely and brutally honest. I'll try to work with him as best I can. I'll even treat him with some cordial respect. But as long as he's a prisoner, he'll think like a prisoner."

Noah frowned in thought. "What if you promised to free him?"

Connor smiled. "That, my friend, is what I call a carrot. It'll be his motivation for helping us. Well, that and us taking him where he wanted to go."

"But will you do it? Will you free him?" Noah asked.

Connor took a few moments to think about his answer. Phendran watched him closely.

"Honestly, I don't know."

"If you think he can tell if you're lying, don't you think he'll sense that you'll double-cross him?"

"Yes."

Noah's eyebrows knitted, and he chewed his bottom lip for a second.

"I expect him to double-cross us."

"What if he doesn't?"

Connor stared at him for a second. "He's responsible for manipulating the Aczars for a thousand years. Do you honestly think he'll not seize any opportunity to change the status quo? I'd be looking for it. So would you. So would anyone."

"Yeah, but if he didn't."

"Okay, let's consider it. If he was true to his word, I'd need to think about what I was allowing into the galaxy. He knows about the Vemus. He might even be able to trace how they've spread throughout this region. We don't know if the Vemus have spread everywhere. I hope not."

Noah was quiet for a few seconds. "Well, we shouldn't condemn him without any proof."

Connor nodded. "I know. It's going to depend on how this goes. What we're about to do. I don't think he's going to have a sudden change of heart just because we're nice to him. However," Connor said before Noah could reply, "I do intend to be straightforward with him. His life will be on the line for as long as I can keep it that way. It's either him or us."

Noah heaved a sigh and nodded.

Phendran regarded both of them. "I think you'll do well against Salpheth. Well enough to try."

"You still think I shouldn't even take the chance?" Connor asked.

"I've already stated as much. All I can do now is help you in any way that I can so we all get what we want."

Connor shared a look with Noah for a second. "Alright, tomorrow we'll see just how serious Salpheth's offer really is."

CHAPTER 9

As the week drew to a close, Ethan noticed a sense of anticipation building among the crew. The alien signal was still being detected as they closed in on the location. He walked through the corridors, heading to the bridge and standing next to Qualmann.

"Good morning, Will."

Qualmann had the late-night watch, but looked as fresh-faced as when he'd arrived for duty.

"Feel like going fishing this morning, sir?" Qualmann asked.

"That depends. How's it look out there?" Ethan asked, lifting his chin toward the main holoscreen.

"Lieutenant Jackson, do you have an update for me?" Qualmann asked.

"Exiting hyperspace in three minutes, Major."

Qualmann flicked his eyebrows. "Right at the top of the minute. How's that for timing?"

Ethan rolled his eyes a little. "Very impressive. Be sure to include that in the ship's log." He pursed his lips, considering. "Maybe even your personal log."

Benjamin Horak turned away from the science officer's workstation to look at them. "Tell me you don't fill your personal log with that kind of stuff."

Qualmann shrugged and stared at him for a moment. "It's personal, Ben."

Ben blinked and cast a quick look Ethan.

"No worries, Benjamin. Just a little easing of the tension," Ethan said. "Tactical, be ready with a full scan once we come out of hyperspace."

"Yes, Major Gates," Seana replied.

A countdown appeared in the lower right corner of the main holoscreen, and when the timer reached zero, the *Ascendant* left hyperspace. The shifting patterns of hyperspace gave way to flashes as the I-Drive bled transit energy in curtains of cerulean glow, and the flashes cycled downward as their velocity quickly decreased until the ship was once again in n-space.

The main holoscreen shifted to display a panoramic view of space with a tactical overlay. An icon appeared, marking the distant source of the distress beacon.

"Sir," Captain Brett said, "scout class ship detected as the source of the signal. No other ships detected in the area."

The HUD updated as scans identified several asteroids. Ethan studied the screen, considering.

Qualmann looked at him. "What do you think?"

"I wonder why a ship that size is out here at all. Was it damaged and got left behind, or was it running from something?"

Qualmann nodded. "We could increase the range of our scans and see if something else gets picked up."

Ethan considered it and then shook his head. "Helm, take us in."

"Yes, Major," Lieutenant Jackson replied.

Ethan walked over to the tactical workstation. "What kind of energy signature does that ship have?"

"Not much that we can tell from this range, sir," Captain Brett said. "If they have protocols like ours, they could be using emergency power to maintain the distress beacon while conserving their main power core."

Ethan nodded. "Carry on, Captain," he said and returned to the command station.

Qualmann sat next to him in the auxiliary station.

It would take them a little over an hour to reach the alien ship. Ethan thought about the reports he'd read about CDF missions during the Krake War. Until that time, space warfare had only been conducted against other humans. None of the evidence with this alien scout ship indicated a trap, but he still wanted to be cautious. Earlier in his career he'd have exercised minimal caution while going straight at an objective, but years in the CDF with increased responsibility had taught him the value of a measured approach.

"Ops, have a subspace-capable comms drone ready to deploy. Include current tactical data package," Ethan said.

"Drone ready for deployment. Ship's logs and tactical data package uploaded, sir," Lieutenant Gooding said. "I have a subroutine updating the drone systems until you order it deployed."

"Very good, Lieutenant," Ethan replied.

Comms drones were an essential risk-mitigation tool in the event of a surprise attack that impeded the ship's communication capabilities.

"Washburn and his recon team are ready," Qualmann said.

Ethan snorted a little. He would've liked to have gone with them to investigate the alien ship. "A week in transit with only drills to occupy them? I bet they're more than ready."

As the *Ascendant* came closer to the alien scout ship, they were able to get more detailed scans of the vessel.

"Ship has taken damage near the engine pod, and the hull shows signs of energy weapons damage. This ship has been in a battle, but some of the damage appears to be the result of an impact with an asteroid or another ship. Our analysis AI doesn't give a high score either, sir," Captain Brett said.

"Comms, has there been any response to our hails?" Ethan asked.

"Negative, Major," Lieutenant Samantha Trickle replied. "No response at all. Their comms system might be disregarding our communication attempts because we're not following their protocols."

Ethan's eyebrows rose, and Lieutenant Trickle smiled. He nodded once. "Understood. Keep monitoring."

The alien scout ship was moving through space, and they matched its speed and trajectory.

"Ops, send the recon team to the ship," Ethan said.

Lieutenant Gooding relayed Ethan's orders.

"No heat signatures detected in the ship," Captain Brett said. "I've relayed the best entry point to the away team."

A recon shuttle left the *Ascendant,* taking Captain Washburn and his team to the alien ship. A comlink was established from the shuttle.

The shuttle flew to the derelict alien scout ship. The once sleek hull was now pockmarked with battle scars, and the metallic panels were streaked with strange, iridescent stains—perhaps remnants of fuel or some kind of alien atmosphere. It was frigate-sized, and depending on the size of the aliens, could have a crew of over a hundred if they were close to the size of Humans.

CDF scout ships were designed for speed and increased scanning capabilities. They weren't meant for fighting battles. Usually, their mandate was to run when faced with a hostile target. They were to report back to the fleet or task force rather than engaging in a conflict. In other instances, scout ships were used as messengers carrying vital intelligence.

"Ascendant," Captain Washburn said, "we've reached the target

coordinates. Thanks for that. The big hole in the side of the ship was a dead giveaway. We could almost dock the shuttle to it."

"Why thank you, Captain. I aim to please," Captain Brett replied dryly.

"There's nothing wrong with your aim, Seana. That's what I like about you. Heading inside. Washburn out."

Ethan chuckled.

He listened as Washburn and his team explored the alien ship. It had no atmosphere, but some systems still had power. He leaned back in the command chair and waited.

CHAPTER 10

"WE'RE ALMOST TO THE BRIDGE," Washburn said. "They've positioned it near engineering in the ship's center."

There were risks inherent to locating the bridge near engineering, but there were always tradeoffs. Main engineering on colonial vessels was home to the power core, computing core, and engines—both sub-light and the I-Drive. All were targets for enemy fire, and although the bridge of the alien ship was located in an armored section of the ship, it was also the part of the ship that would be the most targeted.

"How's the damage inside the ship?" Ethan asked.

"Most of the damage is in line with an explosive delivery system meant to crack a ship wide open. Nothing is left of it, but I wasn't kidding when I said we could almost fly the shuttle inside that hole. None of my teams have encountered any aliens. Crew quarters are empty, if a little strange."

Ethan glanced at Qualmann for a second. "In what way are they strange?"

"The corridors are large enough for us to move through, but the crew quarters have lower ceilings and what I think is a bed is in the middle of the room. Reminds me of a nest. Check this out," Washburn said.

A video recording appeared on Ethan's holoscreen. The room was octagonal, with a smaller, sunken octagonal area in its center. Dark blue cushioning lined the inside, with padded shelves on each side. A person could sit in the "bed," but it wouldn't be comfortable to sleep in.

"Without any bodies to examine, I'm not sure what kind of beings these aliens were. Their control interfaces are easy to use, so I guess they have some kind of hands," Washburn said.

Horak cleared his throat. "That makes sense. Advanced civilizations should be adept at using tools."

Washburn grinned. "Very insightful, Dr. Horak. Thanks for sharing. Any other nuggets of wisdom you'd like to share?"

Horak shook his head, looking irritated, but didn't respond.

"Entering the bridge," Washburn said.

Multiple live video feeds became active from Washburn and his team's suit cameras in their helmets. They pried the door to the bridge open, and lights from the combat suit helmets pierced the darkness.

Near the door was a ledge, and the bridge was at a lower level. This sunken-level design was consistent with what had been observed in crew quarters.

Ethan watched Washburn's camera feed as he peered over the edge.

There were smaller ledges leading down. It wasn't a traditional ladder, but the grouping of the ledges looked big enough to grab.

"Any ideas on this, Dr. Horak?" Washburn asked.

"Perhaps the aliens were large spiders," Horak replied.

Ethan glanced at him, thinking he might've been joking.

Horak was peering at the video feeds. "See the workstations down below? There are no chairs. They're half an octagonal shape, enough room for a multi-limbed being to operate in. Even the interface looks like it supports this," Horak said excitedly.

Washburn leaped down, using his suit jets to control himself in the zero gravity.

One of the other soldiers called him over to a workstation that had power. A pale green holoscreen activated, and they both focused on it.

"Waiting on the translation interface to link up," Washburn said.

The translation program they used had been compiled over the years, with improvements from other alien species they'd encountered.

"The data indicates the ship suffered from a catastrophic malfunction. The crew was abandoning ship when an explosion occurred," Washburn said. He paused for a moment. "Either it was a malfunctioning weapon or a timed detonation meant to trigger after the ship left the battlefield. There are a lot of logs here. Permission to upload this data to the ship?"

Lieutenant Gooding looked at Ethan. "Sir?"

"Granted. Isolate the data from the rest of the computing core. Sandbox protocol," Ethan replied.

Lieutenant Gooding relayed Ethan's orders.

"Uplink established," Washburn said. "Bringing up the recent logs…" he began to say but then stopped. "Is this translation right, Specialist?" he asked a member of his team. A few moments passed. "Understood," Washburn said. "*Ascendant* actual, data repository indicates a fleet engagement with a very large ship moving through space. Once we can decipher their units of measurement, we'll have a better grasp of what kind of ship this was, but the description of the hull is… familiar, sir."

"Understood, Captain," Ethan replied. "Continue the data dump and finish your sweep."

Ethan muted the comlink, and Qualmann looked at him. He bit his lip on an unasked question.

"We don't know. Let's see what the data tells us rather than making the data fit into a box of our own design," Ethan said.

Qualmann nodded. "Understood, sir."

Horak glanced at them. "I don't understand."

Qualmann looked at Ethan for permission to explain. Ethan nodded. "The CDF had engaged a Vemus Alpha that was going to destroy New Earth. It was a massive ship over twenty kilometers in diameter. On another planet, a different strain of Vemus was attempting to build a behemoth-sized ship using all available resources."

Horak nodded. "Ah, I see. You think this could be another Vemus Alpha class ship?" He pressed his lips together for a few seconds, then shrugged. "Other species can build large ships."

Ethan gave him an approving nod. "You're absolutely right. Until we have actual confirmation that the ship in that report is an alpha, I refuse to jump to any conclusions about it."

"Since this ship was leaving the battle, it might've been going for help," Qualmann said.

"True. We'll need to decipher the navigation data to find out where that ship has been and where they were going," Ethan said.

Dr. Horak frowned. "Assuming we can decipher the data, which way would we go?"

"I don't have an answer for that," Ethan replied.

He frowned in confusion. "Really?"

Qualmann chuckled. "How long have you been aboard the ship?"

Dr. Horak blinked. "Six months."

Qualmann bobbed his head. "And in that time, you should know we don't rush to make decisions like that, and certainly not without approval."

Horak thought for a few moments. "Sorry about that. I should know better. I just assumed we'd investigate the potential alpha that might be out there."

Ethan knew others would make the same assumption. "It's alright to ask questions. It's one of the reasons for your appointment. Science officers offer a different viewpoint that has proven to be valuable."

Dr. Horak relaxed a little. "Thanks for that, Major. I'll ask better questions in the future." He rubbed his chin. "We don't even know how long that ship has been out there, or when the battle it was involved in took place."

"Right, and there might not be anyone left who needs help," Ethan said.

The comlink from Captain Washburn chimed. *Ascendant,* preliminary data scan is complete. Looks like these aliens had an unwanted guest aboard. There is evidence of weapons fire near the port side airlock. Looks like they were moving away from the airlock right to the area that we entered the ship. We're not able to detect any biological substances there. Remnants of the invader and the aliens are gone." Washburn paused and peered into the camera. "Major Gates, assuming the translation software is accurate, there is data here that suggests these aliens were engaged with an enemy who could survive in space."

Horak cleared his throat. "What do you mean 'survive in space'?"

"I mean without any type of EVA suit," Washburn said, and then looked at Ethan. "Sir, I'm starting to get a bad feeling about this."

Vemus fighters could survive in space without a spacesuit, which had something to do with their exoskeletal material.

"Understood, Captain," Ethan said. "Finish your sweep, and leave the data link up with a portable power source. Then return to the ship."

"Yes, Major," Washburn said.

The comlink severed, and Ethan looked at Horak. "Get your team to work on that data. Access will be coordinated with Captain Brett and her team."

Dr. Horak nodded and turned back to his workstation to begin contacting his team. A few moments later, he left the bridge.

Qualmann blew out a breath. "This got more complicated."

Ethan nodded. "Yeah. Another species was fighting a Vemus Alpha and were losing the battle."

Qualmann frowned. "How do you figure that?"

"Sending a scout ship for help. Somehow, an enemy combatant snuck onboard the ship. They blew a big hole in their ship to stop it, effectively sacrificing themselves. Vemus fighters don't go down easy, and sometimes they get back up."

Qualmann nodded. "We're going to need to check this out."

Ethan remembered his conversation with Cynergy from a week ago, and he wondered what her reaction would be when she learned that she'd been right. The Vemus weren't as far from them as they'd hoped.

Ethan regarded his XO. "Absolutely."

CHAPTER 11

ETHAN COULD REMEMBER when he'd lost himself for hours or even days reviewing all the data the colony had accumulated about the Vemus, and that knowledge significantly increased after he'd been part of the expeditionary force to return to Old Earth. But with his increased rank, he now had to delegate those efforts to review the treasure trove of data they'd managed to extract from the alien scout ship. He was supposed to rely on his crew, and he had no doubts as to their abilities to perform a thorough and complete analysis of the data. However, he wanted to perform his own research, which he'd been in the middle of when he received reports from Dr. Horak and Captain Brett. In the end, they'd sifted through the data and presented him with the things he was most interested in. It was a preliminary report, and they would present their findings at a meeting.

Cynergy met him on his way to the conference room. She gave him a knowing look, as if to say to him, "See, I told you this would happen."

She also looked troubled.

"What's wrong?" he asked.

She shook her head. "Nothing. I'm just eager to learn what they found."

They entered the conference room, and most of the attendees from Ethan's senior staff were already present. He saw that Qualmann was standing off to the side of the room, speaking with Dr. Horak and Captain Brett.

Ethan sat and said, "Alright, let's begin."

The attendees became quiet, and Qualmann and the others came to the conference table.

Ethan looked at Dr. Horak and Captain Brett. "I've reviewed your preliminary report. I have to admit it came a bit sooner than I expected."

Dr. Horak glanced at Brett for a second, and she nodded for him to speak. "The translation software gains confidence as it learns the alien language. Hence, we were better able to search for the data we were most interested in first. The aliens were engaged in a battle with a Vemus Alpha."

"Was that the name they gave it?" Qualmann asked.

"No," Dr. Horak replied. "The translation is something to the effect of space-faring fighters..." He paused for a moment and glanced at Captain Brett.

"Demons," she said. "Or devils. Take your pick."

Dr. Horak exhaled through his nostrils. "It's a translation."

"It fits," Ethan said.

"Right," Dr. Horak said. "There were descriptions of the various types of Vemus fighters, and our analysis AI attempted to create several images based on the data. Um, I'll put them in the holotank."

The holotank in the middle of the conference table turned on, and several horrific images appeared. They were multi-limbed beings that appeared more insect-like than that of a humanoid encounter.

Dr. Horak was quiet for a few moments, and the rest of them

took in the images. "I must reiterate that these images are an approximation based on alien data."

"Looks pretty accurate to me," Wade Walsh said.

He was a Vemus hybrid and had fought the Vemus remnant in Old Earth's star system for a long time.

"The Vemus use alien DNA and restructure it according to a pre-defined matrix. Then, it will adapt as it subjugates the species under attack," Dr. Horak said and gestured toward the images. "These designs are in line with the strange architecture that was found on the scout ship. We have no idea how many alien species have been attacked by the Vemus, and there could be just as many Vemus variants out there."

Captain Seana Brett nodded. "It's my recommendation that if we were to further investigate these findings, and in the event that we encounter this new variant of Vemus, we should treat them as an unknown entity and use extreme caution before engaging."

Ethan nodded. "What can you tell me about the ship?"

"It's larger than the Alpha that attacked New Earth—over two hundred kilometers with a heavy armament profile. Weapon types range from high-energy weapons to attack drones. There was special emphasis on high-energy weapons."

Cynergy looked at him, and Ethan gestured for her to speak. "Was there anything in the data to support whether the aliens fighting the Vemus Alpha were of the same origin?"

"We're guessing," Dr. Horak said, "and it's our best guess, based on the data retrieved from the scout ship. To be honest, we just don't know. There is evidence to support that they're from the same planet, but until we know more about these aliens, there's no way we can be sure."

"So, an enormous Vemus Alpha," Qualmann said, "and an alien fleet with FTL capability engaged to stop them. There is a possibility of multiple species involved here, a star system with two inhabited planets, or just a star system that is exceptionally rich in materials for building fleets of ship."

Dr. Horak frowned. "All possibilities, and there is the potential for allies."

"That's a big 'maybe,'" Ethan said. "I know the notion that the 'enemy of my enemy is my friend' has been popular for a long time, but I wouldn't let my guard down for it. One of the persistent obstacles the CDF faced during the Krake Wars was difficulty finding Ovarrow worlds willing to coordinate and unite to fight the Krake. It's one of the reasons there was so much secrecy about the CDF presence on those worlds."

Qualmann nodded. "They had to determine whether the Ovarrow of those worlds would be open to an alliance."

"Precisely."

"So, there is the Vemus Alpha and the potential for hostilities from an advanced alien species. Does this mean we won't get approval to investigate this?" Cynergy asked.

Ethan noticed that the other hybrids around the table became very still. It was subtle, but something he was acutely aware of because of his own hybrid nature.

"It's possible," Ethan said. He looked at the others. "We need to review the rest of the findings before I put in any kind of recommendation of what the mission potential is for this." He looked at Captain Brett. "Were you able to decipher their navigation system?"

She nodded. "Yes, but the data is incomplete, so we're working with fragments. However, we have a good idea as to where the scout ship came from. I'll put the data in the holotank."

A star chart became active in the holotank. An icon represented their current location, and then a destination icon appeared.

Ethan studied the data.

"That's beyond the operational limits established for the expeditionary force commanders," Qualmann said.

"Yeah, but," Wade began, "surely they'll give you an exception, given how concrete the data is, right?"

"Let's not get ahead of ourselves," Qualmann said.

Wade's eyes narrowed in irritation. "What are you talking about? We have a heading and a solid lead to pursue here. What more do you need?"

"Quite a bit, actually, which you'd understand if you weren't obsessed with finding another alpha," Qualmann replied. "We don't have limitless supplies. The target coordinates lead us to a battlefield. We don't know how old the scout ship is. The fleet engagement with the alpha could be from hundreds of years ago, or it could be from five years ago. Then, there's the potential for damage to this ship because of automated defenses still active on the ships that were left on the battlefield. I'm sure I can come up with more things if what I've listed so far isn't sufficient for you to exercise some much-needed caution!"

Qualmann's voice had risen by the end.

Wade stared intently at Qualmann, and neither man blinked.

"What's the matter?" Qualmann asked. "Can't think straight when there's an alpha in your sights?"

"There's nothing wrong with my mind. I remember exactly who the enemy is. Do you?" Wade asked and then swept his gaze around to the others. "The Vemus are out there and represent a danger to us all. Investigating this should be our top priority. The *very* top."

"Agreed," Ethan said. The others around the table looked at him, some registering surprise. Qualmann gave him a considering look, and Wade calmed down. "We shine a light in the darkness, and it will be overcome. However, this doesn't give us license to be reckless. The location puts us well out of range of any kind of support, but acknowledging the risk doesn't mean a mission to investigate will immediately be ruled out." He stared at Wade for a moment and the hybrid lowered his chin once. Ethan looked at Qualmann. "We'll need to review whether taking this on is feasible given our current resources. We also need to identify the risks involved." He looked at Wade and the others. "Mission approval doesn't happen in the absence of risk. It's how we make informed decisions."

"Yes, sir," Qualmann said.

Ethan looked at Captain Brett. "Is there anything else we can learn from the scout ship?"

She shook her head. "Negative, sir. I think we've gotten all we can from it. It's important to remember that the ship was significantly damaged. We don't know the limits of their subspace communication capabilities. I've adjusted our comms array detection capabilities to listen for the protocols used by the alien scout ship and haven't detected anything in the direction of the fleet battle or where the ship was heading."

Ethan nodded. "Good work, Captain. This assumes that the direction the ship was heading would've taken them to their home world."

"True, sir. They could've been heading to base or a refueling station," Captain Brett replied.

Ethan looked at Dr. Horak. "Any idea how long the ship has been here?"

"Analysis of the samples gathered from the away team gives a wide age range of five years to five hundred years," Dr. Horak said. "The reason for the wide margin is that we're unable to identify all the materials used in the construction of the alien ship."

Ethan blew out a breath. "Still, five hundred years? Can you narrow it down?"

"I might be able to help with that, sir," Captain Brett said.

"Go ahead, Captain," Ethan replied.

"It would require us going to the location where the battle occurred. Scans of the area would be analyzed and we could model the data that would give us an accurate picture of how the battle took place. We could compare that with samples collected, so a timeline could be established."

Ethan nodded. "I thought as much. Thank you, Captain."

"What will your recommendation be to Colonel Phillips?" Cynergy asked.

"I'll propose two recommendations—one where we go to this location and check it out. The second, we move on until a task force can be assigned to journey to this location together. Both have potential, and we're not under any time constraints," Ethan said.

He thought he saw a flash of disappointment in her eyes, but she hid it well.

They spent the remainder of the meeting going over mission scenarios, which didn't take long. Ethan had already decided how he'd conduct the mission and his proposal. He liked to get feedback from his senior officers and staff because they either confirmed what he was already thinking or provided a better alternative that he hadn't considered yet. Despite going through this, he knew that Cynergy believed they wouldn't get approval. For some reason, she'd lost faith in the Confederation's exploration goals. Ethan didn't agree with her.

He'd kick it up the chain of command, along with his recommendations, and see what Colonel Philips had to say about it.

CHAPTER 12

ETHAN AND QUALMANN waited in the ready room for the comlink to Colonel Phillips to connect. He'd sent in his report and a meeting request came shortly after.

The comlink connected, and a video feed appeared on the holoscreen.

"Colonel Phillips," Ethan said, and both he and Qualmann saluted their superior officer.

Colonel Phillips had a thick, red mustache and beard, but his head was devoid of hair. "Major Gates. Major Qualmann. That's quite the report you sent over."

"Indeed, Colonel," Ethan replied. "The findings warranted high priority."

Colonel Phillips chuckled a little. "I bet you did," he replied and leaned back in his chair. He was twelve light-years from them aboard his own ship. "As you know, priorities for exploration are being expanded upon. We're looking for other civilizations to meet and learn from, but we're also searching for places with the potential of becoming future colonies. Not everything is centered around searching for the Vemus. If they were a more immediate threat, things would be different. This isn't like the Krake War. Distance from the enemy is a huge factor."

"I understand that, Colonel, but this request ticks the boxes of both priorities—one for the Vemus and one for establishing contact with other alien species."

Colonel Phillips regarded him for a long moment. He looked a little tired. "I know," he sighed. "You've given me two well-thought-out proposals, but only one of them has potential to gain any real traction."

"Which one is that, Colonel?" Ethan asked.

"If I were to make you wait for other ships from the task force to arrive, this mission would never get approval. We're spread too far apart, and to be honest, I think this requires more immediate attention. If I were to kick this up the chain to COMCENT, we could both forget about it."

"Seems to be a lot of that going around," Ethan said.

"What do you mean?"

"It seems like people just want to forget the Vemus are out there."

Colonel Phillips nodded. "So do I." He smiled a little. "Sometimes ignorance is bliss, but it'll blindside you if you let it. I get it. Okay, I'm going to grant your approval to investigate this location of the Vemus Alpha. According to your reports, it's a real lead. We'll note the potential of another alien species if we ever decide to go beyond the limits set by COMCENT."

Qualmann cleared his throat. "Colonel, aren't we already doing that by going to look for the alpha?"

"Yes, but in this case, you're also investigating what equates to an alien distress call."

Qualmann became quiet and looked at Ethan.

It was a gray area that Colonel Phillips was exploiting for approval.

"Understood, Colonel," Ethan said.

"I thought you might," Phillips replied. "You'll be out of direct contact with us, but your suggestion of using a communication drone as a relay for mission updates is what really sold this. That, and I think you and your crew are uniquely qualified for this mission." He leaned toward the camera. "I strongly urge you to be cautious. If the area is too hot for you to make contact, I expect you to turn around and come back, using best speed available. Is that understood?"

"Yes, Colonel. I won't put my ship or crew at more risk than absolutely necessary. I hope we'll learn something useful and gain more of an insight into the Vemus."

Colonel Phillips nodded. "Agreed. Happy hunting, Major Gates."

The comlink severed, and Ethan looked at Qualmann.

His XO shook his head a little. "I'm surprised he's letting us move forward with this."

"He's sticking his neck out for us."

Qualmann frowned. "How so?"

"Based on what he said. The conditions for approval were because of the distress beacon. That makes the presence of the Vemus Alpha more of an immediate threat. That's something he can kick up the chain, and no one is really going to give him grief over it."

Qualmann bit his lower lip for a second. "I see."

Ethan regarded him for a moment. "Do you still have reservations about this?"

"Of course, but I also have faith in our crew and our training. We've got our orders. I won't spend time second guessing them."

"I didn't think you would. Brett had a solid proposal for our approach to the target coordinates. Should allow us to get the lay of the area without fully committing ourselves."

Qualmann nodded. "Brett's plan is good. She's a good officer. It's the hybrids I'm concerned with." Ethan waited for him to continue. "They're high strung. I can see them getting impatient about this."

"That could be true for anyone, but I understand your concern. They can be a pushy bunch."

"There are limits to what should be tolerated. That's all I'm trying to say."

Ethan smiled with half his mouth. "They're part of the team. We'll need them, but if they get too far out of line, they'll be sidelined. The same is true for anyone."

Qualmann nodded. "I'm glad to hear you say it." He paused for a second. "I've never been out of communications range before."

"Neither have I," Ethan replied. "Only the people who served during the Krake Wars know about that."

"At least we're not traveling to another universe with no backup of any kind."

"They were brave and more than a little desperate. We might be out of comms range, but at least we won't be completely cut off from everyone else."

CHAPTER 13

NEWS of the new mission had spread quickly. The ship was in transit to the coordinates from the alien scout ship.

Ethan left the showers after an intense workout at the gym. He rotated his routines to alleviate boredom with them. There was also the added bonus of embracing his hybrid nature, which increased his strength and agility. Mostly, his time was spent competing against his own personal best in terms of completion times and ability to navigate a dynamic obstacle course. The obstacle course elevated the challenge based on the capabilities and previous performances of the person participating. He'd decided to test the AI by changing from being fully human to embracing his hybrid nature. The obstacles in his path had quickly adapted, almost as if the AI had anticipated his behavior. Sometimes, it threw obstacles in his path that were impossible to overcome, which was part of the challenge. Knowing when to back off was just as important as when to push harder.

He stopped in the dining hall and grabbed a quick protein-dominant breakfast. Whenever he exercised, he always built up an appetite, unlike Washburn, who sometimes preferred a nap after exerting himself. Within an hour of exerting himself, Ethan would be ravenous with hunger.

He destroyed his meal in record time and hastened out of the dining hall. There were more than a few sidelong glances thrown in his direction. He hurried through the corridors, heading to the conference room near the bridge. He was almost ten minutes late, which he hated, especially since it was his own meeting. He shook his head. He hated being late for any meeting.

He opened the door to a full conference room; conversations quieted as he took his seat.

Ethan glanced at Qualmann. "Lose another bet?"

Qualmann frowned for a moment and then shook his head. "I know better than to bet against you twice. Is that where you were?"

Ethan nodded as he poured himself a cup of coffee from the carafe. "You know me. I get cranky if I don't eat following a work-out. Decided to try to trip up the training AI, and it one-upped me."

Cynergy speared a look at him. "I warned you about doing that."

"I'm fine," he said to her.

Her gaze narrowed. "No, you're not. You're favoring one side. Mid back muscles are tight."

Qualmann grinned a little. "Might want to rethink that safety levels you've got enabled."

Ethan could never fool his wife. Because they were both hybrids and she'd changed him to save his life, they shared an intimate connection that puzzled most people.

"It'll heal," Ethan said.

She knew his sore muscles would heal, but that didn't mean she was happy about it. The training AI sometimes had difficulties with estimating how much to challenge hybrids. All hybrids had different abilities, but they could either embrace their hybrid-ness in small amounts or go at it full tilt. Sometimes body scans were enough to determine those limits, and other times they were less than accurate.

He'd get some downtime to focus on healing, and perhaps he'd ask Cyn to give him one of her amazing massages.

Ethan looked at Qualmann. "I think we can get started." He looked at the others around the conference table. They were his senior staff and team leaders from among their civilian crew members. "Apologies for being late."

Qualmann eyed Ethan for a moment, considering. "Didn't your father used to charge people colonial credits for being late?"

Ethan arched an eyebrow. "He did."

Qualmann smiled like he'd just hooked a fish. "And his standing practice was to reimburse all the attendees if he was late for a meeting."

This drew a few grins from around the room, and Ethan chuckled.

"First, I'm not my father, so there is no standing agreement about tardiness for meetings. And," he said, drawing out the word, "lest any of you get the wrong idea about punctuality, it's still of critical importance. I promise not to be late to another one of these meetings. If I am, I'll investigate the kind of reimbursement measure that Major Qualmann has seen fit to mention. Sound fair?"

Qualmann tipped his head to the side. "I have a few ideas if you need help with coming up with creative measures for reimbursement."

Ethan snorted. "I'm sure you do. Now, let's begin."

Qualmann smiled and turned to address the others. "Colonel Phillips has approved a mission to recon the coordinates found in the alien scout ship. We're to look for survivors, the presence of the Vemus Alpha, and determine the aftermath of the space battle. We're also to assess the alien ship's combat capabilities."

Overall, the reactions from the others around the table showed that they were pleased the mission had been approved.

"Mission prep will begin while we're en route to our destination," Qualmann continued. "We'll drop out of hyperspace as we get closer to the target coordinates to assess the area, at which time we will make adjustments both to the target and the mission preparations as a whole."

More than a few people looked at Ethan, as if sensing something about to be dropped in their laps.

"Because we'll be performing a reconnaissance mission, the CDF will take point," Ethan said.

He could sense Cynergy becoming still next to him as her muscles tightened.

Wade Walsh lifted his hand, signaling he'd like to speak. "What do the rest of us do? Just wait around?"

"Yes," Ethan said, deciding to take this line of questioning directly. "We're entering a combat situation. Condition Two will be our readiness status because of the probable threat in the area."

Cynergy looked at him. "What about the Alpha? What if it's still there?"

"I'll make a decision when and if the presence of the Alpha is confirmed," Ethan replied.

"You'll make the decision? What about the exploration initiative?" Wade asked.

Ethan felt a flash of irritation. Wade knew better than this. "Did you honestly expect me to make a blanket decision that if we find an Alpha, we'll investigate it no matter what?"

Wade blinked, and the words caught in his throat for a second. "No," he said, and frowned. "No, of course not. The way it sounds is that even if we do find an Alpha, there is a chance we might not investigate it at all."

Ethan nodded and allowed his gaze to sweep across the others around the table. "That's exactly how it sounds because it's true."

Some inhaled sharply, while others waited for him to continue. Ethan could almost see the cracks forming in the crew's morale. Members of the CDF understood the need for authority and protocols to follow. It was the civilians who sometimes needed reminding that they simply couldn't do whatever they wanted. This included the hybrids, who were caught between the CDF and civilians, depending on the type of mission.

"An assessment will be made when we reach the target. We'll consider all the options and then I'll decide what our approach will be," Ethan said and paused for a moment. "Command of this ship and this mission is not by committee, so this shouldn't come as a surprise to anyone at this table."

Silence and stillness took hold of the people around the table, and Ethan let it go on for a few moments.

Qualmann caught his eye, looking pleased, and Ethan gave him a nod.

"As we gather data," Qualmann said, "it will be made available to you. I encourage you to perform your own assessments within your own fields of expertise. Many of you will be brought in to consult with our CIC staff to help assess the anomalies we expect to encounter."

Wade cleared his throat, and Qualmann gestured for him to speak. "Can I request to be present for analysis of the Vemus Alpha?"

Qualmann looked at Ethan.

"Yes," Ethan said, and the hybrid looked surprised, leaving Ethan to wonder whether Qualmann's concern about the hybrids was something he needed to take more seriously. "Wade," Ethan said and looked at the others, "this is for all the hybrids: Your input is valuable, especially when it comes to evaluating the Vemus. Of all the people at this table, no one has more experience than all of you."

Wade shared a look with Cynergy. "Thank you, Major Gates.

Our zeal for learning all we can about the Vemus can sometimes be off-putting for some," he said, directing his gaze at Qualmann. Then, he said, "Given how the priorities of the exploration initiatives are changing, some of us were beginning to worry that we would abandon the search for the Vemus altogether."

"The change in priorities is a good thing," Qualmann said. This caused the hybrids and some of the other civilians to bristle. Qualmann kept his gaze on Wade. "Finding more of the Vemus may not be good for everyone. It often comes with loss of life and exposing the Confederation to more risk than it can take on at this time. These are the realities of our current state of readiness." He paused for a second. "And if we do find active Vemus at this location, there is a significant risk of putting hybrids, such as yourself, in harm's way—meaning it might not be acceptable to authorize any mission where a hybrid comes into close contact with a Vemus Alpha."

Wade sneered. "You've got to be kidding me. I've been hunting Vemus since before you were a cadet, much less an officer. I know more about the dangers of facing the Vemus than you ever will."

"That's true of the Old Earth star system, but alien Vemus are another situation entirely," Qualmann said.

Wade gritted his teeth. "Why don't you say what else is on your mind, Major?"

Qualmann showed his teeth. "You know, I think I will. Your experience with the Vemus is commendable, but the last mission with a Vemus Alpha revealed that you're not as immune as you thought you were. So yes, exposing you and others to an Alpha will be weighed heavily against the possibility that you can be compromised."

Wade swung his gaze at Ethan. "Do you agree with this assessment?"

Ethan felt the weight of every gaze at the table. He'd been part of the mission Qualmann had mentioned. He'd been responsible for rescuing the surviving hybrids, but without his father's presence, he might not have been able to.

He regarded Wade for a long moment. "You can't run from the truth. None of us can. Exposure to an Alpha is a concern for us all, but especially for us. It's about time you and the other hybrids accepted this." He softened his gaze. "This is one of those times when experience can work against us."

Wade stood, eyes blazing with anger. "I fought the Alpha to the end."

"I know you did. I was there. I brought you back from the brink."

It was true, and they both knew it. For Ethan to have done that meant that the other hybrids had to submit to him, even if it was only for the time it took to break free of the alien Vemus Alpha's hold on them. This led some scientists to theorize that Ethan was some kind of alpha himself, but he didn't agree with them. It was his connection to Cynergy that had reinforced his will over the others.

Wade looked away, teeth clenched. For a moment, Ethan thought that Wade and some of the other hybrids would leave the meeting.

"I apologize for my outburst," Wade said quietly and sat down.

The meeting settled into more familiar territory with assignments being given, but Wade and other hybrids had become quiet for the duration. Qualmann had been right to bring to light his concerns. Ethan shared them, and he hoped Wade and the others would come to accept it as well. They were valid concerns, and Ethan wasn't only caught in the middle; he also had to worry about his own vulnerability to a Vemus Alpha. It was one of the reasons his XO was his equal in rank and experience. Qualmann would take command of the mission were Ethan to become compromised by the Vemus Alpha.

The meeting ended, and Qualmann asked to speak with him in

his ready room. They entered and Qualmann waited for the door to close.

"Wade is out of control," Qualmann said.

"He had a lapse in judgement and then apologized for it."

Qualmann shook his head and then wavered. "Maybe, but it's unacceptable."

"You're right, it is. If it happens again, he'll be confined to his quarters until he calms down. If that doesn't work, I'll have him thrown in the brig. I won't tolerate insubordination on this ship."

Qualmann regarded him for a moment. "Permission to speak freely."

"It's just us here, Wil."

He nodded and took a moment to consider his words. "The situation with the hybrids is getting worse. I think it's going to continue to get worse."

"Is there a suggestion in that statement somewhere?"

Qualmann frowned. "Could we remove Wade from the duty roster and have him assessed by the doctor before we clear him for duty."

Ethan crossed his arms and rubbed his chin while he considered it. "No," he said finally. "We have regular psych evaluations, and he passed. Now, he might be stressed because of recent developments. We can keep an eye on him, and we should. That holds true for anyone on the ship, but this could become a witch-hunt awfully quick. You know all those evaluations they make us go through as part of the CDF? It's double for hybrids to be part of this. If there was something to be found, it would've been discovered. We've got plenty of time before we arrive at those coordinates. Give them time to adjust."

Qualmann heaved a long sigh through his nostrils, then pressed his lips together for a moment. "I know hybrids have a rough history when it comes to trusting them. I'm trying to do what's best for this mission."

Ethan nodded. "You wouldn't be doing your job if you didn't bring these things up to me, or just as important, bring them up in the meeting. We're not going to coddle anyone, including the hybrids."

"Do you think of yourself as being separate from them?"

Ethan sighed and shook his head, which wavered as his mind changed. "Depends. Sometimes I do, and sometimes I don't. I'm certainly more sympathetic to them. I've been on the receiving end of countless evaluations. It's like a default go-to for people no one knows what to do with." He held up his hand to forestall his XO. "I'm not saying that's what you did, but it happens."

"What's the right course of action?"

"Give them time. As capable as Wade and the others are, they're not the military. We've got it drilled into us to follow orders and maintain the chain of command. They don't. It's as simple as that."

"I'm going to keep an eye on them. I still think they're having an effect on crew morale. I'm concerned that more divisions will form because of this."

Ethan thought about that for a few moments and nodded. "You do that. If you find something that requires more attention, I expect you to bring it to me. It's what I would do if you were in command."

Qualmann nodded and left.

CHAPTER 14

IN THE WEEKS THAT FOLLOWED, he and Cynergy seemed to be on
opposite schedules. Uneasy silences occurred more often than not
when they were together.

They had one more hop before they'd reach the alien battlefield.
Their assessments from so far out hadn't yielded much data, and he
wasn't sure what they would find when they got there. Distance was
a major factor when it came to their scanning capabilities.

He walked into his quarters, and a dim amber light came from
their bedroom.

Cynergy cleared her throat. She sat on the couch to his left and
gave him a tired smile. Wisps of vapor rose from a blue mug on a
side table, and he smelled the faint odor of lavender chamomile tea.

"Waiting up for me?" he asked.

He'd decided to perform a mid-shift inspection during the third
watch. It was a good way to stay in touch with the crew, and it kept
them on their toes.

Cynergy sighed and patted the spot next to her on the couch.

Ethan sat.

She stared at him for a moment. "Do you trust me?"

His eyebrows knitted into a frown. "What kind of question is that?"

She bit her lower lip for a moment. "Why are you having us followed?"

He regarded her for a long moment. Her eyes looked tired but alert.

"There are concerns about Wade and some of the others. Moteki's name keeps popping up as well. Some of the things he says are being reported."

Her full lips pinched tightly. "So, it's true then. You're having us watched?"

Ethan looked at her for a long moment, softening his gaze, knowing that how he answered this would have greater implications. He wasn't going to lie to his wife, nor would he hide from the truth.

"Cyn, I'm in command of the ship, so the official things that happen on it are in my purview."

"Just answer the question!" she snapped.

"Yes. Wade and some of the others are being watched."

"Why?"

"That outburst during our all-hands meeting really kicked it off. Do you remember?"

She thought about it for a second and then nodded, pushing her long blonde hair behind her ear.

"Qualmann came to me after the meeting. It's his job to point out potential risks or concerns about the ship, crew, and our mission."

She sighed. "He doesn't trust us."

His brow furrowed, and his jaw tightened. "I refuse to lump all the hybrids together."

She stared at him for a moment with a knowing look, and he

didn't like what he saw there. "Separate or together, it amounts to the same thing. You don't trust us."

"It's different. Why can't you see that?"

"I've been through this before. Why can't *you* see *that?*"

He looked away for a few seconds and then sighed. "I don't like that this is coming between us. It's a gap, a wedge, right where it shouldn't be."

Her expression softened, and she slowly nodded. "I know—I'm caught in the middle of this, Ethan. On the one hand, there are the other hybrids. For so long we prided ourselves on being immune to the Vemus, and now we aren't. It's like all the prejudice we endured was suddenly justified, and now we have to prove ourselves again."

He shook his head. "It's not justified, and you've got nothing to prove."

"Maybe not to you, but to others it will be. We'll be seen as a problem that needs to be solved. On any mission, the others will be looking over their shoulders instead of focusing on what's important."

"And that's why Wade and others insist on being at the fore-front of anything to do with the Vemus."

"Wouldn't you be?" she asked.

"I understand the motivation, sure. But…" He paused for a moment. "I think of it like a disease. If I'm vulnerable to it, and there isn't a cure, it makes sense to avoid it."

"We can't avoid it. Sooner or later, it'll show up like it always does."

He wasn't sure how to fix this. There were no easy answers. He'd known that taking this kind of command would come with compli-cations, but he always thought they'd find a way through them. Instead, it was forcing a wedge between them.

"Cyn, we can't afford to ignore the facts."

"No, and I wouldn't want you to, but just because we became vulnerable to one Alpha doesn't mean others will have the same effect. What everyone ignores is the fact that it took a long time of constant exposure for the Alpha to begin to assert its will over us. We fought, Ethan. It's not like when the Vemus spread across Earth. What Wade and the others—and me—what we want is to have a say in the decision as to what kind of risk we take on. We're not unreasonable, and sidelining us isn't the answer."

Ethan regarded her for a long moment and then cleared his dry throat. "I almost lost you the last time. I don't want to ever come that close again."

She stood and looked at him, then reached with her hand, and he held it. "I've thought about giving it all up. Go back to New Earth for a while. Get some distance from being way out here."

His eyebrows raised. "Really?"

"Yes, really. I know you're worried about your father. So am I. Maybe it's time for some changes."

There hadn't been any updates about his father's disappearance, and it had been on his mind more lately.

"Yeah," he said with a sigh.

She pulled him to his feet. "Come on. Let's get some sleep."

She led him into the bedroom. While they lay next to each other, he had the uneasy feeling that they were still far apart. It might've been better for them if they hadn't found another Vemus Alpha. Memories of their previous encounter sprang from the darkness in his mind, and the muscles of his stomach tightened. Sometimes he dreamed about it, and he knew Cynergy did too. Those memories didn't often persist, but they also never completely went away either.

CHAPTER 15

THE SHIFTING patterns of hyperspace gave way to flashes while the I-Drive bled transit energy, and the flashes of light cycled downward as their velocity decreased until the *Ascendant* was once again in n-space. They'd just transitioned from going a hundred and seventy-five times the speed of light to the barest fraction of C. Sensors began to come back online.

"Transition complete, Major," Lieutenant Jackson said.

"Acknowledged," Ethan replied. "Tactical, begin scanning the area as soon as the arrays are back online."

"Yes, Major," Lieutenant Brett replied.

The main holoscreen displayed a video feed of the area in front of the ship. The coordinates from the alien scout ship had taken them to a region of space on the outskirts of the Oort clouds of two distant stars, which gleamed a pale blue light in the distance. A wide field of shimmering ice and rock twinkled in a vast expanse, like the individual drops of an ocean frozen in space. Silence swept over the entire bridge as they watched the scene of cold, panoramic beauty that also contained an element of deep mystery. Hidden among the gleaming splendor, the sensor array began highlighting ships with small icons while the computing core continued to evaluate the data as it came in.

Ethan scanned the image, losing count of the enormous asteroids drifting through space. He looked at Qualmann. "This is a good place to engage the enemy. Lots of cover around here."

"Agreed," Qualmann replied with a hint of awe in his voice.

Selecting a location to wage battle was just as important as the capabilities of the fleet's ships. Favorable terrain was a tried-and-true method for ground-based conflicts, and the same was true for space warfare. No matter the environment, any commander who ignored the environment where they engaged the enemy usually ended up on the losing side of the conflict. It could sway the advantage away from an enemy with superior numbers, abilities, or, as in the case with a behemoth-sized Vemus Alpha, superior firepower.

If the data collected from the alien scout ship was correct, there could be a Vemus Alpha located in the region, and it was over a hundred and twenty kilometers long. Captain Grayston, the ship's lead engineer, had estimated the power requirements for a ship that size to be over fifty fusion power-cores, or at least fifteen of their own seventh generation Casimir power cores. Grayston also added a proviso that he had no idea what the capabilities of the alien ships were until they got more data. He was guessing, which Ethan could appreciate. Grayston knew his stuff, and sometimes his guesses were better than other people's facts.

"Sir," Captain Brett said, "I've detected a large concentration of ships in this region." An area on the main holoscreen highlighted as she updated the tactical readout. "Scans are having trouble separating distinct ship hulls from this range. This likely has to do with the asteroid field. No active ships or any kind of power signatures detected between us and them. I recommend we make our way there."

"Very well," Ethan said. "Helm, take us in. Ops, deploy scout drones to cover the targeted region."

His orders were confirmed, and ten scout drones were deployed.

The scout drones raced ahead of the ship. They were subspace capable and the data they collected augmented the ship's scanner array, which gave them a better insight into the battlefield.

"If it's been a while since the battle, any power cores intact on those ships are likely either on standby or depleted," Qualmann said.

Ethan nodded and sent a message to Cynergy, requesting that she come to the bridge.

"So, we're in the right place. Where is the Alpha?" Ethan asked.

"It's easy to get lost in there," Qualmann replied. "That is assuming they were able to stop it. It could've just moved on."

Ethan glanced at the ship count estimates and the numbers widened his eyes. "There are hundreds of ships here," he said. The number jumped to over a thousand, and he whistled softly. "Look at that."

Qualmann glanced at his personal holoscreen. "It says distinct ship counts. They'd outnumber us by almost three to one if we brought our entire fleet here."

"Superior numbers don't guarantee victory," Ethan replied.

He'd studied every fleet engagement the CDF had been part of, and the only battle that came close in scale to this was when the Vemus Alpha attacked New Earth. His father had known they couldn't build enough war ships—crew not withstanding—to defend the star system, so he relied on automated defense platforms throughout the star system. They'd softened the Vemus Alpha as it made its way to New Earth, and in the end, it had taken every weapon and technology they had to stop the Alpha. It still made it to New Earth, but the CDF was able to snatch victory from the jaws of defeat. People like his father, General Hayes, and General Quinn still remembered that battle, but for many others, it had become a historical event separated by decades of peace.

Ethan tried to imagine a similar desperate fight in this place between stars. How many aliens had died here fighting the Vemus? As majestic as the panoramic view was, in reality it was an icy tomb. Hopefully, if they were able to glean some kind of intelligence about the Vemus from these aliens, he would make sure the aliens were honored for it.

"Tactical, are there any habitable planets in either of the two nearest star systems?"

"One moment, Major," Captain Brett said. "Negative, Major. No habitable planets detected."

Ethan pressed his lips together into a thoughtful frown. "So why fight a battle here?"

Qualmann exhaled. "This is a good place to lay a trap."

He considered that for a few seconds. "True, but they'd have to either lure the Alpha here or know it was going to stop here anyway. I wonder how they accomplished that?"

The door to the bridge opened, and Cynergy arrived. She walked over to him at the command center.

"Thanks for coming," Ethan said. "Would you mind sitting with Captain Brett? She is analyzing the scan data, and I'd like you to help with detecting Vemus ship signatures."

Cynergy smiled a little as she nodded and went to sit in the open seat at the tactical workstation.

Qualmann looked at Ethan. "Do you think the Vemus had their own fleet?"

Ethan nodded. "Yes. I know we didn't find a fleet on the planet where we encountered them a couple of years ago, but when the Vemus attacked New Earth, they had a fleet of ships. That Alpha divided its forces as it attacked. It wanted to expose our defenses, while the Alpha arrived later to make its run to the planet. The alien Vemus we encountered didn't get that far. They never left the planet."

Qualmann bobbed his head slowly. "That's right. Can't believe I forgot about that."

"It's a bit closer to home for me than most people," Ethan replied.

Qualmann regarded him for a second. "Yeah, I bet," he said quietly, almost soberly.

The ship drew steadily closer to the battlefield while the scout drones sped ahead. Hours went by quickly as they pieced together the battlefield. All available computing cycles were devoted to the task, which would take many more hours to filter out. The *Ascendant* was bearing a workload that should've been performed by a battle group or small fleet. It wasn't that his ship couldn't handle the colossal task it had been given, but it would take longer to get that clear picture than he really wanted.

Cynergy had found Vemus ships among the wreckage of the alien fleet. According to the data they'd gathered, they'd been utterly destroyed, and the fighting had been vicious. The aliens had made their stand there for some unknown reason, and it just reinforced in Ethan's mind that they needed to be cautious.

The alien fleet had ships beyond larger than CDF's battleship carriers, but they also had a range of support ships that flew with them. They had sleek and purposeful designs whose refinements could only come from a mature spacefaring race.

Twelve hours after they'd arrived, Cynergy leaned back in her chair and turned toward Ethan. "Found it. The Alpha looks like it's caught in the ice among a cluster of asteroids. It's easy for sensors to miss, but I was able to narrow it down based on the Vemus ships we were able to detect."

"I'll put it on the main holoscreen," Captain Brett said.

A sub-window appeared on the main holoscreen, showing a vast dark shape—definitely a ship. It almost blended into the ice and rock, and the scout drone had detected the Alpha far into the ice field.

"Let's focus our scans on that area. Set the priority for the next watch. That will give us better idea by the time we come back on duty," Ethan said.

He clamped his mouth shut to stifle a yawn and looked at Qualmann. "Maintain Condition Two readiness and order the shift change. I want us to have a nice long look at this place before any plans are made."

"Yes, sir," Qualmann said.

The announcement went out to the rest of the ship.

"Comms," Ethan said, "give me a ship-wide broadcast."

"Broadcast channel open, Major," Lieutenant Samantha Trickle replied.

"Crew of the *Ascendant*," Ethan said, "this is Major Gates. I wanted to give you a brief update. We're currently analyzing the alien battlefield. Because of the uniqueness of the location, it's going to take us longer to do a proper assessment than previously expected. We have located the Vemus Alpha among the wreckage of over twelve-hundred ships." He paused for a moment to allow what he'd said to sink in. "A massive battle was fought here, and the potential for acquiring a treasure trove of information is prevalent. Our readiness will remain at Condition Two for the overnight watch, and we'll continue to analyze the battlefield from our current location. Over the next few days, we'll conduct further reconnaissance missions to see what else we can learn about the aliens who died here and the Vemus Alpha they sought to stop. Major Gates, out."

He closed the broadcast channel and left his XO to oversee the change of the watches.

Cynergy walked with him, and they were both quiet. Not only had they found the largest Vemus Alpha, but also the remnants of the advanced alien species who'd fought them. As he walked through the corridors of his ship, he kept thinking of his father's account of what the Phantoms had told him about the Vemus, that they were beyond humanity's ability to deal with. To the Phantoms, this had been stated as a matter of fact, but his father and others wouldn't take the Phantoms at their word, and neither would Ethan.

He wasn't sure where this particular Alpha fit in the Vemus hierarchy. Was it an abnormally large anomaly, or could they expect more like this the farther they explored? What if the Vemus were more powerful than they ever imagined? What if the Phantoms had been right all along? What Ethan decided to do over the next few days could have vast repercussions if the Vemus Alpha they'd found wasn't dead.

CHAPTER 16

THERE WERE times to work through exhaustion or even past the time when Connor should've known better, but after being alive for as long as he had been, he'd learned the value of patience. A night's sleep could make all the difference in the world. It allowed his mind to work on possibilities that he hadn't considered while he was awake. These benefits compounded across the crew. When he *could* take time to consider a problem, it was most often time well spent. The problems with the ship wouldn't be any greater by waiting a single night before going to face Salpheth. Some rest was better than no rest.

Connor had lain awake a long time before sleep finally came, and when he woke the next morning, he didn't have any startling revelation that he hadn't already thought of yet. If anything, he felt more resolved as to the course of action he'd decided upon. At least now he could come at it fresh.

Connor headed to the Dining Hall, and Seger caught up to him in the corridor.

"Good morning, General," Seger said.

"Good morning, Sergeant."

They walked into the quiet Dining Hall, where a couple of people were already eating. They looked over at him as he walked toward the food station.

"So, this is it. You're going to dance with the devil, sir?" Seger asked.

Connor eyed him for a second. "I guess you could say that."

"Better you than me."

Connor scooped some scrambled eggs onto his plate, toast, and a pale-colored bar of protein. At least there was coffee, and he was very appreciative of the eggs.

"Don't like Salpheth?" Connor asked.

"Nope, but I understand why we need him," Seger said and scooped a forkful of scrambled eggs into his mouth. He chewed for a second, seemed to arrive at some kind of conclusion, and said, "Why does it feel like we're playing in someone else's sandbox? Do you know what I mean?"

Connor nodded. "I do, and we are. We don't know all the rules, and we're stumbling in the dark, making our way as best we can."

"That's it. I wish there was more I could do. It feels like we're just waiting at this point."

"Yeah, I know. That's going to change today. Regardless of what happens with Salpheth, we're going to be on the move. Either we get meaningful intelligence from him or we pick one of those buoys we've detected and hope there are resources we can use there."

Seger sipped his coffee and winced. "I miss cream in my coffee. Naya mentioned something about Phendran possibly having data that could help us pinpoint where we are."

"He's trying to figure out how to get the data out of his mind and into our nav computer, but he hasn't found a good way to do that. Aczar computer systems are too different from ours for a direct interface."

Seger pressed his lips together in thought. "What about the other way around?"

Connor frowned. "What do you mean?"

"Well, if we can't get the data out of him, then can he take the data we already have and work through it on his own. Their brains work differently from ours. Faster. I could take him to the Stellar Cartography Holotheater, show what we've already mapped, and just let him do his thing. It might give him a way to physically input the data. It wouldn't be as quick as a data dump, but it's better than nothing."

Connor blinked and regarded the CDF Sergeant for a moment. Seger was an excellent soldier with advanced specialties in weapons and tactics, but he was growing beyond that role. "Did you just think of this now?"

He smiled and nodded. "Just popped into my head, and it makes sense."

"Naya was right. You'd make a good engineer," Connor said and glanced around the Dining Hall.

"Yeah, she's been on me about it."

"You should listen to her. I'm serious. You just thought of a good solution while the rest of us have been scratching our heads about how to bridge that gap with Phendran."

Seger's chest swelled a little at the compliment. "Thank you, General."

"You're welcome. In fact, when we get home, if you want, I could make a way for you to do just that. Only if you want, and don't feel pressure to do it just because I'm offering to help you with this. Understood?"

Seger looked intrigued as he considered it, but then he smoothed his features. "When we get home, I just might just take you up on that offer."

They finished their breakfast, and Connor sent Seger off with Phendran. In the corridor outside the Dining Hall, he stood with Noah, Rhodes, and Kincaid.

Noah looked at Connor. "Know what you're going to say to him?"

Connor shrugged. "Nah, I just thought I'd shoot from the hip."

Rhodes's eyes widened, and Connor chuckled.

"Relax. Yes, I know what I'm going to say to Salpheth," Connor said.

"I wish you'd reconsider and let me go in there with you," Noah said.

Connor shook his head. "No, at least not this time. I'm the only one who goes in there. These are typical negotiating tactics. If a couple of us were going in, Salpheth would seek to manipulate us, play us against each other. This way things are simple."

"He probably knows we're watching the entire exchange," Noah replied.

"Absolutely. In fact, I'm going to tell him that. However, he won't see your reactions. We'll keep him as uninformed as possible."

Rhodes regarded him for a few moments. "You're a shrewd negotiator. I thought I had a good bead on you before the inspection, but I was way off. Way off."

"Thanks. I think," Connor said.

In his experience, a lot of people tended to box him into a particular set of behaviors or beliefs. The fact was that Connor had always had a disciplined mind that was well suited for conflict. In the past, people had accused him of being ruthless or that he pushed too hard, and some of it was true. There *was* something cold and dangerous inside him, which was part of everyone who'd fought on a battlefield. But in these latter years, Connor had honed his skills and impulses into something more constructive. He'd needed to move beyond the mentality of painting the universe in black and white, enemies and threats. Those impulses were still in him, and he'd call on them as needed, but only after he'd exhausted other options. The fruit of that labor was that people were less afraid of him and more willing to work with him.

"We'll monitor you from the bridge," Noah said.

Connor nodded. "Be ready to lock things down if Salpheth demonstrates abilities we haven't seen yet. Oh, and Seger had a good idea about reconciling our lack of nav data with what Phendran has."

He quickly told them Seger's idea.

Noah shook his head. "Brilliant, and so obvious at the same time."

"I thought so," Connor replied.

The group became quiet for a few seconds and then split.

Connor and Kincaid walked away from the others. The CDF captain was unusually quiet, and Connor decided to wait him out. They went down a deck to where the secondary power core was located. Jorath was on monitoring duty.

"I'll have the purge protocol ready to execute on your order, General," Kincaid said. He glanced at Connor's wrist where the SRA was. "Does it ever do anything?"

The SRA was near his wrist computer. "Phendran says it's still going through an evaluation process. Sometimes it raises a question."

"How?"

"It's puts up a holoscreen of its own and puts text on it. I can just speak the answer back to it."

"Does it speak?"

"Not yet. The Aczar brain implants allow the SRA to interact directly with their brains. Thought-for-thought type of communication. I'm not going to allow that, and I don't think it wants to do that."

Kincaid stared at him for a second. "That sounds strange."

Connor nodded. Colonial technology used artificial intelligences for different things, but the SRA was more sophisticated. Sometimes it showed Connor an image as a way of sending a message. It was definitely paying attention and did spark a few thoughts in his mind.

"Do you think Salpheth knows you have it?" Kincaid asked.

"He hasn't mentioned it."

"I wonder how he'd react to learning about it, or that there are Aczar here on the ship."

Connor regarded Kincaid for a long moment. "Why do I get the feeling you're stalling? Do you have concerns you'd like to raise?"

"I'd prefer you not go in there, sir. These are risks I should be taking for you."

Kincaid was part of his protection detail. Duties were assigned to soldiers, but not all of them were wholeheartedly committed. Kincaid genuinely wanted to protect Connor, and he appreciated it.

"You'll watch my back from out here."

"Yes, sir."

They walked toward Jorath, and the Ovarrow gave them a nod.

"The prisoner hasn't moved at all during my shift," Jorath said.

"Understood. I'm going in there," Connor replied.

"Very good, General," Jorath replied and stepped aside.

Kincaid went to the mobile workstation nearby and brought up a holoscreen.

Connor walked down the corridor away from them and sent his credentials to the door control systems. The door to the secondary power core opened, and Connor stepped through.

Beyond the work area, there were monitoring stations available. The large room was isolated from the rest of the ship, with greater emergency-shielding capabilities, including the area where the semi-transparent, amber-colored energy field formed a large sphere around Salpheth. His grayish humanoid form floated in the middle, and his eyes opened, revealing black, almost soulless eyes that regarded Connor intently.

Connor walked toward the edge of the energy field, and Salpheth floated over, causing a momentary shifting of the waves of energy that moved around the field. They reminded Connor of ripples across a lake.

"I've considered your offer of an alliance," Connor said.

Salpheth glanced above him for a second. "The fact that I'm still here indicates you are at least open to the idea."

"I am, provided the data you deliver actually helps us."

"Very well. What assurances do I have that you'll treat me fairly?"

Connor stared at him for a few moments. "What do you want?"

"My freedom, the same as you."

Connor was about to reply but considered his response. "I wouldn't say they're the same."

"You want to be free of me, and I want to be free of you. There is no need to complicate it."

Connor slowly bobbed his head. "I'm looking for assurances of my own."

Salpheth stared at him.

"That you won't attack us if or when I release you."

"That's an easy concession to make. I promise not to attack you or anyone else on your ship, for that matter."

"You'll have to forgive me if I don't take your word for it."

Salpheth titled his head to the side, giving Connor an appraising look.

"This is my offer to you," Connor said. "You help us reach a destination where we can find resources to repair our ship, and we go our separate ways. Betray us, and I will personally see to it that you end up so far in deep space that you will never survive to reach any destination."

"Our goals aren't that much different, General Gates. I told you that I had intended to use your ship to take me to a place where I could secure better accommodations."

"After you killed us."

"I see very little point in trying to convince you otherwise, so let's just agree that the topic is moot at this point, shall we?"

Connor remained quiet and waited for Salpheth to continue.

"There will be resources for you to use, perhaps even another ship to replace this one, and technological wonders you haven't even considered yet. You have everything to gain and nothing to lose."

The edges of Connor's lips lifted a little. "We have a saying. It's actually an old saying, but I think it fits here: When something sounds too good to be true, it usually is."

Salpheth frowned in annoyance, and he leaned toward the edge of the energy field. "Do you always insult the people you're trying to negotiate with?"

Connor shook his head. "No, I plan to be very honest with you. I think you're making promises you can't keep."

"Well, there's only one way to find out."

"Maybe. I plan to qualify everything you say and do with intense scrutiny."

Salpheth smiled. "You and the team of people you no doubt have monitoring this entire exchange."

"They're out there. Watching. Recording. And we have the purge protocol ready to go."

Salpheth's expression darkened.

"I told you I plan on being completely honest with you. This is it. This is the reality of what you're facing."

"And you don't intend to allow me to forget that you hold my life in your hands. I will never forget."

Connor regarded him for a few seconds. "So, we have an understanding."

"I think we do. Now, will you grant me access to your computer system…"

Connor grinned. "And here I thought we had an understanding."

"How else am I supposed to share the knowledge I have to offer?"

"You won't be getting access to our computer system," Connor said and engaged his personal holoscreen. He expanded it to fill the space behind him. "Our sensors have detected these deep space communication buoys. Other than the initial acknowledgment, there are no other kinds of communication."

Salpheth peered at the holoscreen. "That's because the species that created those buoys has moved beyond that method of communication technology."

"So, you've seen this before?"

"Yes, it is ours."

He meant that the Phantoms created it.

"Do they still monitor them?" Connor asked.

"Has anyone contacted you?"

Connor shook his head. "No."

"Then I believe you have your answer. It's impossible for me to say for sure because I've been with the Aczar for so long. However, my guess is that they are no longer monitored. In fact, that is the reason so few of them responded to your broadcast."

There were hundreds of buoys that spread in a number of different directions.

"There used to be many more of them."

Connor frowned. "When we first met, you said the Phantoms have explored galaxies."

"We *have* explored galaxies."

"And you just deployed these buoys to make a communications network across the entire galaxy?"

"Only when required. Sometimes we spent a considerable amount of time in certain regions to study the planets there. My target coordinates were for a resupply station you may have already detected."

Excitement leaped in Connor's chest, and he doubted he was the only one.

Salpheth looked pleased. "I thought that would get your attention."

"What kind of resupply station?"

"The kind that hold stockpiles of resources, automated ship-repair facilities, and many other things. You could say that we commit to the things we're doing."

"And you think they just left it all behind?"

"Of course. It's built from materials gathered in the area."

"What if another species found it?"

"If they could figure out its use, they were welcome to it."

Connor didn't believe Salpheth and said so. "No species is as benevolent as you claim."

"It was interesting observing your response. However, you're still intrigued, and you can't afford to ignore it. I will provide you with protocols to track the buoys. They'll point you to the nearest resupply station."

"I thought you knew where it was."

"I know how to find it, but since I've been…away from things for a while, I suspect the station has moved."

Connor thought about that for a moment. "Why this particular station?"

Salpheth gave him an appraising look. "I was involved with its creation."

"I don't know if I believe you."

"I see. Maybe I've adopted your posture of being completely honest. Now, General Gates, I've laid everything out for you to take us where we both need to go. All you have to do is get us there…if you can."

"Show me the protocol for tracking the buoys," Connor replied.

Salpheth gestured around himself, and a series of symbols in a language that Connor had never seen before appeared. His translation interface analyzed the language and provided a translation.

A text message from Noah appeared on Connor's internal HUD.

We got it.

"Okay, Salpheth. We'll check this out and decide on our next steps."

Salpheth moved back to the middle of the containment field. "I will wait for our next meeting."

Connor left the secondary power core and headed for the bridge.

CHAPTER 17

Connor and Kincaid made their way in silence. This suited Connor, who kept replaying his conversation with Salpheth. Connor knew that he could eliminate Salpheth whenever he chose, so why did meeting with the exiled Phantom always feel like he was the one who was at a significant disadvantage? When he stripped away the various proving statements and assertions, in the end, he was doing exactly what Salpheth wanted. They needed to do it, but it still triggered alarms in his mind that he was missing something.

Kincaid glanced at him a few times as they walked through the corridors.

Naya Corman joined them on their way to the bridge. She was a tall woman with an athletic build and piercing emerald eyes. Her hair was a wild tapestry of auburn and gold that reminded Connor of his wife.

"Noah asked me to join you on the bridge," she said.

"Good," Connor replied.

"I watched your exchange with Salpheth."

"What do you think?"

She tied her long hair into a ponytail. "We always have a choice, but we might not like the choices available to us. I don't like it at all, General. We're doing exactly what he wants us to do, and while it might meet our short-term needs, I'm not sure how it will work out after all that."

"Salpheth said he didn't know what would be there, so whatever he finds will be as much of a surprise to him as it will be for us," Kincaid said.

Connor pressed his lips together while he thought about it. "It's probably safe to assume that he's not being entirely forthright with what he knows. And he's aware that we're suspicious of him."

The door to the bridge opened, and they saw that the main holoscreen was displaying a vast star map. Noah stood off to the side with Rhodes, Cassidy, and Tripp Krin. Tripp was working at the aux workstation nearby, focused intently on the data in front of him.

Noah looked at Connor and the others with him. "We've put the protocols Salpheth showed us into a virtual environment to test them. So far, they check out." Noah gave him a pointed look.

"But we're limited as to what we can test in a virtual sandbox. Understood," Connor said.

Tripp had unruly red hair, pale freckly skin, and an extremely thin frame. He looked up at Connor and then at Noah. "The protocols check out. I'm ready to add them to the new subspace comms suite."

Noah looked at Connor. "I say we use what he shared with us."

They all watched Connor, waiting for his decision. No matter how much he included the others by inviting their input, the decision was his.

"Okay, do it," Connor said.

"It's done," Tripp said. "Initiating new scans."

The protocols augmented the new subspace scan capabilities Noah and Phendran had discovered. The way Connor understood it was that it was part of a focused broadcast. They watched the main holoscreen for a few minutes, and the buoys they'd already detected hadn't changed.

"How long do you think this will take?" Kincaid asked.

"I don't know. This is the first time we've used the new protocols," Noah replied.

Rhodes cleared his throat. "Shouldn't we talk about what Salpheth said?"

Connor looked at him. "Yes, let's do that. Why don't you go first?"

Rhodes looked at the others for a second. "He's making a lot of promises, almost as if he's ticking a bunch of boxes designed to guarantee our cooperation."

"I was thinking the same thing," Noah said and looked at Connor. "And he hardly reacted at all when you pointed that out to him."

"Because he knew it wouldn't change anything. Hundreds of buoys have been detected. If they're anything like ours, they're not worth the trip with limited resources."

Noah nodded. "But a resupply station is worth our attention. Say what you want about Salpheth, he knows what buttons to push. It makes it difficult not to do as he's suggesting."

Rhodes eyed Connor for a second. "Doesn't that make you not want to do what he wants?"

"Yes, and under different circumstances, I wouldn't."

"Maybe we'd be better off doing that. Pick one of the buoys that is near a star system that potentially has the resources we need," Rhodes said.

"There are risks in doing that," Connor said and lifted his chin at Noah.

"The power core degradation issue. It accelerates the more we draw upon it. We have finite resources that, depending on how we use them, will determine how long they last."

Rhodes glanced at his daughter for a second with a concerned frown on his face. Then he shook his head. "There are no good options to pick from."

"No, there aren't," Connor said. "All we can do is balance the risk as best we can."

"How can we do that?" Rhodes asked.

Connor was about to reply when an alert chimed, drawing their attention to the main holoscreen. A new icon appeared, indicating a previously undetected object.

Noah quickly moved to a nearby workstation. "It's just under three hundred light-years away."

Rhodes blew out a breath. "Which means more of a strain on the Infinity Drive."

Connor peered at the new waypoint on the holoscreen. "Is it just an acknowledgment, or did the response provide more data about what's there?"

Noah's hands navigated the interface, and he shook his head. "Just a response, and it's near the coordinates Salpheth provided."

"Near? Not exact?" Rhodes asked.

"It wouldn't be exact because of how much time has passed since Salpheth's capture," Connor replied.

The chevron icon slowly rotated on the main holoscreen. It was brighter than the others because of its recent detection. Their scans wouldn't reveal much more information until they were closer.

"We need to plot a course. How accurate can the new I-Drive protocols be?" Connor asked.

Noah arched an eyebrow. "Are you asking if I can hit the target?"

"Well, yes. I'm keeping count here, and we're zero for two intentional attempts at using those new protocols for the I-Drive."

"That wasn't my fault. The nav system was compromised," Noah said.

Rhodes looked worried but kept quiet.

Connor waited for Noah to continue.

"I can hit the target. It's still a calculation. It's just the velocity that's changed. So, the question is where exactly do you want me to put the ship?" Noah asked.

Connor crossed his arms and then rubbed his chin while he considered it. If the ship arrived too far away, their scans would take too long to return data they could use, but if they arrived too close to the target, they'd be arriving blind.

"Target within two light-years. That should get us close enough to get more of an idea of what's there while not completely committing ourselves," Connor said.

"On it," Noah replied.

Kincaid cleared his throat. "What about Salpheth?" he asked. "If he's lied to us, what should we do?"

The others watched Connor, waiting for his response. They had to know what he was going to say, and what he would do.

"If that's the case, he's out of options and no longer a factor in what we do. I'll purge the secondary power core and we'll be rid of him once and for all," Connor said.

Even though the others had expected it, they each took a moment to absorb it. Kincaid understood, and so did Noah, but the others needed a little more time with it.

"Are we sure that…" Cassidy began and stopped. Then she shook her head. "Never mind. I understand, General Gates."

Noah looked away from his holoscreen at Connor. "I have a course, but I think we need to get in closer. The reason is our sensor array. We need it to be closer."

"How much closer?" Connor asked.

"At least a light-year."

Connor thought for a moment.

"That should still be far enough away, right?" Rhodes asked.

The fact was that there was no way for Connor, or any one of them, to know what the minimum safe distance was from the target. Salpheth had hinted at the technological capabilities the

Phantoms had. They were an intelligent species that traveled across the galaxy and even to other galaxies, unless Salpheth was lying about that. The Phantom Connor encountered had only indicated that they explored this galaxy. Would they have built their resupply stations with integrated defenses against unwanted visitors?

Connor couldn't guarantee it for them. "We'll find out. How soon can we get there?"

Noah glanced at his screen. "You're not going to believe it but about an hour."

Connor gave him a dissatisfied look. "Really—That long?"

Noah frowned and then shook his head. "I could get us there quicker, but I'm trying not to stress the ship's critical systems."

Connor smiled a little. "An hour is fine. We've got to warn the others, and I want everyone to go to their designated stations. EVA suits with their own life support."

Everyone left the bridge, heading for their designated stations. Naya and Tripp returned to main engineering. Rhodes and Cassidy went to the drone maintenance lab with Rabsaris.

After donning their EVA suits, Connor, Noah, and Kincaid returned to the bridge. The others checked in and all were ready. As a precaution, they were strapped in and were on their own individual life support systems supplied through their EVA suits.

Connor sat at the commander's workstation while Noah and Kincaid were at the tactical and operations workstations.

"Ready to depart," Noah said.

"Execute," Connor replied.

A large power-draw came from the core, going directly to the Infinity Drive as they transitioned out of n-space.

"We're in hyperspace," Noah said. He stared at the screen. "Still feels odd to plot a course directly to a set of coordinates."

Kincaid frowned. "What do you mean?"

"He means without moving around star systems and large planetary bodies out there," Connor said.

"These protocols don't put us in the same kind of hyperspace that is normally used. It's different, and it allows us to travel through physical objects in normal space—travel through them without having any kind of impact. It's amazing," Noah said.

Connor opened a broadcast channel to the rest of the ship. "We're on our way. Systems are green across the board. I've made a countdown clock available, and if all goes well, we'll repeat this in under an hour."

He closed the broadcast.

Kincaid looked at Connor. "Seger says they're making progress with Phendran."

"That's good. If they can figure out where we are in relation to Ichlos, we can find a way back to New Earth."

An hour had sounded like a long time, but it really wasn't. Connor considered speaking to Salpheth again but didn't. There was nothing to be gained by it. Either he was telling the truth, or he wasn't.

As the countdown time came to zero, the nav system took them out of hyperspace. The flashes of light cycled downward as their velocity decreased until the ship was once again in n-space, and the ship's sensors began to come back online.

"I-Drive is offline and stable. Analyzing the power core usage," Noah said and then winced. "Definitely had an impact."

Connor checked the data on his workstation and nearly winced himself. He kept thinking about their return trip to New Earth and whether they'd have enough resources to get them there.

He looked at Noah. "That's more of a hit than we thought it was going to be."

"I know," Noah replied and bit his lip in frustration. "The core is old. I…I'm…"

"It's alright. We'll figure it out. First thing first, we need to scan the target," Connor said.

"Right," Noah said. "Scanner array is up. Active scans initiated."

They were a light-year away from the target, which was still a considerable distance. The data they were collecting from that distance was, at best, a year old, so they were relying on scanning through subspace, which gave them current data but was limited in its application.

"You're up, Captain," Connor said.

Kincaid leaned toward his holoscreen. "There's a structure there. The computer model is still working on it."

"Put it on the main holoscreen," Connor said.

A new image appeared, and it was a very distant view of a large space station. It had a wide platform opening at the top, giving it a cone-shaped appearance, but they couldn't see structural details.

"Unbelievable. That's their version of a resupply station? That's bigger than anything we've got back home," Kincaid said.

Connor stared at the image as the computer continued to build the model in front of them. He glanced at Noah. "Looks more like a shipyard than a simple resupply station."

The model finished building.

"We're not going to get more detail than that," Noah said. "We're too far to detect what kind of power signatures it gives off, but we did get a response through Salpheth's protocols, so I think they've got to have some power."

"Regardless, there have to be high grade materials we can use. Can you try to open a comlink to them?"

Noah turned back to his station. "Broadcasting. No response."

Connor frowned, then opened a comlink to Salpheth. The Phantom floated in the middle of the energy field in the secondary power core.

"Your data has led us to the resupply station," Connor said.

Salpheth opened his eyes and came to the edge of the field, staring intently at the holoscreen with the video comlink showing Connor's face.

"I told you it would be there."

"Yes, you did. Why aren't they responding to our communication attempts?"

"Because no one is there. To put it in your own terms, the computer system is basically on standby. That's what I expect to find. Can't you tell what's happening there with your sensors? Are they so rudimentary that they can't detect these things?"

Connor leaned forward to sever the comlink, but Salpheth seemed to have anticipated this.

"Wait, General Gates. Going to the station without me is not recommended. You'll need me to access those systems—" Salpheth said.

Connor severed the comlink and looked at Noah. "Take us in."

CHAPTER 18

"PULSING THE I-DRIVE," Noah said.

Connor watched as the status window on his holoscreen showed a burst of energy going to the I-Drive. They transitioned out of n-space for less than a nanosecond—and were brought within twenty thousand kilometers of the alien resupply station.

Connor frowned in surprise at how close Noah had taken them.

Noah looked at Connor with a pleased expression. "We're breaking all kinds of records right now. This is going to change so many of our space-travel protocols. I could've brought us in closer, but I thought I'd play it safe considering that we haven't done this before."

"Pulsing the I-Drive has been done before," Connor replied.

"Yes, but not with the new protocols. I think it's more efficient —a lot more efficient."

"Okay, well, just keep being cautious. When we get home, I'm sure we'll get new toys to play with so we can really perfect it."

Noah smiled, and for the first time in a while, his smile didn't have any weight to it.

The image of the resupply station updated on the main holoscreen.

A massive cone-shaped structure appeared. It was constructed from some kind of white metallic alloy. The station was over forty kilometers long, but it wasn't enclosed. It had the appearance of a vast skeletal structure, as if construction hadn't been completed. At its widest point near the top, it measured ten kilometers across.

Kincaid whistled in appreciation. "That's not just a resupply station. Look at it. The docks alone could hold half the CDF fleet for maintenance and repairs. It's like they combined a shipyard and a defensive outpost all in one."

Connor read the tactical data. There were turrets, but they seemed to be in a state of partial construction. The station was more complete near the top. Dozens of large asteroids orbited the massive station, and he thought they'd been brought there for their resources.

The incompleteness of the station reminded Connor of skeletal remains. He'd lost count of construction platforms that were no longer working.

"Anything detected by our sensors?" Connor asked.

"Negative, General. No weapons systems. However, I am detecting trace power signatures near the top of the station. It's the areas that are most complete, so that makes sense. We'll have to take a closer look," Kincaid said.

Connor stared at the alien space station on the main holoscreen, allowing himself to absorb what he was witnessing. He needed a minute or two to really take it in and decide their next move. He knew the others were watching the same feed on the holoscreens available at their designated areas.

There were no nearby star systems, and without knowing how to find the station, Connor doubted that anyone would stumble upon it. They were remote and away from everything. Something about it flirted with the edges of Connor's mind, as if his instincts were leading him to a conclusion he wasn't quite ready to see.

"Just like Salpheth said, there isn't anyone here. Noah, take us in for a closer look. Target the top of the station and we'll look for the best place to find what we need," Connor said.

While Noah programmed their course, Connor sent a quick message to the others.

Kincaid cleared his throat. "Sir, the power signatures. There are several of them, and they appear to be in standby or power-saving mode."

Connor nodded and looked at Noah. "Think you can make something to address our failing power core?"

"Routing power to our core is relatively straightforward, but refueling the actual core presents a significant challenge. It'll depend on the kind of fuel they're using for their own power. I won't know until we get closer. Speaking of which, I found a dock for us. It's not one of these external platforms; it's interior, near the top of the cone. Whoever built this certainly had ambitious plans for it."

"I agree. This is more than a simple resupply station. Someone had intended to stage operations here for a long time," Connor said.

Noah stared at him, giving him an appraising look. Then his eyes widened. "No, you don't... really?"

Kincaid frowned. "What?"

Connor shrugged. "I've just wondered how involved Salpheth was in the construction of this place. This isn't some mobile station built with minimal resources, only to be abandoned as they moved on. There is something else going on here."

Kincaid looked at the main holoscreen for a moment. Then he shook his head. "I can't even wrap my brain around that. Could the Phantoms really live that long?"

"I'll ask one the next time I see them," Connor sighed. "I don't know. Maybe. Regardless, Salpheth might've been involved somehow, or maybe he just heard about it, and this was his best option for finding a ship."

The ship flew to the station as they kept a careful watch on the scan data coming to them.

Noah stood and walked over to Connor. He arched his back, stretching for a second. "I've been analyzing the structure of the station. I think what we're seeing here are various construction platforms that were automated. They continued going long after this place was abandoned. There should've been some kind of oversight. I don't think this was the intended design."

Connor thought for a few moments. "Yeah, but forty kilometers' worth of material?"

Noah nodded. "It's a machine. Maybe their computer system didn't know any better. Or maybe whoever built it expected to return long before. Or it could've been an error that spiraled out of control. It'll be interesting to see Salpheth's reaction to this."

"He wants to go to the station. He said we'll need him to get access to the resources available here," Connor said.

"He could be right about that. It's an alien system, but I doubt you'd send Salpheth along with the away team."

Connor shook his head. "No way. We'll take a look for ourselves first, then decide."

Kincaid became still as he looked at Connor.

As much as Connor wanted to be on the away team, he wasn't going and said so.

"I'm glad to hear you say that, General," Kincaid said.

Connor exhaled through his nose and looked at Noah.

Noah grinned a little. "If they only knew."

Kincaid frowned. "Knew what?"

"When we first arrived at New Earth, Connor liked to lead excursions deep into the wild landscape of our home. This was before we'd really mapped it out and were aware of all the dangerous creatures."

Connor shrugged. "We can only rely on recon drones for so long. I still remember the first time you held a rifle."

Noah laughed. "I could shoot a rifle." He looked away with a thoughtful frown. "That was those civilian rifles we were using back then. CAR something. I can't remember."

"Yeah, but I was thinking about the AR-74s. I thought you were going to give Diaz a heart attack a few times," Connor replied.

Their laughter dissolved the tension for a few minutes as both of them remembered those early days of the colony. But it inevitably brought the stark reminder that they were far from home, far from their families and friends.

Connor gritted his teeth for a moment and looked at the alien space station. The resources they needed had to be there. All they had to do was find them.

CHAPTER 19

ETHAN MET with his senior officers in the dimly lit conference room. He'd reviewed the preliminary findings of the scan data before arriving at the conference room. The crew was eager to explore the battlefield, despite the risks. Everyone who served the exploration initiative of the Confederation were volunteers. Going where no one had ever been before was part of their core. Encountering an alien species was something they hoped for, even with the violent history of humanity's previous contact with a new alien species. Tempering the general excitement was a sobering awareness that countless aliens had died there. They'd given their lives to stop the Vemus, and the soldiers of the CDF felt an immediate kinship with them. Standing the line in the face of a powerful enemy was part of the foundation of the CDF his father had built. The founders of the colony had imagined a military was something they wouldn't need. Despite this, Connor had taken a colony that knew very little of war and forged it into a fighting force that withstood the enemy that had crushed Old Earth. Ethan knew that yesterday's victories were no guarantee they would survive another full-scale encounter with the Vemus. It was something he'd heard his father speak of in presentations to graduating military cadets and was meant as a warning that they shouldn't get too comfortable because no one knew when or where an enemy lurking in the darkness would bring their darkness to them.

His father had been on his mind a lot, probably because he was missing, but ever since Ethan had risen through the ranks of the CDF and now had command experience, he saw his father and the burdens he'd carried in a whole new light. He wondered what advice his father would give him about what he was about to do. He doubted his father would leave without exploring the battlefield, not when there was so much they could learn. In all likelihood, he'd advise Ethan to be cautious and rely on the input of his crew. That was how the burden was shared.

Ethan sat at the conference table and the meeting began.

"Captain Brett, you can begin," Ethan said to his senior tactical officer.

She stood, and the holotank became active. "What you're about to see is a high-level recreation of the alien battle with the Vemus Alpha. It's based on the data from our scans of the region, taking into account the current location and orbital velocity of the entire region."

Several hundred small icons appeared, being pursued by the Vemus Alpha.

"Over seventy percent of the simulations indicate that the Vemus Alpha pursued a subset of the alien fleet. This is in line with the theory that the Vemus Alpha was lured to this location. It was then ambushed by the remaining fleet, which was broken into two smaller fleets. They used the asteroid field for cover, and there was evidence of weapons platforms that were deployed as part of the battle."

The simulation continued at a higher speed, which depicted a violent clash of ships.

"Analysis of the damage to the ships indicates that both the alien fleet and Vemus Alpha made liberal use of high-energy weapons, and there are even some indications that they also used payloads of gravitic weapons."

Dr. Benjamin Horak stared intently at the holotank and then looked at Ethan. "I didn't think the CDF used gravity weapons."

"Only in defense against Krake attack drones. Our armor was able to withstand their weapons, so with the use of powerful gravity emitters, they were able to shield the ships. Since gravity-based weapons require a lot of power to be effective, the CDF's R&D for the development of weapons pursued their own version of the Krake attack drones because of their superiority. Those, coupled with our missiles and mag cannons, make up much of our armaments. However, we also employ high-energy weapons. It really depends on the kind of enemy being faced at the time."

Dr. Horak nodded. "Why would these aliens limit themselves to just one particular type of weapons system?"

"We found evidence of multiple weapons systems here," Captain Brett said. "However, energy weapons were the dominant weapons system we've detected so far. As to why..." she shrugged. "It would be tied into their history and the effectiveness of the weapons against their enemies. It's not uncommon for nations to develop niches of effective weapons systems of a certain kind, while other nations develop different kinds of weapons. I think it's safe to assume that these tendencies would be present in other alien species as well."

Ethan nodded. "That's a good thought," he said, and gestured toward the holotank. "But for this kind of battle, if their energy weapons were powerful enough, they might be superior in these kinds of close-quarters fighting."

Captain Brett blinked, then looked at the holotank as if seeing it for the first time. Her shoulders slumped a little and she sighed. "I feel like I just missed the forest for the trees, sir."

"You're not the only one, Captain," Qualmann said.

Ethan shrugged. It seemed obvious to him and was a little surprised it wasn't to the others. "Always keep the battlefield in mind. It's a major factor for deployment and engagement tactics."

Captain Brett nodded. "I will, sir," she replied. "I've compiled a list of ships that are the most intact from which reconnaissance missions can be conducted."

The battlefield simulation disappeared and a list of targets appeared, grouped by ship types. With over twelve hundred ships to choose from, Ethan had expected the list to be much longer.

"There is a secondary list of targets, sir. However, I thought it best to present the best targets for us to explore first," Captain Brett said.

"Understood," Ethan replied.

"Why are there no Vemus ships on this list, or the Alpha for that matter?" Cynergy asked.

"The Vemus ships were little more than frigate or small cruiser class ships. There weren't enough left of them to explore. And while exploring those wrecks is an option, I'm not sure how much intelligence can be gleaned," Captain Brett replied.

Cynergy looked at Ethan. "If there are Vemus bodies intact, we could learn more about how they evolved in this alien species. We could also confirm whether the Vemus ships operated independently or were controlled by the Alpha."

"That's assumed the computing core on any of their ships is intact," Ethan replied.

Cynergy nodded. "We won't know until we take a closer look."

"Agreed, and that's why I've authorized the use of Smart Scout Drones to collect samples and make the first pass of the Vemus ships," Ethan replied.

Cynergy frowned and glanced at Wade for a second.

Wade leaned forward. "There's only so much those smart drones can do."

"They're well suited for this kind of work."

Wade licked his lips. "I thought this would be assigned to us."

"Analysis of the data from the scout drones will be," Ethan replied.

Wade rolled his eyes, and Ethan saw Cynergy shake her head.

"What about authorizing us to scout the Alpha? Not board it, but to take a closer look?" Wade asked.

Ethan shook his head. "It's too soon for that."

"It's just a flyby using the sensor suite on our ship," Wade replied.

"Major Gates has already responded to your request. It was denied," Qualmann said.

Wade's broad shoulders slumped and became tense all at once. "I understand. I was just asking that it be reconsidered."

Qualmann was about to reply, but Ethan held up his hand and he waited.

"Wade…" Ethan said, "and this applies to the other civilians as well…I acknowledge that you and your team could perform better for a recon mission than the scout drones, but it's too soon for that. All you see is the Alpha. What I see is that an alien fleet of twelve hundred ships gave everything to destroy the Alpha. While it appears to be dead in space, it might not be. The Vemus on that ship could be in some kind of stasis. Rushing to get that knowledge gets us nothing and increases the danger for everyone else."

Wade began to speak, and Ethan cut him off. "I'll finish without interruption," he warned.

Wade slowly inhaled a breath and then nodded.

"That Alpha isn't going anywhere. It's not. As of right now, it's doing what it's been doing for the last fifty to seventy years, according to the report. However, when we start poking around, it could wake up. If that happens, we'll get out of here as fast as we possibly can."

Wade frowned. "You'd run?"

Ethan blinked, almost shocked by the sheer size of the blind spot in Wade and the other hybrids. Even Cynergy appeared surprised, which made him cringe inwardly.

"Absolutely. The *Ascendant* has no chance against a ship that size. I don't care how much it's been damaged. As the saying goes, we'd cut bait and run like hell."

Wade looked away and shook his head. "At some point, we've got to take a risk. You have to authorize us to take a closer look at that Alpha. All the answers we've been searching for are there. They have to be. That ship is over a hundred and twenty kilometers long. At best, it represents an end stage of Vemus infestation. We need to learn where it was going. You have no choice but to authorize us to go investigate this."

Ethan stared at Wade for a long moment. There were a few things that couldn't be tolerated while commanding a ship, and a subordinate telling the commanding officer what he had to do was one of them.

Ethan turned to his XO. "Major Qualmann," he said firmly.

"Yes, sir?"

"Strike Wade and the rest of his team from all future missions until further notice. Their access to mission data is hereby revoked."

Wade shot to his feet, along with two others. "You're grounding my team!" His skin darkened as he embraced his hybrid nature and his voiced changed. "You're out of line. You can't remove us from the mission!" His two companions, Moteki and Sekino, stood.

CDF soldiers entered the conference room. Two of them had their sidearms pointed at Wade and the others.

Ethan stood. He'd embraced his own hybrid nature without thinking about it. Immediately, all his senses became more acute, and his perception of the room changed. A burgeoning rumble came from his chest. Wade, Moteki, and Sekino hesitated, shocked by the display.

"Remand them into custody right now. Throw them into the brig," Ethan ordered. His voice was deep and husky.

The soldiers quickly subdued Wade and the others. The people around the conference table stared at Ethan, and he exhaled a long breath as he returned to his natural state. Normally, Ethan didn't showcase his hybrid abilities except during physical training and almost never on the bridge. They were unaccustomed to seeing him like this, so when it happened, it was a shock.

Cynergy cleared her throat. "Major Gates," she said formally, "since my team has been taken off the mission, I'd like to excuse myself and the rest of my team from this meeting."

Ethan regarded her for a long moment. He'd only intended his orders to apply to Wade and some of the others, but that wasn't what he'd said. He wouldn't backtrack now.

Cynergy was stone-faced, but through his connection with her, he knew she was seething and hurt.

"Understood," Ethan replied.

Cynergy and the other hybrids left the conference room in a wake of cold silence.

Qualmann waited a few moments. "Perhaps we should break for a few minutes, sir?"

Ethan shook his head. "No, we'll keep going. Captain Brett, continue."

Captain Brett took a second to smooth her features and began speaking. Ethan didn't hear what she was saying for the first few minutes, but eventually he got his head in the game.

CHAPTER 20

Ships rarely operated in isolation. The Mark V Combat Shuttle maintained a network connection to the *Ascendant* and the scout probes currently flying the battlefield. Ethan stood by himself in front of the holoscreen outside the cockpit. Various sub-windows populated the holoscreen, and he had to admit that getting off the ship for this scouting mission had been the right decision. Qualmann hadn't been surprised to learn of his leaving to accompany Captain Washburn on his scouting mission to the alien ships. Both he and Qualmann rotated participating on away missions, but that didn't necessitate that they go on all the missions. That wasn't practical. However, Ethan had a lot of experience exploring derelict ships, space stations, and abandoned facilities on planets.

Ever since he'd grounded Wade and the other hybrids associated with his team, the gap between him and Cynergy had increased. He'd expected it, but that didn't make it any easier. The rub was that Cyn recognized it as well. She was conflicted, which was understandable. In the twenty-four hours since he'd grounded the hybrids, the friction between them had only intensified. She wasn't surprised to learn that he was going off the ship. She would continue to analyze the scan data coming from the ship's sensors and the scout drones. He knew she'd focus her attention on the Alpha, and it was probably for the best. They needed to learn all they could before launching any missions to explore it.

Someone cleared their throat behind him, and Ethan saw Hash standing there. They'd known each other for years. Hash was a young hybrid who had excellent engineering skills and was an all-around technical expert. While Hash wasn't with the CDF, he'd joined Washburn's command as a civilian specialist.

"Major," Hash said, looking a little uncomfortable.

Ethan had first met Hash when they'd returned to Earth. He'd been the youngest member of Cynergy's squad. Age, experience, and a dedication to learning everything he could about colonial technology had made him an invaluable member of Washburn's team.

"Yeah, Hash, what can I do for you?" Ethan replied.

He smiled a little. "Actually, I was coming here to see what I can do for you."

Ethan frowned and lifted one of his palms. "What do you mean?"

"I know what happened with Wade and the others. They're... intense. I wasn't sure if you had any concerns about me, and if you did, I'd prefer to address them."

The edges of Ethan's lips lifted. "If I had concerns about you, I would've had you removed from Washburn's team." He paused for a moment, and Hash looked more at ease. "Hash, I'm unaware of any concerns about you or your abilities."

Hash nodded. "Good, I just wasn't sure."

"I'm glad you came to me instead of wondering about it. I'd rather you were focused on the mission."

"I am. I promise," Hash replied. He rubbed the top of his wrist with his other palm for a second. "What's going to happen to Wade and the others?"

"Hopefully, they'll calm down, re-evaluate their behavior, and move on."

"You're not going to kick them off the ship?"

Ethan arched an eyebrow. There was only so much he was willing to discuss.

"I'm sorry, Ethan. Uh, Major," he said, looking away.

Ethan chuckled. "Hash, it's okay. We've known each other awhile."

"Captain Washburn has remarked on my lack of following CDF doctrine from time to time."

"Really, even after all this time?"

Hash shrugged. "He called me a social butterfly. I had no idea what that meant. After looking up what a butterfly actually was, I still had no idea what he meant. It's a strange expression."

"On mission, we need discipline. I know you understand that."

Hash gave him a determined nod. "I'm all business when we're on a mission."

"Good." Ethan regarded him for a moment, considering. "As for whether Wade and his team will be removed from the *Ascendant*, I haven't decided yet, and it will also depend on him. He was out of line, and I couldn't ignore it any longer."

"Understood, sir. Thank you for indulging my curiosity."

"Have you studied the data on the alien ship we're going to?" Ethan asked.

Hash nodded. "Constantly. Won't know what we're really dealing with until we get aboard and I can see their internal systems."

"Same here."

"What do you think of it?" Hash asked, gesturing toward the image of the ship they were heading to.

Ethan glanced at the image, though he didn't need to. He'd memorized every curve of it. "It looks like a white whale."

Hash frowned. "Oh yeah, I see it. It's all belly, but with eight dark eyes in the front. The shape is inconsistent with missile tubes, so they could be something else."

The large gray hull had an angular snout with ridge lines on both sides of it that appeared to be some kind of observation area. Along the entire hull were thick black lines that reminded Ethan of veins, as if the ship itself had been alive. It looked bloated, like a bag filled to near bursting. Gaping holes revealed the structure inside, and the ship wasn't hollow in the least. There were many decks remaining, even though most had been destroyed in some kind of explosion.

The ship was as large as a CDF battleship carrier, but it had sustained heavy damage. Large, blackened areas on the whitish-gray hull looked as if they were peeling away like a snake shedding its skin. They'd found over a hundred of these battleship-carrier class ships, but there was evidence of even bigger ships among the ice field. Those larger ships had sustained so much damage that there were mere pieces of them left.

Ethan had decided to target one of the more intact ships, hoping they could retrieve data about the battle that had been fought there. Among the many risks that went with boarding an alien warship was the potential for security systems to become active. CDF ships had security systems in place to repel boarders that went beyond arming the crew. Suppression systems could neutralize an invading force, and Ethan hoped that if the aliens had similar security systems, their power cores were depleted.

The door to the cockpit opened and Captain Washburn stepped out. "We're making our final approach, Major Gates."

"Already?" Ethan asked.

Captain Washburn's expression became deadpanned. "My team is outstanding at their jobs, Major Gates."

Ethan heard a few of the men chuckle from farther inside the shuttle.

"Also, we found an open hangar bay. Makes things easier for

going aboard," Captain Washburn said and frowned. "Technically, we didn't just find it. We knew it was there and knew it was our best bet."

Hash frowned and glanced at Ethan for a second.

"Something on your mind, specialist?" Washburn asked.

"Negative, Captain."

"Go get your kit ready. We'll be there in fifteen."

Hash left them, and Washburn looked at Ethan.

"I have to admit I was going a bit stir crazy on the ship," Washburn said.

"Same here."

Washburn nodded. "Ever regret going into command?"

Ethan frowned. "Command? You mean commanding a ship and the mission?"

Washburn had known Ethan for a while. "You know exactly what I mean, sir."

Ethan chuckled a little. "It means I get to come on missions like these whenever I want."

Washburn pursed his lips with an appreciative nod. "I get that, but what about all the other headaches?"

"You're asking me if I think it's worth it? It is. Look where we are. We're on the absolute fringe. No one has been here before."

Washburn shrugged. "Except for the aliens."

Ethan eyed him for a moment. "Are you considering a career change, Captain Washburn?"

The CDF captain quickly shook his head. "I like watching your back, Major. You go where all the action is."

Ethan had heard this before, and not just from Washburn. Many soldiers sought to serve under his father because of the events that seemed to happen around him, but that also fostered a culture of other soldiers who wanted to avoid serving under him for those same reasons. As Ethan ascended the ranks of the CDF, he'd noticed the same behavior. He'd rather have soldiers eager to serve under him than the opposite.

"I appreciate your enthusiasm."

"It's how I start each and every day."

Ethan didn't doubt it. Washburn was nothing if not consistent with his attitude and proficiency as he executed his tasks.

The hangar bay was completely empty, leaving them to wonder if the aliens had abandoned ship during the battle. They hadn't detected any escape pods or hatches on the outer hull of the ship.

The shuttle flew inside the empty hangar. There weren't any hangar bay doors, and since there was no power, whatever atmospheric shield that had been used was inactive. Ethan spotted shield emitters that were part of the open hangar as they flew by.

The platoon had engaged their combat suits and were on their own life support. The shuttle's pilot transmitted a message to the *Ascendant,* notifying them of their arrival.

The shuttle landed, magnetizing the landing gear to keep them on the floor. Whatever metallic alloy the aliens had used in construction of the ship was reactive to the magnetic properties of the shuttle's landing gear.

The loading ramp of the shuttle opened, and Washburn gave Lieutenant Zach Scout the go-ahead to take point. Ethan watched as the CDF soldiers left the shuttle and began making a sweep of the hangar. He and Washburn were last to descend the ramp and step onto the alien ship.

Ethan paused at the bottom and took in his surroundings. The interior of the ship had pale-gray walls, similar to what they'd observed on the outside. They were smooth and looked as if they'd been well maintained right up until the ship was abandoned.

"Detecting faint power sources nearby," Hash said, gesturing across the hangar.

They walked across the large room. There were wide, open

catwalks above them, constructed from dark materials that contrasted with the lighter walls and ceilings.

Ethan scanned the area as they walked toward an elongated octagonal door. He noted the lack of equipment floating around. In fact, the entire hangar was free of debris of any kind. He couldn't see any maintenance bots or some other way for the area to be so clean. It was as if it had already been picked clean.

"Maybe we're not the first ones to come here," Ethan said.

Washburn gave him a thoughtful frown. "That's a cheerful thought," he said and looked at Hash. "Do you know if the Vemus ever scavenged for materials?"

Hash looked up from his personal holoscreen. "Of course."

Ethan frowned. "Most of the remnants we found in Old Earth's star system weren't scavengers."

Hash nodded. "They lacked an Alpha to direct them, but we encountered Vemus repurposing materials all the time. They'd been tasked with stockpiling and just kept doing it."

Ethan nodded. Hash and the other hybrids had been at the forefront of the scavenging efforts and had to risk encounters with remnant Vemus just to survive.

"I doubt the Vemus are here," Ethan said.

"How can you be sure?" Washburn asked.

Ethan gestured toward the door. "The door is intact." Then, he gestured up to the wide slats above them. "Those look like vents. We'd detect traces of them up there, and the recon drones haven't detected anything."

"I remember that mission—the one when you went to that facility on Mars," Washburn said.

Ethan nodded. That had been when the CDF hadn't known what to do with him. It had been a frustrating time all around.

"Hash," Washburn said, "see if you can get that door to open."

Hash went over to the door control system.

Ethan noted the lack of alien writing on the walls or near the door control systems. The hangar bay walls were devoid of any kind of signs, leaving him to wonder how the crew functioned without them. Even though the colonists relied on neural implants and a connection to the ship's computer systems, they still had signs on the walls and doors indicating direction and functionality.

A small green holoscreen became active above the door control systems, and Ethan watched as Hash navigated the interface. It took a few minutes as their translation interface interpreted the alien language for them.

A flash came from the alien holoscreen, and then the elongated octagonal door began to rise. A dark corridor was beyond, and scout drones sped down it, lighting the way.

Ethan and the others went through the door into the corridor. The door closed behind them, and Hash peered at the door controls.

"It's fine," Hash said. "The corridor functions like an airlock."

A red light flashed, and several of the soldiers brought up their weapons.

"Decontamination protocol," Hash said.

The red flashing lights stopped after a few moments. Then, a pale green light brightened the area near the ceiling.

"We're clear," Hash said.

They went down the wide corridor. There was no interior atmosphere, but the ship's systems still required a decontamination protocol.

Ethan looked at Hash. "Is the door control system isolated from the rest of the ship?"

"I'm not sure, Major. I couldn't get beyond the node that those systems connected to. It could be that part of the security measures were designed into the system."

Ethan nodded, and his opinion of the aliens who'd built this ship increased. Security of the warship hadn't been an afterthought. It had been built into the design of the ship, right down to the smallest detail. Warships were purpose-built and needed to account for the multitude of scenarios they could find themselves in. Even the unthinkable must be considered, especially during an actual war.

"We'll need to find a workstation, but I expect there will be limitations with that as well," Ethan said.

"Agreed. We need to find the bridge or main engineering, assuming the aliens put their computing core near it," Hash said.

"We'll find it," Washburn said.

As they explored the alien ship, they learned that power was limited. Door control systems had their own small power source, but that didn't extend to other parts of the ship. Near the hangar were storage areas they couldn't access. The ship was in some kind of lockdown that limited their access. They'd need to end the lockdown before they could access those areas.

"The elevators are offline," Washburn said. "Lieutenant Scout found some kind of transit shaft, which seems to be their main source of travel throughout the ship."

Washburn led them to an area with several large connecting tubes that resembled a transit station for maglev trains. There were no tracks, but there was the soft glow of amber-colored circles on the floor.

"Any idea where they go?" Ethan asked.

The transit tube curved out of sight. The scout drone flew along it and there was a sharp ascent not far from their location. There was nothing for them to grab, so they couldn't climb it.

"We haven't found any other way to travel through the ship. No ladders, not even those handholds that were on that scout ship," Lieutenant Scout said.

Ethan looked at the amber light on the ground. It had a very slight pulse to it, as if it were on standby.

Washburn looked at Ethan. "Did they just step out into the shaft and hope for the best?"

Ethan thought for a moment and then bobbed his head.

"So, you'll go first, then?" Washburn asked.

"A job like this has Richardson's name all over it."

Washburn grinned. "Private Richardson, you're up."

A CDF soldier ran over to them. "Captain?"

"We need you to examine the amber light over there," Washburn said.

Private Richardson eyed the alien transit tube uncertainly. "Yes, Captain," he replied.

He stepped to the edge, and Sergeant Staggart grabbed his arm. "Hold up there. Let me attach a tether to you in case something happens."

Sergeant Staggart pulled out a metallic strap and attached it to the back of Richardson's combat suit. He checked it. "You're good to go."

Private Richardson stepped to the edge of the platform and hesitated for a moment. Then, he leaped into the air.

The ship had no artificial gravity, so when Richardson hovered in the air, it didn't come as a surprise. Before Richardson could use his suit jets, the amber light in the floor brightened, then flashed. A ring of lights came on at the same time, and some unseen force pulled Richardson down the tube. Staggart braced himself, but the sudden force from the metallic tether made his magboots falter and he stumbled into the tube.

Ethan heard Staggart bellow as he was whisked from view. A long tirade of curses came over the comlink, which was followed by laughter.

"We need one of these on the *Ascendant!* Woohoo!" Staggart shouted in excitement.

"Richardson, are you okay?" Ethan asked.

"I'm fine, Major Gates. This is amazing!"

Washburn looked at Ethan. "Transit tube works."

"Yeah, without the tram."

"I'm slowing down," Richardson said. "I think I can get off at the platform here."

"Do it," Staggart said.

Ethan listened as Richardson grunted in effort.

"Made it. I'm out of the tube," Richardson said.

A few seconds later, Sergeant Staggart joined him.

"It's a heck of a ride. Want us to come back, or should we scout the area, sir?" Sergeant Staggart said.

"No sense in them coming back here," Ethan replied.

"Don't you want to see if they *can* come back?" Washburn asked.

Ethan shook his head. "Negative. They went in that direction because of the angle that Richardson entered the tube. I bet if we changed direction, it would take us in the opposite direction."

"Shouldn't we prove that theory?" Washburn asked.

"Sure, go ahead," Ethan said.

Washburn turned toward the other soldiers. "Private Sykes, you're up. Jump in the opposite direction that Richardson did."

"Yes, Captain," Private Ali Sykes replied.

It worked exactly as Ethan thought it would. Private Sykes didn't travel as far as the others and was able to quickly return.

Ethan looked at Washburn. "Happy?"

"I can barely contain myself."

"Me, too," Ethan said, and leaped into the transit tube.

CHAPTER 21

ETHAN SPED down the transit tube, yet despite his velocity, it felt as if he were floating at a leisurely pace. The movement tricked his brain, and his stomach clenched. Then he began to trust the process. He flew through glowing, amber-colored rings that passed in a blur. The transit tubes must have their own redundant power source, which made sense to Ethan. Since the aliens had to abandon ship after it had been severely damaged, it wouldn't make sense for them to be stranded on the ship away from the nearest escape pod or egress point.

The transit tube curved ahead of him, and he tried to anticipate even a minor gravitational force, but there wasn't any. It was as if he were at the center of a kind of freefall, subject to wherever the transit tube was going to take him. He doubted he could stop in the middle of it even if he wanted to.

"Major Gates," Washburn said. "I'd like to make a design recommendation for future CDF ships to include these transit tubes. Can you imagine it?"

Ethan grinned.

He flew past several platforms—dark and presumably without power—that appeared on his HUD as he passed.

The transit tube angled upward, and he entered a long, straight tunnel. Near the middle was a well-lit platform, and Ethan spotted a couple of soldiers waving toward him.

Ethan's velocity began to slow, and he leaned toward the platform. The artificial gravity emitters sensed his movement and deposited him gently onto the platform. The transition felt as natural as stepping off a moving walkway.

"Quite the ride, wasn't it, sir?" Lieutenant Scout asked.

"Yes, and fast," Ethan agreed. He stepped away from the edge and watched Washburn exit the tube.

They waited a few minutes for the others to arrive. Because the last group had entered the transit tube at the same time, they arrived at the same time. No need for them to move separately, which would simplify the return trip.

They walked across an open area. The only light came from the platform, but that lighting went out as soon as they left sensor range.

"Sir," Lieutenant Scout said, "I have concerns about overuse of the transit tubes. They've got to be using some kind of redundant power source, and we don't know how much is left. I advise we restrict their use."

Ethan nodded. "Agreed. Let's figure out where we are and go from there."

There were multiple elongated octagonal doors, each about five meters across. The area must've been designed for high traffic, or maybe the shape of the alien body was wider. The pale walls reflected the lights from the teams' helmets, giving them the appearance of glowing, and it did help illuminate the area.

"I still say they're some kind of spiders," Private Richardson said to his companion. "Look at the walls. They're the same color as a spiderweb."

Washburn looked at Ethan. "He might be right."

Ethan thought that was a reasonable theory—until they found one, that is. He walked to the center-most door control panel. Hash was already there and had the holoscreen up.

Hash looked at him. "This one is more sophisticated than the one in the hangar. I'm able to get our location, and this corridor will lead us to the bridge."

Ethan peered at the holoscreen, and a translation of the alien language appeared on his HUD. "Central Command or Center Brain?"

Hash nodded, looking amused. "Complete accuracy takes time, but I think CENTCOM works."

When the language analysis AI fed them the translation, it had to present the data in terms they could understand, bridging the gap of understanding between two distinct species.

"Can you get the door open?" Ethan asked.

Hash quickly navigated the alien interface, and the octagonal door lifted. The process was quick. Without an artificial atmosphere, there was no sound to be heard.

Lieutenant Scout took point and had several members of his team move ahead. A scout drone flew behind them, lighting the way.

The corridors themselves were octagonal-shaped.

Hash walked next to Ethan. "Strange architecture. What's their obsession with octagons?"

"It's different from ours, but if the support structure follows the same model as this, the octagonal design actually reinforces itself," Ethan said.

Hash eyed him, looking surprised.

"I like ships and their designs," Ethan replied.

"Evidently so."

They walked down the long corridor, which led them to another wide-open area. The ceiling was the same height as the corridor, but there was something black painted on the pale gray walls. There was a large oval shape that covered the center door. As their lights shined on it, black, reflective, flowing lines jumped to his attention that resembled rivers on a map of a mountain. There was nothing written on them, and Ethan had no idea what they meant. Humanity had a practice of honoring historical leaders or certain ideals in the naming of their ships. Perhaps these aliens were honoring a place that was sacred to them.

Ethan gestured toward the door control panel. "Hash, you're up again."

Hash hastened to the panel and brought up the interface.

Washburn came to Ethan's side. "I'm surprised any of the doors are opening for us."

"You mention this now?" Ethan asked.

"Yeah, didn't they have security protocols? Anyone could just enter the bridge? Seems too easy."

Hash turned toward them. "This is going to take me a few minutes."

Ethan looked at Washburn. "See what you did?"

"Oh, come on. Tell me you're not that superstitious."

"I just call it like I see it. We were doing just fine until you said how easy this all was. Thanks for that," Ethan said and walked over to Hash.

Washburn chuckled as he followed.

"It's some kind of lockdown, sir. I don't have the credentials to override it. I can try running something more aggressive, but then we'd run the risk of triggering an automated security response," Hash said.

Ethan frowned and thought for a moment. "Is there evidence of that?" He looked around the door and the surrounding area. There were no panels that he could see, but that could be by design.

"I did receive a warning when I tried opening the door, sir," Hash replied.

Washburn looked at him. "We've got thermite. We could try making our own door."

"Yeah, I think we might have to do that," Ethan said. "Hash, stand down."

"Sergeant Staggart," Washburn said and gestured toward the door, "we need you to open that door."

"One doorway coming right up, Captain," Staggart replied.

The other soldiers from his squad went with him and they set about applying thermite paste to the alien door. After a few minutes, they cleared the area, and Sergeant Staggart ignited the thermite.

A bright flash came from the paste, and a dark channel had burned into the door. Ethan watched as Sergeant Staggart checked the door and then informed them that it hadn't burned through. They applied more thermite paste inside the channel that had been burned into the door. Once they were finished, there was a flash of light, brighter than before. This time Staggart was able to push a large section of the door through, making the opening they needed to get inside.

"Good work, Sergeant Staggart," Ethan said.

They sent a recon drone in to scout the area, and after being satisfied no automated defenses had been triggered by breaching the door, a squad of soldiers went in. They performed a quick assessment and gave the all-clear for Ethan and the others to come in.

Ethan walked through the newly made doorway and entered the bridge. It was a very large room that was half-moon shaped. A large blank wall was about twenty meters from the entrance, which would have held a large holoscreen. The bridge reminded him of an amphitheater. There were multiple work stations on each level, similar in configuration to what they'd found on the scout ship. About halfway down was a central command area where the commanding officer of the ship likely carried out his duties.

A pale green light came from the workstations, which became

brighter as the CDF soldiers neared them. Steep ramps led down to the lower levels.

Ethan made his way to the central command area. None of the workstations had chairs of any kind. The aliens must've stood the entire time they were on duty. He went to the central workstation, and the interface glowed at his approach. He tentatively waved his hand over the interface, which sensed his movement, and multiple holo-interfaces outlined in a pale green light came online at the same time. This seemed to trigger other workstations to immediately come on also. Then, the main holoscreen flickered to life. It wasn't just a screen but gave an illusion of the depth typically only found in a massive holotank capable of representing three-dimensional space.

Hash went to the adjacent workstation and began navigating the interface.

Washburn came to stand next to Ethan, gesturing toward the main holoscreen. "Impressive."

"Agreed," Ethan replied.

The speed at which the translation interface worked increased as he navigated the alien computer system. He still went slowly, carefully considering the options he selected because the accuracy of the translation software also increased over time.

"There it is," Ethan said.

A three-dimensional map appeared on the main holoscreen. Thousands of icons flashed brightly for a moment and then diminished.

"It's trying to confirm the status of the other ships," Ethan said.

"I don't know if that's a good idea. It could trigger a response from the Alpha," Washburn said.

"How?" Ethan asked.

"I don't know. I'm just trying to be cautious." Washburn eyed him for a moment.

"Their communications capability is down," Ethan said.

Washburn sighed. "You could've led with that. You nearly gave me a heart attack."

Ethan snorted. "I only wish you could've seen the expression on your face. This isn't my first reconnaissance mission."

"I know that," Washburn replied quickly. "This place is…spooky."

"I was thinking it was empty."

"Thank God for that. Surely they could've salvaged something from this ship or any of the others out there."

Ethan thought the same thing. "Maybe they were happy just to escape with their lives."

"Or they were captured by the Vemus and brought to the Alpha."

"I don't think so," Ethan said.

"Why is that?"

"Because that's not how the Vemus do things, even the alien Vemus we encountered. We'd have seen evidence of it here. Exoskeletal material would've been detected on the ship. We would've encountered Vemus fighters in whatever form they had, based on the aliens they subjugated. We haven't seen any of that. I think this is just a big empty ship, and the danger is…" He paused for a second.

"If you say minimal, I'm going to scream," Washburn said.

"Yeah, minimal isn't right, but certainly less than what we expected."

"Sir," Hash said, "I was able to find some tactical data in their records. They were tracking the Vemus Alpha. I'm not sure about some of the data, but I bet you could make more sense of it than I could."

Ethan leaned to the side and looked at the data on Hash's holo-screen. Then he brought it up on his own. The records showed how the Alpha traveled to outer regions of star systems to resupply.

"Doesn't say why they engaged it," Washburn said.

"No, it just refers to them as the enemy. I doubt we'd find historical records here. Something must've happened for them to commit so many ships to stopping the Vemus," Ethan said and paused. He spotted references to the Vemus Alpha and brought those up, reading the data as soon as the translation appeared on his HUD.

"Hash, get a dump of this tactical data to the shuttle's computer. I want it relayed to the ship ASAP," Ethan said.

Washburn blew out a breath. "It says the Vemus Alpha goes from brutal frontal assaults to pretending their combat capabilities have been inhibited."

Ethan nodded. "There's an old saying called 'playing possum' where the animal pretends to be dead to escape a more powerful predator. But with this Alpha, it was to lure the attacking force into believing they had the upper hand."

"Wouldn't that leave them more vulnerable? What if the attacking force just kept firing their weapons on them?"

"True, but that assumes there was more than a singular engagement. Looks like the aliens predicted the Alpha would stop here before ambushing it."

Washburn was quiet for a few seconds. "How do we know the Alpha is dead? Could it still be pretending?"

"For over fifty years? That's the estimated age of this battlefield. What would it be waiting for?"

"When it comes to the Vemus, sometimes I tend to throw solid logic out the window."

Ethan understood exactly what Washburn meant. As much as they knew about the Vemus, their true motivations were a mystery. There were a lot of theories that seemed right, but until they learned more, they could only be theories.

Lieutenant Scout hastened over to them. "Major Gates, I have a priority comlink from the *Ascendant*."

A new comlink became available, and Ethan acknowledged it.

Major Qualmann's face appeared on his internal HUD. "Sir, one of our transport shuttles has been stolen."

Ethan clenched his jaw and waited for Qualmann to continue.

"It was Wade and the other hybrids."

Ethan's gaze narrowed. "How?"

"We're still piecing that together. The short of it is that they used stolen credentials to gain access to the shuttle."

Ethan swallowed hard and stared at Qualmann. "Where is she?"

"Cynergy is with them."

Ethan's world became very still, and Qualmann's response replayed in his mind. His muscles tightened like a coiled spring that had been compressed too long. Cynergy was with them. In defiance of the absolute storm gathering inside his mind, he exhaled a long, even breath. "Tell me the rest."

CHAPTER 22

"THEY LEVERAGED their knowledge of our systems," Qualmann said. "We'd locked out Wade and the others who were in the brig, but not all of the hybrids. We did monitor their system access, but they were still able to bypass it, tricking the system into logging their locations as being in their quarters."

"Did Cynergy help them?" Ethan asked, hating that he had to ask the question at all, but he couldn't rely on his assumptions about his wife.

"The extent of her participation is unclear. I wish I had a clear answer for you."

"Where is the shuttle now?" Ethan asked.

"They disabled the shuttle's locator, but the scout drones we had near the Vemus Alpha detected their approach to it."

"Are their comms systems working?" Ethan asked.

"They haven't replied to any of our communication requests. And we tried a remote override of the shuttle's systems, but they blocked it."

Ethan turned away from the main holoscreen. Washburn noted that he'd become quiet and told Hash to keep analyzing the data.

A surge of anger wanted to overtake Ethan's thoughts, but he ignored it. He would not lose control. "Did they have help?"

What Wade and the others had done was mutinous, and Cynergy was involved.

What did you do, Cyn?

He tried to reason why she would've done this but stopped himself. He needed to focus on facts and solutions.

"We're conducting a full security sweep of the area and anyone who had access to the shuttle. So far, nothing has been uncovered that indicates they had any outside help."

Ethan swore, and Qualmann winced.

"I know. I'm searching for the smoking gun here, but I'm not sure where to find it."

Ethan spun around. "Hash!"

Hash turned toward him.

Ethan jabbed an armored fist in his direction. "Did you know about this?"

"I...what?" Hash stammered.

"Wade stole a combat shuttle. Did you know about this?"

Hash held his hands up. "I had no idea," he replied. "Believe me. I had no idea they were planning anything."

Ethan glared at him, deciding whether to believe him. He embraced his hybrid nature and used subsonic vocalizations to communicate with Hash.

Hash let out a startled gasp, and his voice changed. Ever since his experience with the Vemus Alpha, Ethan could detect things from the other hybrids. It was as if he could force his will on them, compelling them to comply. Sometimes it hurt them.

Hash let out a soft cry. "Ethan, please. I'm not lying. Listen to me."

Ethan did listen. He could hear Hash's heart beating. It was elevated but even. There were none of the subtle bursts he'd come to associate with lying.

"What's going on here?" Washburn asked.

Ethan increased the subsonic vocalizations, and Hash cried out in pain.

"I. Don't. Know. Anything!"

Ethan released his hold on Hash, and Hash gasped for breath. Ethan then released his hybrid nature, and his perceptions returned to normal.

"What did you do to me?" Hash asked.

"I had to be sure you weren't lying to me," Ethan said. He regretted having to be so forceful with Hash, but he couldn't afford to be deceived.

Hash backed away from him.

"Where are you going?" Washburn asked.

Hash gestured toward Ethan. "He attacked me."

Washburn glanced at Ethan. "No, he didn't."

"Not physically. Yes, physically, just not…" Hash stopped speaking.

Ethan sighed. "I used subvocal communication to determine whether Hash was lying to us," he said and told them about the stolen shuttle.

Hash came to stand in front of Ethan. "I'd never go along with that—I've never given you a reason to suspect me of anything."

Ethan felt guilty for what he'd done.

"Did Cyn go with them?" Hash asked.

Ethan gritted his teeth. "Yes."

Hash was silent for a few moments. "You locked them out of the system. I remember that, so the only way I can think that they circumvented it is if they had some kind of procedure stored that would execute if they were cut off from the system."

Ethan frowned and looked at Qualmann on his HUD. "Does that make sense to you?"

"I'll run it by the security team."

Hash cleared his throat. "They couldn't have used their own

account access, but they could've scheduled a program to run using an ordinary maintenance account."

Ethan nodded. "And then, like a set of dominos, once one falls it starts a cascade."

"That wouldn't give them access to the shuttle," Qualmann said.

Ethan frowned. "Actually, it might. They could've set up a device that allowed them remote access to the shuttle. All they'd have to do is trigger it, although that would require them to physically be at the shuttle."

Qualmann swore. "I should've anticipated this."

"No," Ethan said, "*I* should've anticipated this. I knew what they were capable of. Damn it, get me a comlink to that shuttle!"

Qualmann looked away from him for a moment.

A new comlink became available. Ethan seized the comlink session and forced the stolen shuttle to accept the request.

"Cynergy, are you there?" Ethan asked. After a few moments of silence. "Wade?"

No response.

"The Alpha might not be dead. I repeat. The Alpha might not be dead."

Again, there was no response.

Ethan seized his hybrid nature and switched on the microphone inside the shuttle. He checked the location and saw that it was still en route to the Alpha. He closed his eyes and focused on listening. Ethan held up his hand, pausing the question Washburn had been about to ask. He needed focus.

Then, he heard it. They were on the shuttle, but they'd slowed down their vital signs so the shuttle's biometrics wouldn't register them as being there. As far as the shuttle's computer systems were concerned, it was being remotely piloted by the Alpha. The hybrids on the shuttle were so deeply focused that they'd be unable to respond to Ethan or anyone else.

He tried to think of a way to wake them up. He brought up the video feed and saw them in their EVA suits, helmets on. They were on standby, and he couldn't tell who was on the shuttle.

Ethan tried to initiate a remote override, and the system kicked him out. The comlink immediately severed. He tried to reconnect it.

"It won't work," Qualmann said. "It's blocked the signal. It'll time out, eventually."

Ethan released his hybrid nature.

"Sir," Qualmann said, "the hybrids are heading toward the enemy. I need to know how you want to proceed."

Ethan heaved a sigh, knowing exactly what his XO was asking. "We can't let them become compromised by the Alpha. I'm going after them."

"I don't think that's a good idea, sir," Qualmann said.

"I don't have a choice, Will," Ethan replied.

"You don't…Wait a second. Horak, I'm adding you to this comlink."

"I'm here," Dr. Horak said.

"Tell Major Gates what you found."

"Yes. Uh, we think Wade and the others are being compelled to this course of action," Dr. Horak said.

Ethan frowned. "How?"

"Dr. Lorenco helped me with this," Dr. Horak said and looked away for a second. "Lisa, come here, please."

A woman with long brown hair came to sit next to Horak. She was one of the lead medical doctors on the ship.

"Yes, Major, I'm here," Dr. Lorenco said. "Their latest biometric scans showed an alarming spike in brain activity. It was as if something had flipped a switch. These are the same areas of the brain where the survivors of the previous Vemus Alpha encounter experienced trauma from resisting the Alpha."

"They'd have to be exposed to an Alpha signal for that to happen. A sustained level of exposure," Ethan replied.

Dr. Lorenco's eyebrows knitted together. "Not necessarily, sir. For subjugation to happen, then yes, you are correct. But the briefest exposure has spurred them into action."

Ethan shook his head. "There is no way Cynergy would just submit."

Dr. Lorenco nodded. "You're right. She wouldn't and neither would the others. Resistance to an Alpha signal is ingrained in all of you. However, with the survivors, the effect is more intense. What I'm saying is that they might not be in their right minds. They're acting on instinct, and it's compelling them to go to that Alpha, even if it's their intent to destroy it..."

Ethan's shoulders slumped.

"Major Gates," Dr. Horak said, "Cynergy was analyzing the scout drone data, and they detected a very faint radio pulse coming from the ship. I think it's what triggered this. I'm still looking at the data."

Qualmann cleared his throat. "So, you see, Ethan, you going to that ship is a very bad idea."

"Not necessarily," Dr. Lorenco said.

Qualmann shot her a disapproving look.

"These are the facts. Major Gates is highly resistant to the Alpha signal, and since he was able to pull the surviving hybrids away from the other Alpha, he stands the best chance of being able to sever the connection here as well."

Ethan had almost failed. It was his father who had helped him overcome the Alpha. The experience had changed Ethan.

"He could be just as vulnerable as the others," Qualmann said and looked at Ethan. "Sir, I must advise against this course of action."

Ethan pressed his lips together. "There is only one way to find out. I need to hear the signal for myself."

"Sir..." Qualmann began.

"I'm not letting them go without a fight. If I succumb to the signal, Captain Washburn will have me restrained and take me back to the ship. You'll assume command of the mission."

Qualmann regarded him for a long moment. "It's a suicide mission. Even if you're able to resist it, that doesn't mean you'll be able to rescue the others. You have no idea how many Vemus will be waiting for you."

"We don't know if there will be any Vemus alive on that ship. Regardless, if I fail, you'll use the *Ascendant's* weapons to obliterate our location on the Alpha," Ethan replied. "Dr. Horak. Send me a sample of the signal. Dr. Lorenco, I'm granting you access to my biometrics for analysis."

Hash cleared his throat. "Include me, too. I wasn't captured by the Alpha, so it shouldn't affect me."

Washburn called a couple of soldiers over to them and ordered them to watch Ethan and Hash.

"Signal is ready, Major Gates," Dr. Horak said.

"Execute," Ethan replied.

CHAPTER 23

A SMALL SUB-WINDOW appeared on Ethan's HUD, and a transmission of the faint radio pulse played. The only indication that the signal was broadcasting was a series of jumps in the tracking line.

Ethan glanced at Hash. They'd both made their face plates transparent. Hash shook his head.

Ethan embraced his hybrid nature, and immediately his senses increased. "Again," he ordered.

The signal played, and this time Ethan sensed the change right away. It was light but with a powerful intensity that made his stomach clench. The Alpha signal was both foreign and familiar at the same time.

"I can sense it," Ethan said.

"Me, too," Hash confirmed.

"No compulsion," Ethan said.

"Maybe it takes a few minutes," Qualmann said.

"It's possible," Dr. Horak said.

Technically, anything was possible, but Ethan wanted repeated exposure before he moved forward with what he intended to do.

"Cynergy had to have listened to this more than a few times. I'd like to recreate her exposure. Repeat the signal. Put it on a loop," Ethan said.

The signal looped continuously as they waited.

"My reaction has lessened," Ethan said with a thoughtful frown. "It's still strange. I'm aware that it is an Alpha, but it has no hold over me. Dr. Lorenco, can you confirm with the readings from my biometrics?"

"One moment," she replied. "I've compared these readings with your recent baselines, and they're normal, sir. You're not affected by this signal. However, I must caution you that this could change. Constant monitoring is required to ensure there are no surprises."

"I concur," Qualmann said. "Think of it as someone watching your back, sir."

Ethan nodded. "Alright, send over a simple analysis program and I'll assign it to someone." He looked at Captain Washburn.

Washburn glanced at the nearest soldiers, considering. "Private Sykes. You're on monitoring duty for both Major Gates and Specialist Hash. I want to know the moment there is any deviance from the baseline. Is that understood?"

"Yes, Captain," Private Ali Sykes replied. "Should I stay within close proximity to them, sir?"

Washburn considered it for a moment, glancing at Ethan. Then he looked at her. "Within reason. Stay within seven to ten meters when we arrive at the Vemus Alpha."

"Yes, Captain."

Ethan winced. While he didn't like the thought of having a babysitter, he had to trust Washburn's judgement in this because he knew the people under his command better than Ethan did.

"Time for us to get out of here," Ethan said.

"Major Gates," Hash said. "Permission to leave a portable comlink attached to the console here. It can maintain the data dump from the ship's systems until we're out of range."

"Go ahead," Ethan said.

He left the command center workstation, eager to get going. Washburn ordered the soldiers back to the transit tube.

The others dropped the comlink except for Qualmann. Ethan knew his XO. His friend didn't like this development at all. They both knew Ethan was walking a very thin line where regulations were concerned.

"I have a backup platoon departing and will meet you at the Alpha. I don't suppose I can talk you into waiting for them before you go into that ship?" Qualmann asked.

"That'll depend on what we find."

He wasn't about to charge blindly into the Vemus Alpha. Doing that would be asking for trouble, and not just for him but for the soldiers under his command. But time was against them—the longer the others were exposed, the greater their risk of being subjugated by the Vemus.

"Fair enough," Qualmann said and was quiet for a few seconds. "I hate this."

"So do I," Ethan replied.

His original plan for the alpha involved sending scout drones inside the ship for assessment before ordering teams to go anywhere near there. Weighing the risks was to have been first and foremost. Now he had to operate under another set of risks and protocols that didn't favor a more measured approach.

They ran down the corridor, heading back to the transit tube, and he was becoming impatient. If only there was a way to lock down the shuttle and prevent it from reaching the Alpha.

"Ethan, I'm sorry. I should've kept a better watch on them. They should never have been able to escape," Qualmann said.

"Will, it could've easily happened under my watch too. I was there too, and I also thought the security measures we had in place were enough to prevent this. We can do a full review of the whole situation later and determine where there were any shortfalls in our security posture. Then, we'll make improvements and move on."

"Understood."

Ethan came to the transit tube and didn't slow down. He leaped into it and his velocity increased as he was swept away.

"Will, you can't hesitate with this. If the situation becomes hopeless, you blow that Alpha to kingdom come. Nothing left. Scorched earth. No remains. I don't want that thing to have any knowledge of who we are or where we came from. Is that understood?"

Qualmann's gaze became as hard as battle steel. "Yes, Major Gates. I promise you that if the situation is hopeless, I will do as you've ordered."

"Good," Ethan said. "I'll send you an update when we reach the Alpha."

"I've tasked available scout drones to the area, and I have our sensors locked onto it as well. We'll be moving the ship to within tactical range of it by the time you arrive. Good luck," Qualmann said.

The comlink severed.

Ethan had every confidence in his XO. Qualmann would hate following the orders he'd been given, but approving of the orders one had to follow wasn't a luxury for anyone serving in the military. As long as those orders weren't illegal, the requirement was that they were to be carried out as soon as they were given. If the situation became hopeless, this would haunt his friend long after Ethan and the others had been blown into oblivion, and somehow that didn't make him feel any better.

Ethan didn't count the situation as hopeless but expected things to get worse. With the Vemus, things would *always* get worse. Each layer of understanding took them deeper into the darkened pit of knowledge that only promised there was even more for them to learn. However, the more they learned, the less they needed to be afraid. Knowledge and truth were power, and it could light the path for generations to come. That was what both his parents had taught him in their own unique ways. There was no place Ethan wouldn't go for even the slightest chance of rescuing his wife. Would he be as determined if she weren't among them? Maybe, or maybe not, but she *was* there. If Wade and the other hybrids were under the influence of the Alpha, any Alpha, then he owed it to them not to allow them to become victims of the Vemus. They wouldn't want to live like that, and neither would he.

They left the transit tube and raced back to the shuttle. Once they were all onboard, no time was wasted. They left immediately.

Hash looked at him. "The data connection to the bridge is strong. There is a lot for us to retrieve. I've included tactical data, as well as data from their navigation system. It'll take some time to understand it all. Hopefully, it'll help."

Ethan nodded. "Good work, Hash. I appreciate it." He meant it. It was important to have an eye on the future as well as the current situation.

"Thank you," he replied. "I want you to know that I understand why you did what you did to me. I don't like it, but I understand."

"I didn't like doing it."

Hash blew out a breath. "I'm glad. It's an odd talent you've developed."

He frowned. "What do you mean?"

"There are some hybrids who are sensitive to others in interesting ways. They can determine if someone is lying, but your talent goes beyond that. You can force them into submission. Does that make you some kind of alpha in your own right?"

"I don't know. I've talked about it with Cyn, and she didn't know either. I think it happened during the stress of that last Vemus encounter. I became locked in the hybrid state so I could find her. It's had lasting effects on me."

Hash nodded, lips pursed in thought. "It's like any other

muscle. You've got to tear it down to get it to build back stronger. It could be that this is something any of us can do." He frowned and shook his head. "Not that I want to dominate anyone. Not at all."

"Neither do I. I'm sorry it was so painful for you."

Hash nodded. "I'll leave you to it. I want to keep analyzing the data we're receiving from the alien ship. Maybe there's something there we can use to help us."

Hash left him, and Washburn emerged from the cockpit.

"We're on our way. Best speed will get us there in about two hours," he said.

Ethan's eyes widened a little. That time estimate meant pushing the shuttle's engines beyond design specifications.

Washburn nodded once. "I know. The sooner we can get there increases our chances at rescuing the others. Time is just as much a factor as that Alpha is."

Ethan nodded. "Understood. Did you get the latest update from Dr. Lorenco?"

Private Ali Sykes glanced over at them from where she sat about eight meters away.

"I saw it. There are protocols for the combat suit that will subdue you should I determine you've been compromised by the Vemus," Washburn said. He arched an eyebrow. "Sometimes, I fat-fingered these darn holo-interfaces. I'd hate to accidentally initiate the hybrid-suppression protocol."

Ethan grinned a little. "It'll be a whole lot safer for you if you don't," he said, only partially joking. He glanced at Private Sykes, who was watching her personal holoscreen. "Is she up to the task?"

Washburn glanced at her for a second. "Absolutely. Honestly, sometimes women make the best watchers for monitoring duty. That's been my experience. She'll monitor both yours and Hash's vitals as if her life depends on it. She won't get distracted."

"While I can appreciate that single-minded determination in

any soldier, I *am* concerned. She'll need to monitor as we go through the Alpha searching for the others."

Washburn frowned. "Let me tell you something about Private Sykes. Her training records all show top marks for this type of work, and I'll have Richardson watch her back."

Ethan's expression became deadpanned. "Now I'm safe. You're putting my life in the hands of two privates."

"I'll change it if you want, but I know my soldiers, sir," Washburn said.

Ethan considered that. He knew how fast things could change if they did encounter Vemus fighters. They'd need more seasoned soldiers focusing on other things. He heaved a sigh. "No, we'll do it your way."

"You're in good hands, sir."

Ethan brought up the tactical data for the Vemus Alpha. At over a hundred and twenty kilometers, it was larger than any city on New Earth. He'd read about some of the mega-cities of Old Earth that existed before the Vemus Wars. He'd even seen some of the remnants, but even then, it was difficult to imagine them.

Ethan rolled his shoulders. It felt good to be out of the combat suit for a little while. It was being recharged in the shuttle's cradle, which could only recharge six combat suits at a time. They'd all get done before they arrived at their destination.

Washburn eyed him. "They take some getting used to when you haven't worn one in a while. A bit different than the EVA suits."

Ethan chuckled. That was a colossal understatement if he'd ever heard one. Combat suits were vastly different than an EVA suit. Combat suits were purpose-built to withstand the harshest of environments. They were weapons in and of themselves. Their augmentations and configurations allowed the wearers to function in all but the most extreme of environments. He'd made sure they had the latest series NexStar combat suits before they embarked on the exploration mission.

"At least they're resistant to the exoskeletal material," Ethan said and frowned. "As we know it."

Washburn's eyebrows knitted together. "I wish you hadn't said that."

Early CDF encounters with the Vemus had resulted in Vemus exoskeletal material breaching the combat suits in use at the time.

An icon representing the stolen shuttle showed that it was almost to the Alpha.

"I wonder how they'll pick an area to infiltrate the ship," Washburn said.

"Without knowing how much control the Alpha is exerting over them, it's going to be difficult to tell."

It was difficult to keep the hows and whys straight in his head. Dr. Lorenco had posited that the affected hybrids were reacting to the Alpha, which was compelling them to seek it out. What was unclear was whether those who were affected intended to destroy it or serve it. Regardless, the possibility was real that they weren't in control of themselves.

Washburn frowned. "If they're under its direct influence, then wouldn't it bring them right to it?"

"That's just it. According to Dr. Lorenco, it's their reaction to the signal that could be compromised. They could be seeking it out to destroy it."

"Or they could be seeking a way to communicate with it."

Ethan nodded. "Yeah. We'll need to do our own assessment. Our best bet will likely be to follow them."

"You know, what I don't understand is why the Alpha is so big. Was the population of the planet so high that it warranted building a ship that sized?"

"I don't know. It could be that, or it could have to do with available resources."

Washburn nodded slowly. "Makes me wonder how many

worlds out there are currently fighting a war of survival against the Vemus."

That had been the question on all of their minds ever since they'd encountered the Phantoms and the other alien Vemus.

"I wonder how they launched that ship into space. Was it built on the planet like the other one, or was it constructed in space? As for how many worlds are out there fighting the Vemus, that might be a question we'll never be able to answer."

The tactical data refreshed on the holoscreen, giving them the most current data. Beyond the absolute size of the ship, Ethan could see that it had sustained a lot of damage.

Washburn studied the image and looked as if he were struggling to grasp everything he was seeing.

"Think of this as any other tactical assessment. There isn't a spot on that entire ship that hasn't been damaged. It's lodged into a vast sea of ice with some asteroids mixed in. Cobbled together, it's almost as large as a dwarf planet, albeit on the smaller side," Ethan said.

Washburn nodded. "I understand that, but I can't get the alien's tactical assessment out of my mind... how the Alpha pretends to be disabled to lure in unsuspecting forces."

"I doubt we'd rate as an attack force that could threaten them in any way. I think it's dead."

"What about the Alpha signal?"

"Mostly dead then. If that ship could fly, they would've left. Yet we see no activity on the hull of the ship or in the surrounding areas. If there were repairs happening, we would've seen them. Look at the most damaged areas. That ship took quite a beating."

"I hope you're right—about the mostly dead part, but even then, it's still going to be dangerous."

Ethan nodded and continued to study the images of the Alpha. The behemoth hull consisted entirely of the Vemus exoskeletal material. In some areas, it resembled that of a large asteroid, the kind that they'd target for mining if they needed supplies. However, where there was once significant exoskeletal armor, there were now gaping holes so large as to resemble the largest of cave openings. Whoever these aliens had been, they'd certainly done their utmost to destroy the Vemus. Somehow, in the midst of all that damage, at least a small part of the Alpha remained. Did the aliens who'd fought there realize that, or had they all been wiped out?

"How many combat suit heavies do we have?" Ethan asked.

"Six, and we have at least twelve combat drones."

"We're going to need them. When we find the Alpha, I intend to finish what these aliens have started," Ethan said.

"Understood. I'll go get them sorted. Back in a few minutes, sir," Washburn said.

Ethan studied the screen, but his mind wandered, and his gaze went to the icon representing the stolen shuttle. He mostly thought about Cynergy but sometimes the others. How had he missed the truth about what was happening with his wife and the others? He hadn't wanted to believe it. Not really. None of them did.

He gritted his teeth in frustration. If she'd only talked to him, he'd know whether she'd been compromised by the Alpha. It was the not knowing part that really got to him. He'd have to make tough decisions based on very little information, and if he was wrong, it was going to cost not only him but everyone else as well.

CHAPTER 24

THE *PATHFINDER* FLEW CLOSER to the massive station and an alert appeared on the tactical data feed.

"We're being scanned," Kincaid said.

"Understood," Connor replied.

"Should I engage point defense systems?"

"Negative. Don't do anything. Just let the scans run. I was hoping something like that would happen."

Kincaid frowned. "News to me, sir."

"Think of it as flying to any other space dock," Connor said, and another alert appeared.

Noah frowned as he read the alert. "Just received a message indicating a docking platform to go to. I've entered the coordinates. They want us to go to the interior."

"Take us in," Connor said.

The main holoscreen updated to show a path to their destination. The massive alien structure loomed before them, and large doors separated, revealing more of the interior of the station. They flew past the partially completed sections and Connor noticed construction stations that didn't have a hint of power going to them. He was starting to think Noah's theory about those platforms was correct.

They watched in tense silence as they flew toward their destination. Noah blew out a breath in surprise.

"There are other ships here. Our sensors have detected at least three. Large carrier class, but they don't appear to be warships," Noah said.

"Put it on screen," Connor said.

A sub-window opened on the holoscreen, showing a large, dome-shaped, silver ship. The only lighting came from the *Pathfinder* and the docking platform that had power. The ship sat a considerable distance away, barely visible in the dim light. It was all smooth lines and flat surfaces, akin to that of a helmet. Several maintenance platforms surrounded them, but they didn't appear operational.

"Scans show other ships nearby. All docked. Can't detect any power, but our scans might not penetrate the hulls," Noah said.

Pathfinder's nav system had an automated docking protocol that required them to identify the dock, and the ship's computer system guided them safely to it. Connor couldn't see any docking clamps as the ship moved toward an elevated platform of the same white alloy the rest of the station was made from.

"Detecting an artificial gravity field maintaining a point eight-seven G. No atmosphere," Kincaid said.

Pathfinder's size was almost minuscule when compared to the docking platform. Pale circular lights highlighted the platform and path that lead to the station proper.

The maneuvering thrusters brought the *Pathfinder* closer to the platform, and Connor noticed a spike in the gravity field near the ship. They stopped moving, being held in place by artificial gravity emitters that must've been part of the docking platform.

"Cut power to the engines," Connor said.

Noah did as Connor ordered. "Maintaining position."

Nothing was ever completely motionless in space, no matter how large a structure it was. The station itself was moving, and since the *Pathfinder* was within the station's artificial gravitational field, they didn't have to expend energy to maintain their location with the space station.

Connor looked at Kincaid. "All right, you're up, Captain Kincaid. Take Seger and Naya and see if you can find the source of the energy signatures we detected."

"Yes, General," Kincaid said. He opened a comlink to Seger and Naya and began speaking to them as he stepped away from the tactical workstation. He stopped and looked at Connor. "Sir, Seger said Phendran is still in Stellar Cartography."

"Are they almost finished?" Connor asked.

Kincaid relayed the question. "Yes, he said they're wrapping up."

"Okay, I'll have Rabsaris escort the Aczar to the bridge," Connor said and sent Rabsaris a message.

Kincaid left the bridge.

Noah had the external video feeds panning the area outside the ship. "Two hundred meters of open space until we reach the actual station. Can you imagine how many people could live here? This is more of a deep space outpost, or some kind of mobile colony center. There's been a few of those ideas pitched over the years."

Connor couldn't see any vehicles or anything else on the docking platform.

"We've got a couple of scout drones left. I'm going to send them out and see what they detect around us," Noah said.

"Good idea," Connor said.

While Noah worked on getting the scout drones deployed, Connor studied the data feeds from their scans. There were enough materials here to rebuild the *Pathfinder* a thousand times over. They just lacked colonial construction platforms to do the actual work.

"I was hoping we'd find other Phantoms here or a way to communicate with them on our own. I hate this waiting around for them to decide whether to talk to us," Connor said.

"You. They chose to speak with you. No one else. Just you."

"Yeah, well, that has to change."

"Getting tired of being popular?"

"We're more than any single person. And the Confederation will consist of multiple species. How many more are out there? Hopefully, more will join."

Noah pressed his lips together, considering. "You mean allies."

"Look at this place. The Phantoms told us that we couldn't take on the Vemus as we were. We'll need allies if and when we actually do find where the Vemus are located," Connor replied.

"You've got to think of this in the long term. I mean generational terms, as in perhaps hundreds of years or even more. A time where something like this place won't leave us so awestruck."

Connor considered for a few moments. "Reminds me of what the Krake built. The scale of it. They restricted themselves to a single star system and focused on traveling through the multiverse. They conducted operations at that scale and expanded their influence to use entire planets. They could've just as easily sought to expand beyond a single star system. Could you imagine facing something like that?"

"I'm glad we didn't have to."

"Yeah, but they were heading in that direction."

"What does this have to do with the Phantoms?"

"It's the scale of the things a species builds. Remember when the CDF was just a dozen ships and hundreds of automated defense platforms? Now we have a fleet in the hundreds. With more ships being built on Old Earth, our species is poised to have explosive growth beyond anything that ever came before. Now, with the new and improved Infinity Drive, there's no limiting us to a couple of star systems. This opens the door to the entire galaxy. Maybe this is how the Phantoms began, and they see certain similarities with our own development."

Noah stared at him for a long moment. "You've given this a lot of thought."

Connor arched an eyebrow. "And you haven't? Come on, I know better than that."

A few minutes later, Kincaid contacted them.

"General, we're ready to depart," Kincaid said.

"Remember, this is a scouting mission. Keep suit cameras on and we'll monitor you from here," Connor replied.

"Understood, sir," Kincaid said.

Connor muted the audio and put the video feeds from the three people on the away team on the main holoscreen.

Both he and Noah leaned forward to watch as Kincaid led the others off the ship.

Phendran and the other Aczar joined them on the bridge, along with Rabsaris.

Connor looked at Phendran, and the Aczar looked tired. "Are you okay?"

Phendran slowly moved toward a seat and climbed in it. "The merging of data is taxing my strength. I need time to recover."

"Maybe you should go lie down," Connor replied.

"No, I'll be fine. I want to see this," Phendran replied.

Kholva gave Phendran his canister, which contained a liquid formulation that functioned as a restorative for the Aczar. Phendran sipped it appreciatively.

"I will be fine, General Gates. Please carry on with your operation. We'll observe and try to help as we can."

"Very well," Connor replied and gestured for Rabsaris to join him.

Rabsaris sat at the auxiliary workstation and focused on the video feeds.

"Keep a sharp lookout for anything out of the ordinary," Connor said.

It wasn't lost on him that almost everything there was out of the ordinary, but he knew the others would take his meaning. They were to watch out for danger or anything interesting that the away team should investigate.

———

Kincaid opened the airlock and stepped through. Seger followed him and Naya was last.

A ramp extended from the airlock to the docking platform and Kincaid walked down it. As soon as he stepped onto the platform, the area illuminated under his feet. He paused and looked around to see if anything else had happened.

"That's interesting," Kincaid said and stepped away from the ramp.

As the others followed him, their steps caused the ground to momentarily illuminate, sending ripples of light away from them that quickly faded.

"I guess there isn't any sneaking around here," Seger said.

Naya carried a toolkit that was attached to her back. She held a palm scanner and frowned at it. "It's some kind of reactive plating."

Seger chuckled. "Reactive plating...I like that."

She smiled and winked at Seger.

Kincaid surveyed the area, noting that it was a wide, metallic field leading to the space station. They walked across it, and a dimly lit path appeared before them. Kincaid paused for a second before continuing.

"I thought Salpheth said we wouldn't be able to access anything without him." Seger said.

"That's what I heard him say."

"Kinda inviting of them to show us the way to the door."

"Could already be programmed in for anyone who walks on it," Kincaid said and glanced at Naya. "Part of the reactive plating experience. Anyway, let's keep going."

They followed the path, which took them directly toward the station.

"Hold on a second," Seger said. "Let me try something."

"Okay. Go ahead."

Seger walked to the edge of the illuminated path and stepped past the boundary. A second path illuminated under his feet that led in the same direction as the first. The boundary between the two paths was brighter and easy to distinguish.

Seger returned, and the second path became dark. "Just wanted to see if it would let us off this path."

"I think it's just a guide," Naya said.

They continued onward and made their way to the wall. As they closed in, a seam appeared about halfway up, and a section of the wall sank through the ground, revealing a dimly lit interior with a soft, white light. It was almost delicate but also lit the area well.

They stepped through the doorway and the illuminated path went dark. A single bright light appeared on the ground to light the way ahead of them.

Kincaid looked behind them as they moved away from the outside, and the door remained opened. He didn't relish the thought of being trapped there and was relieved it hadn't closed.

They followed the guide farther inside to a wide corridor, at the end of which was a white wall. An area to their right glowed, revealing a panel.

Kincaid walked over to it and touched the panel, but nothing happened. He tried tapping it, swiping his hand across it, and then held his palm there. Nothing.

Naya came over and began scanning. "It's got power, but for some reason, it's not reacting to us at all."

Seger muttered a curse. "The other door is closing," he said, stepping toward it but then stopping. They wouldn't have made it there in time.

Kincaid peered at the alien control panel. "It's got to be some kind of security lockout. Let's go try the door we came in through."

CHAPTER 25

CONNOR WATCHED the video feed from Kincaid and the others.

"They're trapped," Noah said, tensing.

"The control panel won't even react to them," Connor replied.

"Naya," Noah said, "try to open the control panel."

The camera on Naya's helmet was pointed toward the panel. "There are no visible means to open it. I could try my cutting torch."

Connor looked at Phendran. "Any ideas?"

"No, it must require some kind of authentication. I'm afraid Salpheth was telling the truth about needing his assistance to gain entry into the facility."

Connor pressed his lips together in thought. "Naya, try the cutting torch."

"Yes, General," Naya replied.

She pulled out a hand-held plasma torch and approached an area of the wall near the glowing panel. She activated the torch, and a bright burst of light came from it. After holding it in place for a few moments, she slowly brought it down. Despite the extremely high heat from the plasma, the wall was unmarked.

"Not only reactive but heat resistant too," Seger said.

"I've got thermite. We should try that," Kincaid said.

"Don't bother," Naya replied. "The cutting torch burns way hotter than thermite."

"Understood," Kincaid said. "General, I'm not sure what else to do here. We have explosives, but I don't think that would work."

"What about firing their weapons?" Rhodes asked.

Connor shook his head. "No, they're in an enclosed space. Chances are it would ricochet off the walls and they'd hurt themselves. EVA suits don't have armor capable of resisting weapon's discharge."

"I hate to say it, sir," Kincaid said, "but we might need Salpheth's help."

Connor clenched his jaw a little and nodded. "Yeah. Stand by."

He muted the comlink and looked at the others, then focused on Phendran. "What about your SRA? Is it worth you going out there to see if it can interface with the technology?"

Phendran glanced at Noxrey, who was some kind of engineer, but Noxrey also seemed to be at odds with Phendran, so Connor wasn't sure how much he could trust him.

Noxrey looked at Connor. "Have they scanned for other means of communication?"

Connor engaged the comlink to Kincaid. "Captain, try scanning for any type of comms."

Kincaid was quiet for a few moments. "Negative, sir. Nothing gets a return."

"Understood. Stand by," Connor said.

Connor really didn't want to bring Salpheth onto that station, but he was running out of options. He looked at Noah. "Anything that I can think of requires equipment we don't have here."

Noah nodded. "Same."

Connor looked at Phendran. "What kind of weapons can hurt Salpheth?"

Noxrey's eyes widened.

"We need a means to defend ourselves," Connor said and looked at Phendran. "You've seen our weapons, but you know more about Salpheth than we do. He must have some kind of physical limitation."

Phendran nodded. "He's an ascended being but must maintain physicality to function here. Therefore, the force of your weapons would affect him, but they would not eliminate him."

"So, we could deter him," Connor said.

"For a time, and it would cost him to repair his physical form."

"What would it take to stop him permanently?"

Phendran considered it for a few moments and then looked at Noxrey. The two seemed to be having an offline conversation. They arrived at a conclusion, and Phendran looked at Connor. "We only have theories, but the most success I've seen was accomplished by you and your ship."

"You mean the I-drive when Noah was using it to transport him away from the planet," Connor said.

"Yes, this. You forced his hand, and he chose to hide, which led to furthering his own imprisonment. In our history, there have been rebellions against Salpheth with the goal of eliminating him, but all have failed, either because of security forces stopping the rebel factions or that the means used to attempt elimination did not succeed."

Connor looked at Noah. "Can the portable field generator also be used with an artificial gravity emitter?"

Noah frowned in thought, and then he smiled a little, understanding what Connor was asking.

"What good would that do?" Rhodes asked.

"If we can't hurt Salpheth, perhaps we can trap him without an energy field. Anything to give us an edge while giving him the illusion of freedom," Connor replied.

"He'll see through it eventually, but I can definitely rig something up," Noah said. "Actually, Tripp can do it. He's closer to the workshop there anyway."

Connor frowned. Tripp Krin was a technician, not an engineer. "Are you sure about that?"

"Yes. It doesn't require anything special. You're just asking that a couple of emitters be connected to the portable field generator. They can be put on standby, and you can control how powerful the antigravity field becomes," Noah said.

"Okay, have him do it and meet me at the secondary power core," Connor said.

"Wait," Noah said. "Who are you taking with you?"

"I was thinking of Mac and Jorath. They've had weapons training. I want you to stay here."

"What about taking Tripp with you?" Noah asked.

Tripp Krin was a young technician whose experience was in computing core maintenance and upgrades. He had no field experience but performed well with the things he knew best.

"I think out there, he'd be more of a liability than a help."

"He might surprise you. I've been working with him. He knows the field generator, and if things go sideways, you'll need his help. I can help you through him if it comes down to it," Noah said.

Connor knew Noah didn't like being left behind, but if the situation worsened, Connor also knew that after himself, Noah was the most able to get the survivors back home.

"General Gates," Phendran said, "I think it's time Salpheth learned of our presence here. I'd like you to allow Noxrey and I to come with you. We could advise you and help in any other way we can."

Connor looked at him and then at Noxrey for a second. "Phendran, I have no problem allowing you to come with me. However, I'm not convinced Noxrey would be able to help." Connor stared at Noxrey. "Based on your comments and behavior, you're as likely to help Salpheth against us as you are to help us."

To Phendran's credit, he didn't reply or deny what Connor had said. He looked at Noxrey and waited for the Aczar to speak for himself.

Noxrey was quiet for a few moments, which Connor knew was much longer for them than it was for him. The Aczar perceived time differently than the rest of them. Their brains worked faster.

"You have every reason to be suspicious of me," Noxrey said. "My home world will never be the same, and there are links to you coming to the planet as a catalyst for those events. But my Loremaster has reminded me that we were on this path regardless of your visitation. I don't like what has happened to my people. For as much as Salpheth manipulated, he also taught us. If I could think of a way to return him to Ichlos, I would do it. However, I don't believe this is possible, and it is evident that Salpheth will do everything he can *not* to return to Ichlos. This leaves me with very little choice but to help you so we will get to go home. I will be a witness to these events, and they will be recorded by Phendran. I promise not to hinder your efforts to repair your ship, even if it brings you into conflict with Salpheth. The past is very much with me, but I will not be compelled by it any longer. The future of the Aczar will be ours to make, and I desire to be part of that more than I desire Salpheth to be returned to us. I cannot offer you any other than that."

Connor hadn't expected Noxrey's response, but he couldn't find fault with wanting to return home and build a better future. "You can come only under the following condition: You will comply with my orders. We need a hierarchy so everyone knows exactly where they stand and what the expectations are. This is not so I can have power over you. It's for our protection. If I say we leave, then we leave. We're in this together, and we have a better chance if we're aligned against Salpheth. Can you operate under that condition?"

Noxrey glanced at Phendran for a moment. "I will certainly follow your lead, General Gates, but I won't follow blindly. I'm not a member of your military. If there are questions to be raised, I intend to raise them, but only in the spirit of cooperation and preservation."

"Very well. I accept your terms," Connor said.

Noxrey looked surprised for a few seconds before slowly lowering his chin in acknowledgment.

They left the bridge, and Connor saw Phendran frowning at a small green holoscreen above his wrist.

"What's wrong?" Connor asked.

"I'm unable to communicate with your SRA," Phendran replied.

Connor glanced at the metallic band near his wrist computer. Most of the time, he forgot it was there. He peered at it and then gently tapped it. A faint glow came from it for a moment and then disappeared.

"Should I be concerned?" Connor asked, wondering if he should remove it.

"No, this behavior, while unexpected in its timing, isn't a complete surprise. It's been adapting and learning from you. It's processing information, and when it's finished, your SRA's capabilities will increase. I can see that it has expanded in size to accommodate the necessary growth."

Connor's eyebrows raised in surprise. The SRA didn't appear larger than it had been before. "I don't know what to think about it. You keep referring to it as *my* SRA."

"Because it *is* yours. Its origins may have been with mine, but it has moved beyond that. I'm amazed that the process happened so quickly. Perhaps our SRAs are better suited to your species than my own."

Connor frowned, trying to follow the implications of that. Humanity had used neural implants for hundreds of years, but the interface was highly restricted, even with the use of artificial intelligence. The SRA had a much more intimate connection with the

Aczar, who thought of them as a partner or a friend. His experience with the SRA hadn't been extensive, and it hadn't shown anything like a personality that he could detect. Their exchanges were formal, with a few question-and-answer sessions. He knew it was observing him, and sometimes it offered a reaction, particularly after he'd come from a meeting with Salpheth. It would show him a small image of Salpheth within the energy field, but it applied a heat map to the image. Somehow, his SRA was able to detect subtle variances from within Salpheth during his interviews with the prisoner. Connor wasn't sure what that meant, and he didn't think the SRA did either. He thought the SRA was trying to be helpful and provide an observation that might've been otherwise overlooked.

Mac met Connor and the others at the secondary power core. Jorath was already there. The Ovarrow handed Mac an AR-74 rifle, and Mac took it with a confused expression.

"I don't understand, General. What is it you need from me?" Mac asked.

"I need your help, Mac. By the way you're holding the rifle, I already know you've been trained in its use in the CDF. I need you to come with me on escort duty. The others are locked inside the station, and we're going to get them out."

Mac frowned and glanced at the weapon for a moment, then inhaled a deep breath and sighed. "Understood, General Gates."

"Don't put the EVA suit on just yet," Connor said to them. "I'll go to Salpheth first and call you both in."

Phendran and Noxrey gave him a firm nod.

Mac glanced nervously at the door to the secondary power core, muttering under his breath. He took up a position next to Jorath.

Connor walked down the corridor and entered the room. Salpheth hovered in the middle of the energy field, pretending he hadn't noticed Connor enter.

Tripp Krin came in and Connor gestured for him to wait over to the side.

Connor stepped toward the energy field and disabled some of the safety locks that held it in place. "You were right," Connor said. "We need you to access the station."

Salpheth regarded Connor for a long moment. "I'm glad you finally see reason. Bring down this energy field, and we'll go together."

Connor grinned and shook his head, then gestured for Tripp to go inside the chamber and begin the transition of the energy field. "You didn't seriously think it would be that easy, did you?"

Salpheth glanced at Tripp for a few seconds, then looked at Connor. "How do you plan to allow me access to the station if I'm trapped inside there?"

"You can guide us. Tell us what to do and we'll do it for you."

Salpheth shook his head. "That won't work. I need to directly interface with the station's systems. They're designed for us. You don't have the necessary skills or technology to achieve those ends."

Connor smiled and sent a message via his comlink to Phendran. The two Aczar walked down the corridor and entered the room.

Salpheth stared at them, shocked. Then he looked at Connor.

"I assure you they are here. This isn't some kind of deception," Connor replied.

Phendran regarded Salpheth. "We are here to ensure you do not deceive them."

Salpheth seemed to have recovered from his initial shock. "Aczar, here? Loremaster Phendran, I should've anticipated this. Your compliance scores were always dangerously close to the fringe of acceptable behavior. How have you come to be here?"

"I am no longer answerable to you, Salpheth. How we came to be here is none of your concern."

Salpheth glanced at Noxrey for a second, then looked at Phendran. "You've broken through your societal constraints. Truly remarkable progress you've made. I hope you realize where your will to do this originated."

Connor laughed, and the sound of it shocked the others. "As if Phendran or any other Aczar needs you to make up their own mind. Stop trying to manipulate them."

Salpheth watched Connor for a moment, considering. "I see why you kept them from me. Always testing. You humans are always testing, convinced of your own cleverness, but now you're running out of options. I see this now. I'm ready to leave."

Connor looked at Phendran.

"There is no more to be learned here, General. We should make our way to the others," Phendran said.

Connor nodded. "Okay, Tripp, initiate the transfer."

The energy field was maintained by a small power generator, and Tripp attached his portable field generator to it. The field generator sat on a grav pallet that floated in the air. The energy field holding Salpheth constricted in size, becoming small enough to fit through the corridor, and Salpheth watched in concern as the edges of the energy field closed in on him.

"Ready for transport, General," Tripp said.

Tripp made a passing motion toward Connor, and a new data connection appeared on his wrist computer. Both he and Tripp shared control of the energy field and the grav pallet.

"Let's go," Connor said.

Tripp guided the portable energy field out of the secondary power core, and Connor and the others followed. Salpheth seemed to have lost interest in them, except for the few times he turned toward Phendran. Connor suspected that the presence of the Aczar was making him alter whatever he was planning.

They made their way to the airlock. As Connor and some of the others put on their EVA suits, Mac and Jorath kept their weapons pointed at Salpheth.

Once they were outside the ship, Salpheth stared intently at the space station. A range of emotions seemed to cross the Phantom's face.

Connor came to his side. "It's been a while, hasn't it?"

Salpheth looked at him. "I've never been here before."

"Then how did you know it was here?"

"I knew it was being built, but the effort was going to be abandoned."

"Any idea why?"

"When I can access the systems, I will have a better idea," Salpheth said. He was quiet for a few moments. "How far did your team make it before they were contained?"

"You could've warned me about the security lockdown procedure."

"I did warn you. I told you that you wouldn't be able to access the station without my help."

"How are you going to be able to access the station?"

Salpheth was about to reply but stopped. "I will show you."

The ground felt solid, even if the reactive plating glowed beneath their feet. When they were about halfway to the station a comlink came from the ship.

"Connor," Noah said, having initiated a private comms channel, "I'm going to move the ship."

Connor blinked and turned back toward the *Pathfinder*. "What?"

"Not far. There's one of those carrier class ships on the neighboring docking platform. I'm not sure if it's by design, but their hangar bay is accessible. But more important than that is that there seems to be a repair station inside it."

Connor looked to his right. In the far distance, he could barely see the large ship he knew was there. "What are you going to do?"

"I'm going to try to use the repair station—"

"Noah, I don't like this. What if the *Pathfinder* gets trapped? How do you even know it'll work on the ship?"

"Well, I sent a recon drone to one of the smaller repair stations. The station scanned the drone and applied some kind of repair kit that improved the drone's outer plating. I'm hoping it can do the same for our ship. It also repaired the drone's sensor array. The scans must've been able to determine the functionality of the array because it's back to being fully operational. And it detected a significant power source located on the ship."

"Huh," Connor said thoughtfully while he considered the information.

"If this works, we might not need Salpheth's help as much as he suspects we do."

Connor glanced at Salpheth for a second. If Noah was wrong, the ship could be irrevocably damaged. "It really just fixed the drone? No interface or anything like that?"

"None. I was shocked. I honestly thought that either nothing was going to happen, or the drone would be lost. It must operate on some kind of autonomous diagnostic and repair protocol."

Connor nodded. He still didn't like the idea because of so many potential unknowns. "What can you tell me about this power core?"

"Other than that it's there and it's significant, not much. We'd need to investigate. I don't like putting all our eggs in one basket with Salpheth, and this gives us a viable alternative. My thinking is that if they can generate this kind of power signature while being docked here, there's a good chance it can do more than that, and they might have materials we can use to refuel our own power core."

Connor sighed. "Just be careful, Noah. If the station has some kind of security lockdown, a ship certainly has one as well."

"I know, but remember all those other alien facilities we've been to? We were able to use what was already there. Since the repair station is working, there could be an active data connection to the ship itself. I could use that to gain access to their systems. This is worth taking the risk."

Connor could hear the excitement in Noah's voice. He was

committed, and Connor couldn't blame him. "Alright, go ahead. Send me status updates every fifteen minutes."

"Will do," Noah said and closed the comlink.

Connor looked at Salpheth and was surprised to find the Phantom watching him. Connor calmly regarded him, and Salpheth turned back around.

Could Salpheth have somehow heard his conversation with Noah? Not unless he'd hacked their comlinks, which he would've been able to detect.

"This is quite the facility," Connor said.

Salpheth looked around, seemingly unimpressed. "It's adequate for our needs. As I've said, this was a resupply station for staging exploratory operations."

"The place looks hardly used."

"It was likely no longer required."

"And they just left the other ships here? We detected some as we arrived."

Salpheth smiled, probably thinking Connor had accidentally revealed this information to him. He hadn't.

"We're a pragmatic race."

Connor nodded and continued walking in silence.

Behind him, the *Pathfinder* maneuvered away from the dock. The others were so focused on reaching the station that they hadn't noticed, and Connor decided not to tell them yet. They needed to focus on what they were about to do.

CHAPTER 26

THE NEXSTAR COMBAT suit's diagnostic cycle neared completion as Ethan stood before it. The outer alloy was charcoal-colored, with a dark red CDF emblem on the shoulders. It didn't stand out from the other suits in any way, which stemmed from military practice to prevent the enemy from identifying commanding officers on the field. But that only applied to the outer appearance of the armor. Their HUDs identified combat-suit wearers, which eliminated the need for identifying marks on the physical suits themselves.

The combat suit was split open from the neck to the feet, and he stepped inside. He transferred his credentials to the suit computer and his preferences immediately caused adjustments to the suit's interior to fit his specifications. The process only took a second or two and then the suit closed, encasing him in a protective shell. Ethan kept the helmet retracted into the storage compartment that sat just behind and below his neck. Once all processes completed, he left the shuttle's assembly area and headed toward the cockpit where Washburn was speaking with Hash.

"All I'm saying is that we've never been closer to finding it out," Hash said.

"You're right. Any idea *how* we find out?" Washburn asked, glancing at Ethan. "Hash was just telling me about how we've never been closer to finding the source of all Vemus."

Ethan looked at Hash for a second. "He's right. That Alpha out there has reached a predetermined stage in its development, which compels it to seek out the next part of the hierarchy."

Washburn nodded. "Yes, but we don't know whether the super-Alpha is the next step or if it's another level. If the super-Alpha is smart, it would use multiple layers of security to not only ensure its survival but ensure that only the best or the strongest Vemus actually reach it successfully."

"Well said," Ethan replied. "I've been thinking… with this particular Alpha being so large, maybe it didn't come from a single planet at all. Maybe it's made up of multiple sub-Alphas from different planets, and it reached a stage in its development that compels it to seek out the super-Alpha."

Hash looked worried, and his eyes widened a little. "There could be multiple types of Vemus on that ship."

Ethan nodded. "It puts the battle that was fought here into a new perspective, doesn't it?"

Washburn slowly shook his head and sighed. "Thanks for that."

Ethan frowned. "Huh?"

"I finally get my head around what we're facing, and you throw another thought-log onto the fire."

Ethan chuckled a little. The edges of Hash's lips lifted, and he shrugged.

Washburn rolled his eyes. "Better the devil you know than the one you didn't see coming."

"As long as we're aware of the risk," Ethan replied. "If we could find the nav data from that ship and figure out where it was going, we could stop stumbling around in the dark so much. Come at this problem at its source."

Washburn scratched an itch near his ear. "The Phantoms could be right, and this is too big a problem for us to handle."

"Maybe, but at least we'd have definitive proof of it. Then we could study it. Take our time. Build ourselves up and eventually find a way to stop it."

Washburn heaved a sigh. "Reminds me of the missions I read about from the Krake War."

Hash frowned. "I've heard of the Krake War, but I don't know about the missions."

"The Krake kept their homeworld a secret," Ethan said. "They used other worlds as staging places to conduct experiments and other kinds of operations against Ovarrow worlds. The CDF began sending teams into alternate universes to gather data about the Krake and the other Ovarrow. Eventually, this led to gaining allies, and we enabled the Ovarrow in other universes to communicate with each other. Basically, we were casting a wide sensor net."

Washburn nodded. "And even then we had very little warning when the Krake did attack. If we have to employ similar tactics, we could be facing similar circumstances here."

"The alternative would be to bury our head in the sand and pretend that the Vemus aren't out there," Ethan said, then bobbed his head once. "Granted, the scale of this is on a much larger battlefield."

Hash frowned. "What do you mean?"

"The galaxy is a big place. We don't know how far the Vemus infestation goes or who else could be out there."

Hash considered that for a moment, then said. "True, and our range is limited. It still takes us about a month to travel sixty light-years between Old Earth and New Earth."

"Yes, and the only reason it's that fast is because we've mapped it out. We know the safe ways to get there," Ethan replied. "My point is that we might not see the end of the Vemus. It could be our descendants who do that, but the groundwork will be established right now, during our time."

Washburn stared at him with a furrowed brow. "I hope you're wrong."

Hash exhaled through his nostrils. "To be honest, I don't know what to hope for. I'd rather take it as it comes."

Washburn arched an eyebrow at him, and Hash shrugged.

"Maybe us Old Earthers have a thing or two to teach you colony types."

"Hash is right," Ethan said. "As much as we'd like to stuff the Vemus into a box of our own understanding, it might not work out that way. However, this mission... this we can focus on, and if we find an opportunity to better understand the Vemus, all the better for us."

The cockpit door opened. "Captain! Collins is sick."

Groaning could be heard from inside the cockpit.

Washburn went through the door, and Ethan followed. Lieutenant Collins was doubled over, looking pale and about to pass out.

"Get him out of the chair," Ethan said.

Washburn helped Collins to his feet, and he cried out. Hash called out for the medic, then helped Washburn carry Collins from the cockpit.

Ethan glanced at the copilot, a young woman named Rachel Thiesen. She looked alarmed.

"What happened to him, Lieutenant?" Ethan asked, sitting in the pilot's seat.

"He'd been complaining about his stomach during the mission, sir, but he went to the autodoc and he said he felt better. Then, I noticed he started looking pale and sweaty, as if he had a fever. I was about to say something to him about it when he cried out in pain. I took the flight controls and called for help."

Ethan looked at the holoscreen. They were approaching the Vemus Alpha, which was surrounded by a debris field of asteroids and ice. Thiesen had control of the shuttle, but Ethan could tell she was a little out of her depth with this kind of flying.

"Are you feeling sick, too?" Ethan asked.

Lieutenant Thiesen grimaced. "I think it's just nerves, Major. I should be fine—" she cried out in pain.

Ethan yelled for help and took control of the shuttle. He'd maintained his flight status on a number of ships, including this combat shuttle. Sometimes, he missed the days of leading a squadron of Talon V Stinger class attack groups.

Washburn rushed through the door and hovered over Thiesen. "Easy, you're going to be okay. Are you able to stand up?"

Thiesen tried to stand and winced as she favored her right side.

"That's good. Here, give me your arm. We'll get you to the autodoc," Washburn said. "Major—"

"I'm fine, Captain. Take care of them," Ethan said.

He checked the flight plan and confirmed their location. The HUD showed their intended path, leading them to the stolen shuttle. He kept the ship on course.

A few minutes later, Washburn returned to the cockpit. "Both of them have some kind of parasite. Not sure where they could've picked it up."

"Are they going to be alright?"

"They've been given something for the pain, but they'll be out of action for a while. Are you alright taking us in?"

"With my eyes closed."

Washburn sat in the seat next to him and looked at the controls. "Came out of nowhere. I hope it doesn't spread. No one else has complained of any symptoms, but Wasbesky is pulling data from their biochips and checking their biometrics. If anyone has this bug, they'll get treatment."

He eyed Ethan for a moment. "Are you feeling okay, sir?"

Ethan chuckled. "I'm fine."

"Hash said he was, too. Said something about hybrids not being as susceptible to parasites as the rest of us."

Ethan blew out a breath. "That's only partially true. We have biochips, and we screen for this. It's probably something new, and that's why it was missed."

Washburn speared a look out of the cockpit. "Oh, so he was playing with me then."

"I can't rule out retribution being involved," Ethan said.

Washburn let out a shallow grin. "He's a crafty one."

Ethan flew near a spinning asteroid, and Washburn gasped. "That was close," he said.

"No, it wasn't," Ethan replied.

"Just remember we're not in a Talon V, sir."

Ethan grinned. "I'm well aware of that, Captain. Would you like to take over?"

"You look like you're having so much fun," Washburn replied, then sighed. "You're the better pilot, and I wouldn't want to scratch the paint."

Ethan's piloting prowess had persisted. He loved flying, whether it was atmospheric flight or space travel. It was just part of who he was, but leading attack squadrons was his past, and commanding warships was his future.

They flew toward the Alpha. The exoskeletal material the hull was made of appeared both familiar and foreign to him at the same time. The way the behemoth ship was lodged in the ice and rock reminded him of a dying leviathan that sometimes washed up on the shores of New Earth. They were dark colored, which made for excellent camouflage in the deep, and even dying they were dangerous to approach.

The damage to the Vemus Alpha was ever more apparent as they flew closer to it. They were on a direct course to intercept, which kept them away from flying along the ship. No energy signatures had been detected, but Ethan wasn't taking any chances. The shuttle's weapons systems and the point defense flak cannons were active. The automated system also destroyed smaller asteroids as they flew past.

One of the biggest misconceptions about traveling through space was that it was endless darkness and emptiness. While there *were* vast areas of darkness, there were also vast areas of stunning brilliance. Even here, among the bones of a fleet of ships that had done everything they could to destroy the Vemus Alpha, was a vast sea of ice that reflected the light coming from two nearby star systems. The view was majestic and mysterious, and it had a certain amount of physical beauty to it that was appealing to Ethan's eyes.

They flew toward a wide-open gap in the Alpha. It was almost twenty kilometers wide, and the inside was a mixture of shifting shadows. Ethan reduced their speed and allowed the shuttle's scanners to penetrate the gloom.

Multiple icons from the CDF scout probes appeared on the main holoscreen. They'd mapped the area, and the video feed was enhanced so they could see the interior of the ship.

"The damage is consistent with the alien weapons we saw," Washburn said.

The Vemus Alpha had been gutted, and the farther they flew inside the ship, the more Ethan began to believe that the aliens had achieved their objective of destroying it. But some part of it had survived. The shuttle's sensors detected an Alpha signal. It was stronger, but it was concentrated somewhere ahead of them.

It was difficult to distinguish the different decks inside the Alpha. It was unlike any Vemus ship Ethan had ever seen and didn't match the records they had of the Vemus that had come from Old Earth. Those had taken over Old Earth ships from its military and essentially anything they could get their hands on, so the insides of those ships were a little familiar.

The inside of the Alpha resembled the inside of a living biological creature. It was full of roundedness, half tunnels that rose up and down, and also coiled.

"That's different," Washburn said, unable to keep the awe from his voice. "It looks like…" his voice trailed off.

Ethan's jaw tightened. "The inside of a dead body."

Washburn blew out a breath. "Who ever heard of a hundred-and twenty-kilometer living creature?"

Ethan frowned. "Actually, I have."

Washburn shot him a perplexed look. "Really?"

He nodded. "The planet that the second colony went to encountered an intelligent plant species that had spread across entire continents. It had maintained some kind of equilibrium with the other creatures, but it was by far the most intelligent species on the planet."

"The amount of information you've got in that head of yours is staggering."

"Not really. I know some of the people who visited the planet and rescued the colony."

"We learn about that stuff through news feeds or in a class-room, but your family and friends lived through it. You've got to admit that it had an effect on you."

"If by effect you mean I was around people who talked about it, then yes. It wasn't a news story to them. It wasn't just some briefing or historical record. They talked about it. Their experiences were real to them. It's much like talking to any of the original colonists, the ones who traveled on the Ark. They remember Old Earth and settling on New Earth. There is value and insight in listening to them."

Washburn nodded slowly. "Still, this is different. I expected the interior to resemble the alien ships we were on. It looks a little like it, but it's different."

"At least there are no weapon's systems active," Ethan said.

"Yeah," Washburn replied. "So, this thing eventually gets

defeated, or the two fleets annihilate each other and it just sits here calling for help? Did it think anyone would answer the call?"

"We're here," Ethan said.

"No way for it to know we'd come. My point is that would it just have sent a distress signal into space until it couldn't survive anymore?"

"It might be as simple as that."

"It's like a machine."

"I don't think so. If we were trapped somewhere, we'd call for help for as long as we were able if it was our best option for survival."

The area condensed the farther they flew inside the Alpha, and the stolen shuttle was only a few kilometers ahead of them.

"Scout drones show this opening going all the way through the ship."

"Good. We won't be restricted on egress points," Ethan said.

Sensors picked up the stolen shuttle and Ethan got his first glimpse of it. The tail section stuck out of an improvised landing zone that had just enough clearance to accommodate it. Clamps stuck out of the landing gear, securing the shuttle in place.

"Doesn't look damaged at all. That's good. We can recover it," Washburn said.

Lights from the stolen shuttle illuminated the dark area, also reflecting off the ice that looked as if it had encroached on the area nearby.

"They made a landing area by cutting through the ice," Ethan said.

He eased their shuttle near the other and increased a burst of energy from the engine pods. It quickly vaporized the ice, and soon there was an area large enough for Ethan to land. He deployed the landing gear and brought the shuttle down. Then he engaged the locking clamps, which burrowed into the ice.

He brought up a sub-window and attempted to establish a

comlink to the shuttle. It didn't work. "Going to have to use a hard line then," Ethan said.

"I can do that," Washburn replied.

He targeted a maintenance port on the other shuttle and sent a cable to it. It took a few seconds for the link to establish, and then Ethan stood.

"Have Thiesen and Collins work on resetting the shuttle's systems once the autodoc clears them," Ethan said.

His pilots were out of commission and wouldn't be on the away team. At least they could get the stolen shuttle back under their control.

Washburn looked at him. "Do you think they set a trap?"

Ethan shook his head. "No, they were more concerned with getting here, not keeping the shuttle for themselves."

"Okay, the reason I asked is that they might have to go to the shuttle to disable whatever was used to lock us out," Washburn said.

They left the cockpit.

"Hash," Ethan called, and the civilian specialist came over to him. "Where would you install a device to override security protocols on a shuttle like this?"

Hash frowned in thought. "A few areas could work—the cockpit stations, the computing core, or the auxiliary maintenance access point. I'd start with those. I can go over and check them if you want me to."

Ethan shook his head. "No, you're with me," he said and looked at Washburn. "Let them know. Think they'll need someone to watch their backs?"

They were sick, and even though the autodoc would be able to cure them, they might need someone to watch out for them.

"I'll assign someone," Washburn said.

Ethan and Hash headed to the back of the shuttle. They engaged their helmets, going to their own life support. Then, they retrieved their weapons.

Hash hesitated before reaching for his.

"Take it, Hash," Ethan said. "If you start to feel off, let me know, and hopefully our watchers will detect it," he said, gesturing toward Richardson and Sykes.

"We've got your back," Richardson said.

Hash took his weapon and his tech kit. "I was fine until just now."

"It's just pre-mission jitters," Ethan said, checking his weapon.

"Yeah, I know. It's been a lifetime since it's happened to me." Hash was quiet for a moment. "I'm worried about the others."

Ethan nodded. "Me, too. Let's go get them back."

He called out to the other members of the team. They confirmed their combat suit status and then checked the person nearest to them.

Certain parts of the shuttle were sealed off as the artificial atmosphere was closed off. The pressure reduced until it was at near vacuum levels, matching the outside. Then the side hatch opened, and the soldiers on point exited the shuttle.

Ethan waited for the first squads to exit and then followed. He stepped off the shuttle to the glistening ice on the ground. The tread on his boots adapted to the terrain so they wouldn't slip.

"Tracking twelve EVA suits coming from that direction," Lieutenant Franco said.

Scout drones flew away from them, and the scout team led the way.

The interior of the Vemus Alpha resembled living tissue, but it was solid beneath their feet, as solid as any metallic hull Ethan had ever stood upon. He searched the area, looking for any sign of Vemus fighters. They left the shuttles and went into the dark depths of the Vemus Alpha.

The ground was sloped on either side, and sections were seemingly joined together with thick blade cables. The smooth cables went from the ground to the ceiling, giving the corridor the appearance of a giant throat. There were other connecting cables along the walls like veins.

Ethan peered ahead, trying to see the end of the tunnel but couldn't. He checked the time on his HUD. Cynergy and the other hybrids had a forty-six-minute head start on them.

He almost embraced his hybrid nature but hesitated. What if he became vulnerable to the Alpha? He needed to limit his exposure to it. Embracing his hybrid nature might accelerate the process. He needed to treat it as a limited resource to be used sparingly.

"Hash," Ethan said.

"Yes, Major?" Hash asked.

He made the comlink private. "I think we should embrace our hybrid natures only if it's absolutely necessary."

"Okay," Hash replied, drawing out the word. "But we listened to the signal and had no reaction at all."

"Yes, but I think we should limit our exposure. Treat it like a limited resource."

Hash was quiet for a few seconds. "Are you sensing anything now?"

"Not at all. We should be cautious, but I don't have anything solid to back it up."

"How are you going to find Cynergy without elevating the hybrid in us?"

Hash was one of the smartest people Ethan knew, but sometimes he put certain ideas in a box and limited himself. This was particularly interesting because there were a bunch of times Hash had used out-of-the-box thinking to come up with a solution. They all had their blind spots.

Hash sighed. "Never mind, I…it took me a few seconds to figure out what you were saying. I'm just a little on edge being here. This place is creepy. I feel like we're inside the body of a giant."

"No worries, Hash. Stay focused. Let me know if the drones detect any strange signals," Ethan replied.

"Will do, sir."

They reached the end of the corridor and entered a vast circular chamber. It was a convergence point for an extensive tunnel network. The blackened exoskeletal material had streaks of white in some areas. There were hundreds of decks, both above them and below them. Many of them had huge channels cut through them. The battle damage had penetrated far into the Alpha, and knowing a few things about the energy required to do this kind of damage left him feeling humbled and awed at the same time.

"Energy signature detected, Major," Lieutenant Franco said.

Ethan walked over to him. "Where?"

"It's on the other side of this chamber. It appears to be some kind of atmospheric shield. I'll make the video feed from the drone available, sir."

A video feed showed a corridor entrance with a faint, silvery, semi-translucent shield that went from floor to ceiling.

Washburn peered at it. "That's where the others went."

Ethan glanced at the pathway that went around the chamber. It was over three hundred meters to the other side, and the pathway was blocked. They'd have to climb over the debris if they were to take the paths.

Then Ethan stared across the way. The location of the scout drone was a few dozen decks above them.

"Our suit jets can get us there faster than if we climb," Ethan said.

Washburn looked toward the target. "Lieutenant?" he asked.

"Major Gates is right," Lieutenant Franco said. "With the low gravity, we can cover the distance, no problem."

"You're up, then," Washburn said.

"Sometimes it takes a former pilot to see these things," Ethan said.

"I was about to suggest the same thing. You just beat me to the punch."

Ethan smiled. "Sure you were."

The CDF platoon leaped into the air, using their suit-jets to guide them to the target. The coordinates were set based on the location of the scout drone, and the combat suit computer controlled the suit jets to get them there safely.

Ethan was poised to take over the flight controls of his combat suit, just in case. He glanced beneath him and the massive opening curved from view thousands of meters below. He tried to think of a reason there was such a huge open space in the middle of the Alpha and couldn't come up with anything tangible.

By the time he reached the other side, two squads of soldiers were in the corridor just outside the shield. Scout drones easily penetrated the shield with no resistance. Atmospheric shields were designed to withstand pressure from an artificial atmosphere, but solid objects could move through them easily.

Ethan looked at the drone sensor data.

"Not breathable for us, but it's not going to harm the suits," Washburn said.

"Agreed. Let's move out," Ethan replied.

They passed through the shield and into a corridor lined with moisture and condensation along the walls. Faint hissing noises could be heard from farther along the corridor, as if it were filled with venomous reptiles waiting to ambush them.

They were able to get a more accurate location of the EVA suit signals. The hybrids had paired off, and Ethan saw that Cynergy was with Walsh. They weren't moving and seemed to be in a centralized location. The others appeared as if they were exploring the area.

Ethan initiated a comlink to Cynergy, but it went unanswered. He frowned. If she'd ignored his comlink request, he'd be able to see that, but his request going unanswered meant that she might not have been able to acknowledge it. She could be distracted by the Alpha, or something else prevented her from responding.

"Try to reach others, Lieutenant," Ethan said.

"Yes, Major," Lieutenant Franco said. "Sending out a broadcast to the others,"

"Wait!" Ethan said, and Lieutenant Franco paused. "Direct comlinks only. No broadcasts."

"Understood, sir," Lieutenant Franco replied.

While he did that, Hash came over to him. "Why can't we broadcast a signal?"

"The Alpha might sense it, and it could trigger a response," Ethan replied.

"But direct comlinks won't trigger a response?"

"Different Vemus have had different responses. In our war with them, they could sense comlinks. We updated our protocols, and when we returned to New Earth, the remnant Vemus were unable to detect them. I have no idea whether the Vemus here will detect it or not."

"Understood, sir," Hash replied. "Can I scan for data links?"

Ethan considered it. "Yes, go ahead."

Lieutenant Franco turned toward him. "I've gotten no responses from the hybrids, sir."

Washburn looked at Ethan. "We need to go after them. We could split into three teams, cover more ground?"

"Do it," Ethan replied.

They reached the end of the corridor and split up. Splitting into smaller teams was the quickest way to reach all the others. Some of them seemed to be staying in a particular area, and Ethan wondered if they were trapped.

"If they were trapped, why wouldn't they respond to the comlink request?" Washburn asked.

More than a few thoughts came to Ethan's mind, and none of them were helpful or worth voicing aloud.

"We'll find out as soon as we reach one. The closest are Moteki and Sekino," Ethan replied.

Washburn didn't reply.

As they continued down the dark corridor, they could see that the exoskeletal material that made up the walls and the floor was dead, with no life signs at all. If it had been alive, they'd be in even more danger. Vemus exoskeletal material fulfilled a variety of functions beyond armored protection. It was also a method of transport and communication.

They reached the end of the corridor and entered an open room. To the side were smaller circular rooms, with what appeared to be dormant workstations. Ethan peered inside one of the smaller rooms. In the center was a large table that looked as if it had been grown from the floor. Up to half a meter of thick fog covered most of the floor.

Moteki and Sekino were in one of the smaller areas on the other side of the larger, open room. Pale yellow light emanated around them. Ethan and the others made their way across and found the two hybrids leaning on a table. Their EVA suits had been retracted, exposing their hands to the glowing surface.

Lieutenant Franco called out to the hybrids, but there was no response. He looked at Ethan. "Orders, Major?"

Ethan stared at the two hybrids, then looked at Washburn. "I'm going to see if I can sense them."

"Understood," Washburn said. "Sykes, keep an eye on changes in Major Gates's biometrics."

"Yes, Captain," she replied.

Hash looked at Ethan. "Should I change as well?"

"No," Ethan said. "Just wait."

Hash stared at him for a long moment and then nodded.

Ethan stepped away from the others and looked into the open doorway to where Moteki and Sekino stood. Their skin was black and showed a buildup of bulbous, roughened textures, covered by a complex network of purplish lines.

Ethan embraced his hybrid nature. Because the Alpha had an

artificial atmosphere, his highly acute senses were able to detect the others. Their heart beats were elevated but in perfect unison with one another.

His combat suit detected a magnetic field surrounding the glowing table, and then he heard the Alpha signal. It was coming through as if the table itself was a mode of communication. He tried to determine what it was trying to communicate, but it was like hearing a whisper spoken from the end of a very long tunnel. He could tell it was there but couldn't understand what was being said.

He enabled his combat suit's speakers and began a subsonic form of communication. Moteki and Sekino's hands jerked toward the edge of the table, and their heart rates quickened. Ethan increased the intensity of his subvocal communication, adding an edge to it that they wouldn't be able to ignore.

He heard a rumbling coming from them.

"What's happening?" Washburn asked.

Ethan stepped closer. "There's something wrong—"

Both hybrids spun around and sprang out of their EVA suits. A shudder went through them both and they collapsed to the ground, writhing in pain.

Lieutenant Franco and Sergeant Tramell looked back at Ethan. They had their weapons pointed at the hybrids.

"Orders, Major?" Lieutenant Franco said, his voice tight with tension.

"Give them some room," Ethan said. Because of his current hybrid state, his voice was deeper and more commanding than normal.

Washburn looked at Ethan. "I don't like this. What's happening to them? Is this the Alpha, or are they fighting it?"

The ground was covered in a swirling fog, and it obscured Ethan's view of them. An alarm appeared on his HUD, and he already knew what it meant. By now, the others had seen it, too.

They were too late for Moteki and Sekino.

The former hybrids lunged to their feet, an animalistic scream sounding from their mouths.

They were no longer hybrids.

Moteki and Sekino had become Vemus.

CHAPTER 27

ETHAN SNATCHED up his weapon and fired. High-density explosive darts penetrated Moteki's chest and exploded, making a grisly hole. Moteki stumbled backward, and Ethan cried out as he fired his weapon at Sekino. He'd known them since he'd been turned into a hybrid. Both had been good men, smart and loyal.

And they weren't dead.

They flopped on the ground, the wet thud bringing a bitter taste to his mouth. As Vemus fighters, they would keep attacking until there was nothing left. Even now, Ethan could see that what would've been a deadly wound to any normal person had begun to regenerate at an alarming rate.

Ethan changed his ammo configuration to specialized incendiary rounds and ordered the other soldiers to do the same.

They fired their weapons at the two Vemus fighters. The incendiary rounds fired at a much slower rate, expanding once they hit their target and burning through them. They'd been specifically designed for combating the Vemus.

Smoke rose from the two Vemus fighters as their bodies were

burned away, becoming ash in seconds. Two CDF soldiers checked the area and confirmed the deaths.

Hash moved toward the table, and several soldiers began shouting, pointing their weapons at him.

Hash froze. "Wait. Wait! Damn it, I'm one of you!"

He made his face shield transparent.

Ethan stared at him.

"What are you are doing, Specialist?" Washburn asked.

"We can't communicate with the others, right? Our comlinks won't go through. I need to check the EVA suits to figure out what communication protocols they were using," Hash replied, and looked at the others. "Stop pointing your weapons at me. Did you see me with my hands on that table? No, you didn't. I'm safely tucked away in my combat suit just like the rest of you."

The soldiers glanced at Ethan.

"Lower your weapons," he said.

The soldiers lowered their weapons, and Hash gave him a nod.

Ethan glanced at Private Sykes. She was monitoring both his and Hash's biochips.

"Still all clear, Major," Sykes said.

Ethan nodded, then looked at Hash. "Go on. Make it quick."

Hash hastened to the nearest EVA suit on the ground and opened the access panel on the back.

Washburn turned to Ethan. "You fired your weapon before we could even react. How did you know they were too far gone?"

"They attacked when I tried to force them to acknowledge me. It's something hybrids can do. I knew in that moment that they were gone."

"But not before?"

"It's not like a power switch. They were communicating with the Alpha through that table," Ethan said.

Chunks of table had been blown out of it from their weapons' fire. It was no longer glowing.

"So, the Alpha is still alive, or at least some part of it is," Washburn said.

Ethan glanced at a doorway that led to another corridor. Every part of him wanted to find Cynergy. They had a connection, and she wouldn't succumb to the Alpha like Moteki and Sekino had. He clung to that, but he also knew he was walking a line the width of a razor's edge.

Washburn turned to Hash. "Time's up, Specialist."

"I've got it," Hash said, stepping back from the EVA suit. "They used a secure communications module, closing off comms from everyone but each other. Making the protocols available."

"Don't you need the module?" Washburn asked.

"No, I've created virtual ones."

Washburn looked at Ethan. "Should we try to contact them?"

Ethan frowned. "I don't know. It could trigger a reaction that speeds up the process, but *not* doing it might let the hooks of the Vemus Alpha dig deeper into them." He inhaled a breath and held it for a moment while he thought. "Franco, you and Staggart are on point. Move out," he ordered.

They couldn't afford to wait and left the room.

Washburn came next to Ethan as they moved down another corridor. "They only reacted when you tried to force an acknowledgment. Maybe don't force it and see what happens."

"Maybe, but even the slightest provocation could cause the Alpha to respond."

Washburn was quiet for a few seconds. "This is so messed up. We're damned if we do, and we're damned if we don't. Regardless, we need to give the other teams some guidance. They need to be warned that the people we're trying to save might already be compromised by the enemy."

Ethan gritted his teeth, knowing Washburn was right. He couldn't let them go in there blind, but he also didn't want them to just eliminate the hybrids.

"You're right. They need to be warned about what they could be walking in on. The table, or alien console, has to be the key. Physical contact is the key. They need to use extreme caution if any hybrids are in physical contact with an active console."

"What do you want them to do?"

"Separate them from the console. Destroy it. Maybe cutting them off will allow them to recover from what the Alpha is doing to them. If they're still, they are to disarm them and bring them back to the shuttle, ASAP."

Washburn nodded. "Understood."

Sometimes there was an intrinsic loneliness to being in command. He'd come across this concept during his training, and he'd witness the aftereffects in his father. How long was what he was about to say going to haunt him?

"If they're too far gone, they are to be eliminated and their bodies disposed of so the Alpha cannot get to them."

"Yes, sir," Washburn replied.

"And if they're not at an active console but are searching for it, they're to be restrained and brought back to the ship. Suffering from a compulsion isn't the same as being assimilated by the Alpha. It's vitally important that they understand the difference. It's a judgement call," Ethan said.

"Understood. I'll relay that to the others," Washburn said and moved ahead of him.

Hash followed close behind.

"Did you sense it?" Ethan asked.

"No, I didn't. I stayed normal—uh, like this."

Ethan frowned. He'd heard the slip-up. At one time, no hybrid Ethan had ever met would say that appearing human was their "normal" state. Was Hash questioning that now?

"It's alright, Hash."

"No, it's not. They...It had them so quickly."

He meant the Alpha. Ethan knew that during the Vemus War,

people had been converted into Vemus in as little as a few minutes. The process was fast.

"Do you think we're more vulnerable than the others?" Hash asked.

Ethan swallowed hard. He wanted to reassure his friend, but he couldn't lie to him. "I don't know."

Hash became quiet after that.

A hybrid's immunity from the Vemus had been the source of their strength. It almost gave them a reason to exist, and it was being taken from them. How would the other hybrids react when news of this got out?

Ethan looked at Cynergy's location on his HUD. She and Walsh had stopped moving. Was she attached to one of the consoles now, too? Was the Alpha even now breaking past her defenses?

Another hybrid had almost made it to her. His name was Torren, and he was still moving, so maybe there was a chance for him.

Ethan opened a comlink using the protocols Hash provided. The comlink established.

"Torren, it's me, Ethan."

Torren gasped. "Major Gates! Can you hear it?"

"Hear what?" he asked.

He'd quickened his pace, and Washburn ordered the others to move faster.

"I can't stop it. I've tried to, but it keeps taunting me."

Taunting him? Was Dr. Lorenco right about the Alpha's effect on the hybrids? Was this some kind of competition as a way of luring them in?

"Torren, we're making our way to you. Can you stop moving? Can you wait for us?"

"You're here? You're not on the ship?" Torren asked. He sounded confused. "We stole the shuttle. We knew it was wrong," he said, sounding like he was climbing over something. "Cynergy warned us not to do it. She tried to stop him, but he wouldn't listen."

Hearing that made Ethan want to seize his connection to Cynergy. It had always been a reassuring presence, but he didn't trust himself to do it right then. He wasn't sure what effect it would have on her.

"It's okay, Torren. We'll sort that out back on the ship. Right now, you need help. The Alpha is trying to bring you to it. Don't let it. Everything it's doing is a lie. Its only objective is to control you."

"It'll never control me, I won't let it. I've got to destroy it."

Ethan winced. Torren sounded more irritated than before. "That's what we're here to do. All you have to do is wait for us. Can you do that?"

"You are? I don't see you," Torren said.

"We're almost to you," Ethan said and muted the comlink. "Two hundred meters," he said to Washburn.

Washburn called out to Lieutenant Franco, and they raced ahead.

"I have to go. They're just ahead. I'm almost to them."

"No," Ethan said. "Just wait. Twenty seconds. You can do it. Just wait."

Ethan embraced his hybrid nature, then shouted. "Stop!"

Torren gasped and cried out.

A silvery light appeared at the end of the corridor where Franco and Staggart had run. Ethan came to the end just in time to see the CDF soldiers tackle Torren to the ground. He had part of his EVA suit off, but his skin was normal. He'd let go of his hybrid nature. Angry red blotches appeared on his hands, and Staggart stuffed Torren back into his EVA suit.

"Nighty, night," Staggart said as he initiated the suppression protocols.

Torren slipped into unconsciousness.

Ethan sighed with relief, but it was short-lived. They were in a wide-open tunnel, and a metallic catwalk led toward the center.

Ethan peered at it. There were several off-ramps from the center, and Cynergy was standing by one of the glowing tables. Walsh was at her side, each had a hand on the table. A larger creature crouched near the center of the tunnel, with thick, glowing cables connected to it. Most of them were blackened and dead, but six of them were active.

"Is that the Alpha?" Washburn asked in disbelief.

For a ship over a hundred and twenty kilometers in length, the Alpha should've been much larger. The creature had legs like a spider that was folded toward itself. It was a mass of exoskeletal material, and he couldn't see its head.

"It has to be," Ethan said.

Behind the Alpha lay an open space, devastated by the alien attack. The alien weapons must've penetrated even there.

Ethan peered through the gloom. "No—it's what's left of the Alpha. See across that wide expanse? This whole ship was the Alpha. The atmospheric shield ends just beyond the center of the platform."

Washburn ordered the CDF heavies to target the Alpha. They had large railguns mounted on their backs, which could do a lot of damage. But it was the attack drones that would do the most damage.

"There are no Vemus fighters. Where did they all go?" Hash asked.

Ethan shook his head. Had all the Vemus been cannibalized to keep the Alpha alive?

"Permission to destroy the Alpha, sir?" Washburn asked.

"Wait."

"Major, they're attached to the console, which means they've been compromised. I have to destroy the Alpha."

"I'm ordering you to wait," Ethan snapped. "I didn't come this far just to write them off."

Washburn stared at him for a long moment. "Sykes?"

"Still all clear, Captain," Private Sykes replied.

Ethan had embraced his hybrid nature, and while he could detect the Alpha, it had no influence over him.

Ethan started to move, but Washburn blocked his path. He gritted his teeth. "Captain, get out of my way."

Washburn didn't raise his weapon. Ethan was watching for it. Embracing his hybrid nature had increased his reaction times, and the CDF captain couldn't match him, even in a combat suit.

"Sir," Washburn said, "let me send my soldiers there."

"No. Now get out of my way."

Washburn didn't move. He held up an armored hand in a placating gesture.

"Captain," Sergeant Staggart said, "the man's wife is in danger! If you don't move, I'm going to move you. I'll accept whatever comes from it."

"Damn it, Sergeant, stay out of this," Washburn said.

"Tom," Ethan said, and Washburn turned toward him. "Cover my six. Keep Hash and Sykes with you. They'll know if I'm gone and be able to advise you. If things go south, you obliterate that entire area. But there's no way I'm going to leave without her."

Washburn swore bitterly and got out of the way, then ordered three soldiers to go with him.

Ethan went past him, with Sergeant Staggart in tow.

"I've got your back, Major Gates," Staggart said. "And if you turn into one of those things. I'll make a quick end to it, I promise. I won't let that thing have you."

Staggart had a no-nonsense attitude that Ethan liked. "Thank you, Sergeant."

"If it's all the same, I'd rather not do that."

Ethan chuckled a little. "Understood."

Ethan started running, and Sergeant Staggart and the other soldiers tried to keep up. Combat suits enabled the wearers to move fast, and the suit's only limitations came from the person inside them. Because Ethan was able to augment his own body due to his hybrid nature, the other soldiers could never keep up with him and he sped ahead of them.

He closed the distance, keeping his gaze on his wife, and then he glanced at the Alpha remnant on the nearby platform. A pulsing shudder swept over its alien body as a subsonic Alpha signal came from it, and Ethan built up a mental barrier in his mind to block it out. He focused his attention on Cynergy, bringing their intimate connection to the forefront of his mind, using it like a shield.

The Alpha signal stalled, but Ethan knew that wouldn't last. Contrary to what most people thought, a Vemus Alpha wasn't a mindless biological machine. It was both clever and highly intelligent. It would withdraw and assess before making an even stronger push. His unique connection to Cynergy was likely something it hadn't encountered before.

Ethan rushed down the ramp to where Cynergy stood with one dark hand out of her EVA suit, palm on the glowing table. He peered inside her helmet. She was in a partial state of hybridness. Her long, dark-blonde hair was pushed to the side, as if she'd hastily put her helmet on. The skin on her face was that of a pale human, with patches of dark that came from her hybrid nature.

Walsh was completely in his hybrid state and now had both his palms on the table. Glowing tendrils were fused to the top of his hand.

"Ethan," Cynergy said.

She stared at him with a mixture of relief and strain. One of her eyes was blue and the other was a bright jade surrounded by dark skin.

"Cyn, you have to let it go," Ethan said.

She was on the other side of the table, and he slowed down. He thought he saw Walsh twitch but couldn't be sure.

"I'm on the verge of finding it. The data is there," Cynergy said.

Her voice sounded distant, as if her mind were focused on things he couldn't see.

Sergeant Staggart and the other soldiers arrived. Ethan could hear them breathing heavily through the comlink. He held up his hand, not wanting the soldiers to interrupt.

Staggart told the other soldiers to cover the Alpha.

The Alpha signal returned—stronger and more intense. The huge creature began to shift its weight.

"Hold your fire," Ethan said.

Cynergy cried out, and his connection to her wavered as if pieces of it were being shredded away. It was actually slipping away.

"No," Ethan said, his hybrid voice firm and unyielding as he injected the subsonic overtones of his command into it.

Cynergy inhaled a breath, and her gaze locked onto his. "The source, Ethan. It's going to the Alpha Prime, just like we thought."

They'd spent countless hours talking about the existence of a Vemus Super Alpha that spread its seed across many star systems.

He shook his head. "No, it's not, Cyn. The aliens stopped it. It's not going anywhere. All that's left is a remnant."

With a haggard expression, she squeezed her eyes shut for a long moment, and Ethan stepped toward her. The glowing tabletop brightened, and something dark and menacing swirled under the surface.

"But that information is there. I can see it. I can almost get to it," Cynergy said.

His connection to her slipped farther from him, and he realized that if he didn't stop her, he'd lose her.

"It's lying to you," Ethan said.

"No, it can't be."

A soft growl came from Walsh, and his eyes opened. "It's there. This Alpha was traveling to the source. It promises to take us there."

The intensity of the Alpha signal changed and seemed to circumvent Ethan's mental barriers, coming through his link to Cynergy.

"You will come. You've come for us, and we go to join the Prime. All will journey there and the answers you seek are there, sub-species. Allow us in. I am in you already, sub-species," the Alpha said.

Cynergy moaned, and glowing tendrils began to rise from the table, seeking out her hand.

"No!" Ethan growled.

He lunged toward her, slammed his fist on the tendrils, and shouted, "Kill it!"

The CDF soldiers fired their weapons at the Alpha, and Walsh dove toward him, knocking him off balance. Ethan stumbled for a second, then regained his balance. He lifted his weapon and fired it at Walsh. Incendiary rounds tore through the remains of his EVA suit and began to consume it with fire. Walsh was gone, and the newly born Vemus fighter lunged toward him. Ethan continued to fire his weapon on full auto. The Vemus that had been Walsh staggered back, the damage to his body so severe that he could hardly stand. Ethan kicked him back, and the Vemus fighter was sent careening off the platform.

He turned toward Cynergy, and she watched him. One of her hands was still on the table, tendrils attached to it. The CDF soldiers were firing their weapons at the Alpha, but the signal was strong.

Cynergy held up her other hand, and the EVA suit retracted, exposing the dark hybrid skin. She was still there; the Vemus hadn't taken over, but there was no denying its presence.

The soldiers shouted something, but Ethan ignored them. They were focused on killing the Alpha, and he was focused on saving his wife.

He could snatch her from the Alpha just as he'd done before. The armor covering his hand opened, and he grabbed Cynergy's outstretched hand.

"Let go of it," Ethan commanded.

He felt a swirling torrent of turmoil coming through his connection to Cynergy. She was deep into the Alpha. Assurances came through the connection, promising a return to who she'd been, but Ethan knew it was a lie. She was slipping from him. Even now, the Alpha was trickling into her.

"We can be together, even now," Cynergy said. "This is the only way to find the Prime."

It was a lie.

The Vemus Alpha was becoming desperate. It sensed Cynergy's longing to find the source of all Vemus and was using it to manipulate and control her.

Ethan didn't respond but put everything he had into his connection with her, calling to her as she'd done to him when she'd changed him into a hybrid. The Alpha recoiled as if it had been shoved, and then Ethan felt something seize him. An almost indomitable will pressed in on him, surrounding him, but Ethan wouldn't give up. He would never give up, even if it killed him.

A blaring truth became apparent to him as everything was being stripped away: Even a dying Alpha could hurt them.

CHAPTER 28

ETHAN'S AWARENESS of the Alpha increased, and he suspected it was gleaning information about him simultaneously. Cynergy was caught in the middle. For some reason, the Alpha seized on their encounter with the other alien Vemus, and it was able to pull knowledge from Ethan before he realized it.

At the same time, Ethan decided to do some digging of his own into the Alpha, searching for something he could use against it. After a few moments, he stopped. He was being goaded into this reaction, and he knew that if he gave the enemy what it wanted, he would be defeated. He'd stopped, but Ethan's mind was bare before it. Knowledge of humanity was within the Alpha's grasp.

"You're a mindless slave, and you will never control us," Ethan said.

"You'll be assimilated like the rest. Awareness of your species will be brought back, and soon, they will come for you."

"But you'll never control us. Not really. You rewrite them. You override what's there and take control of our bodies, but you'll never have what's important. Even now, you're being destroyed, and we will die knowing that you'll never get what you're looking for.

How many species do you need to conquer before you learn that most will never submit? We will never submit!"

Ethan sought out Cynergy, and they unified and strengthened each other in both body and mind.

"We are incomprehensible to you," said the Alpha.

"No, you're a creature that only knows subservience to a hierarchy without ever asking why. You just do, because if you dared question it, you'd be overruled. You're a mindless slave, no better than an animal, and you will never control us," Ethan said.

He gripped Cynergy's hand and pointed his weapon at the growling table.

A thick tentacle burst from the table and knocked him off his feet. He held onto Cynergy and they rolled to the edge of the platform. The soldiers nearby were shouting, and he could hear their weapons being fired. Something felt different inside him. Through his connection to Cynergy, he couldn't determine where he ended and she began, and within them was a whisper of the Alpha. Somehow, it had gotten a fingerhold.

Bright flashes surrounded them. Then everything seemed to tilt to the side. Something cold pierced his arm, and he gritted his teeth, knowing what was happening. Everything was wrong. He felt Cynergy's confusion, and it made him start to panic, even as everything slowed down in his mind. Detachment set in, and it was like he was observing his surroundings without comprehending what was really going on.

Then everything faded to oblivion.

Captain Tom Washburn looked down at his friend. Ethan's combat suit had been partially removed, and there was some kind of covering that connected him to Cynergy. It was similar to the Vemus exoskeletal material but not quite. It was dark and looked more like when they became hybrids. Washburn couldn't remember exactly how Ethan referred to it.

"Status, Captain," Major Qualmann said, his voice coming over the comlink.

"I…I'm not sure, sir," Washburn said.

Private Sykes stood next to him. "The medical suppression protocols have caused them both to lose consciousness, but something isn't right. It's like their signals are crossed. I don't know what to make of it."

"Are they a danger to you?" Qualmann asked.

"Need a moment, Major," Washburn replied.

He muted the channel and called Hash over. "I need your opinion."

Hash looked down at Ethan and Cynergy and then at Washburn. "I'm not sure what you want from me."

"Are they compromised? Has the Alpha infected them?"

Hash peered down at them, and his skin color changed as he embraced his hybrid nature. He focused for a few moments, frowning intently. Then he looked at Washburn. "I don't know. I can't tell. They're not Vemus, but they're not like they were before, either. They need a real doctor to examine them."

Washburn nodded and activated the comlink to the ship. "Negative, sir. If they were Vemus, they would've attacked, but something isn't right. They need medical attention, and we should use quarantine protocols to be safe."

"Understood, Captain. Carry them out of there. Our weapons are locked on your location. Bring all the survivors out of there," Major Qualmann said.

The comlink severed, and Washburn looked up at the platform where the remnant of the Vemus Alpha had been. It was a smoking ruin, but there were still glowing tendrils that went elsewhere on the ship. He ordered the soldiers to carry Ethan and Cynergy back to the shuttle. Lieutenant Franco joined him, along with Sergeant Staggart.

"We've got to get out of here. Major Qualmann intends to finish what those aliens started. What's the status of the other teams?" Washburn asked.

"Three hybrids were rescued, but the rest had become Vemus and had to be killed," Lieutenant Franco said.

Sergeant Staggart heaved a sigh. "Damn."

Twelve hybrids had come to the Alpha, and only four survived. Washburn didn't know what to say about that.

"Let's move out. Staggart, did you see what happened?" Washburn asked.

"Cynergy spoke to Major Gates, but I think there was something wrong with her. The way he spoke sounded like he was talking to the Alpha. He told us to kill it, and then things got crazy. Something swirled in that table as if it was some kind of cocoon. I can't wait to get out of here. This whole place is just wrong."

They backtracked the way they'd entered the area, moving as quickly as they could. Washburn kept going over what had happened in his mind. It had all unfolded so fast. He glanced at the soldiers carrying Ethan and Cynergy. They were still joined by some kind of skin growth, and the soldiers were careful not to disturb it.

The backup platoon met them along the way. Captain Olson brought grav pallets with them so they could easily carry the survivors. The hybrids were unconscious and would remain so until they returned to the ship.

They made it back to the shuttle and left the massive Alpha behind. Once they reached the minimum safe distance, the *Ascendant* fired several HADES VII missiles at the Alpha. Using navigation data from the scout drones, the missiles flew deep into the innards of the ship. Then, the detonation of their powerful fusion warheads annihilated the middle of the ship, breaking up the rock and ice that had kept it together.

Washburn found Hash sitting at the workstation just outside the cockpit. His brow was furrowed in concentration, and his eyes were closed.

Washburn sat next to him and waited.

Hash opened his eyes. "Sensors haven't detected the Alpha signal since the *Ascendant's* weapons destroyed that area, sir." Hash looked unsettled and scared, and lines of worry creased his forehead.

"Don't you think they're tracking that on the ship?"

He nodded quickly. "No, I realize that. I just wanted to listen for myself."

Washburn's gaze narrowed a little. "You were trying to see if you were vulnerable to the signal."

Hash swallowed hard, and he glanced at Private Sykes, who watched them. He sighed and looked at Washburn. "I had to know."

"Are you?"

Hash slowly shook his head, looking relieved.

"That's good."

"It doesn't feel good. Not when eight of my friends have died, and another three might be infected. Won't know for sure until later. Then, there's Ethan and Cynergy."

Washburn could tell Hash felt guilty that he'd managed to come out of this mission unscathed. That was a normal reaction, and Washburn wouldn't chastise him about it.

"We'll figure it out. We're not going to abandon them, so you don't have to worry about that," Washburn said.

Hash looked away from them and wiped his eyes.

"Rest. We'll know more once we get back to the ship." Washburn then stood and went to check on the others.

When they returned to the ship, they were instructed to land the shuttle in a designated area of the main hangar bay and were then subjected to quarantine protocols. The ship's doctors examined them and allowed most of them access to the ship.

Washburn and Hash stayed behind, waiting to hear from the doctors about Ethan. Washburn had known Ethan for years and respected him. He'd served under different officers throughout his military career, and he counted himself fortunate to serve under Ethan Gates.

Washburn sat at a table just outside the mobile medical unit in the hangar. His nutrient-dense recovery cocktail was empty, and he rolled the metallic canister around lazily. Major Qualmann walked over to him, and Washburn moved to stand.

"Sit," Qualmann ordered and sat next to him. He eyed Washburn for a moment. "What are you still doing here?"

"Waiting, Major."

Qualmann glanced to where Ethan was being kept, then nodded. "I understand."

Washburn stared at him for a long moment. "It happened on my watch, sir."

Major Qualmann shook his head, looking tired. "Let me tell you something: Ethan is a force of nature. His instincts are unparalleled whether we're in a fight or just scouting an area. He knew the risks. You were given an impossible task."

"I tried to watch out for him, just like he ordered me to." Washburn felt weighed down and exhausted.

Qualmann leaned back in his chair, crossing his arms. "Whenever we do something that involves crossing paths with the Vemus, somehow it changes the rules. It's like we're playing a deadly game and we don't know all the rules yet."

Washburn stared at him, eyebrows raised.

Qualmann gave him a tired smile. "You don't think I second-guess myself after a mission? We all do. It's how we improve. Re-evaluate, don't beat yourself up. You did everything you could. Now we just have to wait and see if any other pieces are going to fall away."

Washburn considered that for a few seconds. "Thank you, sir."

Qualmann stood. "Come on. Let's go see what the doctors learned."

Washburn stood. "They're not out yet."

"They don't have all the time in the world. I've got to report this in, and I need answers."

They walked to the mobile medical unit, and Washburn watched as Major Qualmann requested a status from the doctors.

The door to the mobile unit opened, and Dr. Lorenco waved them inside. "They're not contaminated," she said.

Washburn followed Qualmann inside, and Hash joined them.

There were five cordoned off areas where the hybrids were recuperating. All were still sedated. Washburn tried not to look where Ethan and Cynergy were because the sight still disturbed him.

"The others are going to be fine. I recommend that we move them to the medical bay for observation. They'll need to be monitored, and my recommendation is that they do not return to active duty," Dr. Lorenco said.

"You want them to sit on their hands for months?" Qualmann asked.

"I don't think you'll get much pushback from them. I don't have a treatment plan because we're not exactly sure what the trigger for their behavior was. Honestly, they should be taken back to New Earth."

Washburn blew out a breath. "This has been going on for months. It started up in earnest when Major Gates canceled the mission to investigate an anomalous Vemus detection. Things further spiraled when we encountered that scout ship."

"He makes a good point," Qualmann said. "Maybe the pressure got to them. Permission granted to move them to the medical bay, but I will post a security detail there."

Dr. Lorenco looked as if she wanted to say something but stopped. "Very well, Major."

Qualmann moved to stand outside the area where Ethan and Cynergy were. They were still in a heightened hybrid state, and some kind of exoskeletal material covered their hands and forearms.

"Now that you've got the easy stuff out of the way, tell me about them," Qualmann said.

"We've kept them sedated, and my recommendation is to put them in stasis," Dr. Lorenco said.

Qualmann's eyes widened. "Stasis?"

Lorenco nodded. "We have medical protocols to help hybrids return to their normal state of equilibrium, but I'm reluctant to do that here."

"What is that stuff covering their hands? Is that what's keeping them connected? Is that part of the Alpha?"

"I've compared samples of the Alpha that was brought back from the ship with the material covering their hands, and it isn't a match."

"That's good," Qualmann said and frowned. "Isn't it?"

"I don't know, sir. It doesn't match the Alpha, but it also doesn't match either Ethan or Cynergy."

Qualmann peered at them for a few seconds. "Can you surgically remove it?"

"Our scans indicate that the covering appears surface level, but it actually reaches the deeper tissue and has even infiltrated down to the bones."

"Will it spread?"

"Right now, they're stable. Putting them in stasis is their best bet. It'll give us time to study what has happened to them. And, honestly, this is beyond my expertise. I think they should be taken back to New Earth. There are specialists who know more about hybrids than I do."

Washburn cleared his throat. "His sister is a hybrid specialist. She's done work on actually reversing them from being a hybrid."

Hash nodded. "Dr. Lauren Diaz. Her research is somewhat controversial, but in light of this development, it might gain more traction."

Dr. Lorenco smiled. "I'm aware of her work. I would like to consult with her and the research board of specialist on New Earth before I attempt any kind of treatment."

Washburn watched as Qualmann considered it and wondered what he was thinking. He was glad that decisions like this were above his rank.

Dr. Lorenco cleared her throat. "I know this isn't the answer you wanted. I wish there was something I could do that would fix whatever is going on with them, but I can't. That's the long and short of it. Major Qualmann, will you allow me to put Major Gates and his wife in stasis?"

Qualmann heaved a sigh, and his shoulders slumped for a second. "Do it. Send me your current report so I can inform my superiors. Then we'll take it from there."

"Understood, sir," Dr. Lorenco said and went to speak with her staff.

Qualmann left the mobile medical unit, and Washburn and Hash followed him.

"What's going to happen now?" Hash asked.

Qualmann stopped and turned toward them, looking tired. "In all likelihood, they'll be going back to New Earth."

"Major," Washburn said, "I'd like to be assigned escort duty."

"So would I, but it might not be in the cards for us. Both of you go get some rest. That's an order."

Major Qualmann left them.

Hash glanced back at the mobile medical unit. A medical capsule was being brought to it that was large enough to accommodate both Ethan and Cynergy.

"Doesn't seem right," Hash said.

Washburn shook his head. "Were you able to sense anything in there now that we're back on the ship? I know you guys have very acute senses."

Hash looked as if he'd been caught doing something he shouldn't have been doing. "I thought I was quick enough that no one would notice."

"Well, I noticed."

"I think it's them, but at the same time there's more, but it's not the Alpha. I'm not sure what that means."

Washburn bit his lip for a second. "I don't know what's going to happen to them, but I think they're going to need help from someone like you."

Hash frowned. "Me?"

"A hybrid. Someone with training or is sensitive to other hybrids. I don't know how to say it, but do you understand what I mean?"

Hash looked away for a second. "I think so."

Washburn speared a look at him. "Can I trust you with this?"

Hash nodded. "I'll do everything I can. I promise."

Washburn inhaled a deep breath and sighed. "Alright. Let's get out of here. I've got some things I need to do before I hit the rack."

"Do you need help?"

Washburn regarded him for a moment, then tipped his head to the side. "Sure thing. Come on."

CHAPTER 29

NOAH OPENED A COMLINK TO RABSARIS. "Hey, can you come up to the bridge? I'm moving the ship."

"Are you serious?"

"Yeah, I need your help."

"I'll be right there," Rabsaris said.

Noah glanced at Kholva and Vorix, his two Aczar companions. They regarded him with twin expressions, though Vorix's facial features and body were slenderer because she was female. They were careful observers, and he'd been trying to build up a rapport with them.

"Is there a way we can be of assistance?" Kholva asked.

Noah thought about it for a second and then gestured toward a workstation next to him. He activated the holoscreen. "Those are external video feeds. I need you to watch for anything out of the ordinary."

Kholva and Vorix went to the workstation and sat. Their feet didn't reach the floor.

Vorix looked at Noah. "Can you qualify what is out of the ordinary?"

Noah had multiple holoscreens up and he was multitasking to his limit. He paused and looked at them, then grinned a little. "Right, point taken. Everything right now is out of the ordinary. Okay, let's try this. We're going to the adjacent docking platform. I want to know if you see anything changing. Just keep me informed of what you see."

Kholva and Vorix shared a look, and Noah thought they looked amused for a moment, but it could've been excitement.

"We understand," Kholva replied.

"Good," Noah said and turned his attention back to his own screens.

A few minutes later, Rabsaris entered the bridge, and with him were Cassidy, Grace Mendel, and Reed Davis. Before the door shut, Tim Hopper came in. He looked as if he'd been running. They were the only other people on the ship.

"Sorry, I can't see staying in the kitchen by myself. Is it alright if I join you?" Tim asked.

The ship was lonely enough with so few of them aboard, and with all that was going on, being together and comforting each other was much better than being alone.

"Yes, just stay over to the side. Maybe stay with Grace and Reed," Noah said.

Grace and Reed were specialists that were part of Naya's team. They moved to the side where the communication workstation was.

"Rabsaris, I need you at Operations. Cassidy, you join him," Noah said.

Noah sat at the tactical workstation. One of his holoscreens showed the configuration of the command interface, while the others displayed data feeds from the ship's sensors. He also had the navigation interface.

Rabsaris sat at the workstation and opened the holoscreen. "Do you know how many years it's been since I've had this kind of training? I'm better at fixing the components of these systems than using them."

Noah nodded. "I know, but you're all I've got. Would you prefer that I put one of the others in that chair?"

Rabsaris stared at Noah for a moment. The others were very young. A specialist was barely more than a cadet, and while Tripp was a technician, his expertise was on basic computer systems.

Noah regarded Cassidy. She was very intelligent and had spent her time aboard the ship learning all she could. She was a requisitions auditor, so she had some knowledge but no practical application experience.

Cassidy gave him a determined nod. "What do you need us to do?"

"We're moving the ship. Long story short, I found that the ship on the adjacent docking platform has repair capabilities in their hangar bay. It seems to be operational. I'm taking the ship there, hoping it'll help us with some of our hull issues and perhaps even the sensors that are broken. Also, I've detected a significant power source. That ship might have everything we need to help us get home."

Rabsaris frowned. "What about the others?"

"I've informed Connor," Noah said.

Cassidy glanced worriedly at the video feed that showed the others making their way to the station. Then she looked at Noah. "I understand. We're covering as many avenues to get us home as possible."

Rabsaris nodded, his shoulders slumping a little. "Oh, I get it. Let's do this."

Noah programmed the nav system with their destination, which then showed a simulation of where the ship was heading.

"Wait," Rabsaris said. "What if the other ship has defense systems? They might not like another ship coming to their hangar bay."

"It didn't seem to mind when I sent the recon probe there. In fact, it fixed it," Noah said.

He authorized the nav system to move the ship, relying on the ship's computer. Maneuvering thrusters came online, and as they exerted force, the ship moved away from the docking platform. Somehow, the artificial gravity from the station determined that the ship was leaving and dialed back the gravity field accordingly.

Noah watched as the ship moved away from the docking platform. He was still amazed at the scale of the station. The adjacent docking platform was much larger than the one they were at. There were two behemoth-sized ships already in dock, but there was a huge gap between them.

One of the ships looked like a large, elongated dorsal fin that had been stretched. It was mostly white but with grayish tones. The hull had smooth lines and was pleasing to the eyes. Noah suspected it had been built for aesthetics as well as functionality. There were multiple bands along the length of the entire ship, and each of the bands displayed shiny chrome accents. Everyone on the bridge watched the image of the alien ship on the main holoscreen in silence. The Phantoms had built this station and perhaps even these ships, only to abandon them.

"The power signature seems small in comparison to the rest of the ship," Cassidy said.

"If their power cores are in any way similar to ours, it could be in standby. It only requires the most minuscule of fuel to be left in an active state, so the systems could be brought back online relatively quickly," Noah answered.

"A ship that size must have more than a single power core," Rabsaris said.

Noah nodded. "I agree."

No point defense system came online, and no communication attempts of any kind came from the alien ship. As the *Pathfinder* flew toward the docking platform, an area nearby illuminated. The automated systems assumed their ship was going to dock there.

Noah held his breath as their maneuvering thrusters altered their course, bringing them toward the ship. The automated systems could have safety measures in place to protect the platform and the other ships docked there.

The *Pathfinder* flew in a controlled manner, so its approach to the other ship was intentional. The alien monitoring systems didn't take any action to correct them, and Noah heaved a sigh of relief.

Cassidy glanced at him.

"I wasn't sure if they'd allow this to happen," Noah said.

"Who, the station or the ship's monitoring systems?"

"Both."

The nav system highlighted their target coordinates on a subwindow on the main holoscreen. It was within the ship's hangar and would take them right to the repair station, which was designed to accommodate ships larger than the *Pathfinder*.

The hangar bay was wide open, and as they made their final approach, Noah saw that it was open all the way to the other side.

"It's over a kilometer wide!" Rabsaris said.

Automated systems detected their approach, and silvery ambient lighting began to come online surrounding the hangar bay. Given the design, Noah expected that perhaps the Phantoms had used a shield to contain an artificial atmosphere but then began to question their decision. With this much open space, maintaining an artificial atmosphere would be a huge effort and a lot of wasted space. It was more pragmatic to maintain specific areas for artificial atmosphere. Noah had served on design review boards for future ship-building initiatives that included features like this.

The repair station had an open metallic framework of cross sections that reminded Noah of a cradle apparatus designed for holding things in place. As they approached the repair station, bright overhead lights came online, and Noah adjusted their approach to align in the center of the lights, believing them to be a guide.

As the ship flew into place, side walls swung down on either side of them.

"Detecting an artificial gravity field," Rabsaris said.

Noah disabled their maneuvering thrusters, allowing the station's artificial gravity field to bring them into position. Their ship came to a complete stop, and bright flashing lights surrounded them for a few moments.

"They're scanning us," Noah said.

Large robotic arms came down from the ceiling and began scanning specific areas of the ship. They focused on key areas like the remaining engine pods and the scanner array.

A proximity alarm burst onto Noah's tactical holoscreen. The point defense system was registering the action of the repair station. Noah acknowledged the alarm and set the system to monitor mode.

Rabsaris looked at him. "Is this what happened to the drone?"

"Yes, they did an assessment first. Then they used some kind of nanorobotic material over the entire drone. It actually improved the drone's hull and exterior components."

"Wonder if they will try to access the interior of the ship," Cassidy said.

"What do we do if they try?" Rabsaris asked.

"I thought about that, and I don't think they will. I mean, if we open the doors they might send in a drone of their own or something like that, but I don't want that to happen."

Cassidy frowned. "Why not?"

"Because repairing the hull and sensor array is much simpler than our power core and other critical systems in main engineering," Noah replied.

Kholva turned toward Noah. "They've extended a docking tube to one of our airlocks."

Noah blinked, unsure if he'd heard the translation correctly, then glanced at the video feed Kholva was monitoring. "Right, to the airlock," Noah said.

He changed the video feed to show the outside of the airlock, which showed a docking tube extending to their ship. The end of it was large enough to cover the entire airlock door. There was some kind of dark material on the end that looked as if it were in a fluid-like state. Sensors outside the door indicated that the docking tube had sealed, but there wasn't an artificial atmosphere.

Noah looked at Rabsaris. "I've got an idea. How many recon drones are in the robotics lab?"

"None. We lost them on Ichlos," Rabsaris said.

Noah shook his head in frustration. He should've remembered that. "What about the repair drones?"

"Just partials. I've been using some for parts to keep the others online."

Noah nodded. "Good. Assign a repair drone to carry some of the others to the maintenance hatch in the forward section."

Rabsaris turned toward his holoscreen and brought up a sub-window. After a few moments, he looked at Noah. "Done. You think they'll repair them?"

"Yes, and then they can do some scouting for us," Noah said.

Three maintenance drones in various states of disrepair were placed just outside the top hatch, and Noah waited. It didn't take long for one of the robotic arms from the repair station to investigate. The pale-colored arm split into smaller appendages as it assessed the drones. Then it sprayed a small silvery mist over them.

"They look like nano swarms," Noah said.

Kholva looked at him. "This technology is similar to our SRA. It's an adaptable nanorobotic particle capable of restoring machines and other structures. It can also be used to manipulate other objects and defense."

Noah had seen the Aczar SRAs in action and had a lot of respect for their capabilities.

"They've restored the drones. It's complete. Look, they're checking in, showing up as fully functional on the ship's computer systems," Rabsaris said.

"That's good. Bring them back inside the ship. I want to send them through the airlock to scout the way for us," Noah said.

Rabsaris nodded. "Understood."

Cassidy regarded Noah for a few seconds. "Are you intending to go on that ship?"

"That'll depend on what the drones find," Noah replied.

Cassidy's eye widened and she looked at the main holoscreen for a second. "Why?"

Noah stopped working for a second and looked at the others. He heaved a sigh. "There's something I need to share with you. The degradation issue with our main power core is accelerating faster than I anticipated. It's even faster than the ship's computer systems predicted. To put this as simply as possible, we need power. Pure and simple. There might be materials on that ship to help us rebuild our power core."

Rabsaris looked away. He'd known about it, but the others were surprised.

"I had no idea it had accelerated so much," Cassidy said. "I knew you were worried."

Noah gave her a patient look and then included the others. "Look, we can't lose hope. We have a way forward now, and it's going to involve taking a few risks. Some of the best things are on the other side of our greatest fear."

The others considered it for a few moments, and eventually, each returned their gaze with renewed determination.

Tripp, Grace, and Reed had a quiet side conversation for a few moments.

"Excuse me," Tripp said. "Should we allow the restored maintenance drones access to the ship? Maybe we should escort them to the airlock."

Noah nodded. "Good idea, Tripp."

"Actually, it was Grace's idea."

Noah smiled at her. He pulled out his sidearm and held it up. "Take this with you. If they start behaving strangely, take them out."

Tripp hastened over and took the pistol. Then he, Grace, and Reed left the bridge.

They spent the next fifteen minutes watching as the repair station restored the hull of their ship and the external systems. Sensor arrays went through a diagnostic and reported back that they were in absolutely pristine condition.

"The battle steel hull plating has a different color now," Cassidy said. "It's more like the alloy of their ship."

"We were concerned about the hull failing in certain sections, but those alerts are gone," Rabsaris said.

Noah brought up another sub-window. "Better than the specs were when the ship was built."

Noah received a message from Tripp. "They've escorted the drones to the airlock."

He brought up the video feed showing the docking tube. The drones moved through the docking tube and entered an open area. It was dimly lit, and they couldn't see much. A pillar rose from the floor with a flourish of grayish metallic particles, as if it were being constructed at that precise moment. A metallic screen formed at the top of the pillar and began to glow with a faint azure glow. Noah stared at the video feed, his mouth partially agape for a moment. "That looks familiar," he said.

Rabsaris stared at him in shock.

"You're right. It's similar to what we saw on Ichlos," Cassidy said.

Rabsaris glanced at the Aczars for a second and then at Noah. "So, what do we do?"

Noah looked at the Aczar, who were students of Phendran.

"The technology Salpheth shared with us must be based on the same technology used here," Kholva said.

Noah bit his lip for a second, thinking. "You're students of Phendran. Do you know what this is? Do you have knowledge of this…you know," he said and tapped the side of his head.

"No, Loremaster training is many years ahead of us," Kholva said, and then gestured toward the main holoscreen. "This appears to be a data terminal. I think they want your input."

Rabsaris blew out a breath. "I don't like this. If they figure out that we don't belong here, it could be bad for us."

Noah pursed his lips in thought. The edges of the alien console glowed, but it was otherwise blank. He considered using one of the mechanical arms on the maintenance drone to manipulate the screen but then decided against it. Instead, he enabled the external speakers on the drone.

"How are they going to hear us?" Rabsaris said.

"There is an artificial atmosphere. We can't breathe it, but it's enough for sound to travel," Noah said.

Rabsaris peered at the sensor feed. "Yeah, but what if they can't understand it? We won't know what it'll sound like."

Noah enabled the comlink to the drone. "Hello? Thank you for repairing our ship. Is there anyone there?"

The alien console flashed, and symbols flew across the screen faster than he could read. Noah frowned and then broadcast a communications package through the maintenance drone. He wasn't sure if they could understand it, but he thought it might help.

The symbols continued to scroll across the screen for a few more seconds and then became blank. Noah leaned forward, peering at the video feed, waiting for some kind of reaction from the console.

A thin cord of metallic material extended from the console and disappeared from the video feed. Then, a new data connection registered on the drone's control interface.

"It's plugged into the data port," Noah said.

A new sub-window opened on Noah's screen. It was from the drone. ::*Greetings initiated with foreign species. Your request for assistance has been granted. Please wait while more systems are brought online.*::

Noah's eyes widened, and the breath caught in his throat.

"They understood you," Cassidy said.

Noah was about to reply, when multiple sub-windows opened as something began accessing the *Pathfinder's* computer systems.

"They're in the system," Rabsaris said. "Look at it. They're accessing our records. Should we try to stop this?"

They looked at Noah, and for a moment, and he kinda felt like Connor did when people looked to him for answers. "I don't know how they'd react if we severed the connection."

"The message said they were going to help us. Maybe this is their way of checking us out," Cassidy said.

Noah slowly bobbed his head. "I think you're right."

"I don't know about this. It doesn't feel right," Rabsaris said.

"That's because it's out of our control. None of this feels right. I think…we should let them finish, and see what they do," Noah said.

"We don't even know who 'they' are. Is it someone or is it something?" Cassidy said.

"Good question," Noah replied.

"I wish we had an answer," Rabsaris said.

Noah nodded and thought for a few moments. Then he engaged the comlink. "Who are you?" he asked, thinking that starting with a simple question was best.

The answer he received both perplexed and intrigued him. There was a significant opportunity there, but he had to be careful or everything around them would unravel.

CHAPTER 30

Tripp was first to notice that the ship was missing. He turned his wide-eyed gaze toward Connor.

"It's fine," Connor said, then gestured ahead of them. "Keep going."

Tripp frowned for a second, but grasped that Connor wanted him to keep quiet.

As they made their way along the same path that Kincaid had taken earlier, Salpheth began to speak.

"We can't go in that way," Salpheth said.

"Why not?" Connor asked.

"Because it's locked down and I won't be able to access it."

Mac and Jorath watched Salpheth.

"Deception," Phendran cried. "You're manipulating us!"

Salpheth regarded the Aczar for a long moment. "How rebellious you've become."

"Your attempts to deflect are insufficient."

Salpheth regarded Phendran for several seconds and then looked at Connor. "Your companions triggered a lockdown. I need to access the computer systems from inside the station to lift it.

Now, does that sound like I'm trying to deceive you? Do you design access to your own facilities where security protocols can be overridden from outside?"

Connor considered Salpheth's words for a few seconds. "Where are you taking us?"

"The lockdown will affect the entrances in this area, so I'm taking you outside of that area."

Connor tried to pick out the truth from the lies and couldn't decide which was what. "How can you tell there's a lockdown?"

Salpheth tilted his head to the side, staring at him. "Your companions confirmed it for me. The consoles here won't come on for anyone. Now, before you ask how I know this, I'll just tell you. This isn't the first resupply station I've ever been to. I know the security protocols that are in place. They can only be lifted from inside the facility. If you'd like, I can demonstrate to you that I'm unable to gain access to the station over there." He gestured to where Kincaid and the others had found a door.

Connor smiled a little. "Well, since you offered, why not?" He looked at Tripp and gestured toward their original destination.

Salpheth looked resigned and didn't say anything else.

They crossed the distance to the hidden door. It was just a smooth wall, but the area Kincaid had gone through was highlighted on Connor's HUD.

"Time to release me from the energy field," Salpheth said.

"Not yet," Connor said.

He accessed the controls to the portable energy field and engaged the artificial gravity emitters, then partially disengaged the energy field. About forty percent of the field closest to the station's walls disappeared, making the field look like a partially drawn curtain.

A hungry gleam appeared on Salpheth's face. He extended his pale hand toward the edge of the field, tentatively stopping at where the barrier had been. Then he pushed beyond it. The Phantom's hand extended a couple of feet and then he hastily pulled it back, glaring at Connor.

He didn't offer Salpheth an explanation.

"You seek to hold me with an artificial gravity field?"

"I do. You didn't think I'd just let you out of there and hope for the best. Do you want to test it?" Connor asked.

Salpheth gave him an appraising look for a moment, then gestured to be moved closer to where the control panel had been. A small area on the wall began to glow, and Salpheth tried to use the interface, but it wouldn't respond to him.

"See, I can't do anything with it. No one can," Salpheth said.

Connor stared at him for a moment. "I don't believe you. Maybe you need the proper motivation. I'll just constrict the gravity field."

Salpheth clenched his jaw, narrowing his gaze. When the gravity field closed in around him, causing even the partially engaged energy field to close in on him, his eyes widened, and he hunched his shoulders, making his body as small as possible.

"Stop! I'm not lying to you. There is nothing to be gained by this. I'm telling you the truth."

There was a deadly part of Connor that would always be there, no matter how long it had been since he'd experienced that side of himself. Sometimes it surprised him, and other times it felt like an old, familiar pair of shoes. It was the part of himself that could do the things most people couldn't. He didn't love it or hate it because it was just part of who he was. It wasn't his favorite part of himself, but he knew there were times when it was necessary. It was time that Salpheth learned exactly who Connor was. He gritted his teeth, staring coldly at Salpheth. "I don't believe you, Salpheth."

He looked at the control interface for the artificial gravity field and moved the slider to make the field both more powerful and smaller.

Salpheth flinched as he professed his innocence.

"Open the door!" Connor shouted. "Open it, or I'll crush you."

Mac shifted on his feet but kept his weapon pointed at Salpheth.

Jorath simply stared at him.

After a few moments had passed, Connor expanded the field. "Try it again."

Salpheth growled as he stood. "To try again is pointless. But do as you will. It won't change anything."

Connor stared at him and the seconds seemed to gather off to the side. "Fine, we'll try it your way."

Salpheth blinked in surprise and then gestured. "Over there," he said roughly.

As they walked along the wall, Salpheth stared at him thoughtfully. "I've underestimated you, General Gates. There is a ruthlessness to you that I suspected was there but hadn't actually seen."

Connor didn't reply. Nothing Salpheth said could be trusted, and this was just another tactic. He really wanted to be done with all this. If he'd had any chance of rescuing the others without Salpheth, he would've taken it and been done with him.

"Shall I tell you about my species?" Salpheth asked.

Connor looked at him, and Salpheth smirked.

"You'd like to tell me 'No,' but you also know the value of gathering data," Salpheth said, and paused for a moment. "We're explorers. I believe I've told you this before. Phendran knows some of our history. You can confirm it with him if you suspect I'm lying to you."

Connor glanced at Phendran for a second and then looked at Salpheth. "You bet I will."

Salpheth grinned. "It doesn't have to be this contentious between us. I understand why you did what you did. You can't trust me. If our roles were reversed, I would've done something similar. So, we share a bit of common ground, you and I."

Connor didn't agree but kept quiet. One thing he'd learned over the years was that the longer someone spoke, the more they revealed about themselves. Salpheth would prove who he was, one way or the other. Connor knew it was true for people, the Ovarrow, and the Krake. He hadn't been around the Aczar long enough, but he suspected it was true for them, too. He wasn't sure whether this applied to the Phantoms. Their life spans were much longer than Humans, so perhaps they could deceive better than others could.

"We left our world and made our new home among the great expanse. We studied star systems and planets, learning about different species. It renewed our unique place. Our world was surrounded by light, unlike the outer spiral arms of this galaxy, where things are dark."

Salpheth absently gestured toward an area of the wall toward the edge of the docking platform. Connor glanced back the way they'd come, and they were nearly two hundred meters from where Kincaid had entered the facility.

"We observed star nations rise and then collapse, which further confirmed our greatness and how few species ever achieve what we had," Salpheth continued. He regarded Connor for a moment. "I see that your species has this potential."

"No, you don't," Connor said. "You don't know anything about my species."

"But I know you've been contacted by members of my race. They've taken a somewhat active role in your development. I don't think you understand how rare this is."

"Sure, we're special. Now get us inside."

To the outside observer, it would appear that Connor was being rude, but he knew one of the best ways to glean information from an insufferably proud being was to act like you didn't want to hear what they had to say and that what they were saying wasn't as impressive as they thought.

"It has made me revise my estimation of you," Salpheth said.

They moved him toward the wall with the energy field still only partially engaged. Salpheth lifted his hand toward the wall and a new control panel appeared. It had a glowing rectangular surface that was more inside the wall than on the surface. The pale wall of the panel became semi-translucent, but Salpheth was able to interact with the alien symbols.

A large rectangular door sank into the ground, revealing a dark corridor beyond. An azure glow brightened along the ceiling and floors, illuminating the area.

Salpheth gestured inside, looking pleased. "As promised," he said.

Connor and the others peered inside.

"Can you open the other door now?" Connor asked.

Salpheth shook his head. "Not here. We have to go inside. The sooner we do that, the sooner we both get what we want. Then you'll see that an alliance with me isn't as disastrous as you had feared."

Connor thought he saw Phendran glaring at Salpheth, but the Aczar didn't say anything.

Connor looked at him. "Why are you trying so hard? What do you want from us?"

"You, General Gates," Salpheth said. "Surely you know the benefits that alliances can have for everyone involved. There is much we can learn from one another."

Connor chuckled. "You just finished telling me about how special your species is. How you've seen young spacefaring species fail. What could you possibly learn from me that you don't already know?"

"There is an opportunity here for both of us to benefit from. You want to learn more about the Phantoms, and I'm willing to teach you, share our knowledge. And in return, you support me with my work."

Connor cringed inwardly. Did Salpheth really believe Connor would agree to this? "For someone who professes to know so much about other species, you'd have to know that no single person has the power to make a binding agreement on behalf of his entire species."

Salpheth regarded him for a long moment. "I suspect you wield a lot of influence. More than you're comfortable admitting."

They walked down the corridor and came to another door.

"It's worth considering," Salpheth said.

"What is it you need our help with?"

"We've encountered many species in this galaxy, including a living spacefaring species that spreads itself to many worlds. It absorbs them. You refer to them as the Vemus. What did my Phantom brethren tell you about them?" Salpheth asked.

Connor gestured toward the wall. "Aren't you going to open the door?"

Salpheth stared at him for a moment and then accessed the door controls. Connor watched as Salpheth navigated through the control interface. Another door opened, but this one was only four meters wide.

Bright lights burst from the room on the other side, showing a wide expanse of pedestals with semi-translucent shafts above. Waves of purplish energy shimmered across them.

Connor felt his SRA shift inside his EVA. His SRA squirmed, as if it was moving from his wrist toward his gloved hand. An access port on his forearm opened, and a metallic substance with the consistency of mercury slithered out. It circled his arm with a faint greenish glow.

Connor looked at Salpheth, but he was watching the rows of pedestals across the room. Inside the containment fields above them were metallic humanoid figures. Floating above their heads was what looked like a circle of liquid metal. They were a meter and a half tall, but something about them made Connor uneasy. There were hundreds of them in the room, maybe even a thousand.

"What the heck is this?" Mac asked.

"They appear to be in some kind of stasis," Jorath said.

Tripp stared at the pedestals and shifted his focus back to Salpheth.

Phendran and Noxrey peered up at the containment fields.

"Yes," Salpheth said, stretching out the word. "You know what they are." Connor looked at him. "These are a form of the SRAs that the Aczar are so keen to use, but I find it surprising that you, General Gates, now have an SRA of your own."

Connor looked down at his arm before he could stop himself.

"You are no doubt familiar with their capabilities, as much as the Aczar were able to develop with my help."

"What is this?" Connor asked.

"Don't you recognize a fighting force when you see one? Fighting, serving, and any application I can think of, these SRAs will do for me."

Connor looked around the room, taking in the sight and potential.

"There are many more here."

"Are you telling me that this resupply station is filled with these..."

"They're not complete SRAs yet, so 'drone' will serve your vernacular just fine. Think of the application for which they can be used. I know the Vemus are of great concern to you. They have an interesting hierarchy, don't they?"

Connor regarded him for a long moment. "What do you know about it?"

"You never answered my question. What did my brethren tell you about the Vemus?"

Connor's gaze narrowed as he considered his reply. "They said that the Vemus were a considerable threat."

Salpheth pursed his lips for a moment. "They must've expanded since I last studied them. What else did they say? Surely you asked... demanded more information from them."

Salpheth wasn't wrong about that. Connor remembered his encounter with the Phantoms.

"They said the Vemus were too much of a threat for us to deal with right now. They advised us to build ourselves up before seeking them out."

Salpheth slowly shook his head. "Typical. Instead of giving you actual help, they advise you to take a path that has zero certainty of success."

"There are no guarantees. *You* can't guarantee anything, so what have I really lost?"

Salpheth made a sweeping gesture. "This is one of many incubators on this station. There is much more I can show you."

Connor peered across the room. "You were going to help us free our companions. Why don't you deliver on that promise before we talk about anything else."

"Very well, General Gates."

They made their way through the room, careful not to disturb anything. Connor looked up at one of the containment fields, peering at the figure inside. The head was smooth and featureless. It would've been easy to underestimate these drones based on their size, but he knew what Aczar SRAs could do, and these were more independent.

They left the room and entered a long corridor, and Salpheth looked at him.

"Have you wondered why nothing was done about the Vemus?"

As they walked along the corridor, parts of the walls became transparent, and they could see storage rooms filled with equipment and vehicles on one side, and more of those SRA incubators on the other. Connor wanted to ask Phendran about it but knew better than to do that in front of Salpheth.

"I thought maybe they were too much for you to handle," Connor replied.

Salpheth grinned. "Now you're trying to get me to reveal something."

"The Vemus aren't an issue for your species because somehow you don't have to stay in n-space with the rest of us," Connor said.

"That's not a bad theory," Salpheth replied. The Phantom looked around with increasing excitement, as if something he'd been hoping and longing for was finally within his grasp.

"Why do you want an alliance with me?" Connor asked.

"As capable as the SRAs are, they need overseers. Even Phendran will tell you that it takes years for their SRAs to form a harmonious relationship with them," Salpheth said, and his gaze narrowed, considering. "That doesn't seem to be your experience, though. An interesting development. One I hadn't anticipated."

The farther they went into the station, the more Connor felt like they would never get out of there. Despite the artificial gravity field and the energy containment field, Salpheth was becoming increasingly sure of himself, as if his captivity wasn't as much of an obstacle as it once had been. Connor needed to think beyond what was happening or events could get away from him.

Salpheth looked at Phendran. "I once believed I would eventually convince *you* to bring me here."

"Now, that's something I don't understand," Connor said. "First, you convince the Aczar to abandon exploration, and now you tell us that you once thought they'd bring you here?"

"The Aczar required a lot of refinement," Salpheth replied.

"They were afraid to go above ground. Was that part of your plan?"

"There were some missteps during our interactions."

Connor stared at him for a long moment. "If you're so superior to everyone else, why would there be any missteps? Why were you left on that planet?"

They reached the end of the corridor, and Salpheth gestured toward the door. "I should probably open that."

Tripp looked at Connor. He was controlling the grav pallet that Salpheth's containment field rode on.

Connor walked toward the door. "What if *I* opened it?"

Salpheth's hand jerked up. "Don't!"

Connor raised his hand toward the panel.

"If you do that, you'll start another lockdown," Salpheth warned.

He couldn't tell if Salpheth was lying to him. If he tried to open the door and Salpheth was right, they'd be locked in, but if the door opened, Salpheth's lies would be exposed.

Connor looked at the control panel. He couldn't read the alien language, so he had no idea what option to use. Why would selecting the wrong option result in the entire area being locked down? The more he thought about it, the more implausible it seemed.

Many thoughts came to the forefront of his mind, as if his brain had been processing information and was now bringing it forward.

"Tell me which option to select," Connor said.

Salpheth hesitated.

His hand drew closer to the panel. "Tell me, or I'll just guess." He glanced at the panel, and for a second, a perfect translation appeared on his HUD. He blinked and it was gone. It had happened so fast that he thought he must've imagined it.

"General Gates," Salpheth said, "you asked a question before that I haven't answered. I'm well aware that you cannot make decisions for your entire species. My offer of an alliance was to be extended to your Confederation. Have the Phantoms joined your Confederation?"

Connor frowned, as much from Salpheth's question as from what he'd seen. "They have not."

"I see. In the next room there is a control station. It's where I can lift the lockdown that has trapped your companions."

Connor lifted his chin, his gaze narrowing. "The Vemus. In

many ways, they seem like a biological weapon that's out of control."

Salpheth blinked in surprise. It was one of the first honest responses Connor had seen from him, and it confirmed that he was closer to the truth than he'd been before.

"We never found the source of them. We only encountered the worlds that they'd invaded," Salpheth said.

"So, for a thousand years or more, the Vemus have been spreading?"

"Your guess is as good as mine. You already know where I've been all this time."

Connor's earlier encounter with the Phantoms revealed that while they were aware of the Vemus, they were sure that they were beyond Humanity's ability to deal with. What he hadn't considered was that the Vemus might be beyond the Phantom's ability to deal with.

He looked at Salpheth for a long moment. Some of the things Salpheth had said to him tumbled around in his head, and a small part of him was seriously considering taking him up on his offer of an alliance. If the Vemus had been around for so long, the Phantoms might be right about whether Humanity would defeat them. With the Vemus, there would always be war. Wondering if there was some kind of great evil in the galaxy was one thing, but knowing about it was something else entirely. What alliance wouldn't he consider if it meant they could defeat the Vemus one day. This line of thinking represented a slippery slope in his mind, but what if Salpheth was telling him the truth?

He stared at Salpheth and immediately thought, what if Salpheth was lying to him? What would it mean for the rest of them? If they formed an alliance with Salpheth, how hard would it be to leave the alliance later on? Salpheth had his own goals, and they probably didn't align with the Confederation's. He glanced at Phendran, who watched him intently. Salpheth said that he manipulated the Aczar into rebellion because of their reluctance to move beyond the fears that had driven them to Ichlos. Had Salpheth tried to reason with the Aczar and they simply wouldn't listen? Phendran would know, unless that knowledge had been erased from their archive.

A wave of shimmering light washed over the alien drones in rooms beyond the corridor. Some of the humanoid figures moved a little, as if they were rousing from a deep sleep.

Mac muttered a curse. "This doesn't look good."

"He's correct, General Gates," Salpheth said. "I must open the door and get to the control center to prevent the SRAs from coming online. If they do, they'll be following protection protocols, and none of us are authorized to be here. I have to shut them down. Please, let me open the door."

Connor stared at Salpheth for a long moment and then moved out of the way.

CHAPTER 31

SALPHETH OPENED THE DOOR, and Connor engaged the energy field so that it surrounded Salpheth. The Phantom shouted, but Connor ignored him and went into the room.

They entered the vast chamber they'd glimpsed through the translucent walls in the corridor. It was a massive room, as large as a vast storage facility. Pedestals with shimmering containment fields sent mesmerizing ripples of light to the ceiling high above them.

Large, dome-shaped workstations stood near the spread-out pedestals. Holoscreens activated, displaying scrolling text in the Phantom language.

Connor looked at Mac. "Have you located the others?"

Mac nodded. "I've been tracking them since we entered the station. Making the waypoint available to you."

Jorath peered at the Phantom SRAs. The metallic humanoid forms jerked from within the containment field, as they received a jolt. The swirling crowns of liquid metal began to sink toward them. "We should leave this area," he warned.

Connor searched for the control station and spotted a central work area about seventy meters from their location.

"Tripp," Connor said, "let's move. Stay close to Mac."

The young technician had become distracted by their surroundings. He gave Connor a nod. "Yes, General."

They quickly made their way to the control system. Once they started moving, Salpheth became quiet. He was getting what he wanted, so why would he inhibit progress toward his intended goal?

As they went past the rows of pedestals, Connor spotted small holoscreens near the base. Again, a flash of a translation appeared on his HUD. It was a status window, something about them being on standby.

He looked at Phendran. "Can you read their language?"

Phendran shook his head. "No, this language is foreign to me. Can you?"

Salpheth turned toward them, his dark eyes narrowing with calculating interest.

Connor shook his head. He wasn't sure if Salpheth believed him.

They quickly made their way to a central location, a nexus of where the entire room seemed to converge. The control system was on a large, raised platform with four large holoscreens above four workstations that looked as if they had grown from the floor.

"General Gates, you must let me out of this containment field. It's not as simple as opening the door. I must authenticate with the system. It will only work for my species. If you don't, the automated defense systems will use the SRAs to kill us all."

Phendran looked at Connor. "You shouldn't trust him. He will betray you."

Connor nodded and began to walk up to the nearest workstation.

"No, General Gates. You don't know what you're doing!"

Connor gestured for Phendran to come with him, and Noxrey followed.

"This reminds me of your technology," Connor said.

"The design is similar, but it is also vastly different. I cannot decipher the language on the holoscreens," Phendran said.

Noxrey peered at them and then at the surrounding area. "Power is being routed to all the pedestals. These SRAs are being powered on—activated. Salpheth might be telling the truth."

Connor stared at the data on the holoscreen, and a perfect translation appeared for a brief moment. He gasped and leaned forward as a dull headache erupted in his head.

"General, are you okay?" Mac asked.

Phendran and Noxrey watched him intently.

"For a second, I could read what was on the screen. It happened before and I thought I imagined it. It's like something is locked away inside my head," Connor said.

His vision blurred, and he gritted his teeth.

Salpheth bellowed and slammed into the energy field, sending harsh eddies of energy across the field.

Connor stared at the holoscreen, and every time he blinked, it went from an alien language to something he could read. He caught snippets of words. A list of active systems.

He heard Mac speaking but couldn't understand what he was saying. He squeezed his eyes shut for a couple of seconds and when he opened them, a lance of pain went through his skull. Connor gritted his teeth, forcing his eyes to remain open. He stared at the holoscreen through sheer force of will, ignoring the pain.

He was looking at several command prompts, and they required input. One had to do with the security lockdown. There were several areas throughout the station that were locked down. Connor had no idea which one was where Kincaid and the others were, so he selected the options to end them all.

A bright flash came from the side as Tripp screamed. "Watch out!"

An unseen force shoved Connor into the workstation, and he

tumbled over it. A high-pitched ringing sounded in his ears, and his rifle slipped from his grasp, clattering out of reach.

Salpheth was suddenly in his line of sight, standing where Connor had been a moment before. He was out of his containment field. A bright flash emanated from Salpheth's pale skin as Mac and Jorath fired their weapons, but the shots had no effect. The darts just ricocheted off.

Salpheth glared down at Connor for a moment, and in the next he'd seized him, lifting him off the floor. Before Connor could do anything, Salpheth flung him to the side, and Connor flew over the workstation, crashing to the ground.

Connor pushed himself up and spotted his rifle nearby. He scrambled toward it, but Salpheth was too fast. He kicked the rifle away and raised his powerful fists into the air. Connor flinched, scrambling back, and raised his arm to block the incoming blow on instinct. As Salpheth's fist came down, a metallic shield opened around Connor's arm a meter across. Salpheth's fists slammed into the shield and bounced off in a burst of green energy, shoving the Phantom back.

Connor's eyes widened as he realized that his SRA had protected him, just as he'd seen the Aczar's SRAs do on Ichlos.

Salpheth's eyes widened in shock as his gaze sank to Connor's SRA. Then, snarling, he lunged toward Connor.

Gritting his teeth, Connor pushed off the ground, meeting Salpheth's attack head on. At the last moment, he pivoted to the side, using his shield to push Salpheth off balance. A burst of force came from his SRA, and Salpheth crashed into nearby pedestals. The containment fields above them came down and the metallic drones sank gracefully to the ground as if gravity didn't affect them. They slowly raised their heads as if being roused from a deep sleep.

Connor spun around toward his rifle and snatched it off the ground, bringing it up to aim at the Phantom drones. They surrounded Salpheth, blocking him from view and ushering him away for some reason.

He looked for the others and found Mac helping Tripp to his feet. Jorath scanned the area, weapon ready.

Connor sprinted over to them. "What happened?"

"Those things attacked the containment field. They came out of nowhere," Tripp said.

There were scorch marks on his EVA suit.

"General!" Mac shouted and began firing his weapon.

Connor did the same.

Phantom drones began coming toward him, and he fired his weapon at them. Large, high-density darts slammed into the drones, knocking them back, but the damage done to them was only temporary. Connor aimed for the chest at first, which only slowed them down. Then he aimed toward the feet, and they stumbled.

Salpheth fought the drones surrounding him, and the small metallic machines flew away from him as he swiped them away.

"Mac, you're on point. Get us to the others. Jorath, you're with me covering our six," Connor said.

Mac turned and began moving toward the waypoint where the others were. Tripp stayed with him. He had his sidearm out but wasn't firing. Phendran and Noxrey were close behind them. Their SRAs had spread to encase them in a protective suit.

Jorath was at his side, and the Ovarrow soldier fired his weapon at Salpheth, but the Phantom was hardly affected at all.

"Save your ammo," Connor said.

More of the pedestals sank to the ground, and as if the entire room had begun moving at once, their containment fields disappeared and more of the Phantom drones came online.

Salpheth waded through them, making his way to the control center.

Connor needed to prevent Salpheth from using the console.

Connor engaged the secondary ammunition configuration, which he'd set to explosive rounds, and fired at one of the workstations. The explosive rounds penetrated and then exploded, hurling pieces across the large room. The workstation lost form and sank into the ground.

Salpheth screamed at Connor.

Connor aimed for the next workstation, and Salpheth quickly grabbed one of the drones, throwing it at Connor.

Explosive rounds hit the humanoid drone. Its form wavered, becoming a solid metallic sphere for a moment, but the explosion Connor anticipated never happened. The drone had absorbed the force but didn't attack as it went through some kind of repair cycle.

Connor swung his weapon toward the workstation again. Salpheth was trying to seize control of the entire station. Connor fired at the workstation, destroying it, but Salpheth howled in triumph.

"You're too late!"

Jorath, copying Connor's tactic, destroyed the other workstation and the entire control center.

The only weapon Connor had that could hurt Salpheth was his own SRA, but to get to him, he'd have to go through the hundreds of drones that were coming online.

"General Gates, we must leave," Jorath said.

He'd backed up a few steps, and Connor glared at Salpheth. The grav pallet with the mobile energy field had been destroyed. There was no way for him to capture the rogue Phantom again. Salpheth had his freedom, and Connor and the others were going to die if they stayed there.

Connor fired his weapon at the ground in front of Salpheth, and the explosive force pushed the Phantom back. Salpheth lunged toward a group of SRA drones. Their eyes gleamed in white light for a moment before becoming as dark as Salpheth's. He was taking control of them.

Connor turned toward Jorath. "Go. Go. Go!"

He quickly moved away from Salpheth and his growing army of drones. The drones that had been released from their containment fields seemed to follow a latent protocol, attacking the nearest threat around them.

Connor fired his last explosive round, and his ammunition configuration automatically switched to his primary ammunition source.

An SRA drone lunged toward Connor's side, and his own SRA expanded to protect him. Connor pushed the drone away, and his SRA released a force that propelled it through the air.

They quickly moved back to the waypoint where Mac and Tripp had gone. Mac was firing his weapon at the pedestals, destroying them, which interrupted the reactivation process that was occurring. Phendran and Noxrey defended Mac's sides from attacking drones. They were protecting Tripp, who was trying to get the door control panel to work.

Tripp turned toward them. "General, I can't get it open. The lockdown must still be effective here."

Connor hastened to the door and saw that the controls were locked out. The pain in his head had faded and the translations were coming much easier. A short distance away, he spotted a small workstation. He looked at Mac. "Hold this position. I'm going to get the door open. Tripp, cover them as well."

Connor ran toward the small workstation and weaved his way around the pedestals that hadn't been activated yet. Bright flashes of light came from the central area where Salpheth was. Connor glanced in that direction and saw a huge battle going on between the unmodified drones and the ones that Salpheth had somehow brought under his control. Salpheth must've celebrated too soon. He wasn't in control of the station.

The workstation was a smooth, metallic desk that, like the others, appeared to have grown from the ground. Connor forced himself to look away from the central area and put his SRA over the workstation. A holoscreen became active, and his SRA emitted a green glow. Alien symbols scrolled across, and then a translation appeared on his HUD.

Security override in progress…

Permanent decommission of the facility has been halted.

Connor stared at it, and a thin tendril from his SRA extended toward the holoscreen. The interface reacted to it and a status list appeared. Connor quickly read through the options, and he blinked. The station wasn't supposed to be there. The Phantoms had never meant for it to stay active for so long. Either Salpheth or someone helping him had somehow stalled the decommissioning process.

Connor brought up the control interface for the decommission protocol to close the facility. The stations' SRAs had been meant to carry out the final disassembly of the entire station. The materials were supposed to have been processed by the construction platforms to decommission the station. Those protocols were still active, but the process had been halted.

General Gates, you must engage the decommission protocol before the security subsystems are overridden.

Connor frowned as the words appeared on his HUD. "Who is this?" he asked.

SRA Designation KMTB74720103.

His SRA glowed green around the edges, and Connor stared at it. Their interactions had not been spoken before. He shoved away the tumult of questions coming to his mind and tried to find the decommission protocol as his SRA had advised him. It wasn't as simple as finding the option and engaging it. Each time he made a selection, it brought him to a new sub-window, asking for another confirmation.

"Can you speed this up?" Connor asked, looking over his shoulder. More of the Phantom drones were gathering at the center.

A new sub-window opened on the holoscreen, and several tendrils came out of his SRA, navigating the interface. Connor searched for the door-control systems in the area. The Phantom interface was quite intuitive, but the lockdown was slowly taking over the system as Salpheth continued to battle for control. Connor tried to find a system for emergency protocols.

"Evacuation functions. Please tell me they wouldn't decommission the station with people trapped inside," Connor said.

A new sub-window appeared in front of him, and Connor selected the emergency evacuation systems. As soon as he selected that option, Connor looked around in shock as all the doors in the area opened at the same time.

Salpheth bellowed in rage and began searching for Connor.

Connor squatted a little and started to pull his hand out of the holo-interface but stopped because tendrils of his SRA were still in the system. Sub-windows flashed across the screen in rapid succession.

"Give me a remote session so we can get out of here, and keep searching for some kind of master control for the decommission process because we can't keep answering hundreds of prompts," Connor said.

The tendrils from his SRA withdrew from the holo-interface and rejoined the band on his forearm. The band was larger than it had been before, covering his entire forearm.

Connor left the console but saw a new data connection available on his HUD. He began to race back toward the others and saw that Kincaid and Seger had joined them, helping to defend the area from the Phantom attack drones. Behind them, the doors began to close.

Connor gestured behind them. "Get out of here! I'll meet you on the other side!"

Kincaid looked at him, and Connor ran through the nearest metallic door. It had paused midway from closing. The data connection to the Phantom Space Station flashed, and Connor glanced at it. A data window projected into view, and he saw a bunch of sub-windows. Somehow, his SRA was still navigating the interface. He wasn't sure what it could and couldn't do.

Connor ran down the corridor, and a comlink came from Kincaid. He glanced behind him and saw hundreds of Phantom attack drones entering the corridor. They must've stopped the door from closing.

"General, what's your status?" Kincaid asked.

"Running from the enemy. Get back to the docking platform. I'll meet you there—"

Something hit Connor hard, and he slammed into the wall of the corridor, then rolled to the floor, stunned. Then, it grabbed Connor's arm and lifted him into the air. His body swung around, bringing him face to face with Salpheth's hateful gaze.

"I've had just about enough of you, General Gates," he snarled.

Connor squeezed the trigger of his rifle, firing blindly at the ground at Salpheth's feet.

Salpheth swung Connor around, squeezing his arm, and Connor realized he was trying to crush his SRA. A heat alert registered on Connor's HUD, and he recognized that it was because of his proximity to Salpheth.

Connor tried to jerk his arm back, and his legs swung toward the wall. He lifted his feet and pushed off the corridor, and at the same time Salpheth's hand blew apart in a bright flash of light. Connor's SRA had become a multitude of jagged spikes, and Salpheth howled in pain.

Connor stumbled and moved out of reach a short distance from the Phantom. Salpheth stared at his arm in shock, seeing a stump where his hand had been.

Connor blinked. He'd hurt the Phantom. His SRA had hurt the Phantom.

Phantom attack drones armed with their own SRAs flooded the corridor, coming toward them at a frenzied pace.

"There will be no escape for you!" Salpheth shouted.

Connor ran toward the Phantom, and his SRA extended, becoming a sharp metallic lance with a greenish glow along the edges. Salpheth disappeared before he could hit him and instantly reappeared farther down the corridor among the loyal attack drones that were dead set on reaching Connor.

"General! Take cover!" Kincaid shouted as he ran toward him, throwing a plasma grenade toward Salpheth and the attack drones.

Connor dove to the ground, and the force of the explosion shoved him along the floor. Heat proximity warnings appeared on his HUD.

Kincaid helped Connor to his feet. "Come on, General, we've got to get out of here."

They sped down the corridor at an all-out run. Seger and Jorath were at the door, providing cover. Connor looked over his shoulder and could see Salpheth far down the corridor. An army of Phantom drones charged toward them.

CHAPTER 32

As soon as Connor was through the door, he and Kincaid slowed down. "Covering fire!"

Seger and Jorath retreated, and the four of them fired their weapons at the oncoming army of Phantom drones that was charging toward them. Their weapons were having an effect on them, but as the drones dropped to the ground, the others leaped over them in rapid succession.

Connor glanced over his shoulder to find the others. Mac, Tripp, and Naya were running toward the empty docking platform, looking for a way to cross to where Noah had taken the ship. There *had* been a way to reach the adjacent platform, but the way was now cut off by a wall. It must've been part of the lockdown, something new that Salpheth had done.

"General!" Kincaid shouted.

Connor spun. A group of Phantom drones popped into existence near them, well ahead of the charging army. Phendran and Noxrey darted toward them. Their SRAs had become some kind of edged weapon, and they attacked the drones with blinding speed.

Salpheth had been able to teleport the drones closer to them.

The Phantom drones didn't carry any weapons, instead their hands had become a powered lance. Two of them burst away from the group and were on Kincaid in seconds. Jolts of energy caused Kincaid to fall. Connor moved toward him, raising his own SRA up. It raced ahead of him, becoming a lance and piercing the two drones that were atop Kincaid. Connor flung his arm to the side, and with added strength from his own SRA, the drones were hurled far away from them. Connor reached down and helped Kincaid to his feet.

Now that they knew Salpheth could teleport a small attack force to them, they stayed alert for it. Connor and the others retreated, and Phendran and Noxrey rejoined them.

Connor opened a comlink to Noah. "We can't reach you. The way has been cut off."

"Connor, thank God!" Noah said. "Right. Right. Hold on. I have a way to get you out of there. Okay, I just need to bring it up."

Connor shook his head and checked the ammunition level in his rifle. "We're running low on ammo. Just bring the ship and pick us up. Give me an ETA when you got it."

Kincaid looked at him and Connor gestured toward where the others were. "Tactical retreat!"

They started running toward the others in spurts, pausing to fire their weapons at the Phantom drones that were running at them.

Connor lost track of Salpheth. The drones stopped teleporting closer to them. That was one less problem, but he lost count of the drones that were racing toward them like a nightmarish scene from the depths of his imagination.

"I'm out," Mac said.

"So am I," Jorath replied.

Connor tossed his rifle at Mac. "Use this one."

Mac caught the rifle and swung it toward the drones.

Their weapons could only slow them down, disabling the drones for a short period of time. Only the SRAs had catastrophic effects on them, and only Phendran, Noxrey, and Connor had them. With the number of drones coming at them, the three of them would quickly be overwhelmed, SRAs or not.

Connor scanned behind them, looking for their ship. "Noah! Where are you?"

Regretting that he'd agreed to let Noah take their only means of escape, Connor looked for a place where they could make their final stand. The problem was that there wasn't anything nearby.

They reached the others, and his data link to the space station flashed around the edges, calling his attention to it. Connor ignored it, instead focusing on the comlink to Noah.

"No way I can make it to you on the ship. I have an alternative. You're going to have to trust me," Noah said.

Connor gritted his teeth and shook his head.

"There should be an area nearby that's glowing orange."

Connor spun around, searching. "No orange. What the heck are you…"

Farther away along the edge of the docking platform, a large circle of the reactive plating illuminated with an orange glow.

"Go to the orange area. You all need to step inside it. You've only got one shot at this," Noah said.

Connor gestured toward the area, telling the others to go there. "What it is?"

"It's a transit pad. It's similar to the mode of travel the Aczars used on their planet."

How did the transit pad work? He recalled Phendran telling them the technology was limited and required something at the destination to receive them. They didn't have anything like that on the *Pathfinder*.

Connor and the others ran to the transit pad. The others got on, but Connor stayed out of it. The data connection to the station came to prominence on his HUD.

"General, what you are doing?" Kincaid asked.

A message from his SRA appeared on his HUD.

Search complete. Master decommission control initiated by...

A group of Phantom symbols identified the individual who had authorized the decommission protocol for the station.

Kincaid came over to him.

"Stay on the pad," Connor said.

He was worried that if he stepped on the pad, his connection to the station's computer systems would be cut off.

Kincaid nodded. "Sergeant, we need to buy him some time."

They fired their weapons at the drones. There was no end to them coming from the station.

Connor looked away and focused on the data comlink.

His SRA had found the command authorization to decommission the station, but it had been stopped.

"Connor, what are you waiting for? That army is going to overwhelm you any second."

"I know," Connor said.

He found the master control list and saw where the entire process had stalled. It was some kind of clean sweep maintenance protocol that could allow for the resources used to construct the station to be reused. He killed the priority for the process, and the decommission protocol resumed. Long lists of protocols scrolled up the screen too fast for him to read.

Kincaid grabbed Connor's EVA suit and hauled him back to the transit pad.

Connor looked up, watching the horde of Phantom drones about to reach them. Then, there was a bright flash, and they were instantly in some kind of large hangar bay.

"The *Pathfinder!*" Tripp shouted.

The ship's hull gleamed in the light as if it had been newly constructed. Tracking lights illuminated the ground near the landing skids.

"Go!" Connor said.

They ran across the hangar as the loading ramp extended from the closest airlock. They hastened up the ramp and into the airlock. Once it cycled, the door opened, giving them access to the ship.

"Noah, we're aboard. Get us out of here," Connor said.

"Why? Those drones can't reach us here," Noah said.

"Because the station is about to decommission itself. We don't have much time. Get the *Pathfinder* out of here."

"Uh, that's going to be a problem."

"What problem? I saw the outside of the ship. It looks fresh out of the shipyards."

"I know, but the problems with the power core haven't been fixed. There's nothing here for us to use to refuel the core. The *Pathfinder* alone is not going to get us home."

Connor jogged through the ship. "I'm coming to the bridge."

"I'm not on the bridge," Noah replied.

Connor stopped. "What do you mean you're not on the bridge? Where the heck are you?"

CHAPTER 33

"I'm on the alien ship. The transit pad brought you to the hangar outside of our ship, right?" Noah replied.

He sounded like he was multitasking.

Connor glanced down the corridor toward the bridge. Noah was on the alien ship and was obviously working on something. A warning appeared on his HUD. The data connection to the station was stalling, as if experiencing severe latency issues delaying the refresh of the data.

A message from his SRA appeared on his HUD.

Connectivity issues unavoidable.

"Understood," Connor said.

"What?" Noah asked.

"Not you. Fill me in. Our time is running out," he said, continuing toward the bridge. "I know you've got an idea of how to get us out of here. Just tell me what you need me to do."

"You're not going to like it, but here it is," Noah said.

He was right. Connor hated that idea. It was terrible and fraught with extreme risk, but it might just be crazy enough to get them out of this.

He made it to the bridge. Kincaid and Phendran followed him. The others went to their stations, while Seger, Naya, and Noxrey continued to main engineering.

"The power relays are already in place," Noah said, "you know, from when the ship was connected to the umbilical back home. I'm going to route power from the alien ship to our core."

Connor shook his head. "Noah, how are you going to manage the power flow? You'll overload the entire system."

"I can do it. You just need to prep the Infinity Drive."

Connor hastened to the command chair and accessed the I-Drive interface through the nav computer. He entered the set of coordinates that would take them away from the station and then frowned.

"The nav computer won't let me input coordinates because of insufficient power," Connor said, his voice tight with frustration.

"Okay, you'll need to disable the safety protocols."

Connor's eyes widened. "You can't be serious."

"You said we had to go. This is how we get out of here."

Connor gritted his teeth in frustration. Disabling safety protocols didn't just affect the power requirements but the stability of the I-Drive itself and half a dozen other systems designed to keep them alive. All his experience screamed that doing this was going to result in the destruction of their ship.

"Please trust me. This is the only way," Noah said.

Connor inhaled a deep breath and did as Noah asked. With the safety protocols disabled, the nav computer allowed the coordinates to be locked in.

An alert flashed from his SRA.

Execution of decommission protocols is imminent. Massive power surge is detected on the station.

"We're out of time, Noah!"

"Okay, executing."

The I-Drive began to draw power from the core, causing the

bridge lights to dim momentarily as energy redirected to the drive systems. Alerts appeared, warning that the current draw would drain the remaining core, but then they stopped and a message flashed about an unknown power source. More alerts appeared as the power spiked, but then whatever protocols Noah had put in place brought the flow under control.

Another warning appeared, this time from the I-Drive. Connor frowned.

"Why is the field so large?" Kincaid asked.

The I-Drive created a field that bent space and built a bubble around the ship. It was often referred to as taking them out of n-space, putting them in hyperspace. For some reason, the field being created was beyond the known acceptable limits for a ship the *Pathfinder's* size. Connor was about to abort, but if he did that, they'd be caught up in the Phantom decommission protocols for the station.

He lowered his hand and stared at the main holoscreen. "Hold on."

The I-Drive engaged.

Power spiked to the I-Drive. The surge was beyond anything their power core could've managed, even at full capacity. Seconds passed and the I-Drive disengaged.

Connor released the breath he'd been holding for what felt like minutes and read the message on the screen. "Successful transit."

Automated diagnostic protocols began analyzing the I-Drive, as well as the ship's systems.

"Where are we?" Kincaid asked.

"A light-hour from the station," Connor replied. The comlink to Noah had disconnected. He opened another comlink. "Noah, are you there?"

"Yes, we made it," Noah said, sounding relieved. "I'm on my way back to the ship. I'll explain everything when I get there."

The comlink severed.

Kincaid looked at him. "What about the station?"

The *Pathfinder* was inside the hangar of a massive alien ship. However, their sensors were receiving data from reconnaissance drones. Connor stared at the data feeds, and then a video feed came to prominence.

"It's gone. The station is completely gone."

Phendran looked at Connor. "Where has the station gone?"

Connor quickly brought up a recording from the recon drones. It showed a massive field surrounding the station, and then it disappeared out of n-space. "The Phantoms only visit n-space. Maybe their decommission protocols reclaimed the resources to whatever higher band of existence they reside in."

Phendran stared at the main holoscreen. "Then Salpheth is gone. Finally, my species can move on from the blight of his influence."

Salpheth had said that he was the reason the Aczar like Phendran had begun to rebel from established societal norms.

Connor carefully considered his response. "It's going to take time to figure out where you stand on what he did and how much his influence will continue to impact your species."

Phendran slowly nodded. "Yes, I believe in this you are correct. Especially after the shock of it gives way to acceptance."

"General," Kincaid said. He sat at the tactical workstation. "I'm reviewing the final moments of the station, and I think another ship escaped before it was destroyed."

"What have you got?"

"Nothing visual. It's just a noted spacial disturbance, but it's similar to a ship going into hyperspace. It's going away from the station."

Connor looked at the data and sighed. After all they'd gone through, Salpheth had escaped with a ship of his own.

Phendran looked at Connor. "Is it possible for us to trace where he went?"

"It's complicated. The data is partial and only gives an indication as to what direction he was heading. He might've done what we did, just going a short distance away. Then he'll get his bearings and go wherever he intends to go. We don't have the means to track him at this point. Our best option is to return home." Connor frowned and stared at the holoscreen. "Assuming that the alien ship still has power enough to get us there and we can figure out where New Earth is relative to our location."

Phendran nodded. "I've been working on that, and I do have options for you to consider."

Connor gave him a tired smile. "Let's regroup and figure out our current status," he said and stood up. "And I want to take a look at this alien ship Noah was so keen on taking with us."

"It's massive, sir," Kincaid said.

A video feed came to prominence on the main holoscreen. The colossal silhouette of the Phantom ship showed a vast ivory hull with a metallic sheen that was almost fluid. It glimmered with a subtle iridescence, catching the starlight in soft waves of silver.

What Kincaid *hadn't* mentioned was that this ship was also a treasure trove of knowledge and advancements beyond their dreams.

CHAPTER 34

OVER THE NEXT FOUR HOURS, Connor and the others reviewed what had happened to them. They were out of immediate danger—as in they weren't likely to be attacked by Salpheth—but there were still significant problems that must be addressed. When all they faced were large problems, that tended to become the norm. Mac insisted that they allow the autodoc to have a look at Connor and the others who had been on the station.

When Connor removed the EVA suit, his SRA transferred to his wrist on its own. Kincaid had been watching, and the CDF captain looked uncomfortable that Connor still wore it. But given how the SRA had saved his life, and was instrumental in escaping the space station, Connor was more receptive to having it around.

Connor sat in the medical center and allowed the autodoc to scan him for injuries. He had some bruises, for sure, but the autodoc warned him about increased neural activity in his brain. He'd been able to decipher the Phantom language, and he wondered if it had been implanted in him somehow from his encounter with them the first time. The autodoc would never be able to figure that out. It would require the doctors back home to help him work through it.

Connor glanced at the SRA, a band of flexible metal near his wrist computer. "I think it's time you and I had a talk."

The SRA took on a slight green glow.

Agreed.

The words appeared on his internal HUD via his neural implant.

"Are you able to speak aloud?"

"Yes, I have this ability. Communication can also occur without speaking."

The SRA's voice was similar to his own and also reminded him of his son.

Connor frowned. Communicate without speaking? "You mean like the Aczar do?"

"Precisely. It's a type of thought communication, but over time, I will be able to decipher your emotions as well. And in like manner, you will be able to understand my thoughts and emotions."

Connor bit his lip in a thoughtful frown. SRAs had emotions? The Aczar had explained that the SRAs were sentient, but Connor was still surprised by that sometimes.

"Don't take this the wrong way, but what if that makes me uncomfortable? Can you decipher my thoughts anytime you want?"

"Communication only works at both yours and my discretion."

It was gratifying to learn that he could shield his thoughts from the SRA, but he planned on speaking to Phendran about it.

"Okay. That's good. I need to address you as someone—you need a name. I can't remember the identifier you used before."

"KMTB74720103 is a translation from the identifier of the Aczar."

"What do you want to be called?" Connor asked.

"I could pick a name at random, but that seems insufficient, particularly when your species regards names as being of extreme import."

"They *are* important."

"So, it should be unique with no other like it, but that doesn't align with what I've observed."

Connor considered for a few moments. "It doesn't have to be a name no one else has ever used. I'm not the only person who was ever named Connor."

"Perhaps I should call myself Connor then?"

The question sounded genuine, and Connor suppressed a grin. "I think that would be confusing."

"I understand, but I'm at a loss as to which name to choose. Could you give me a name?"

Connor pressed his lips together, considering. "I could if you really want me to."

"I think I would like that, but if I thought the name wasn't appropriate, I could just choose another one."

Connor grinned. "Okay. Let me think. Hmm, this is tougher than I thought it would be." Memories of himself and Lenora picking out names for their children came to his mind, bringing a bittersweet pang to his chest. "You protected me from Salpheth," Connor said.

"Yes, he would've eliminated us both and would terminate our bond."

"I'm still learning about SRAs, but I've seen them protect the Aczar. Phendran described it as a partnership."

"Yes, this is an apt description. Does this help you pick a name for me?"

Connor nodded. "It does. How about Joshua?"

"What meaning does Joshua have for you?"

"I used to know someone who had that name. He was a good man. It's a very good name. There was also a famous teacher who tried to protect and help people, and I think it would be a good fit for you."

"Protect and help. A teacher. One who imparts knowledge. One who is capable of learning. I like this reference. I will be called Joshua from now on."

Connor looked down at his wrist. "Okay, Joshua, it is then."

A few seconds of silence passed.

"Thank you for naming me, Connor."

He smiled. "You're welcome."

Connor left the autodoc to find Mac waiting for him outside the room. "I'm fine."

Mac's eyebrows raised. "I'm surprised. What the heck are you made of?"

Connor chuckled. "I'll be sore later, but no broken bones or internal bleeding from brunt-force trauma."

Mac's gaze slid to Connor's SRA. "And that?"

"Saved my life, and yours," Connor replied.

"If you say so. The Phantoms used them to control those drones...robots... whatever the heck they were." He shook his head. "General, I'd like to go home now."

Connor gave him a solemn look. "Me, too, Mac. Me, too."

They went to the dining hall, and the others were already there, waiting for them. Silence descended, and Connor gave them a wave.

"Cleared for duty," Connor said.

"That's good," Noah said. "I was just telling them about the alien ship."

"Keep going because there's a lot I don't understand."

Noah nodded. "Okay. It actually makes much more sense after learning about your encounter—the whole decommission process. The ship had active repair capabilities, which fixed all the issues we had with the hull. I think it can do more, but I doubt you'd want to allow it access to our internal systems."

Connor shook his head. "It's okay to just take our gains and go back home. Does the alien ship have sufficient power to get us home?"

Noah smiled. "Yes. Even though the ship had been at the station for such a long time, the power core didn't suffer from the same degradation that ours would've. I can't wait to study it."

Rhodes cleared his throat. "So, you really think we can use the alien ship to get us home? Are you proposing that we fly it?"

"No, flying the alien ship isn't an option. The power is there. I've analyzed the data from the micro jump, so the protocols to manage the power flow will work even better than before. However, creating a field large enough to accommodate the alien ship would be a strain on the I-Drive."

"So, we limit the number of times we enter hyperspace."

Noah nodded. "Honestly, I say we only do it one more time."

"Only one?" Connor asked. "That doesn't give us any margin of error. What if we miss the mark or the I-Drive fails during our return trip?"

"I, I know. If the I-Drive fails, the same safety protocols will gracefully take us out of hyperspace."

Connor arched an eyebrow. "You had me disable the safety protocols."

"Only for that time. Naya and I were able to update the checks that the nav system does to account for the new power source."

Connor pursed his lips and nodded as he glanced at Naya for a second. "That's good. I was worried we'd have to make this journey without any safety protocols."

"Let me see if I understand the order of events here. Is that alright?" Rhodes asked.

Connor nodded.

"So, this space station—resupply station is what Salpheth called it—was to be decommissioned, and somehow that process was halted. The Phantoms arrived in their ships and left them in this semi-standby state that allowed anyone to access them? That doesn't seem right."

"Well," Noah said, "if I think about what would be available at a resupply station, I think it's safe to assume it would have some kind of repair functionality. This would be at the station, and a ship the size of the alien vessel was designed to travel vast distances from any kind of supply line. We do the same thing with our own ships but on a much smaller scale."

Rhodes bobbed his head slowly. "I can follow that logic and it makes sense, but why would they allow just anyone to access them?"

"The repair station was automated. It assesses and repairs. It has to be designed to service all kinds of ships. I tested it with one of our recon drones before bringing the ship there. When we went aboard the ship, I encountered the security measures you might expect, but not too extensively. I think the Phantoms might have been part of, or were building, a Confederation of their own. The alien ship's computer system knew I wasn't a Phantom, but it allowed me to use the ship's resources. In fact, that's what it asked me."

Rhodes frowned. "So, the Phantoms are benevolent toward strangers?"

"Maybe, but we can't be sure," Connor said, and looked at Noah. "We can't be sure that the alien ship had a crew aboard when it arrived at the station."

"Huh," Rhodes said. "You mean the ship returned to the station by some kind of automated process?"

Connor nodded.

"I hadn't considered that until you mentioned it earlier," Noah said.

"They were decommissioning the site. Maybe the ships that were docked were part of the process," Connor said.

"That's a lot of resources to be unaccounted for," Rhodes said.

"To us, absolutely, but to them? Maybe not," Connor replied.

"The ship does have a nav system, and it's extensive," Noah said and then shook his head. "I need to get my mouth under control. They're extensive for a particular region of space. Between their records, observations from our sensors, and Phendran's knowledge, I have a good idea of where we are and how to get back home."

The others in the dining hall perked up at this, and Connor enjoyed seeing them hopeful, but they were guarded as well. It had been a very long time.

"We need to be careful," Connor said. "How close to home could you get us?"

"Definitely within subspace communications range," Noah replied.

Rhodes grinned and shared a look with his daughter. "Outstanding. That would put us within about twenty light-years from New Earth."

Noah nodded and regarded Connor for a long moment. "Yes, but I think we can do better than that. We *need* to do better than that."

Rhodes frowned and looked at Connor. "I feel like I'm missing something."

"We might only have one last use of the I-Drive, so we need to get as close to New Earth as possible. However, since we're flying in the belly of an alien ship, there are defenses in place to protect against someone from showing up unannounced."

Rhodes sighed, his shoulders slumping a little. "What about the alien ship? Surely it has something like the Infinity Drive. I know you said we couldn't fly it, but why not?"

Noah blew out a breath. "The alien ship does have a means of propulsion that includes FTL, but I have no idea how it works. We're better off using what we know."

Rhodes sighed, conceding the point.

Connor looked at the others. "So here we are again."

Some of the others grinned nervously.

"I say we go for it. Let's go home," Kincaid said.

Seger nodded. "Yes."

The others offered their affirmation in support of finally going home, except for the Aczar. Phendran and the others remained quiet as they observed the meeting.

Connor looked at them. "I intend to keep my promise to all of you."

"Thank you, General Gates," Phendran replied.

Noxrey, Kholva, and Vorix echoed the sentiment.

Connor stood. "Noah, Kincaid, Rhodes, and Phendran, please come with me to the bridge. Everyone else, please return to your stations. And if anyone would like to offer any prayers for our safe return home, have at it. We need all the help we can get."

"One minute," Seger said. "Gather around everyone."

They did, and Connor could feel the bond they'd forged on this voyage. He gestured for Phendran and the others to join them while Seger led them in prayer.

They left the dining hall and were soon on the bridge.

Noah sat next to Connor and arched an eyebrow. "You know, we could claim salvage rights to the alien ship." Connor stared at him. "All of us, I mean. Not just me."

Connor shook his head. "Glad you're focused on the important things."

"It's a tremendous opportunity," Noah said and grinned.

They were thousands of light-years from home. None of them had forgotten that, but maybe it was because they'd survived so many trials that they had been forged anew. What had been impossible for them to even consider was now not only possible but would change everything back home.

Noah stared at him, considering. "Come on, Connor. Enjoy the moment."

"I was thinking about Salpheth," he replied. "He knows about us. Maybe not where we are exactly, but I wonder how much trouble he's going to cause us in the future."

Noah frowned, looking concerned for a second. "I understand, but we can't change what happened. I also think he'll focus his attention on others first."

Salpheth was definitely the type to seek revenge. Connor had known that after the first time they'd spoken. Salpheth would focus on going after those who were responsible for leaving him behind. He wondered what the Phantoms would do about it. Would Salpheth go after them directly, or would he choose subterfuge instead, drawing the Phantoms out, using their interest in Humanity as a lure?

"It's a problem for another day," Connor said, and gave his friend a sidelong look. "What was it you called that? A future-Noah problem?"

Noah grinned with a nod.

"Yeah, so I guess it's a future problem for us to consider, as well as the Vemus."

"Okay, Connor, you need to stop. We haven't even gotten home yet, and you're already thinking about tomorrow's problems."

"I can't help it. It's how my brain works."

"Well, how about crafting a message so the CDF doesn't open fire on us when we reach New Earth?" Noah said.

"Fine," Connor said and recorded a message to broadcast when they arrived home. *When,* not if.

Kincaid cleared his throat. "Can you put the flight plan on the main holoscreen? I'd like to see it."

"Yeah, one minute," Noah said and finished what he was doing in the nav system. "There it is."

A large star map appeared on the main holoscreen. On one side was an icon that represented the *Pathfinder,* and on the other side of the holoscreen was the New Earth star system.

"This will be a nonstop journey," Connor said.

Kincaid stared at the holoscreen. "You're going to put us that close to New Earth? What about the defense platforms and the fleet patrols?"

"I thought of putting us near the lunar shipyards, but that would trigger most of the automated defenses in the region," Noah said.

"I wish I had your confidence," Kincaid said.

"Are the coordinates locked in?" Connor asked.

"Yes, General Gates," Noah replied.

Connor sent an alert to the rest of the ship, informing them that they were about to leave. Then he looked at Noah. "Take us home."

"Engaging the I-Drive," Noah said.

Using the experimental protocols that had taken them thousands of light-years from home, they were finally on the journey back. The weight of responsibility pressed on Connor's shoulders as the lives of everyone aboard hung in the balance of this one desperate attempt to return to the world they'd feared they might never see again.

"We're in hyperspace," Noah confirmed. "Power draw is stable."

Noah had explained to him how he'd routed power from the alien ship to the *Pathfinder*. The alien ship had multiple power cores, and Noah thought they were using a reserve core to draw power from.

When the event that caused the *Pathfinder* to leave New Earth occurred, they'd traveled over five thousand light-years. It hadn't happened all at once but in bursts before they were able to stop the process. The event occurred during a major computing core upgrade, and the entire system had been thrown into a loop that would've repeated until the critical systems of the ship were no longer operational.

They were pushing the Infinity Drive well beyond the design specifications for maintaining the field around the ship. In theory, they had a better than average chance of making it home in one shot. Connor preferred to make the journey in smaller increments, but the *Pathfinder* couldn't survive it. The critical systems were limping along as it was. This was their all or nothing moment.

Kincaid blew out a breath and looked away from the main holoscreen. "We have ten hours of this. It didn't feel like ten hours to get all the way out here."

"We need to accommodate the field around the alien ship, which means we have to travel slower," Noah replied.

Kincaid rolled his eyes and looked at Connor. "Travel slower, he says."

Noah blinked for a second and then chuckled.

Connor opened a broadcast comlink to the others. "We're in hyperspace. I-Drive is stable. Remain at your stations for now."

He closed the comlink.

They were strapped into their chairs, and all of them watched the main holoscreen. Connor waited an hour of consistent performance before he gave the all-clear for people to leave their stations.

Kincaid stood. "I'm going to take a walk, General."

"I'll be here," Connor replied.

Kincaid left the bridge.

Phendran watched the various data feeds on the holoscreen.

Noah glanced over at him. "You're not going to leave the bridge, are you?"

Connor shook his head. "Neither are you."

Noah smiled. "I know. I feel like if I'm here and something goes wrong, this is the best place for me to be so I can help."

"We're both waiting for the other shoe to drop."

Noah was quiet for a few moments. "We're stable now. I could increase our velocity, and if the system becomes unstable, I could back it off."

"I like consistency. If we're stable at this speed, why alter it at all?"

Noah leaned over to Connor. "Because this whole thing is built from a patchwork of efforts. We don't know if the alien power core will hold out. I think it will, but there's no way for me to know for sure. What if something goes wrong?"

"I understand the concern, but sometimes it's not worth the risk. I think we should ride this out."

Noah inhaled a breath and leaned back in his chair. "Okay."

"But," Connor said, and Noah looked at him, "can you have an emergency protocol in place, just in case?"

He frowned. "What do you mean?"

"If the system starts to degrade, could we increase our velocity before the safety protocols take us out of hyperspace?"

"You want me to maximize our speed before we stop?"

Connor nodded.

"And I thought *I* was playing fast and loose with this."

"You know how it goes. Better to not need it and have it than the alternative."

Noah nodded. "Let me see what I can put together."

Connor watched Noah as he worked. After about fifteen minutes, he had a solution.

"This should work. I hope we never have to use it," Noah said.

A klaxon alarm sounded, and multiple alerts appeared on the main holoscreen. The I-Drive was becoming unstable.

"We're losing drive coils. They're failing—just giving out," Noah said.

"How much time do we have?"

Noah peered at his holoscreen for a second. "Not enough."

"You've got to do it."

More alarms appeared on the screen, which triggered alarms throughout the ship, warning the passengers to return to their stations.

Noah brought up the emergency procedure they had just hoped they wouldn't have to use. "Execute."

A blinding surge of energy erupted from the alien power core, racing through the ship's systems and flooding into the I-Drive with a force that made the deck plates vibrate beneath their feet. Power fluctuated throughout the ship, and more alerts appeared from the damage-control system. I-Drive failure was imminent.

Connor gritted his teeth, holding on to the armrests of his chair.

Then, the power cut off from the bridge. Everything went dark for a brief moment before emergency lighting came on, and the main holoscreen blanked out before coming back on.

"I-Drive is offline," Noah said.

Connor stared at his holoscreen. "We're on emergency power."

That wasn't good because emergency power wasn't going to last them very long.

"The system overloaded."

"Yeah, but where are we?" Connor asked.

Noah read the data on his holoscreen and shook his head. "I don't know."

"What about the power from the alien ship?"

"The link was cut off during the overload. I can probably re-establish the link, but that'll require a visual inspection to make sure there was no damage," Noah replied.

Connor navigated the holo-interface and brought up the communications system. "We've got subspace," he said and frowned.

A comlink established.

"Unknown alien ship. You are in protected space. Please respond to this communication, or I will be forced to consider your intentions hostile. I repeat. This is Colonel James Rush from the Colonial Defense Force ship *Valkyrie.*"

Connor accepted the comlink. "This is General Connor Gates, transmitting my authentication using CDF encrypted protocols."

Connor sent the data packet. "Please confirm your receipt of the package."

There was a long pause as they waited for a reply.

"I repeat," Connor said and stated his name. "We're aboard the *Pathfinder* and have commandeered the alien ship that is on your sensors. Scans will show a hangar bay on mid ship with access available on both the port and starboard sides."

"Hold while we confirm," Colonel Rush said.

Connor could imagine the flurry of activity that was happening on the bridge of the *Valkyrie*.

"Colonel Rush, we're experiencing power issues, and I don't know how long this comlink will last. On board our ship are survivors from the Whitehall R&D Facility. I'm going to send you a list of people who are here with me."

Colonel Rush cleared his throat. "General Gates, it's good to hear your voice, but you have to realize the enormity of this. We have protocols to follow. Do you realize where you are?"

Connor blew out a breath. "As a matter of fact, we're not sure. We were traveling back to New Earth, but our I-Drive failed. Can you tell us where we are?"

"Voice identity confirmed. Excellent," Colonel Rush said. "Okay, General, the *Valkyrie* is ready to render assistance. As for where you are, let me show you."

A video feed was added to the comlink, showing them a high resolution of the alien ship. Then, the camera feed pivoted away from them, and Connor saw a distant view of a bright blue planet —New Earth, with its surrounding rings.

The stunning view of their home nearly stole the breath from his lungs.

Connor's throat became thick with emotion, and he leaned back in his seat.

"Welcome home, General Gates. Sending an emergency response team to you now," Colonel Rush said.

Connor cleared his throat. "Thank you, Colonel," he said, his voice thick with emotion.

"A lot of people are going to be happy to hear of your return. We've been searching for you…"

Colonel Rush kept talking, and Connor could barely keep up. It was as if all the emotion he'd kept locked inside the walls of his heart had burst forth with the knowledge that they were finally home. They'd made it, but their worries had gnawed away at them —a ship that was barely holding together, experimental technology they were just beginning to understand, and a dangerous alien prisoner. Maybe he should've taken Salpheth out when he'd had the chance. How long could Salpheth have survived if he'd just left him in the deep dark, far away from any star system?

Connor heaved a sigh, releasing a whole lot of the tension he'd been carrying.

Noah smiled, his eyes brimming with tears. He quickly wiped them away and exhaled a long breath.

Connor looked at him. "We did it. All of us."

"General," Colonel Rush said, "I've just relayed a message back to COMCENT. Not that this will come as a surprise to you, but I'm to get you back to the planet ASAP. We're figuring out what to do with an alien ship. Sit tight and wait for the rescue."

"Colonel Rush, this is Noah Barker. The alien ship's engines are offline, and we haven't used them."

"We'll need several space tugs to handle a ship this size," Connor replied.

"Understood. If you don't mind, I'll stay on the comlink until the away team makes it to the ship."

Connor smiled. "Thank you, Colonel."

"There will be hot meals waiting for you. Best food in the fleet."

"Looking forward to it."

CHAPTER 35

THEIR TIME on the *Valkyrie* went by so quickly that it seemed that no sooner had they arrived than they were being taken to New Earth. Quarantine protocols were followed, and they also went through decontamination protocols. Rhodes was annoyed that they weren't allowed to contact anyone on New Earth and that news of their return was being delayed. Connor assured him it was just until they could be debriefed and that their families would be notified. Surprisingly—or maybe not—Rhodes accepted Connor's explanation with a level of understanding and respect that simply hadn't been there before this whole thing happened.

"I guess a few more hours won't make much of a difference," Rhodes said.

Connor insisted that Phendran and the other Aczar stay with them, at least until they arrived on New Earth.

"You'll be treated as an ambassador for the Aczar. You won't be locked away or anything like that. You will have a security detail assigned to you. It'll be someone who will help you, and they're going to watch you," Connor said.

"This is acceptable and expected," Phendran replied.

"I know you're concerned about returning to Ichlos. I assure you I'll do everything in my power to make that happen. It's going to take time, though."

Noah chuckled, and Phendran looked at him. "You have no idea how persistent Connor can be. He'll get you home."

Being among so many people, with the occasional Ovarrow thrown into the mix, was enough of a reminder to Phendran and the other Aczar that they were far from home. They'd never encountered another species before.

"I'm beginning to understand how you felt while on Ichlos," Phendran said.

Connor nodded. "This is new. *You're* new, so there will be a lot of curiosity, but don't forget, we've encountered other alien species before. I think you'll find that we can be welcoming while you're with us. You'll be meeting with a team that specializes in diplomacy, but you'll always be able to contact me."

Phendran regarded him for a moment. "You must be anxious to return to your family."

Connor smiled. "I am."

"He's not the only one," Rhodes said. "After a thorough debriefing."

Connor chuckled. "Your family will be there, Glen. The CDF isn't heartless."

The transport shuttle flew out of the *Valkyries'* hangar. It would be a short trip to the planet. They were going to the CDF base at Sanctuary.

Connor looked at the others on the shuttle. They'd had a CDF squad assigned to escort them, but it was mainly just the survivors. They'd been given a change of clothes, dark blue ship suits that were common on warships. They'd also had time to get cleaned up and have a meal. Colonel Rush was right; it was some of the best food he'd had in a very long time.

Kincaid and Cassidy were speaking quietly together. They

smiled a lot more now. Rhodes watched them with a pensive expression. Then he looked at Connor and shrugged.

Seger blew out a breath. "I'm looking forward to the break."

Connor arched an eyebrow. "You think you're getting a break, Sergeant?"

Seger grinned. "Just need a few minutes and then I'll be right as rain, General."

Connor laughed. "You've earned it. I haven't forgotten about our conversation. If you want to pursue other opportunities in the CDF, particularly in engineering, all you have to do is let me know."

"Thank you, sir. I will," Seger replied.

Naya rolled her eyes. "As if you need to even consider it," she said and looked at Connor. "He already told me he was going to take you up on that offer."

Seger gave her a sidelong glance. "Is there anything else you'd like to decide for me?"

Naya smiled. "I have a list."

Seger laughed, and some of the others joined in.

"You asked for that," Connor said.

Seger shrugged. "What can I say? Naya wouldn't know what to do without me."

"Oh please, you keep following me around like a lost puppy."

It was interesting watching the others. Some of them lapsed into reflective silences, each contemplating their own thoughts. They all looked exhausted, and Connor wasn't immune to that himself.

Mac sat across from Connor and gave him a knowing look. "I'm going on vacation as soon as we're done."

"You don't want to know if you got hazard pay or anything else?" Connor asked.

Mac frowned and then shook his head. "Sheesh. Hazard pay? Heh."

Noah looked up from his personal holoscreen. "Wait? We're not getting paid for this? I would've thought a bonus would be appropriate. Maybe even priority parking or a free meal?"

Connor smiled. "You're not thinking big enough."

Noah pressed his lips together. "You're right. Swimming pools all around. Personal shuttle service, and assurances that we'll be able to study the alien ship."

Connor shook his head. "Swimming pools? Really?"

Noah shrugged. "Not all of us live by a lake. I was just thinking about it. Can't you tell I'm giddy to be home?"

"Only you would use that word," Connor said and then looked at the others.

They all returned to side conversations or just closed their eyes for a little while until the shuttle reached their destination.

Rhodes regarded Connor for a long moment. "I've heard about this with you."

Connor frowned. "What do you mean?"

"You build teams. It doesn't matter who's with you; you find a way to make it all work together. This is the first time I've seen it for myself."

Connor chuckled. "Do I live up to the legend?"

Rhodes shook his head. "No, General Gates. The legend doesn't even come close. I know we had our differences when this whole thing started, but I'm glad I decided to listen to you rather than trying to fight you on things."

"I'm glad you did, too."

The pilot announced that they were almost to the LZ.

Noah looked at Connor. "I thought I'd be more tired than this."

"You are. It's all the coffee you drank. You're going to crash, and after you wake up you'll realize just how exhausted you really are."

"There are worse things. At least we'll be home," Noah replied.

The shuttle landed, and the side doors opened. Connor and the others rose from their seats and descended the loading ramp,

Connor pausing to inhale a deep breath of fresh air. The sun shined brightly overhead, and even though it was the height of the day, he could still see New Earth's rings stretched across the horizon.

The air was warm, and all of them stopped a short distance from the shuttle. Environmental recordings on a ship could only do so much to create the illusion of being on a planet. Connor watched as birds flew in the distance and a breeze made the nearby trees sway a little.

They were ushered into a rover and brought to one of the nearby buildings. Over the next few hours, CDF medical doctors gave them a thorough examination. They'd been briefed that the Aczar were with them, and Phendran allowed the doctors to give them a cursory examination. He assured them that he carried no foreign viruses or contagions that would be detrimental to them or New Earth.

Then the debriefing meetings began. Connor could've found a way to send word to Lenora, but he knew she'd already been notified. However, that didn't stop Noah from attempting to send a message to his wife, but it was blocked.

"Security lockdown. The building is a blackout site," Noah said.

Connor chuckled. "I'm surprised you hadn't figured that out before you tried. They're on their way here."

"No, I know that. I just wanted to... you know."

Connor nodded. "Yeah, I definitely know."

A few minutes later, they were escorted away from the others. Both Connor and Noah were brought into a room with a small conference table in it. Across the room a side door opened, and General Nathan Hayes walked in.

He was of average height, trim in build, and experienced in leadership, having led the CDF for a long time. Nathan could balance the rigors of command while working with the colonial government. Connor remembered recruiting him when the CDF was just getting started. He'd watched him grow in his leadership capabilities, and he was a friend. He was also Connor's superior officer, and Connor saluted him.

Nathan regarded the two of them for a long moment. "You two are a sight for sore eyes, let me tell you."

"It's good to see you, Nathan," Connor said.

"You've come to debrief us personally?" Noah asked.

"Nothing but the best for you, but before we get to all that... Noah, Kara is already here. Go out that door, and Sergeant Donnelly will take you to her. We'll catch up in a little while."

Noah didn't quite run out of the room, but he didn't take his time either.

Connor smiled, watching him go.

"Lenora is on her way as well," Nathan said. He looked as if he was about to say more but gestured for them to sit instead.

Connor sat, and a groan escaped his lips as he did.

Nathan chuckled. "I know you're tired."

"Nah, I'm fine."

He rolled his eyes. "Yeah, right. I looked at some of the *Pathfinder's* logs while you were en route here."

Connor had kept a log of events shortly after he'd realized a rescue wasn't going to happen anytime soon. He also encouraged other people to do the same.

"So, I can skip the debrief, then?" Connor asked.

Nathan grinned. "The logs will help, but that's only half the story."

"There are people who were unaccounted for when the event took place," Connor began.

"Lives were lost," Nathan confirmed, his tone softening with regret.

Connor knew it but had hoped that perhaps he'd been wrong. "It took us a while to figure out what happened."

Nathan sighed. "We're still trying to figure out what happened. The investigation team was running in circles until Noah's wife basically took over. Not just her, but a certain general's wife and daughter got involved as well."

Connor smiled a little. "I bet."

"Look, there will be time to mourn the lost."

"But we need to be concerned about figuring out what happened. I can shed some light on it, and Noah can shine even more light on the technical stuff," Connor said. He poured himself some water from a pitcher and drank. "We did it. Noah was on the right path to make a major breakthrough with the Infinity Drive. He said he'd already done it but couldn't track the probes. It never occurred to him that the probes had traveled beyond subspace comms range. We traveled over five thousand light-years in under an hour. Not only that, but we traveled through the planet. That's why it took us so long to figure out where we were."

Nathan leaned back in the chair and bobbed his head once. "We knew it had something to do with the I-Drive, but we hadn't considered that you actually went through the planet. We've been searching in the wrong direction."

"We thought we might've destroyed the planet. The I-drive was never meant to be used while planet-side."

Nathan considered that for a moment and then slowly shook his head. "How did it happen?"

Connor explained to Nathan what they'd discovered, how the Phantoms had somehow interfered with their computer upgrade, which caused a cascade of events. Now that they were back, they could access the rest of the data at the R&D facility and piece together a complete picture.

"I don't like the thought of them monitoring us, despite our security precautions," Nathan said.

"I don't either, but I think it was for our protection," Connor said.

He told Nathan about Salpheth, the Aczar, and everything else that happened. He told him as much as he could remember, but it was a preliminary report at best.

Nathan shook his head. "Once again you find yourself in the middle of…I don't even know what to call it. A breakthrough doesn't quite cover it. First Contact doesn't encapsulate it either. Then there's Salpheth, some kind of rogue Phantom they abandoned."

"He knew about the Vemus," Connor said, his voice dropping to a grave tone that underscored the threat this knowledge represented.

Nathan frowned, looking concerned.

"He knew more about them than he let on," Connor continued.

Nathan pressed his lips together for a second. "What do you mean?"

"I recorded all our sessions, even when we went to the station. The analysts can pick it apart. Salpheth tried to recruit us. He probably knew it wouldn't work, but that didn't stop him from trying. We have to figure out how much of what he told me was the truth and how much was misdirection. I haven't gone back to review the sessions."

"If only the Phantoms were here to answer the question for us," Nathan said.

"You have no idea how many times I've thought the same thing. Something significant happened to them at the time they left Salpheth behind on Ichlos." Connor frowned. "No, it would be before Ichlos. Phendran can help clarify. The Aczar journeyed to Ichlos with Salpheth and then abandoned space travel. But going back to the Phantoms, maybe they had their own breakthrough. I don't know. For beings of light, they sure do cast a lot of shadows."

"How poetic," Nathan said.

"That's me. I'm refined."

A soft chuckle bubbled up from Nathan's chest.

"I promised Phendran we would take them home," Connor said with quiet resolve. "It's a debt we owe them for their help."

Nathan's eyebrows raised. "I understand that, but their planet is over five thousand light-years away?"

"Well, we already did it once."

"You know that will take time. We'll need to fully understand the experimental protocols for the I-Drive and what the effects are on the drive itself. I'm not saying it's not possible; I'm saying that it's going to take time," Nathan said and frowned. "Look at me. I'm saying these things like you don't already know them."

Connor smiled. "I know."

Nathan glanced at Connor's wrist. "Is that it?"

Connor lifted his arm. "This is Joshua."

His SRA shifted on his arm and expanded to form a nondescript humanoid head. "Greetings, General Hayes."

Nathan's mouth hung open for a moment, and he looked at Connor. "You named it?"

"I think it's a 'him.' I named him."

Nathan considered this for a second and then looked at the SRA. "Hello, Joshua," he said and gave Connor a worried look. "I know you're one to push the envelope, but this concerns me."

"I assure you, General Hayes, that I intend to cooperate in any way that I can to put your concerns to rest," Joshua said.

Nathan bit his lip for a moment, then leaned forward a little. "I appreciate that, but this is quite complicated. Connor, you have to know how this complicates things."

He nodded. "I do. Joshua, it's complicated because of my security access and that I'm part of the senior leadership in the CDF. I have clearance, and you don't."

"How do I get clearance?" Joshua asked.

Nathan blinked, and Connor smiled a little, raising his eyebrows. "I see this is even more complicated than I originally thought." Nathan pressed his lips together. "Could you remove it if you wanted to?"

Connor glanced at his SRA, and it came off his wrist and seemed to gather on the table.

Nathan regarded him for a moment, his eyes narrowed with cautious scrutiny. "Do you feel any different?"

"No."

Nathan narrowed his gaze.

"It was a temporary arrangement with Phendran so we could interface with their technology. But then Joshua decided to stay with me. At the time, we didn't communicate much. It's similar to the training of one of our own AIs, but this is different. The Aczar believe their SRAs have true sentience. They are paired at a young age and the relationship or bond increases as they grow. However, both parties can choose to separate if they want."

Nathan glanced at Joshua for a few moments.

"He saved my life, Nathan. Don't let this current form fool you."

"I thought you were trying to set me at ease."

Connor snorted. "It's the truth as I understand it. Salpheth was both troubled and intrigued by the fact that an SRA was able to sever its bond with an Aczar and form a new one with another species. You should've seen it. You *will* see it. Phendran and the others all have SRAs. It's part of their clothing. Their SRAs helped them adapt to our atmosphere. I've never seen anything like it. I think the Aczar have a lot to offer and should be brought into the Confederation."

Nathan rubbed his eyebrow for a second. "Okay, I understand. You know how this is going to go."

"They'll want to study Joshua and make sure he's not manipulating me. I've told him."

Joshua looked up at Nathan. "I have nothing to hide. I protect and help those I have a connection with; however I'm not what you'd consider a slave. I have autonomy."

"Then you could just as easily hurt the person you say you're protecting," Nathan replied.

Joshua was quiet for a moment. "This is possible. Trust will take time to establish. Education will be the key to understanding and building a solid foundation."

Nathan slowly bobbed his head. "What happens to you if your host dies?"

"Depends on the bond. If it is harmonious, I could merge with another SRA that has paired with a descendant, but quite often, our existence as we know it ceases."

"So, you die," Nathan said.

"We revert to a non-bonded state and can choose to join with another."

"What if there is no one else?" Nathan asked.

"Then our substance will break down and become non-functional."

"They die," Connor said.

Nathan looked away for a moment. "Thank you for answering my questions, Joshua."

A metallic strand came from the SRA and went back to Connor's arm.

"That's going to take some getting used to," Nathan said.

"The Phantoms used a similar technology," Connor said.

"We're not going to figure this all out here, but this is going to require thorough study. Not to mention that alien ship you brought back with you."

"Noah described it as a 'treasure trove of information,'" Connor said.

"Yes, but will the Phantoms allow us to keep it?"

Connor frowned. He hadn't considered that and said so.

"Well, I guess we'll deal with that as well," Nathan said and looked at Connor for a few moments. "I'm trying to think of the implications of all these developments, and honestly, I'm having trouble keeping up. The Phantoms warned us to stop exploring and build ourselves up. But with this," he said, lifting his hand up for a moment, "we might not have much of a choice."

"We'll find a way through it. The more we learn, the better prepared we can be."

Nathan arched an eyebrow. "You want to go after Salpheth."

Connor pursed his lips for a second. "I feel responsible for his release. He's dangerous."

"And you want to take the Aczar back to their planet and be part of the diplomatic mission."

"I hadn't thought that far, to be honest."

Nathan regarded him for a long moment, considering. "Maybe it's time to let others bear the burden."

"What do you mean?"

"We've all sacrificed for the colony, for Old Earth, and now with the Confederation becoming our future. What I'm saying is that you don't need to be at the forefront of what comes next."

"I didn't seek this out, Nathan."

He smiled a little. "I know that. And yet, I've watched circumstances pull you back in. I'm here to tell you that it doesn't have to be you. What if I told you that maybe you're worth more here at home than out there," he said, gesturing above them. "I'm serious, Connor. I can see the look in your eye, and I know that look. It's the kind that makes you step forward, and you might feel like you don't have a choice. I'm telling you that you do."

This wasn't the first time they'd had this conversation, and it echoed some of the conversations Connor had had with Lenora over the years. "So, what do you think I should do?"

Nathan smiled. "After you get settled, reunite with Lenora and your family. Then assign the task of going after Salpheth, diplomatic relations with Aczar, and probably a host of other things that I can't think of on the spot... but assign those tasks to others. They're ready to take on the burden. Our roles are to step back and guide. It's time for the torch to be passed."

Connor crossed his arms. "I've tried. If you recall, I didn't want to go back to Old Earth."

Nathan waved away the comment. "It's all in the past. No need to revisit all that. You've fought more battles than all of us, but you have other significant talents that sometimes get overlooked—pushing the I-Drive R&D project with Noah, knowing it was worth pursuing, training people, whether they're soldiers, officers, or even civilians. You've got a knack for spotting the areas where we fall short. That's going to be very important where the Confederation is concerned."

Connor blew out a breath. "I don't want to leave New Earth," he said and paused for a moment. "You know, Lenora and I talked about having more kids."

Nathan's eye twitched, and the edges of his lips lifted.

Connor's gaze narrowed. "Seriously?"

Nathan sighed, looking amused, but there was a weight to it that Connor didn't understand. "Yes, I was trying to avoid it, but I only just learned about it myself. Congratulations, Connor, you're going to be a father again."

A surge of emotion brought a wide smile to his face, and Connor felt his eyes tighten a little. He looked away from his friend. "Lenora is on her way?" he asked, ready to stand up.

"She's en route. She'll be here soon," Nathan replied.

Connor swallowed hard and nodded. "So that's why you wanted to talk about this. Next steps and all that."

Nathan's expression sobered. "There's more."

Connor didn't like the solemn expression on his face. "What is it?"

"Ethan and Cynergy. They had another encounter with the

Vemus. Hybrids aren't as immune from them as we thought," Nathan began and told Connor what happened to Ethan.

Connor remembered their last encounter with a Vemus Alpha, and the lasting effects were something that was of great concern.

"They were brought back home in stasis, and the doctors were able to separate them. Ethan has come out of it but not Cynergy. She became worse. The doctors had no choice but to keep her in stasis while they worked on the problem," Nathan said.

Connor took a few moments to absorb what he'd been told. "What about the hybrid reversal treatment?"

"It's on the table, but they don't know whether it will work on Cynergy. Ethan is against trying it."

"I bet he wants to exhaust all the options."

"Yes, but he thinks the best way to help her is to find more Vemus."

Connor blinked, unable to follow the logic.

"That was my reaction as well. It doesn't make sense to me. I think he needs time."

Connor doubted it. He knew his son. It would take a lot for him to change his mind. They couldn't force treatment on Cynergy, especially if they didn't know whether it would save her life.

"Thanks for telling me."

Nathan sighed. "I wish I didn't have to. Ethan is already pushing to return to his command."

"Yeah, he'll have to wait."

"It gets complicated where Ethan is concerned, and these events don't help."

"No, they don't. Anyone can become compromised. Ethan believes that his unique insights and that of the other hybrids will help us ultimately defeat the Vemus. I agree with him, but I don't know what it will cost."

Nathan was quiet for a few moments. "There are valid arguments all around. It's another thing we're not going to figure out here."

"There is a lot of that happening."

Nathan chuckled. "Policies are changing, and that will affect our strategy for exploration and a whole bunch of other things. I'm glad *I* don't have to make the decision. You and I will have input, but these things are beyond the scope of just the CDF."

"And yet another reason to stay on New Earth and influence those policies."

"You could always retire."

"I think your wife would kill me."

Nathan chuckled. "Probably."

"You know we had the mindset that if we made certain sacrifices, we would be sparing future generations. That was okay while we were restricted to our own star system. This might change due to the enormity of…" Connor's voice trailed off.

"The galaxy? This breakthrough with the I-Drive certainly expands where we can go."

Connor blew out a breath and stood. "You know what? I'm not going to worry about this right now."

Nathan frowned and stood. "Where are you going?"

"Lenora is here," Connor said.

"How did you know?"

Connor laughed. "I know a thing or two about getting around lockdowns."

Nathan arched an eyebrow.

"Plus, I heard her," Connor said and headed for the door.

Nathan grinned. "Get out of here."

CHAPTER 36

CONNOR LEFT the conference room and spotted Lenora walking down the corridor toward him, his heart leaping in his chest at the sight of her familiar silhouette. When she saw him, she ran past her CDF escorts and leaped into his arms with a jubilant shout.

They held each other for a few moments, and one of the soldiers cleared his throat.

"General Gates, there is a room right here you can use if you want privacy."

Connor glanced at the room and then shook his head. "I'm going outside."

"Yes, General."

Lenora stared at him as if she didn't trust her eyes, her long auburn hair catching the light as she shook her head in disbelief, and Connor just enjoyed the moment because he felt the same.

"Come on, let's take a walk," Connor said.

The CDF soldiers followed behind them, giving them plenty of space for a private conversation as they left the building and walked along the sidewalk.

Lenora wiped her eyes and shook her head. "Every single time," she said, wiping away her tears.

Her gaze—a mixture of relief, love, and the lingering fear that he might disappear again—sent a knife twisting right into his chest, and he leaned toward her. "I'm sorry, Lenora."

She shook her head, looking away from him for a few seconds. "If you'd taken any longer, I was going to have to come looking for you."

He chuckled.

Lenora blew out a breath and fell into his arms, pressing her face into his chest. "I know it's not your fault." Her voice cracked a little. "I'm just so happy you're home."

Connor swallowed hard. "Me, too."

They walked, and Lenora told him about Ethan and Cynergy, who'd been brought back to New Earth a few days before.

"I hate seeing her like that," Lenora said. "She deserves better than to be a victim of the Vemus."

"I hope they can figure out a way to help her."

Lenora held his arm while they walked. Connor didn't think she'd let him go more than a few feet from her, not that he wanted to.

"I'm not going anywhere, Lenora."

"You'd better not because we need you here. Didn't you say you wanted to catch up with Diaz?" She smiled.

Connor laughed. His friend Diaz had a veritable village of children and grandchildren now.

"I hear we're already making some headway with that," Connor said.

Lenora stared at him for a second and rolled her eyes a little. "Nathan."

"He's very happy for us. He basically said that we should let the next generation take all the risks now."

Lenora arched an eyebrow. "I think he missed that by at least one generation. What happens now?"

"We go see Ethan."

"Lauren is there, too. They...have strong opinions about how best to help Cynergy."

His daughter had long been a proponent of giving hybrids the option to be free of the Vemus once and for all. It was an option that many of the hybrid population had pursued, but not all of them. It was part of who they were.

"We're family. We'll figure this out."

"I've been thinking," Lenora said. "If we started working together, the next time something like this happened, at least we'd be in it together. What do you think?"

At first he was amused by her comment, but there was an underlying fear that he didn't like to see in his wife. Thinking about his voyage on the *Pathfinder,* he was glad Lenora hadn't been there. He'd never want to put her life in danger like that. He'd protect her from that for as long as he lived.

"I'd like that," Connor said.

Lenora's eyes widened. "Noah and Kara found a way to make it work. Why can't we?"

"You make it sound so easy, but we work in completely different fields."

"I didn't say it would be easy, but most of the time, the best things never are."

They headed for the medical center where Ethan and Cynergy were being treated. The other surviving hybrids were being held under observation somewhere else. Connor sent a quick message to Nathan, informing him where he was going. He had to be debriefed just like the others, but given the circumstances, some leniency was warranted.

They went through a security checkpoint. Connor was out of uniform in a generic blue ship suit, and the soldiers on duty straightened themselves when they realized who he was. They walked down a few corridors, entering the secure wing, and his daughter rounded the corner with a determined stride. Her eyes widened for a moment, and she rushed forward.

"Lauren," Connor said, hugging his daughter. She clung to him in a way that reminded him of the little girl he'd carried to bed. Sometimes, he saw hints of the child she'd been in the accomplished woman she was now.

"Dad," she said, giving him an appraising look. "You look like you've lost weight. I knew there wasn't enough food on that ship when you…"

Connor smiled. "I'm fine. I'll eat everything you put in front of me, but first, tell me about them." He lifted his chin to the nearby room where Ethan and Cynergy were.

Lauren glanced at Lenora.

"I told him some things already," Lenora said.

Lauren nodded and licked her lips for a second. "High level. Their encounter with the Vemus Alpha caused exoskeletal material to grow, and it connected the two of them. Ethan is fine. The material was comprised partly of the alpha, as well as both Ethan and Cynergy. Ethan said they'd been struck by the alpha. Some kind of tentacle burst from a holding-tank table they were using to interact with it. I think it was the alpha's last-ditch effort to survive through them."

Connor considered that information for a moment, and then slowly nodded. "Okay. And then?"

"The decision to put them into stasis and bring them back here was best thing that could have been done for them. I was able to surgically remove the exoskeletal material."

Connor frowned. "How?"

"I used an altered version of what you used to kill the Alpha during the Vemus Wars."

She was keeping it high level, and he appreciated not getting caught up in the details.

"Exposure caused the exoskeletal material to break down, and I was able to cut it away enough to separate them," Lauren continued. "I was then able to remove the rest of it. Ethan quickly recovered, and Cynergy didn't."

"Why not? What's wrong with her?" Connor asked.

The door to the room opened, and Ethan walked out. He wore light gray hospital pants and shirt. His feet were bare.

Connor observed Ethan for a second and saw the worry and frustration in his gaze as his son came over and gave him a hug. Connor glanced around and then looked at his daughter. Ethan and Lauren wouldn't look at each other. He'd seen that stubborn determination in both of them from time to time.

He looked at Lauren. "You were saying?"

Lauren looked at Ethan. "Why don't you explain it?"

"Cyn was exposed to the Vemus. She was trying to learn where the Alpha Prime was located. The exposure has left her body confused."

Lauren leveled her gaze at him, and Ethan looked at Connor. "It was turning her into a Vemus. I was able to stop it. She fought it. She's still fighting it."

Connor glanced through the open door and saw the edge of a stasis tube inside. He looked at Lauren. "What exactly is the risk here?"

Ethan started to speak, but Connor held up his hand for him to be quiet.

Lauren looked at her brother, and her gaze softened. "She's in stasis, so the process has been stalled. The fact that she's a hybrid makes her resistant to the conversion. That and Ethan's intervention."

"Okay, can you reverse it?"

"No, she can't," Ethan said.

"Yes, I can," Lauren said and looked at Connor.

Ethan began to speak, and Connor looked at him. "Let me catch up for a second."

Ethan looked away and sighed. "Okay."

"It's not without risk," Lauren said. "The only way that I can see to help her is to eliminate her hybrid state. She would be completely human."

"And the risk is that she'll die if it doesn't work," Ethan said.

Connor shared a look with Lenora for a moment. Both of them had had to make choices when there seemed like there was no good outcome to be had.

Connor looked at his son. "Have you tried reaching her?"

"Not while she's in stasis."

His family watched him, waiting for him to weigh in, and Ethan's gaze narrowed a little.

"I'm her husband, and the decision for her care is mine. If the situation were reversed, Cynergy would be making the decision," Ethan said, his voice tight with barely contained frustration as his hands clenched at his sides.

Connor was quiet for a few moments. "Do you mind if I go see her?"

Ethan blinked, the request surprising him. He nodded. "Yes, of course, Dad."

Connor looked at Lenora and Lauren. "Please give us a minute."

Lauren looked as if she wanted to speak, but Lenora put her arm around her shoulder, speaking softly to her as they walked down the corridor.

Connor looked at his son. Ethan's jaw muscles twitched beneath his unshaven face, his posture tense and guarded as he stood with his back slightly to the wall, much like a cornered animal that was on the verge of lashing out. Connor tipped his head toward the door. "Show me," he said and smiled a little in reassurance.

Ethan led him into the hospital room, and they crossed over to where the stasis pod was. Connor noticed that it had been moved toward the window. Sunlight bathed the top half of the stasis pod, and Connor looked at Cynergy.

She certainly looked as if she were stuck in a partially transformed state between being hybrid and human, but it was more than that. Her dark skin and pattern of darkened areas were more severe than he remembered. There was a buildup of darkened skin along her neck and arms, and Connor suspected it could be found down the length of her body. It was similar to what he'd seen on Vemus fighters but to a lesser degree.

Seeing Cynergy suffering like this made his throat thicken. He loved his daughter-in-law. The person she was, her strength and intelligence, complimented his son's. Together, they were complete. But Connor knew that his own fear of losing Cynergy was nothing when compared with Ethan's.

Father and son looked at Cynergy while minutes went by in silence, the soft hum of medical equipment and their own measured breathing the only sounds in the sterile room. The weight of the world was riding on Ethan's shoulders, and Connor knew it.

Connor lifted his gaze to his son.

Ethan winced. "I know what you're going to say."

Connor frowned. "Do you, now?"

Ethan nodded, and the move was rigid. "You're going to insist that Lauren be allowed to reverse her hybrid nature."

Connor shook his head. "As you already said, the decision is yours. You're Cynergy's husband. She trusts you with her life, even now. That's what this is." Ethan blinked in surprise, and Connor continued. "She's trusting you to make the most rational choice for her wellbeing. It's part of marriage, son. If the situation were reversed, I'd say the exact same thing to her. Do you believe me?"

Ethan considered it and then sighed. "Yes."

The edges of Connor's lips lifted a little. "Good."

"Dad, this isn't what she wants. Cynergy doesn't want to be changed. Being a hybrid is who she is."

Connor nodded. "Yeah, I know. But it's also something she can live without," he replied with quiet certainty, speaking the difficult truth that Ethan needed to hear.

"But—"

"Please, just hear me out," Connor said calmly. "When it's all said and done, do you think Cynergy loves being a hybrid more than she loves you?"

Ethan frowned and shook his head. "No."

"Would she rather die for the chance to remain a hybrid than spend the rest of her life with you?"

Ethan's shoulders slumped. "It's not that simple."

"Yes, it is. It's really that simple. You're right. There are no good options here, but when you lay it all down, what's best for her?"

"I can help her."

"Maybe you can. I don't know. But if you can't…"

Ethan clenched his jaw for a few seconds. "If I can't…"

"She'll die. You can't keep her in stasis forever. What kind of life is that? For her. For you. It's not a long-term solution."

Ethan swallowed hard. "I'm worried I won't be able to help her."

"Then be ready to do whatever is necessary. Cynergy will understand. You want to give her the best chance at life you possibly can. The problem is, that it might not be the life either of you expected. What's the alternative?" Connor asked and then gestured toward the stasis pod. "She's suffering, and so are you. I know keeping her in stasis is like hitting a pause button, but it's not fair to her or to you."

Ethan's gaze sank toward the pod.

"Your sister would do anything to help you. She's trying to

protect you the best way she knows how. And she happens to be an authority in this. But, if you want to seek out another opinion, then do it. There are other medical experts out there."

Ethan chuckled bitterly. "Lauren already connected me with three other specialists—she did that this morning," he said, shaking his head.

Connor grinned with approval. "She's thorough."

Ethan smiled, and his smile had a little less weight to it.

"Tell me what you want to do. What can you live with?"

Ethan inhaled a breath and held it while he looked at his wife. "I want to try to reach Cyn first, and if that doesn't work, then Lauren can…she can do what she can."

"Then that's what we'll do."

Ethan blinked. "Really?"

"Why does it have to be one or the other?"

"I never really thought of it like that."

Connor glanced out into the hall. "Time is an issue. There's nothing wrong with having a backup plan, but I think it needs to be done in tandem to minimize the risk to Cynergy."

"I just… I didn't think…" Ethan heaved a sigh. "I should've thought of this."

"You would've, eventually. Come on, let's see what they think," Connor said.

Ethan nodded.

Connor started to walk out of the room, but Ethan called out to him. He turned toward his son.

Ethan stared at him for a long moment. "Thank you, Dad."

Connor returned his son's gaze. "Always."

———

It didn't take that long for the arrangements to be made for Cynergy's procedure. Connor and Lenora stood in the observation area with a bird's-eye view of the operating room. Lauren and Ethan were in hospital scrubs, waiting off to the side while another doctor oversaw the procedure.

Lenora looked up at Connor. "I'm glad you were able to get him to see reason."

"He wouldn't have allowed this otherwise," Connor said.

Once they removed Cynergy from the stasis pod, Ethan would try to reverse what the Vemus Alpha had done to her. If her condition became worse, the doctors would begin the process to reverse the hybrid in her.

Two CDF soldiers entered the observation area. They stopped and snapped a salute to Connor.

"General Gates, I'm Captain Tom Washburn. Sergeant Staggart and I served on the *Ascendant.* We were with Ethan when the encounter with the Vemus Alpha occurred. Do you mind if we observe the procedure?"

"Come in," Connor said.

"Thank you, General," Captain Washburn said.

The two soldiers looked down at the operating room with solemn concern of men who had fought alongside their commander. When Ethan noticed them, a flash of recognition crossed his weary face, and lifted his chin in greeting. They waved back, their gesture conveying both respect and solidarity.

Washburn looked at Connor. "Most of the crew wanted to be here."

Connor nodded in understanding.

Lenora leaned toward Connor. "Ethan reminds me of you sometimes. I'm glad he has people to watch his back."

The comlink to the observation room became active, and the doctor informed them that the procedure was about to begin.

———

Connor sat next to his son outside the recovery room. Ethan looked as if he hadn't slept in days, and the past few hours had drained him.

"You did everything you could," Connor said.

"It happened so fast."

"When we fought the Vemus, the conversion took anywhere from a few minutes to thirty seconds. It's relentless once it gets a foothold."

Ethan nodded. "They're going to monitor through the night, but they don't expect to her to wake up until tomorrow."

"I guess we'll wait here until tomorrow, then."

Ethan looked at him. "You've got to be exhausted. You only just got back. Why don't you get some sleep?"

Connor shrugged. "I can sleep anywhere. I know you're going to go in there soon. I'll be out here or close by somewhere."

Ethan sat up and stretched his back for a second. "I keep trying to figure out what I'm supposed to do."

Connor frowned. "What do you mean?"

"Cyn won't be a hybrid anymore."

"You'll figure it out."

Ethan bit his lip for a second. "The Vemus are still out there."

"Yeah," Connor agreed. "But they're not here today. We've got time."

Ethan was quiet for a few moments. "I don't know whether to keep searching for them or if we should listen to what the Phantoms advised us to do."

"We'll figure it out. The collective 'we,' that is. I don't have the answer either." Connor shook his head and sighed. "That's a problem for tomorrow. Right now, all you need to focus on is in that room behind us."

After an extremely close call that left even the doctors saying they weren't sure whether Cynergy could be helped, the procedure began to work. Connor thought that perhaps, on some level,

Cynergy had decided to let the hybrid in her go. If she'd clung to it, she would've died. He hoped that Ethan eventually arrived at the same conclusion. He thought he'd failed, but Cynergy was still alive, and over the past few hours her recovery had continued to progress.

Ethan stood. "I'm going inside for a bit."

"It's about time."

Ethan chuckled tiredly and went into the room.

Connor waited a few minutes and stood. He accessed the video feed for the recovery room, and saw Ethan sprawled out in a chair, asleep. He held Cynergy's hand.

Connor smiled and closed the video feed.

Lenora came to his side. "Now it's your turn to get some sleep."

Connor glanced around. "I don't think they'd approve if we just took a vacant room."

Lenora grinned and shook her head. "Actually, there's a room just down the hall. I told them that technically you were still under observation."

"I guess you're right."

Lenora led him to the room for visiting family. "Why does the thought of bending the rules a little appeal to you so much?"

Connor shrugged. "It's a character flaw, I guess."

They closed the door, and Lenora dimmed the lights. The room was small and only had one bed barely large enough to fit them both. They laid down and Connor drifted off to sleep with Lenora in the crook of his arm. It was the best sleep he'd had in a very long time.

CHAPTER 37

ETHAN WOKE to someone gently rubbing the back of his head.

"Ethan," Cynergy said quietly.

He opened his eyes and sat up. He'd been resting his head on the hospital bed; his body ached from sitting awkwardly in a chair.

Cynergy watched him. The back of the bed was raised enough for her to sit upright. Her skin was back to its normal pale color, and her long dark blonde hair was pulled over her left shoulder. Her lips were pale and she looked tired, but in her honey-brown eyes he saw something he hadn't seen in a while—peace. She emanated calmness, as if she'd finally gotten the rest she'd been robbed of for so long.

"How do you feel?" Ethan asked.

The edges of her full lips lifted. "Better. A lot better," she replied softly, a quiet gratitude in her tone.

A wave of relief swept over him, his chest loosening and his jaw unclenching as the tension drained from his body. "That's good. That's really good," Ethan said, and a little bit of fear crept into his thoughts. Did she realize she wasn't a hybrid anymore? Would she hate him because of what he'd allowed to happen? At least she was alive.

"Ethan," she breathed, and reached for his hand, "I know."

Ethan blinked, but held onto her hand, afraid she might snatch it away.

"I know I'm not a hybrid anymore."

There was nothing accusing in her tone, but her words hurt, twisting in his chest like a knife. He swallowed hard, his fingers tightening around hers. "I'm sorry, Cyn. I had no other choice. You would've become a Vemus if I hadn't let them. I couldn't let that happen."

Her chin trembled, and she reached with her other hand to cover his. "I understand. It's not your fault. I wouldn't listen to you. If I had, maybe none of this would've happened."

Ethan looked away and sighed. "I wish I'd been able to stop you."

Her eyebrows gathered, and she sighed. "I wish I'd been able to stop myself. I should never have put you in that position."

He just looked at her for a moment, trying to think of a reply to make her feel better. He hated seeing so much pain and regret in her eyes.

Understanding passed between them, and she asked, "How bad was it?"

"It was bad. The Alpha was able to subjugate them," Ethan said and told her about the other hybrids.

Cynergy closed her eyes and shook her head. "I tried to stop them, but then I couldn't."

"Cyn, the doctors believe there was a response designed to make you seek out the Alpha, even with the intention of destroying it after learning what you could from it. You and the others were playing into its hands."

She frowned. "But not you?"

"I felt some of the compulsion, but I think I was able to resist because my exposure to the Alpha wasn't as much as yours and the others."

"Yeah, but not everyone who went with us were part of that other mission where we encountered the Alpha."

"I know. I think it's because of the way hybrids interact with each other," Ethan said, his expression thoughtful as he tried to make sense of what had happened. "Maybe some of those behaviors or longings were transferred to the others? I don't know. It's the best I can come up for now. Maybe we'll figure a better explanation later."

Cynergy's gaze sank to her lap, then she inhaled a breath. "Ethan, I'm sorry. I put your life in danger, and other people's lives in danger. I don't know where we go from here. What's going to happen now?"

Ethan cleared his throat. "They'll be an investigation. Mission reports will be reviewed. We'll give our own reports, and we'll have to stand before a review board."

She bit her lip, and her eyes became misty. "Your command. You're going to lose the *Ascendant*. You worked so hard for this."

Ethan shook his head and leaned toward her. "I don't care about that. You almost died. I almost lost you. The CDF will never come between us."

Her head tilted to the side. "Ethan, the CDF is in your blood."

He smiled wryly. "They haven't kicked me out yet. I'm not afraid of a formal review and investigation. What kind of commanding officer would I be if I couldn't stand by my own record? If they determine the *Ascendant* should be taken away from me, then that's what happens. We'll figure it out." He paused for a moment. "But I don't think they will."

"Why not?"

"The Vemus are still out there. They need people to explore and find them. People who can learn what we can about them so we're not blindsided in the future. And there are other species out there fighting them. Hopefully, we're not in this alone."

She shook her head. "They're never going to allow me on another expedition."

"Yes, they will. Cyn, you weren't in your right mind. We learn from our mistakes and we move forward. That's how we excel. That's what separates us from everyone else. It's why we're still here."

She was quiet for a few moments, considering what he'd said. "I don't know how much I could really contribute anymore."

He'd been waiting for her to say this. She equated her value as a person with being a hybrid. Every instinct in him shouted for him to snuff out this flame of doubt before it became an inferno. He wanted to make her see reason, but he knew that being forceful wasn't the best way to accomplish this. That would only confirm to her that he shared her fear, which he wouldn't do to her.

"Cyn," Ethan said calmly. She looked at him, vulnerable and sad. "Being a hybrid was part of who you were, and the knowledge of it is still with you, but you're so much more than that. You're more than what you were able to do. If I lost my arm, would I be any less than I am now? No, and neither are you." He leaned forward and held her hand. "You're exactly who you've always been —intelligent, beautiful, and the most courageous woman I've ever met. I'm lucky that you're my wife. It's something I'm thankful for every day, no matter what happens."

Tears leaked out of her eyes, and he held her in his arms. She buried her face in his chest and sobbed.

"Thank you," she whispered.

He held her. Eventually, she pulled away and he let her go. He looked into her eyes, and instead of despair beginning to take root, he saw hope. He didn't know what the future had in store for them, but they would face it together. And that was worth any trial life threw at them, even the Vemus.

AUTHOR NOTE

Thank you for reading *Forsaken Outpost* - Book 18 in the First Colony series. I hope you've enjoyed this journey with me.

This is the second book in a multi-part story that began with *Pathfinder*. When I started writing this particular arc, I knew it was too expansive to fit into a single volume. This decision has allowed me to deeply develop new storylines and characters—elements that have always been the cornerstone of my writing and this series in particular.

The First Colony universe continues to expand well beyond its initial boundaries. There are more stories waiting to be told and characters you've yet to meet as the torch passes from one generation to the next. I'm thrilled about the future of this series and hope you share that excitement.

Your support has been the foundation of everything—without you, there would be no First Colony series. When I began this journey in 2017, I never imagined I'd still be writing in this universe eight years later, and that's all thanks to readers like you.

If you enjoyed *Forsaken Outpost*, please consider leaving a review. Reviews significantly help with discoverability and send a powerful message to potential readers that this series is worth their valuable time.

Thank you again for accompanying me on this adventure.

~Ken

If you're looking for another series to read consider reading the Federation Chronicles. Learn more by visiting:

https://kenlozito.com/federation-chronicles/

ABOUT THE AUTHOR

I've written multiple science fiction and fantasy series. Books have been my way to escape everyday life since I was a teenager to my current ripe old(?) age. What started out as a love of stories has turned into a full-blown passion for writing them.

Overall, I'm just a fan of really good stories regardless of genre. I love the heroic tales, redemption stories, the last stand, or just a good old fashion adventure. Those are the types of stories I like to write. Stories with rich and interesting characters and then I put them into dangerous and sometimes morally gray situations.

My ultimate intent for writing stories is to provide fun escapism for readers. I write stories that I would like to read, and I hope you enjoy them as well.

If you have questions or comments about any of my works I would love to hear from you, even if it's only to drop by to say hello at KenLozito.com

Thanks again for reading *First Colony - Forsaken Outpost*

Don't be shy about emails, I love getting them, and try to respond to everyone.

ALSO BY KEN LOZITO

Space Raiders - Dark Menace

Federation Chronicles

Acheron Inheritance

Acheron Salvation

Acheron Redemption

Acheron Rising (Prequel Novella)

Ascension Series

Star Shroud

Star Divide

Star Alliance

Infinity's Edge

Rising Force

Ascension

Safanarion Order Series

Road to Shandara

Echoes of a Gloried Past

Amidst the Rising Shadows

Heir of Shandara

If you would like to be notified when my next book is released visit kenlozito.com

Made in United States
Orlando, FL
10 April 2025

60367277R00187